THE
RIVER
PALACE

GILBERT MORRIS

THE **R**IVER **P**ALACE

A WATER WHEEL NOVEL

B&H
PUBLISHING GROUP
NASHVILLE, TENNESSEE

Published by B&H Publishing Group,
Nashville, Tennessee

Dewey Decimal Classification: F
Subject Heading: STEAMBOATS—FICTION / LOVE
STORIES \ HELPING BEHAVIOR—FICTION

1 2 3 4 5 6 7 8 • 16 15 14 13

CHAPTER ONE

"Looky there at them stinkin' bluebellies, Gage. Ain't they disgustin'? They got on new uniforms and most of 'em is fat as sucklin' pigs."

Gage Kennon, standing next to his friend Ebenezer Jones, studied the Union troops bringing the supply wagons into their camp just across the river from Appomattox Court House, Virginia. He took in the unfaded blue uniforms, the shining brass buttons, the glittering gold braid of the officers, the polished sword hilts, the mirror-shined boots. In contrast, the Army of Northern Virginia was scarecrow ragged and thin. Many of them had no shirts, only blankets thrown over their shoulders. His friend Eb had no shoes; his feet were wrapped in green cowhide strips.

Still, Gage felt a moment of pride. *We're still dangerous,* he thought, his brow lowering. *Like half-starved wolves or cougars.* But he merely agreed in his low voice, "You're right, Eb. They are right pretty."

1

"I've a mind not to eat their rations. Gits my craw to take charity from them," Eb complained.

"They're probably our rations," Gage said. "I heard they took our supply train that was on the way to Lynchburg. Besides, if we don't eat them, the bluebellies will, and they'll just get fatter and more rosy-cheeked than they already are."

"Hmph!" Eb grunted. "Then I'm gonna eat till I'm bursten!"

The previous day their beloved leader General Robert E. Lee had returned to the remnants of the Army of Northern Virginia, now in April 1865 a scant twenty-seven thousand men. He had surrendered to General Ulysses S. Grant at Appomattox Court House. General Lee had dressed immaculately for the sorrowful occasion, wearing a brand-new gray uniform, boots with decorative red stitching, spotless white gauntlets, and a sword with a bejeweled hilt. The men had crowded around him and his beloved horse, Traveler, sometimes gently touching the horse, murmuring words of comfort and support. Many cast themselves to the ground and wept unashamedly.

General Grant's terms of surrender were generous, indeed. No Confederate soldier was to be imprisoned or prosecuted for treason; they were free men. All who had their own personal mounts were to keep them, for General Grant had understood that most of the men were farmers, and he was anxious for them to return to their homes and begin their pastoral life again with their draft animals. Admitting to General Lee that General Sheridan's U.S. Cavalry had captured their wagon train, Grant had ordered thirty thousand rations for the defeated army.

The Rebels stood watching the long line of wagons, escorted by cavalry, file into the valley and begin to line up at the edge of their camp. The Union soldiers curiously looked over the sea of men, standing with shoulders thrown back and arms crossed defiantly. Some of them particularly noted Gage Kennon, for he was six feet tall, head and shoulders above most men. He was one of the few that still wore a Confederate uniform, a gray shell jacket with sergeant's stripes on the sleeves and trousers with the blue ribbon of the infantry down the side, tucked into knee-high cavalry boots. His friend Eb was only five-five, tough and leathery, dressed in humble butternut homespun, and he stared back at the Union soldiers with contempt.

There was no stampede to the longed-for food. The men waited until the quartermasters were ready with the rations, and then filed along to get their salt pork and hardtack quietly, in good order. When the Union cook handed Gage his ration wrapped in a muslin rag, Gage quietly said, "Thank you, Private." The man was too surprised to reply.

Eb and Gage returned to their tents and sat together on Gage's oilcloth poncho to eat. It had rained during the night, and their camp was a sea of stinking mud. The dawn was dismal and chilly, with low dun-colored clouds hiding all traces of the sun. Despite the vast crowd of men in gray and blue in the wide valley, it was quiet. The Confederate soldiers said little, and when they did talk their voices were low. The Union soldiers also spoke in murmurs, even the officers giving their perfunctory orders quietly.

Eb said, "These here ain't our rations. Marse Robert woulda got us some cornmeal to make hoecakes, instead of these sheet-iron crackers."

"They didn't have to give us anything at all," Gage said mildly. "Look at the bright side, Eb. All these weevils in the hardtack are extra meat."

Soon it was time to break camp for the last time. The men folded up their tents and gathered their rucksacks as if they were precious jewels, then slowly formed ranks for their last dread duty as Confederate soldiers: giving up their arms. They marched with their old swinging, swaggering step to an unnamed road, little more now than a mud wagon trail. Across it stood the Federals, a sea of dark blue. Eb and Gage stood side by side with what was left of their company, the Sons of the South Sharpshooters. Their commander, the dashing and fierce General John B. Gordon, rode at the head of the column, with rounded shoulders and downcast face.

Then suddenly the commander receiving the surrender of the Army of Northern Virginia, Brigadier General Joshua Chamberlain, gave an order in a clear clarion call. "Carry arms!" Bugles sounded, and the distinctive susurration of shifting arms sounded on the clear air. General Gordon looked up in wonder; their enemies were saluting them. With a steely ringing sound he drew his sword, then touched it to his boot toe, honor answering honor.

Two days later General Chamberlain wrote:

> *Before us in proud humiliation stood the embodiment of manhood; men whom neither toils nor sufferings, nor the fact of death, nor disaster nor hopelessness could bend from their resolve; standing before us now, thin, worn, famished, but erect, and with eyes looking level into ours, waking memories that bound us together as no other bond;—was not such manhood to be welcomed back into a Union so tested and assured?*

Eb and Gage laid down their rifles, threw down their cartridge boxes, and went to the corrals where the horses were. Mounting in silence, they rode away from the forlorn valley.

ABOUT TWO MILES BACK east, as the army had been making their last desperate run to escape the encircling Federals, Gage and Eb had blundered through an almost impenetrable pine thicket about thirty yards wide. At the base of a tall skinny pine tree they had buried their rifles in Eb's oilcloth. As they resumed their running fight, they took two rifles from dead Union soldiers that hadn't been retrieved from the field yet.

Gage went in an arrow-straight line to the thicket and found the tree. Soon they had retrieved their precious Whitworth rifles, the top-of-the-line weapon for sharpshooters. Gage had also buried his M1841 Mississippi rifle, the first gun he had been issued when he had joined the Confederate Army. He hadn't used it very much.

The time came for the two men to part, and the hardship showed on both of their faces. Gage stuck out his hand and Eb took it, and they shook, hard. "Ebenezer Jones, it's been a privilege and an honor to serve with you," Gage said quietly. "God bless you, keep you, and prosper you and yours, my friend."

Eb was choking back tears, but he managed to say, "And to you, my good friend."

Ebenezer Jones rode west. Gage rode east. Neither of them looked back.

GAGE KENNON WAS A solitary man.

The Union Army had offered to let the defeated rebels use the railroads to return to their homes. Gage could have chosen any of a dozen railroad lines to take him east and south, but he didn't. Instead he chose to travel the entire distance, over a thousand miles, down country on horse-back. For the last four years he had been in the company of thousands of men, eating with them, marching with them, talking to them (somewhat), listening to them (continu-ally), sleeping with them, and awaking to them. He longed to be alone, truly alone, as deeply as a thirsty man desires water. Instead of taking a couple of weeks by train, he knew it would take him a couple of months to reach New Orleans. As he rode out of the Appomattox River Valley, for the first time in many long months his heart was lifted up, and he looked forward to the coming days of seclusion and privacy.

He patted his horse's neck. "How 'bout it, boy? We're finally going home. It'll take us awhile, but I'll bet you in the next week or so we'll be out of this desert and we can find you some real forage." Normally southern Virginia and northern Tennessee could hardly be characterized as a desert, but the countryside had been ravaged by the war. Farms were stripped of crops and animals, pastures were bald, even most of the woodlands were sparse as the armies had cut down thousands of trees to make videttes or crude log huts for the long winter camps. The horse snorted dis-dainfully in agreement with Gage.

Gage had named his horse Cayenne, for he was such a bright chestnut he was almost as red as the pepper. A tall horse, he was over sixteen hands, which was good for Gage, who had long legs. Cayenne had beautiful glossy black points, stockings and mane and tail, and he was a sturdily built horse, though not heavy-limbed. Now after four years of war, his ribs showed and his coat was dull, but he still had stamina and strength. Gage reflected acerbically that Cayenne's was the only company he could enjoy just now. Their temperaments were much alike. Cayenne was a calm, composed, easygoing horse.

He skirted the Cumberland Mountains, heading for the Cumberland Gap. It took him sixteen days to reach the tiny village named for the pass. It was April 26, 1865, and Gage had missed going to church on Easter Sunday, which had been on the sixteenth. On that day he had been six days from Appomattox, in a scanty pine wilderness at the foot of the mountains. Now, even though it was a Wednesday, Gage thought he might find a little church in the outpost and pray for awhile.

The town of Cumberland Gap had a post office, a saloon, a mercantile store, a church, and a huddle of perhaps two dozen log cabins. Gage went first to the mercantile store to get some supplies, hoping they might actually have some. Although the Gap was of great strategic importance as an east-west gateway, there had been only minor skirmishes there in the war, and it had never been occupied by either army.

Some men were on the single main street, but no horses or buggies. Gage hitched Cayenne to the post in front of the general store and went in. Several men were seated and standing around a potbellied stove that had a low fire. They were talking loudly, then grew quiet when Gage entered. He touched his hat and said, "Good day, gentlemen. Looking for some supplies, if you've got any on hand."

The storekeeper, a short bald man with a snowy white apron, came forward to shake his hand. "Good to see you, Sergeant. You from these parts, are you?"

"No, sir, I'm on my way home." Gage looked around the well-stocked shelves, the barrels of crackers and pickles, the joints of meat hanging along the back wall. "It's been a long time since I've seen this much tucker all in one place. There's a couple of things I sure could use, and I bet you've got them. Coffee, cornmeal, any vegetables I can get my hands on, and oats and molasses for my horse."

The storekeeper went around the counter and started gathering the items Gage had named. "Er—Sergeant, the Yanks have already been here and told me that our Confederate money is outlawed, so—er—that is—"

"Don't worry, sir, I've got coins," Gage said.

The storekeeper brightened considerably. "Well, that's good news. And I'm glad you've come now, Sergeant, because I expect any day now there's going to be patrols out hunting you boys down one by one, the country's in such an uproar."

Gage frowned. "What are we in an uproar about now?"

A low murmur sounded from the men around the stove. The storekeeper answered, "You haven't heard? Abraham Lincoln was shot. Killed dead by a Confederate sympathizer, some crazy fool of an actor. Back on Good Friday, it was, April 14."

"What! Oh, no," Gage groaned. "Crazy fool's too good a name for him, cowardly madman sounds more like it to me."

The storekeeper nodded in agreement. "They're blaming us, you know. Every last man of us. Like we knew that lowdown snake, like any honorable gentleman would put a bullet in the president's head. He was just watching a play, and that varmint sneaked up behind and shot him in the back of the head, right in front of his wife! Even though we thought he was our deadliest enemy, no son of the South could think of such a terrible thing. Anyway, Sergeant, if you're traveling, and especially if you're armed, you'd better keep a sharp lookout for any Yanks buzzing around. They're mad as hornets and looking for trouble."

"Can't say I blame 'em," Gage said regretfully. "Thanks for the warning, sir. I'll take the back roads from now on, for certain." Gage gave the man the one dollar and eleven cents he owed.

The storekeeper stared down at the coins in his hand. "Didn't know any of you poor boys had any money left a-tall," he murmured. "Most of us surely don't."

"Had it when I joined up," Gage told him, "and somehow I couldn't find much I cared to spend it on in the last four years. Thank you again, sir."

Gage was very glad now that he'd decided not to take up the Yankees' charitable offer of the railroad travel. He figured all that Federal goodwill was gone for good now. Even though he hadn't planned to visit any of the larger towns and cities on his way, he now decided to give them all a wide berth.

In ten more days he was on the outskirts of Nashville, and he made a long circle around the city. On the far outskirts he saw only ragged farmers on foot or in shabby wagons with skinny, tired horses. At the south of the city he breathed easier for the first time since Cumberland Gap. He was at the north end of the Natchez Trace, the old road that led from Nashville down to Natchez, Mississippi. All four hundred forty miles of the wide path had first been cleared by Native Americans—mostly Choctaw and Chickasaw—who first followed the bison and deer as they made their way from the Mississippi Delta north to the salt licks in Tennessee. Then the Indians began using it as a trade route, then were joined by the European settlers, and at the beginning of the century the United States Army began blazing the trail because of the success of the booming trade route. Finally the "Kaintocks" came, farmers from Kentucky and Tennessee, who floated their goods on flatboats down the northern rivers until they reached the Mississippi. In Natchez and New Orleans they sold their goods, including their wooden rafts, and walked back north up the Trace.

But by 1815 to the west, Memphis had developed its own roads and railroads to the Mississippi River, and to the east Nashville had done the same. Instead of wooden rafts, great steamers carried freight on the river. The Trace had returned to the woods it had been ages ago, although it was still a passable wagon track. But what Gage loved about it was that because all of the transportation was concentrated to the east and west, the Trace had been virtually untouched during the war. The woods were thick and green, the clearings had verdant grasses, the thousands of streams and brooks were clean and sparkling and had known no blood-currents from men in blue and gray. The hunting was easy pickings; Gage could take his choice of wild turkeys, deer, rabbit, squirrels, quail, and any kind of fish he had ever heard of. In the weeks he followed the Trace, both he and Cayenne put on weight and muscle. As they steadily went south and it grew deliciously warm, Gage was able to take all the baths he wanted in the icy springs and brooks along the way; his fine blond hair grew thick and strong again, and Cayenne's mahogany coat and sable points gleamed in the occasional shots of sunlight through the green-shadowed roof of trees. Gage started remembering that he was a young man of twenty-five, instead of a tired old man twice that age.

He reached Natchez, Mississippi, at the end of May. He'd heard no news since the middle of April, and he still didn't want to. He skirted Natchez and started south on the myriad of roads that ran along the Mississippi River, choosing the one that seemed to hug Ol' Miss closely but still went due south. When he was about fifteen miles south of Natchez he decided to find a good camping spot and maybe stay for a day or two. It was a humid bright morning, and again Gabe blessed the warmth. The winters in Virginia had been long and cruel, and he wasn't at all acclimated to cold weather. New Orleans was rarely, *rarely*, cold. Gage hoped he would never again know a cold, bitter night.

The road Gage was following was a narrow but well-traveled track of red dirt with mostly pine forests on either side. Occasionally a wagon road turned off to an unseen farm or plantation. But he had seen no other traveler on the road for two days.

As he topped a small rise he saw a curious sight ahead. Gage's eyesight was preternaturally keen, and though the figure was many yards in front of him, Gage could tell that it was a man walking along the side of the road. But he appeared to be all dressed in white, which was odd. And he was making his way very slowly, in an uneven gait. As Gage neared him he saw that the man was wearing small clothes, a white undershirt and white cotton underpants. He was barefooted. The only things he had were a blue kepi cap on his head and a canteen slung at his side. He moved very slowly; and now Gage saw a lurid red blood stain on the left side of the back of his undershirt. Though he surely must have heard Gage's approach, he didn't turn around.

Gage reined Cayenne down to a slow *clop-clop* as he came alongside the man. The stranger looked up, a ghostly pale face with great shadowed dark eyes under the Union blue forage cap with a captain's gold braid and insignia on it. His canteen had "U.S. ARMY" stamped on it. Both of the man's hands were pressed to his left side. Gage had thought he had been limping because of injury to his legs, but now he saw that the man was practically staggering from weakness.

"Hello, Billy Yank," Gage said.

"Hello, Johnny Reb," the man said as jauntily as he could manage, and then turned to look straight ahead down the road.

They walked a few feet. "Looks like you're in somewhat of a situation here, Billy Yank," Gage said.

"Yep."

"Seems like you could use some help."

"Yep."

Gage dismounted and started walking by him. "I'm Gage Kennon."

"Pleased to meet you, Reb. I'm Dennis Wainwright. My friends call me Denny, but you can call me Captain Wainwright."

"I'll do that," Gage said slowly, "as long as you're above ground. Don't reckon that's going to be too long if you keep bleeding all over the place like you're doing now."

"Oh, you noticed? Yeah, that's because I've been shot," Wainwright said sarcastically.

After another drawn-out silence Gage said, "I'll help you, if you want, Captain."

The man stopped and turned to Gage, swaying precariously. "You will? Why would you do a thing like that?"

"I'd hate for our genteel Southern ladies to see a Yank wandering around in his johnnies," Gage said lightly. "They'd swoon, I guess."

"Don't think so, Reb. At least some of them . . ." And then he dropped like a stone, unconscious.

Gage untied his saddle roll and took out his oilcloth and folded-up tent. "Stay here, Cayenne," he instructed the horse, and walked straight off the road into the woods. After about a hundred feet he stopped to listen; there, he could hear water. A little further on was a shallow little brook running over white stones. Four tall longleaf pines stood close by, their thick tops grown close enough for a canopy. Gage took out his Bowie knife and cut away all the vines and undergrowth, and laid the tent down on the thick aromatic-scented bed of pine straw. Then he returned to the road and picked up the injured Wainwright. "C'mon, Cayenne, cool drink of water just ahead." The horse followed him obediently.

As Gage carried the man he studied him more carefully. He had light brown hair that still had some curl, though it was dank and limp. His features were clean and boyish, with a small nose and generous mouth upturned at the corners as if he were about to smile. It was hard to tell how old he was, because his face was so gray and drawn, but Gage thought he was probably about his own age. He wasn't a big man, maybe five-eight and slender, but he was dead weight and it was a hard go to carry him. Gage could feel heat radiating from his body; he was fevered.

When he reached the pallet under the trees Gage laid him down as gently as if he were an infant. The first thing he did was go to the stream and wash out his canteen again and again, then filled it with the cold water. Gage returned to him and saw that he was rousing. His face had the pallor of a dead man, his lips had no color, and his breath was coming in short pants. He struggled to sit up.

"Lay back down, Captain, sir," Gage said mockingly. "If you sit up you're just going to pass out again. Here, drink this, but not a lot, and not too fast."

Wainwright took a couple of small sips, then shivered. "Good, but cold. I'm cold."

"I know, you've got fever."

Cayenne was wading in the water, drinking happily. Gage said, "C'mere, boy, you gonna make me wade out in my fancy boots?" The horse came back to the side of the stream, and Gage took his saddlebags and rucksack off.

Kneeling at Wainwright's side, he said steadily, "I can make you more comfortable, but I think I'd better take a look at that gunshot first." Wainwright nodded mutely, and Gage pulled up the thin cotton shirt. The bullet had entered his left side, above and to the right of his hipbone. "Let me see your back." Groaning a little, Wainwright shifted to his side, and Gage saw the exit wound. He had had lots of experience with gunshot wounds, and he reflected that the man must have been shot at very close range. Usually exit wounds were much larger than entrance wounds, but this hole was about the same size as where the bullet had entered Wainwright's side.

"Not too bad," he said evenly. "A straight through-and-through, and it missed all the important parts, I guess. Except maybe your rib."

Wainwright lay back down, nodding weakly with relief. "I thought so, but I couldn't tell, really."

Gage pulled the tail of his shirt up closer to look at it. His face grew grave, and when his eyes met Wainwright's bleary gaze he saw that Wainwright knew the news wasn't all good. Wainwright said ironically, "Nice round hole in my best undershirt." Some of the cloth must have gone into the wound, and that meant that the chance of sepsis was high, indeed.

Gage sat back on his heels and thought. Wainwright watched him warily. "When did this happen?" Gage asked.

"Last evening, about six."

Glancing at the sun, Gage muttered, "Sixteen hours, give or take. Where were you going?"

"About eight miles southeast there's a settlement, Cold Spring. I don't know if they'd help me but I figured they might at least bury me."

"You want to try to make it there?" Gage asked.

With desperate weariness Wainwright answered, "Don't think so, Reb. I'm pretty sure that bullet broke my rib, and it hurts more than the gunshot, every time I breathe. I can't make it that far."

"I saw a wagon road about a half mile up, it might go to a homestead. Maybe you could—"

"No!" Wainwright muttered with vehemence. "No, thanks. That's where I was running from, Reb. Take my word for it, I'd get no help there. So whatever you can do, just do it."

"It's going to hurt," Gage warned. "I don't have any laudanum, or even whiskey."

"I heard that at the end you boys had to live through amputations without anything," Wainwright said in weak defiance. "If a Reb can do it, I can do it."

"Okay. I'm going to go clear a place right by the stream, in the sunlight, to lay you down. I'm going to need direct sun to see into that wound. I'll have to try and get that piece of your shirt out, and it might take some digging. You understand, Captain?"

"Yeah," he said faintly. "I understand." He laid back and closed his eyes.

Gage got his oilcloth, then rummaged in his rucksack and came up with his toothbrush, soap, a paper-thin hand towel he'd been using for almost two years, and his "housewife," a cleverly-made small sewing kit. He went to the stream, took out his Bowie knife, rubbed his toothbrush against the cake of carbolic soap, and began to scrub his knife. Then he plunged a thick needle into the cake of soap, and threaded it with black thread. When everything was completely rinsed in the fast-flowing stream, he laid them down on the clean towel. Then, using the side of his boots, he kicked away all the rocks and stones from the riverside, clearing about a six-by-three space down to the wet earth and laid the oilcloth down on it.

Returning to Wainwright he asked, "Can you walk?"

"Yeah, I can walk," he said with determination. But Gage had to help him stand up, then he threw Wainwright's arm around his neck to support him. "You can make it, Billy Yank. See? Right over here, just lie down on it."

With relief Denny laid down on the oilcloth. Gage lifted his shoulders and stripped off his shirt. He dipped it into the stream, and then wrung it out, the droplets colored pink from Denny's blood. Then he folded it, folded it, until it was a small, thick rectangle. "Here you go," he said kindly, and handed it to Denny. Denny took it, breathed deeply, then stuck it between his teeth.

Gage sponged away all the blood from Denny's side until the wound was a clean, round hole. He made two small incisions, like a cross, with the wound at the center. Pulling the tiny flaps open, Gage moved so that the brilliant sun struck the wound just right. Leaning down he scrutinized it with his sharp eyes, occasionally sponging away welling blood. He thought, he was almost sure, he could see the tiny piece of lint, about a half-inch down in the hole. Taking his Bowie knife, he inserted it into the wound, and with small, precise movements turned it so that the curved tip would be against where he thought the fabric was. Then ever so slowly, he began to pull the knife back up to the surface of Denny's skin. Of necessity he had to keep the needle-sharp point of the blade against the side of the wound track so that the fabric would come along with it. During the whole thing Denny panted, painful grunting animal sounds, but he didn't cry out. Gage admired him exceedingly for it.

Finally the tip of the knife came out, dripping blood. Carefully Gage moved it just far enough away from the wound and held it stone still. He took his thumb and forefinger and ran it down the blade . . . yes, there it was, the feel of a tiny, soft, wet piece of fabric. He held it securely, dipping it into the water, then brought it up. With the utmost care he smoothed it out. It was a perfect circle. The edges weren't even ragged, for they had been scorched closed.

Denny took the rag out of his mouth and said weakly, "Is it . . ."

"I got it," Gage said with satisfaction. Then he went on in a businesslike voice, "Now I've got to wash that wound out good, Captain. Can you turn over on your stomach?"

"Yeah," he answered, and tried. Then he said, "No."

Gage turned him. He emptied his canteen, then filled it up with fresh water. Pressing the mouth of the canteen so it would encircle the exit wound, he pressed it down against Denny's skin so all the water filtered through the straight line of the bullet's exit and entry. He did this several times, and Denny began to shiver uncontrollably, though his skin was hot. Turning Denny back over, Gage quickly stitched up the incisions he'd made and saw with satisfaction that the bleeding stopped. The exit wound couldn't be stitched; it was just a round hole. Folding up his hand towel, he pressed it to Denny's back.

Gage said, "That's it. Hang on just a minute, Yank." He went back to the tree stand and piled even more pine needles under the tent so that the pallet would be well cushioned. Then he took his wool blanket out of his saddlebag; he had happily put it away about two-thirds of the way down the Natchez Trace, and now he was glad that he hadn't thrown it away. Hurrying back to Denny, he could see that he was conscious, but only barely. He picked him up and carried him back to the campsite and laid him down, making sure the pad was pressed securely against his back. Then he covered him with the wool blanket.

"It's kinda itchy, I know," he said. "But I guess you're tough enough to take it. You did good, Billy Yank. You did real good."

Denny managed a weak smile, then closed his eyes with exhaustion.

Gage gathered firewood and built a fire. Then he went hunting, and after about ten minutes he came back with a fat wild turkey. Denny still slept. Now there were two red spots on his cheeks, and his hands felt hot, but he no longer had fever-chills.

Gage cleaned the turkey and butchered it until he had several good-sized, moist dark meat pieces. Adding water to his eight-inch cast-iron skillet, he arranged river rocks for a flat surface above the small, hot fire. He boiled the meat until it was falling to pieces, skimmed off the grease, and the broth was rich and thick. It smelled delicious.

He made himself a nice thick pile of pine needles and laid the oilcloth over it. By the glowing afternoon sun he read for awhile. Denny slept on.

Cayenne wandered back into camp, and Gage unsaddled him and brushed him thoroughly, taking particular care with his mane and tail. The horse was looking better and healthier every day. When Gage finished, he petted his soft nose and Cayenne nudged him affectionately. "Can't fix you any hot mash right now, boy, that Billy Yank's using our only pan. I will in the morning, though."

Gage laid down on his pallet again to read the Bible, as he did every day. As the sun set, it cast orange and crimson rays in the near clearing, and he laid the book down on his chest to look at them. He thought how long it had been since he'd had such a peaceful few moments of simple enjoyment, watching the light shimmer and slowly darken to violet and deep purple and then soften to a gentle dying gray.

"Am I alive?" he heard Denny whisper.

He turned to him, and saw that his eyes were closed. "You're alive, Billy Yank."

Denny opened his eyes to stare at him. "You . . . you helped me. You saved me."

Gage shrugged. "Hope you would have done the same thing for me."

"But I probably wouldn't have," Denny said. "Why? Why did you?"

Gage answered quietly, "Because I had to. I've killed men, I've watched them die, I've walked away from them when they were wounded. It was war. But this is different. I don't walk away from anyone who needs help, not if I've got that help to give."

After a moment Denny said, "Yeah. Yeah, I see that. Uh, what did you say your name was?"

"Gage. Gage Kennon."

"Thank you, Gage Kennon. Thanks for everything."

"You're welcome, Captain."

Wainwright said with a weak grin, "You can call me Denny."

CHAPTER TWO

Captain Dennis Wainwright woke up. He hated to move because of the pain it caused him. He didn't even open his eyes. He just laid there, comfortable and warm on his forest bed, reflecting how lucky he was that Gage Kennon had come along. Denny knew that in the hours after he'd been shot he had lost an immense amount of blood, and he'd known that he just might bleed to death on that deserted road. He figured that the only reason he had lived as long as he did was because he was generally a healthy man with a robust constitution. The only times he was ill was with occasional catarrh in wintertime.

He pondered about his savior for awhile. Gage Kennon was an odd bird. He was tall and broad-shouldered, with a set jaw, firm mouth, and somber twilight-blue eyes. At first he was an intimidating figure, until he started talking. He was soft-spoken, but more than that, his whole attitude and demeanor was that of an easygoing man, relaxed and even-tempered. It was at odds with what Denny knew his wartime record must be. Denny had seen Gage's Whitworth rifle, expensive weapons, imported from England, and they were issued to only one elite group of men—sharpshooters. Whitworth Sharpshooters were legendary. They had played havoc on the Union armies, particularly officers. Somehow Denny had always thought that such men must be coldly savage, stony-eyed assassins. Gage Kennon was nothing like that.

Denny heard a soft rustling right near his head, and he opened his eyes. A pretty doe was nibbling on a trailing vine wrapped around the tree behind him. She chewed and regarded him with velvety brown eyes. She was only about two feet away from him, and suddenly Denny wondered how on earth anyone could ever shoot such a gentle, lovely creature. He smiled at her; she watched him curiously as she delicately chewed. Denny thought how odd it was that this animal was so much prettier than any woman he had ever known. No human had such soft sweet, brown eyes, and no human ever evinced such purity and innocence as the doe radiated. After awhile he must have made some small movement, for she started and bounded away.

With a sigh Denny managed to pull himself up to a sitting position. Gingerly he looked at the wound on his stomach. It was oozing a small amount of blood and serous fluid, but his skin looked pink, with no sign of infection. The wound on his back, he knew, kept opening up and bleeding as he moved. He reached around to feel it, grimacing with pain from his broken rib. The skin on his back felt cool, not hot.

Shifting a little, he moaned, and was distressed to hear the pitiful sound in the quiet forest. He looked around for Gage. He didn't want the man to hear him mewling like a kitten. But his companion wasn't in sight. Now Denny saw that Gage's second rifle, the M1841, was lying beside his pallet. So was Gage's "mucket," which was basically a big, thick tin cup with a handle and a hinged lid. It had turkey broth in it, still warm. His canteen was there, filled with fresh, cold water. He remembered waking a couple of times during the night with a high fever, alternately shivering and then sweating, and Gage bathing him, and insisting that he take only small sips of water. Now he drank thirstily; he was sure his fever was gone. He had not slept well at all. Every time he moved the stabbing pain from his ribs woke him up, and then he had trouble going back to sleep. He felt exhausted and feeble.

Denny considered the fact that Gage had left him with a loaded rifle, another puzzle of the man. Suppose Denny just shot him when he returned? Gage Kennon didn't know him, didn't know the first thing about him. Yesterday Denny had been too bad off to make any explanations. Suppose he was a deserter? A Confederate helping a Yankee deserter would be in a deadly position; he would certainly be hanged along with the deserter. And Denny could just be a common murdering thief who'd gotten shot while attempting some robbery. None of these things had any relation to the truth, but Gage Kennon didn't know that.

Suddenly Denny decided that he wasn't going to shoot any more deer. That little doe had been at his mercy just as surely as he had been at Gage Kennon's mercy. Mercy he had been shown, and mercy he would give. It was only fair.

COLD SPRING SETTLEMENT WAS just like a thousand other places throughout the South, a small village with such trade establishments that could be supported by surrounding farms and plantations. Gage noticed that the livery stable was closed, the stable doors sagging open; a dry goods store was empty with boarded-up windows; and goats came in and out of a tiny storefront that had a milliner's falling-down sign above the open door.

One two-story clapboard building seemed intact, however, and above the narrow front porch was a faded sign: Pinckney's General Store. Gage hitched up Cayenne and went in. A small bell jangled as he opened the door.

The store was deserted, but then Gage heard footsteps on stairs and a weary-looking woman with graying hair came through the curtained door at the back of the room. She stared at him suspiciously and demanded, "Are you a Yankee?"

"No, ma'am. I'm just on my way home to New Orleans from Appomattox."

A spasm of pain crossed her face. "I beg your pardon, sir. It's just that since the surrender the Yankees aren't always wearing their uniforms, and no Union man is welcome in my place. But you are. I'm Mrs. Pinckney. What can I do for you?"

"If you've got some medicinal supplies, ma'am, I really need some laudanum, and some bandaging. Maybe muslin or any cotton fabric that hasn't been dyed?"

"Oh? Are you injured, sir?" she asked, looking him up and down.

"No, ma'am. It's a man I met on the road. He's been shot. I patched him up yesterday, but he's in a lot of pain, and I didn't have a single thing to make good bandages."

"Well, sir, why don't you bring him here? I've got a little shed out back—it used to house my pony and cart, until the Yankees confiscated them," she finished acidly. "Anyway, it would make a nice little shelter, and I've got some supplies that you're welcome to."

Quietly Gage said, "That's very generous of you, ma'am, but this fellow is a Union captain."

Her face twisted darkly. "Then I can't help you."

"I see. So you don't feel that you could sell me any supplies, ma'am?"

"You have money? Real money, not Confederate bills?"

"I have U.S. money, ma'am."

"Then I'll sell you what you want, because you're one of ours," she said disdainfully. "But it's a shame for you to waste your money helping the scum of the earth, as far as I'm concerned. My husband died at the Bloody Angle. He raised a company here, and out of the twenty-eight men that went with him, only sixteen came back, some of them crippled. And since '63 those Yankee brutes up in Natchez have made our lives miserable. They've taken our crops, livestock, our horses, our wagons, sometimes they've stolen things out of people's homes, furniture and the silver and the like. 'Confiscated' them, they say, so as not to give shelter and comfort to the enemy!" she spat out. Then with an effort she calmed herself and her face drew back into hopelessly weary lines. "Anyway, laudanum and bandages, you said? I do have one bottle of laudanum left. And I have a length of unbleached cotton, it's good quality, like for bedlinens. It'll cost you," she warned.

"All right. May I have the bottle of laudanum and about three yards of the cotton. Also if you have toothbrushes, I'd like two. And I saw that bushel of green peas over there, ma'am. They're fresh, aren't they? I'd really like to have a good mess of them."

"Yes, sir," she said, still with somewhat ill grace, and began to gather the items. When she finished she meticulously added up the cost. "I'm sorry, sir, but I've got to charge you three dollars for the laudanum. It's the last I have, and I don't know when I'll be able to get more. So your total is going to be four dollars and eight cents."

Gage reached into his little leather bag of coins and pulled out a ten-dollar copper eagle.

She took the heavy coin in her work-hardened hand and turned it over. "Mister, I don't have the change for this. I've got exactly twenty-eight cents in cash to my name."

"Oh, sorry, ma'am," Gabe said uncertainly. "I didn't think . . . but I've only got eighty-three cents in change left . . . uh—what else could I . . . ? I don't guess you have any men's shoes, do you, ma'am?"

To his consternation, her eyes filled with tears. She turned and almost ran to the back of the room and through the curtain and he heard her fast, hard footsteps up the stairs. Uncertainly he wondered what to do. His purchases were neatly stacked on the counter, but the lady had been holding his ten-dollar coin when she dashed off. He had just decided to pack up his things in his rucksack and leave quietly when she came back into the room. She wasn't weeping now, but she looked sad. In her hands was a brand-new pair of tan leather brogans, those sturdy half-boots that working men and soldiers had worn for decades.

"My sister-in-law ordered these for her son when she found out he was on his way home," she said in a low, shaky voice. "He'd written to her before, telling her that his shoes were so patched they were more patch than shoe. Then when he got home last summer he'd lost both his legs. I had ordered them for her for three dollars. Would you like to buy them, sir?"

"Yes, ma'am, that's just what I need," he said kindly. "Thank you very much." He picked them up and stuffed them into his knapsack. "God bless you, ma'am, you've been very kind. I'll say a prayer for you tonight."

"But—but I still owe you three dollars!" she blurted out.

"You just keep that, ma'am. My Bible tells me that if I take care of a widow my trouble will be repaid tenfold, so you don't feel like you're in my debt in any way. Good day, ma'am."

ON THE WAY BACK to camp Gage reflected on his odd experiences with his money.

When he had a steady job back in New Orleans, he had taught himself to be a frugal man. He didn't mind spending his money on something that made him happy. He had paid a high rent, considering his salary, on an upstairs flat in the French Quarter, one second-floor part of a wing of an old Spanish villa built in the traditional three-sided structure enclosing a courtyard. His rooms were of peach-colored plaster that molded and mildewed constantly, and he had to scrub them with boracic acid to kill the fungus. There was no glass in the windows, only shutters. But the courtyard below was delightful, with old roses lining the walls and jasmine and passion flower vines crawling up the single cottonwood tree in the center. The courtyard was paved with ancient Spanish cobblestones, and in the cracks thick green moss and tiny purple wild violets grew all year round. His rent had been about a third of his earnings, but he thought it was well worth it.

He had found, also, that if he kept his savings in unusual coinage he was less likely to spend it on impulse purchases. It was easy to get new and different coins at the New Orleans Mint, so any extra money Gage had he exchanged for new issues or unique offerings by private banks. He had one "dixie" left, the showy red ten-dollar bill issued by the New Orleans bank, the *Banque des citoyens de la*

Louisiane, in 1860. The French word for "ten" is *dix*, and so the English-speaking citizens of New Orleans had called it the "dixie." It had amused Gage that the term had become an affectionate label for the entire South, and "Dixieland" an anthem for the Confederacy. Most of the soldiers that weren't from Louisiana had no idea why they were fighting for "Dixie," and it had been a source of great interest when Gage showed the bill around to them.

Of course, the bill was worthless now. New Orleans had been occupied in early 1862, and the Federals had immediately not only condemned Confederate currency of government issue, but they had also outlawed currency issued by private Southern banks, soundly backed or not.

And the ten-dollar eagle coin was the last Federal money he had besides the eighty-three cents in other coins. It didn't bother Gage. It had to be done. That ten dollars wasn't doing anyone, including him, a bit of good in his pocket. He had carried it all through the war. Many, many times he had been tempted to buy food, for General Robert E. Lee had strictly enforced bans on looting. But somehow it made him feel guilty that he couldn't buy enough food for his regiment, so he had shared their rations, or lack of them, with a good conscience. He had been the most skilled hunter, and almost all of the fresh meat they'd gotten had been from him. That made him feel much more satisfied than buying some delicacies for him and his half-a-dozen or so close buddies.

When he got back to camp he found Denny staggering around in his drawers, barefooted, gathering kindling for the fire. He was clutching at his left side, breathing raggedly, and his face was distorted with pain. He looked like a decrepit old man.

"Why don't you lie down before you fall down?" Gage said acidly as he dismounted. "'Cause then I'd have to carry you around again."

"I'm just trying to get a few little sticks," Denny said grumpily. "You'd think I was a puny four-year-old girl, no more than I can lift. Where have you been?"

"To Cold Spring, to get some supplies. Sit down, I want to check that wound."

Obediently Denny sat on his pallet, and Gage looked over his side and back. "Looks good, skin looks pink. I got some stuff to make a bandage that'll go tight around you. I think if we keep pressure on that hole in your back it'll heal faster. And a good pressure bandage will probably help keep that busted rib from shifting around so much." Gage pulled the length of cotton out of his rucksack and started tearing it into long strips.

"You make your living patching up shot Yankees, Johnny Reb?" Denny asked caustically.

"No, I made my living shooting them," Gage retorted. "And I'm a better shot than whoever plunked that one into you. Are you going to tell me how you ended up in this predicament?"

"There is a young lady, Marie Joslin, that lives at Winningham Plantation, down that road about half a mile from here. I've been stationed in Natchez since '63, and we—er—made friends. Marie's a real friendly young lady," Denny said, his brown eyes alight. "Her father was a major in the 11th Mississippi Cavalry, and he got killed at Antietam. Her two older brothers were in the Jeff Davis cavalry, and she had a young brother, only twelve years old when the war started, that the older brothers took with them as drummer boy. So it was just her and her mother, you see. I kind of looked out for them."

"Did you," Gage said knowingly. "Miss Joslin's mother too?"

"Uh—she didn't much care for me, as a matter of fact, or any Union soldier for that matter. We did sort of confiscate some stuff from the plantation. Giving aid and comfort to the enemy, you know. Some of our men got rowdy, and some windows were broken, some things were missing from the mansion, things like that. But I went back and called on Miss Joslin to apologize, and after she met me on a personal basis she liked me. So in the last year or so I've been calling on her, bringing her and her mother gifts, you know, food and chocolates and scent and things like that. Mrs. Joslin didn't ever warm up to me, unfortunately, but Marie did," he finished with a rakish smile.

"I'm guessing that her mother didn't rob you and shoot you," Gage observed.

"I was coming to that part," Denny sighed. "I was calling on Marie, and I didn't know her brothers had gotten home from Appomattox. They came running out when I got to the house, yelling that scary Rebel yell and some other unfriendly things. Seeing that I wasn't going to get the warm welcome I was accustomed to, I turned my horse and headed back up the road. They caught up with me, and there were three of them on fast horses, and so they sort of surrounded me and ambushed me."

"You shoot any of 'em?" Gage asked curiously.

"They didn't have a single firearm between them, and I'm not going to shoot an unarmed man. I tried to kind of beat them back with the flat of my saber, but it didn't do any good. They pulled me off my horse and proceeded to strip me. That's when I got shot."

"With your own gun, huh," Gage said. "That must have been aggravating."

"It was an accident, really. The kid—I guess he's about sixteen now—took my belt off and pulled my Colt out of the holster. It has a hair trigger, and it just went off," Denny said regretfully. "I think the kid was more scared than I was. And the two brothers—well, I guess they were scared too. Shooting a Union officer, after the surrender? Not good at all. So they mounted back up in a hurry and took off back to the plantation."

Gage asked evenly, "Are you going to have them arrested?"

"Nah, that's way too much dramatics for me," Denny said airily. "I've got no desire to see that kid hang. Or the brothers, either."

"Why not?"

Denny shrugged. "Guess I'm not too sure I wouldn't feel the same way if it had been my sister cuddling up to some smooth-talking Johnny Reb. And those men never meant to kill me, they just wanted to embarrass me. Which indeed they did, since I ended up toddling down the road in my drawers. At least they left me my canteen, and my kepi cap. They took my slouch hat with the gold braid, though," he said regretfully. "And I had just got it broke in."

"Yeah, but stealing your horse, that's not a prank," Gage said, frowning. "And I don't know what other valuables you might have had, but whatever, it's still robbery."

"I know. I've thought about it. But to get my horse and my belongings back I guess I'd have to turn them in, and like I said, none of it's worth hanging a kid."

Gage reflected that it took a merciful man to have that attitude. He had seen many men, older and supposedly wiser than Denny, in positions of power that would never think of showing such understanding and compassion. "So, are you deserted, Captain Wainwright?" he asked lightly.

"Do I need to hotfoot you back to Natchez to report yourself undeserted?"

"No, my unit was the 10th Missouri, and we were mustered out of service June 1. I was just making one last call on Miss Joslin before I took a steamer to New Orleans."

"You're going to New Orleans instead of home? I mean, I assume you're from Missouri."

"St. Louis," Denny replied. "But my Uncle Zeke is in New Orleans and I'm going to visit him. I mean, I was going to visit him. Now I'm flat broke and a long way from New Orleans."

Casually Gage said, "I'm from New Orleans, and that's where I'm headed. It's about a hundred and sixty miles from here. That's not really too far, considering where I've come from."

Denny studied him. "Yeah, but you've got a horse. One horse. And I don't even have any shoes. I'd like to come with you, Gage, if you'd give me a chance to get a little stronger—and for my feet to get tougher, I guess. It's asking a lot, I know, but I can repay you for your trouble. At least I can when I catch up to Uncle Zeke."

Gage thought for a few moments, then said, "Okay, Billy Yank. We'll figure it out when you're fit to travel. But we can stay here for a few days, I was planning on camping out here and taking a rest anyway. Me and Cayenne have been traveling long and hard. I don't mind a few days out of the saddle, and I'm pretty sure Cayenne's really looking forward to it."

"Thanks, Gage," Denny said in a low voice.

"Aw, forget it." Gage had padded Denny's two wounds thickly, then had wrapped a tight cingulum around him. He stood up and said, "I'm going to get a fire going and make us some coffee. And then I'm going to cook us up some fresh sweet green peas. I've been hankering for vegetables

for four years now. Quartermasters told us that we needed
to eat fresh vegetables, and they sure wished they had some
to give us, but there was no such thing for us boys. They
recommended we eat wild onions. I hope I never have to
eat another onion again as long as I live."

Gage busied himself laying the fire and making coffee.
He had a small two-cup coffeepot and one tin mug. He
and Denny shared, both of them savoring the rich dark
brew. Gage liked his coffee strong and black, in true New
Orleans tradition.

"So what about you, Gage?" Denny asked. "What's your
story?"

"I joined up in June of '61, I soldiered, I surrendered at
Appomattox," Gabe said shortly. "Now I'm going home."

"You're from New Orleans, huh," Denny said, his eyes
narrowing. "What unit did you join?"

"1st Louisiana Tigers," Gage said proudly. "Tiger Rifles
battalion."

"You're a Louisiana Tiger! You people are supposed to
be the—I mean, you're famous."

"Infamous, you mean," Gage said carelessly. "I know a
lot of our boys were kinda rowdy, we were mostly just
tough guys from the docks that didn't know any better.
But there was never a faint heart among them, they fought
hard and never gave ground and died without complaint
or regret. I couldn't have asked for better men to have
served with."

Denny nodded. "Yeah, I heard the Tigers were about the
baddest boys to face, either on the battlefield, or off. I gotta
tell you, you sure ain't what we all thought the Louisiana
Tigers were like." He nodded toward Gage's Bible, which
was lying on his pallet. "Bet you kinda stood out from the
crowd."

Gage grinned. "Yeah, I did. Because I was the only clerk in the regiment."

"You're a clerk?" Denny asked with astonishment. So Gage wasn't a cold-blooded assassin, and he wasn't the typical scum-of-the-earth Louisiana Tiger, but Denny still hadn't pictured him as a clerk.

"I am. A sugar clerk, as a matter of fact. Ask me anything about refining sugar, I'm an expert."

"A sugar clerk," Denny said faintly, shaking his head. "What about family?"

"No family," Gage answered evenly, staring into the distance.

"None? No wife? Parents?"

"I'm an orphan. There was a girl once, but it seems like she couldn't wait for me. She got married in the spring of '63," Gage said with no apparent bitterness. "Anyway, New Orleans is the only home I've ever known, and from what I've seen it's the only home I'll ever want. How about you, Denny? Your family?"

"My parents live in St. Louis. I have one sister, ten years older, married with two kids. She and her husband live in Pittsburgh. Personally, I think Pittsburgh is aptly named. It is a pit of a burg."

"But you aren't going to go home to see your parents?" Gage asked.

Denny made a face. "Let's just say we didn't part on very good terms. In fact, I joined the army because it irritated my father so much. Oh, don't get me wrong, he's a Union man. But he wanted me to stay at home and work in the family business, which is textile manufacturing. I do not want to be a textile manufacturer when I grow up."

"So the war didn't make a grown man out of you, boy? I'll tell you what, I thought I was going on a great adventure for six months or so. After First Bull Run I figured out just how dumb I was, and I grew up right there and then."

"I was at First Bull Run," Denny said, somewhat abashed. "At least, I heard the battle. I was aide-de-camp to General Theo Runyan, and we were dispatched to protect the army's rear. As it happened, the rear of the army outran us. In fact, the whole army ran right over us, they were retreating faster than we were. I had more trouble keeping my seat on my horse than I did having to fight any Rebs. That's kinda the story of my army career. One cushy posting after another. Guess I'm just a companionable fellow, I always ended up arranging dinners or parties for some general."

"Doesn't matter. You did your duty." Finishing the last dregs of the coffee, Gage rose and said, "You're looking like you're about to have the vapors, Billy Yank. You'd better rest some. I'm going hunting, and I'll wake you up when supper's ready."

Denny nodded tiredly, then laid down on his pallet. Immediately his eyes began fluttering. "Hey, Gage?" he said drowsily. "Don't kill any deer." Then he fell fast asleep.

"YOU'VE GOT TO BE kidding me," Denny rasped. "I'm not wearing that!"

Gage stood in front of him holding the clothes he had offered him. The outfit was a blood-crimson shirt that had huge brass buttons with a tiger's head imprinted on them. The trousers were calf-length, full in the legs, of wide blue and white vertical stripes. The outfit included white leather gaiters and a red stocking cap with a long tassel. "Okay," Gage shrugged. "You can go in your drawers if you want. Come to think of it, in New Orleans probably no one will give you a second look." He started folding up the clothes to replace them in his saddlebag.

"Wait, wait," Denny said grudgingly. "I'm sorry, it just kinda took me by surprise. I always thought those Louisiana Tiger Zouave outfits looked more like circus costumes than military uniforms. It's kinda hard to picture you in it, too. I thought you were a Whitworth Sharpshooter, you've got a decent uniform!"

"This was my first uniform," Gage said. "The sharp-shooters weren't an organized unit, you know. We just got picked out and they attached us to whatever units were going to the front. We found out real quick that wearing Zouave uniforms aren't very smart for sharpshooters. We looked like giant parrots up in the trees."

He handed the clothes to Denny, who resignedly began to put them on.

Gage said, "And here's some shoes. I got no time to wait for you to limp all the way to New Orleans in your bare feet."

He handed Denny the brogans he'd bought at Cold Spring, and Denny looked them over carefully. "These weren't your army issue, they're brand new. You bought them?"

"Yeah. You owe me three dollars. No, dummy, the gaiters go over the trousers and the boots." He knelt and arranged the knee-high gaiters correctly, buckled them, then stood back and looked Denny up and down. "Now you look like a real Tiger, the scum of the earth."

"I'm not wearing that stupid sock on my head, I'm wear-ing my own kepi," Denny said stubbornly.

"Fine with me, Captain Yank. Okay, now you go ahead and ride Cayenne. You're better but I don't want you trying to walk and falling out two miles down the road."

In the last five days, with Gabe's cinched bandaging and the laudanum that helped Denny sleep the night through, he had improved tremendously. Denny complained that the laudanum gave him weird nightmares, and he told Gabe he should have gotten a good, strong brandy instead. Gabe had retorted that he was awfully bossy for a beggar, which abashed Denny. But he did insist on smaller doses of the drug, and still he seemed to sleep soundly.

Gabe figured that if he let Denny ride and if they took frequent breaks for him to rest, they could still make pretty good time. Gabe could march three or four miles an hour for ten hours at a time. He expected to reach New Orleans in five, maybe six days.

His plan worked. After two days Denny insisted on walking some, and he had regained so much strength that he could walk fairly briskly for a couple of hours. That third day of their travels they made forty miles. But that night Denny developed a slight cough. Anxiously Gage checked his wounds, but they were healing quickly, and there was no sign of tender red skin around them that would indicate an infection. Denny said, "Forget it, Gage, I'm fine. I usually get sniffles in winter, but maybe I'm inflicted with spring sniffles this year."

In northern Louisiana Gage had no trouble finding good camping spots. It was a verdant, rich land with plenty of lakes, rivers, and streams. That night after they finished supper, Denny and Gage talked for a long time, lingering over their coffee. "You said you were a clerk, is that right?" Denny asked, recalling their conversation a couple of days before.

"Yeah. A sugar clerk." Gage took a sip of coffee from the tin cup he and Denny shared, and a half-smile played on his lips.

Denny sighed. Getting this man to talk about himself was like trying to pull a tooth with big pliers. "So tell me about it, Gage. Tell me about you and New Orleans."

"Actually I'm a very boring person," he said with that secret amusement showing on his face. "I was an orphan, and I lived in the New Orleans Orphanage for Poor and Destitute Boys until I was sixteen. You have to leave then, you know, to go to work."

"So were you born there, at the orphanage? Did you know about your parents?"

"No, I was left there, on the front steps, in a cradle. The headmaster told me, when I got older, that it was a nice, well-made cradle, and I was wearing a good-quality gown and was wrapped in a homemade cotton quilt. The only other thing was a piece of paper pinned to the quilt that read 'Gabriel Kennon.'"

"So your real name's Gabriel."

"Yeah, but when I was little I guess I couldn't say it plain, I told the other boys my name was Gaje-ul. Pretty soon everyone started calling me Gage, and in my opinion that wears a little better than Gabriel. Anyway, I never knew anything about my mother or my father. The orphanage had a really good education for the boys besides just the three R's: history; English, American, and French literature; music; advanced mathematics; chemistry; drafting; even basic engineering. As it turned out, I was pretty good with mathematics, and at sixteen I got a job as a clerk for Urquard Sugar Refinery. By the time I was eighteen I was their head bookkeeper. I was still working there when I joined up."

Curiously Denny asked, "But what—how was your life? You said there was a lady—one lady? And, I mean, what did you do for fun, when you weren't being a Super Sugar Clerk?"

Gage shrugged. "This lady, I don't know . . . I guess I just wasn't exciting, or dashing, or something. I told you I'm a boring fellow. I love hunting, I always have, and I spent most of my spare time north of the city, wandering around the bayous and the canebrakes and the little patches of woods. I'm a Christian, and I go to church, I don't drink or go to saloons. I like plays and concerts and I'd go to the theater sometimes, but that's about it."

His dark blue eyes lit up and he continued, "One thing I did a lot, and I guess except for wandering around in the woods, I enjoyed most of all. I loved to go to the French Market, just to see all the different people, the bustle, all the different languages, the cultures. I'd go to one of the coffee stands and buy a *café au lait*—that's the only time I have coffee with cream—and a beignet, and walk around and look at all the stalls. Then I'd go out to the wharves and walk up and down. I loved seeing the steamers coming in, from the little tramp freight-haulers to the big luxurious floating palaces. I tried to imagine where they'd been, what the staterooms were like, the engine rooms, how the passengers lived, the places they'd seen. From the time I was sixteen years old, I'd gone to the docks at least once a week and spent hours and hours there."

"Really?" Denny said with great interest. "Did you ever get to travel on a steamboat?"

Gage shook his head. "No, I didn't want to take a deck passage on the cheap packets, that wouldn't be any fun. And I couldn't afford a stateroom on one of the nice ones."

Denny started to say something, but he had a coughing spell and said his throat hurt. They settled down to sleep.

The next day Denny's cough grew more persistent. It still wasn't a deep wet or very hoarse cough, but it caused him extreme pain because of his cracked rib. He rode all day, spasmodically grabbing his side when he coughed.

His eyes grew red, and his nose started running constantly. At about noon Gage said, "Denny, you're not looking too good, and I know you're hurting something fierce when you cough. Why don't we stop now and let you get some rest?"

"No," Denny said stubbornly. "I'm okay, I'm not going to let a little girly sniffle stop us. You said we'd reach Lake Pontchartrain this evening, let's do it."

In the late afternoon they reached the north shore of Lake Pontchartrain. To round it and go due south to the city was about another thirty miles. "I know this country well," Gage told Denny. "I've hunted and camped all around here since I was a boy. See that ridge running east-west on the south shore? There's good forest there. It's the best camping north of the city, because all the rest of the country around here is either plantation fields or swamp. That ridge is surrounded by swamp, but I know a path that's above water most of the time. I figure it's probably dry now, we haven't had any rain for the last few days. You feel like going on for another three hours or so?"

Denny said gamely, "Sure I do. I don't want to camp out in the swamp or in a sugarcane field."

Denny had been amazed at the change in climate, scenery, and wildlife as they had traveled further south in Louisiana. Natchez was a typical Deep South city, quick warm springtimes that started in March, hot in July and August, rainy and chill in September, and mildly cold in the short winters.

Southern Louisiana was like a different continent. It was blazing hot from sunrise to sunset, with humidity so high that one's clothes and hair always felt slightly damp. The nights were close and wet, with falling dew as thick as rain. Often a dramatic thunderstorm would brew, growling and dark, and torrents of water fell from the skies for an hour or so. Then the fiery sun would charge back out into the azure blue sky to turn the land into steaming greenscapes.

Gage forged ahead, leading them around the perimeter of the lake. It was sometimes difficult to tell where the lake's shores were, for Lake Pontchartrain was low-lying and brackish, and surrounding it was a wide swath of mud. They crossed a small still bayou, the green water only knee-deep, and then began a slight upward climb to the ridge Gage had pointed out. It was about a two-mile-long range of low-lying mounds that were covered with water oak, cypress, and tupelo trees. Because they were so tall and lush, they made an almost impenetrable canopy so there was very little wilderness undergrowth. Denny was coughing more now, so at the first likely place they came to Gage said, "Let's go ahead and make camp here. I'm getting tired." It was still about two hours until sunset.

Denny said, "Okay, you have walked the whole day today, Gage. Even though I've been riding I feel kinda droopy and achy myself." Gage unsaddled Cayenne, who immediately began nibbling the kelly-green springy grass. Denny set about making camp underneath an enormous tupelo tree. As soon as he had spread out his pallet on the soft turf, he laid down. "Think I'll rest for awhile." He coughed and then blew his nose, using Gage's only handkerchief.

Gage made their campfire and put coffee on, using the water from his canteen. He regretted that they hadn't been able to make camp about a half-mile to the east, because he knew of a freshwater spring there. But it was no good camping by the stream, because it was lined with tupelo trees, and the exposed tangle of roots from the trees spread for yards and yards around the stream. Anyway, he knew that Denny couldn't make it any farther. No matter what he said, Gage knew that Denny didn't have a summer cold.

The sun was riding low in the west, a spectacular sunset that shot dark orange and madder-red beams through the trees. The air was heavy, an odd but not unpleasant mixture of the fishy smell of the lake, rich wet earth, and night-blooming moonflowers that were thick around their campsite.

Denny was coughing and scratching his head. "You have lice, Johnny Reb?" he asked petulantly. "My head itches like it's an anthill."

"I don't have lice, Yank," Gage said shortly. Denny coughed, now a thick wet grunt, and sniffled. Gage sat up alertly. "C'mere, Denny, stand here for a minute." Gage pointed to a place beneath the tree where the last sunrays were blazing through.

"Why?"

"Just do it." With an exaggerated sigh Denny came to stand in front of Gage. In the strong light on his head, Gage parted his hair in several places, staring closely at Denny's scalp.

"It is lice, isn't it," Denny said grumpily.

"No, it isn't lice. It's measles."

"What! I don't have measles!"

Patiently Gage asked, "Have you been around anyone with measles lately?"

"No, I haven't," Denny snapped. "I've only been around you."

"For the last eleven days. How about before that? While you were still in Natchez?"

"No, I—oh. I forgot. I went to see my friend L. B. in the infirmary that day before I left to go see Marie. Yeah. He had measles." Denny sighed, which made him cough. "Sorry, Gage. I uh, was hoping by now I'd be more able—I mean—"

"Never mind, Denny," Gage said. "You can't help catching measles if you've never had them and you get within a mile of someone who does. In the summer of '62 my regiment had 242 cases of the measles in three months. At least I know how to nurse 'em."

"So you caught them?" Denny asked as he laid back down on his pallet.

"Not then, I had them when I was a kid. In the orphanage we passed 'em around until every last one of us, and our nurses and the headmaster, all had them." Gage didn't want to tell Denny that there had been a certain amount of fatal cases, both at the orphanage and in his regiment. Measles themselves were a fairly mild disease, but in small sickly children and in men who weren't at a general good level of health, measles often resulted in pneumonia. No one, including the doctors, knew how to prevent that, or to cure it once a patient had it. This worried Gage, for though Denny seemed on the whole to be an energetic and healthy young man, he was definitely still weak from getting shot. That was a great shock to the system, no matter how healthy the man or how light the wound.

"Wish we had some tea now, instead of coffee," Gage said, pouring out the strong brew into his tin cup. He added some molasses to it and gave it to Denny. "Here, this tastes kind of odd, but it'll help your throat."

Denny took a sip and said, "Not bad, actually. Smoky taste of coffee, smoky taste of molasses. Thanks, Gage. Hey, I don't know anything about measles, except the spots. So I know I'm going to be red polka-dotted, but what else?"

"Oh, you've already got a little cough and a runny nose. You'll probably have a low fever at night. Isn't it odd how if you get fevered it's almost always at night, and it goes away in the morning? Anyway, don't worry about it, Denny, you'll be fine in a day or two," Gabe lied. Though the rash only lasted between four days and a week, sometimes the cough, continuous runny nose, muscle aches, and fever could last up to two weeks.

"Yeah, I never get sick. I'll kick this quick," Denny said weakly. "But I am tired, Gage. I'm not very hungry, so I think I'll go ahead and go to sleep."

"Take some laudanum first," Gage said, pulling the dark blue bottle from his rucksack. "Maybe then you'll sleep good, even if you do get a fever." He could tell that Denny was already feverish; his eyes had that telltale dullness, and his cheeks were flushed. Denny took a swallow of the medicine and immediately closed his eyes.

A mourning dove sang its bittersweet song, and the perfume of the moonflowers overpowered the other earthy smells. A low lopsided Louisiana moon slowly rose, casting its sterile light over the land. Gage watched it, savoring the haunting sight. In over a thousand nights, he had never seen a moon shine on his home. He was thankful for it all: the dove, the spreading tupelo tree shelter, the giant white sweet moonflowers, the solemn moon. He thanked God, and prayed for Denny.

CHAPTER THREE

Baba Simza leaned over the kettle and inhaled deeply. The low light from the campfire made her face appear as a disembodied apparition, for she was dressed all in black and had a black *diklo* wrapped around her hair. "Ahh," she breathed with satisfaction. *"Av akai,* Nadyha, Niçu. This incense will make your heart beat strong, it will steady your nerves."

Nadyha, a tall, slim girl also dressed in black, made a face as she leaned over the potion. *"Puridaia* Simza, your incense stinks, the valerian rides over the balm and the lavender. Besides, we're not afraid or nervous. We're going to have *pias, baro pias."*

Her brother Niçu, a slender but wiry young man, obediently bent over the pot and breathed in. "Okay, *Puridaia,* my heart's beating and my nerves are steady. I don't get it, Nadyha, what big fun are you talking about? You've already got a forest of weeds out here. Why do we have to go get more weeds?" he complained.

Mirella, Niçu's wife, was seated by Baba Simza at the campfire. She said with amusement, "Don't pretend like you don't want to do it, Niçu. This is just the kind of prank you love to pull on the *gaje*."

"The wisdom of the prudent is to understand his way. And the mouth of fools poureth out foolishness," Baba Simza said triumphantly. Then, to take away the sting, she grinned at her grandson. "I'm glad you and Nadyha are taking back the treasures from them. Those *gaje* are *magerd' o choros*."

They were Gypsies, though they never called themselves that, they called themselves Romany, and it was Romany words they used interspersed with English. Simza was a sixty-year-old woman, her face sun-creased and darkened, her hands strong and work-hardened. She was the *Phuri Dae*, the wise woman of their *vitsi*, or clan. Nadyha and Niçu were her grandchildren—her favorite grandchildren, as a matter of fact, because she had eighteen. Niçu's wife, Mirella, she also considered her grandchild, for when a Romany woman married she became a member of her husband's family.

Nadyha, Simza admitted to herself, was especially beloved. She had been a pretty child, and now that she was twenty she was an amazingly beautiful young woman. As happened occasionally in their *vitsi*, Nadyha had been born with fairer skin than was usual with the Romany. Her complexion was a light tawny shade, instead of the normal earth-brown hues. Instead of dark black-brown eyes, even at birth hers were hazel, golden brown around the irises shading into dark green, and her eyebrows were lighter than her ebony hair. Her nose was small, her mouth wide and generous but not lush, her face a gentle oval. Children born with these unusual looks were rare in their *vitsi*, and they were usually considered especially gifted, intelligent people. It had proved true with Nadhya; she was a skillful weaver and seamstress, at a very young age she had become, under Simza's tutelage, an expert *drabengri*, a medicine-woman, a healer. She could sing well, she played the guitar with an expertise that had far surpassed her teachers. She had a way with animals that no one had ever seen. All Romany, especially the Vlach-Roma, as they were, loved horses; in fact, they considered horses their brothers. But Nadhya loved all animals, even those that the Romany thought unclean, and they seemed to return her love without stint.

But none of these things were why Simza thought Nadhya so special. It was her spirit, her heart, her love of freedom and independence, her stubborn will, her determination to enjoy the things in life to the utmost, whether it was growing herbs or nursing a wounded bird or playing the guitar. She was strong, and sometimes angry and bitter, but Simza thought that Nadyha would surely grow in wisdom as she got older, and when she found a good husband. If she ever did consent to such a thing, Simza thought with an inward sigh. Nadyha seemed to have nothing but resentment and disdain for men.

Her elder brother, Niçu, was much like her in temperament, but his features were those typical of Romany men: black hair; brown-black eyes; his cheekbones a high, bony prominence; his face long with a sharp square chin. His complexion was that of a lighter brown than some, though the Romany complexion came in many different shades. But their skin had none of the copper tint of the Indian, or the olive tint of Araby. Uniformly the Romany skin was of plain but varying shades of brown, with no red or yellow hue.

His wife, Mirella, was one of the prettier *Roma*, for sometimes the severity of their features—which made the men look dramatic and fiery—made the women appear hard and sharp. Mirella had a long face with a pointed chin and a long, thin nose, but her lips were small and full, and her dark eyes danced with happiness. At least, in the normal course of life she was happy. She loved her husband so much; her dream since she had been a small child was to marry Niçu. They had been married for two years now, and Mirella had lost two children. Sometimes the sorrow showed, at times when she was unaware, mostly when Niçu was not present. But she was a good-natured young woman, easily amused and entertained, and she was only nineteen. She and Niçu had plenty of time.

Now Nadyha chuckled at her grandmother calling the Blue Beasts "wicked thieves," for it might be said—and would be said, always, of the Gypsies—that she and Niçu were the thieves. Sometimes this made Nadyha very angry, but now it amused her. She took Niçu's arm and said, "Let thy foolish words cease, fool, and let us understandeth our wayeth." She often made fun of Simza's biblical quotes, which were always in King James English.

"Go with *amaro deary Dovvel*," Simza called after them.

They melted into the dense forest in a northerly direction. It was mid-June, and the night would have been too warm, except for the falling damps. A maize-yellow half moon lit their way, though they didn't need it, for they had walked and ridden this path since they were small children. To a stranger, the woods would look dark and threatening, tall cypress and oak looming above, trailing their long ghostly Spanish moss-beards. But to Nadyha and Niçu it was their home, night or day. An owl's cry sounded, and they looked up to see if it would dive-bomb them, as the larger males often would. But though he kept hooting derisively at them they never saw him.

They crossed over a ribbon of deep black swamp, on a sturdy cypress bridge that had been built by the Romany in their great-grandfather's time. Then the ground slowly fell until they were walking across great fields of tobacco, now shabby and fallow. The Union soldiers had no time for sowing and reaping, and the Negroes that could have claimed rights to the fields seemed not to want to do such labor since they had been freed back in 1862.

These had been the Perrados fields for over a hundred years, as the Gypsies had been Perrados Gypsies for that span, too. Now the Blue Beasts had stolen Manuel Perrados's money, his home, and finally his and his sons' lives. The eldest son, Jerome, had been killed at Gettysburg, and the younger son, Christophe, had died in Spotsylvania. Manuel Perrados was seventy-four years old, and had lost his second wife, Genevieve, ten years previously in the yellow fever epidemic that had crippled New Orleans. He had never ceased to grieve for her, and had been so devastated by the loss of both his sons, that when the Union Army decided that his taxes for his considerable holdings would be $8,000, he quietly had a massive heart attack and died.

Manuel Perrados's great-great-grandfather had immigrated to New Orleans from Madrid in 1762, bringing with him nineteen Gypsy slaves and two black slaves. He had bought in this new Promised Land a fertile tract of land just north of New Orleans, along Bayou Sauvage, and started raising tobacco. It didn't take long before Perrados Tobacco was famous for its smooth richness, and the Perrados family grew richer along with their tobacco, and bought more and more land until their plantation sprawled across forty thousand acres. Manuel Perrados's great-grandfather had built the lavish Spanish plantation home along the banks of soft-flowing Bayou Sauvage. And it was then, and it was Nadyha's and Niçu's great-great-grandfather, that had saved all of the Perrados horses, fine mounts imported from Spain at great expense, from a barn fire. Their Gypsy ancestor had been badly burnt and had died within two days. With overwhelming gratitude Xavier Perrados had set his Gypsies free; and because he had always been a fair and just master, his Gypsies stayed with him, and they became paid and valuable employees. He had even started a school for the Gypsy children, hiring a schoolteacher that taught them to read and write both in English and in French, for Xavier Perrados had married a Frenchwoman, and the burgeoning Creole culture in New Orleans was already heavily Francophile.

Both Nadyha and Niçu were tall, with long legs, and they walked quickly. Soon they came to the grounds of the Perrados mansion, several acres of landscaped grounds surrounding the great house. It was an old Spanish villa of a warm peach-colored plaster, the main hall of two stories, the two perpendicular wings one-storied. The doors and windows were all graceful arches. In the central courtyard were beds of roses, old roses that scented the entire grounds, surrounding an enormous five-tiered fountain, eight feet high, with a sculpture of a lovely Grecian woman holding an urn from which the water gushed.

Nadyha and Niçu didn't go toward the front of the villa, however, for they had no desire to see how it was now damaged. When Major William Wining had taken the Perrados mansion for his headquarters, it had been the elegant old villa's death sentence. He and his men lazily quartered their horses in the courtyard, and now the rosebeds were all trampled and ruined. The horses drank from the fountain, and often when the soldiers got drunk they jumped into it and played silly games. On one night of debauchery they had decided to use the Grecian lady for target practice. Evidently they were so drunk that their aim was bad, because she hadn't been shot to pieces. Part of her face was chipped, and the lip of the urn was half-gone, and the crook of her left elbow was missing. That same night they had decided to have horse races, making the winning post Manuel Perrados's library. The horses had galloped up the fine marble staircase, chipping and cracking every step.

On this night it seemed every window had a lantern or two shining in it, and Nadyha and Niçu could hear two dozen men singing a vulgar song and laughing uproariously. "Filthy frogs," Nadyha muttered darkly. In ancient Romany, "frog" was the name of the devil.

She led Niçu closer to the house, toward the left wing. Here was a summerhouse, surrounded by oaks, with the lawn green and maNiçured in Manuel Perrados's time. Now it was overgrown with weeds. She went to a soaring magnolia tree, set apart and encircled by a low wrought-iron fence. Beside the tree, on either side, were two plants, with many tall, slender reed-like stalks and long, thin leaves.

As they stepped over the knee-high fence, Nadyha said, "These are the ones, Niçu. And for your information, they're not weeds, they're *elachi*, and these seeds are Grains of Paradise. Here, you have to cut them, see?" She knelt by one plant. Straggling out messily from the bases of the plants' stalks were long, skinny tendrils with pods on them about the size of green peas. Nadhya took a long knife from the sheath on her belt and cut some of the tendrils close to the base of a stalk. "Don't cut the plant," she warned her brother. "It's going to be hard enough for me to get them to grow without them being wounded."

"You mean we're going to have to dig up—never mind," Niçu said resignedly. Now he knew why Nadyha had a spade stuck in her belt. He knelt on the other side of the tree and began harvesting the green strings running along the ground. He had thought, since apparently this plant was so special that his grandmother had called it a treasure, that it might have a strong scent, but he sniffed of the tendrils and smelled nothing but earth, and the heavy perfume of the magnolia blooms above him.

From the house now came sounds of heavy boots stamping. Nadyha and Niçu stopped cutting and looked up alertly. Then another song burst forth, some martial song with a heavy beat. The men were marching, probably around the long, Spanish oak dining table, so old it was black with age. A gunshot sounded, then another, as they sang. They were probably firing their guns into the air, ruining the delicately modeled plaster ceiling. Grimly Nadyha and Niçu went back to their work.

After they had cleared all the tendrils and carefully put them in their rucksacks, without a word Niçu pulled the spade out of Nadhya's belt and started digging. "Be careful, you're not digging a ditch," Nadhya scolded. "Don't touch the taproot, dig a ways around the base of the plant in a circle."

"*Hai, Kralisi* Nadhya," he retorted sarcastically.

She watched him critically for a few moments, and saw that in spite of his put-on impatience he was digging carefully and gently. Then, taking hold of a low limb of the magnolia tree, she swung herself up and climbed about halfway up the tree. Straddling a thick branch, she looked up, to both sides, down to the branches below. Finally, on a skinny twig shooting off the branch she was sitting on, in the uncertain moonlight she saw the perfect magnolia bloom. It glowed white and pure, with no shadow of a bruise on it, and it was as big as a dinner plate. Holding to the trunk of the tree with her left hand, she stretched out precariously far to reach the twig, which was bent with the flower's weight. Reaching under the bloom, she managed to get her thumb and forefinger on the short stem and snapped it. Holding it carefully she climbed down one-handed.

Niçu had finished digging up the plants, which were lying on their sides with wet clods of earth clinging to their short, thick roots. "Got it?" he asked as she jumped down from the tree.

"See?" she said proudly, holding the flower out to him.

He saw the perfection of it and smiled a little. "*Misto kedast tute, Phei.*"

"Thank you, Brother." She retrieved a basket she had made, closely and intricately woven, from her bag. It was filled with wet Spanish moss, and tenderly she nestled the magnolia bloom into it. Then she and Niçu stepped back over the fence and went past the villa, to the grounds far behind. Here was a cemetery, with a high iron gate and cleverly wrought into the arch above the gate was the name "Perrados." As was necessary here, the dead weren't buried, because the land was so low-lying that graves often filled with water and floated up the coffins. The graveyard had many, many white tombs, some of them pillared like Grecian temples, most of them with ornate carvings. Nadyha and Niçu went straight to one tomb that was large but unadorned, except for a marble pediment that read: *Manuel and Genevieve Perrados, Beloved of God.*

At the center of the door Nadyha laid down the basket with the magnolia blossom. Manuel Perrados had loved magnolia blooms dearly. Together they said, "Good night, *Kako* Perrados, *Kaki* Perrados. We are glad you are with *amaro deary Dovvel.*"

Then they made their way to an obscure corner of the graveyard, where long white plaster walls had been built, so that the tombs were made as a mausoleum, stacked three-high. On the door of each was a cone-shaped tin holder, most all of them holding bouquets of dried herbs. The tomb they sought was almost in the middle of the third wall, with the inscription *Guaril, rom Simza* on it—Nadyha and Niçu's paternal grandfather, Simza's husband. Taking a chain from around his neck, Niçu hung it upon the holder. It was a humble tin chain, but the links were as delicate as spun silver, and an elaborately carved tin cross hung from it. Niçu had made it.

Nadyha said, "*Purodod* Guaril, Baba Simza says to tell you that you are still her most *ves' tacha*, and still her best *te' sorthene*. She will join you soon at *deary Dovvel*'s table." Then she and Niçu spoke the same farewell they had given the Perrados, and returned to the great magnolia tree.

The soldiers were still singing drunkenly, and marching and shouting and shooting. Nadyha and Niçu picked up the two plants and started to leave. But Nadyha stopped and looked thoughtfully at the wrought-iron fence.

"No, Nadyha," Niçu said in a warning tone. "Those pieces are short but they're heavy. Not that you couldn't carry them," he added hastily at the baleful glance Nadyha turned on him. "But we couldn't haul them and be careful with the plants at the same time, could we?"

"I guess not," she said reluctantly. "Oh, well, we can just come back and get it. Maybe we'll come in the full moon, so I can see better, and I can save some of poor *Kako* Perrados's favorite rosebushes."

"If you figure on stealing the fountain, you'd better let me know ahead of time," Niçu grumbled. "I'll have to build a big, heavy cart to haul it."

WHEN THEY WALKED INTO the firelight of their camp, Simza and Mirella both burst into laughter. The plants, being very old, had multiplied richly over the years, so that the bunch of stalks was about two feet in diameter, and both plants were about four feet tall. Nadyha and Niçu had continuously shifted their long, fat burdens on their way back to camp, but carrying them was awkward. As soon as they had seen the light of their wagons through the trees they had both held the plants upright in front of them. They looked like two bushes with long legs.

"I thought you said these were grains," Niçu complained as he set his plant down underneath one nature's wall of their camp, a huge, drooping weeping willow tree. "If these things are grains then I'm an ant."

Nadyha set her plant down and hurried to the pump to wash her hands. Both she and Niçu were covered in mud, for they had left as much dirt clinging to the roots of the plants as possible. They washed up and went to sit by the campfire. Mirella had made them a pot of chicory tea with orange peel, Niçu's favorite. It was spicy and refreshing, but it was not a stimulant; in fact, chicory tea had a slight sedative effect.

Nadyha said, "I'm going to rest for a little while, but then I'll take care of the *elachi*, Baba Simza."

The old woman nodded, then stood up and stretched. "That's good, Nadyha. They'll wither and die in the night. I'm going to bed."

They bid her good night. Niçu went and sat on his wagon steps to remove and clean his muddy boots. Mirella asked Nadyha, "Do you want me to help you with the *elachi*?"

"No, there's no need. I already have the beds fixed, all I have to do is set them in it and water them," Nadyha answered. "You go ahead and go to bed, *Phei*." Nadyha called Mirella, "Sister," and loved her like one.

When Nadyha finished her tea she took her plants to the beds she had prepared, raised beds underneath a nearby oak tree. With some difficulty she got them planted just right, with the taproot securely covered, and then quickly put small spadefuls of light, sandy soil around them. With her watering can she hauled water to them and poured only one canful each.

When she finished she put out the campfire, tended to her animals, and readied herself for bed. Lying there, looking out of the wide opening in the back of her wagon at the tree-roof overhead, she could not get her mind to rest as her body longed to.

She thought about the day coming, of all the things she hoped to do, and there were many. She wished it was time to go to town, to sell their wares, but that was still at least two weeks away. Nadyha was restless, impatient, eager for new things, experiences, sights, even people. She loved her family, but she was young and passionate and such a calm lifestyle often frustrated her.

She thought of her brother and Mirella. They loved each other so much, and though they weren't demonstrative Nadyha could clearly sense the passion between them. She herself had passion, physical desires, but they were unformed, nameless, and certainly had no object. She even tried to make up an imaginary lover, a man that she desired and could love, but she simply couldn't do it. For the most part she despised men, at least *gaje* men, and even some *romoro*.

As was the custom of her people, at fourteen years of age her family and another family had decided on her betrothal to one fifteen-year-old Ferka, a skinny, stupid boy that pawed her as soon as they were out of sight of any others. She had threatened to stab him with her knife, and then had told Baba Simza, who as the *Phuri Dae* held more authority than even her father, that she would never marry Ferka nor anyone else. Baba Simza had seen that Nadyha had her mind set, and she knew it was useless to try to make Nadyha do anything, anything at all, against her will. So Baba Simza and Nadyha's father had called off the betrothal. Still, just about the entire *vitsi* had abused her, called her names, told her she would be a withered old woman at twenty if she didn't marry. But Nadyha had remained stubborn, and now she was twenty and she was neither withered nor old. And she was still just as determined not to marry as she had been at fourteen.

At sixteen she had been just like all other young girls; and she had developed a crush on the younger son of the house, Christophe Perrados. He was eight years older than she was, and she thought he was the handsomest, kindest man in the world. He had taken very little interest in his family's Gypsies, until Nadyha had begun to find excuses to seek him out. But even at such a foolish age, Nadyha was sharp and insightful. She had quickly seen that Christophe would indeed return her affection, physically. But she learned that he regarded marriage with a Gypsy with a sort of disdainful amusement. He had gone to war, and had died, and Nadyha had been grieved. But the memory of the painful experience had made her very suspicious of men.

Trying hard to understand her unease, her unquiet, she thought that perhaps it was because of her blood. The Romany were wanderers, they had been for ages untold. Her *vitsi* were one of the few exceptions to the rule. Perhaps she wanted a life of always moving, always leaving one place and arriving at another, each day new and different?

But Nadyha knew that wasn't it at all. She would like to see other places, to experience different things, to learn of other lands and peoples. But she loved her home, at heart.

Wearily Nadyha then thought of God. Perhaps her restive soul needed to be close to Him, as Baba Simza was. But Nadyha couldn't countenance that. Nadyha had a lot of anger in her, and much resentment, and bitterness because of many things, both personal and because of her despised race. She didn't understand how, if God was so good, the world and people could be so very bad. It didn't make sense to her.

Realizing that these ruminations were only making her more wakeful, she made herself lie still and began to try to formulate her new song. It was a poignant, bittersweet song about being a stranger, of longing for home and comfort. But neither the music nor the perfect words would come, and soon she fell asleep with the few notes in a minor key echoing in her troubled mind.

CHAPTER FOUR

Denny was much worse.

It had been two days since Gage had first realized that Denny had the measles, and in the last two nights Denny had steadily grown weaker and more listless. He had broken out in the characteristic rash. To Gage it seemed much more widespread than usual; you could hardly touch a fingertip to bare skin, and Denny complained that he itched terribly. His fever had been constant, and though it never seemed very high, Gage knew how much a two-day fever could sap the strength of even a healthy man.

But it wasn't the fever or the rash that was affecting Denny so perniciously; it was the cough. Because of his cracked rib, combined with weakness, he was obviously in torturous pain every time the cough wracked him. Gage had watched him closely, observing the course of his illness, and he knew that there was a very good chance that Denny would go into pneumonia. Gage felt utterly helpless. All he knew, as far as nursing went, was to keep the sick person as comfortable as possible, bathe them in cool water when they had high fevers, and feed them weak broth or gruel. The day before, Denny had refused anything except occasional sips of water, complaining that his throat hurt too much to swallow food. Gage thought that he probably had the stinging white ulcers inside his mouth and throat that sometimes developed with measles.

Gage had risen and dressed and saddled Cayenne in the gray, cool predawn. As soon as the bright yellow sunlight seeped into their camp through the filtering trees, the air immediately grew hotter. Denny groaned a little and threw off his red Zouave shirt that Gage had used to cover him. Slowly his eyes opened, and he asked Gage in a hoarse whisper, "Can I have some water?"

Gage had to help him sit up to drink from the canteen, he was so weak. Then he began coughing, a thick wet sound. His face turned gray with pain and when the cough ended he fell back on his makeshift pillow, thick bundles of soft grass that Gage rolled up in some of the cotton he'd bought for Denny's bandages. Gage thought that he seemed a little more comfortable in a half-sitting position.

"Listen, Billy Yank," Gage said. "I'm going to go get us some fresh water. I'll come back and make sure you're okay, but then I'm riding into town to get you some medicine."

It was a sign of how sick Denny was that he mumbled indifferently, "Okay, Johnny Reb." For the last two days Denny had argued with Gage vehemently, either about trying to ride into New Orleans to a doctor, or for Gage to go for medicine. He kept insisting that as soon as the rash disappeared, he'd be fine. He had gotten it into his head that the rash caused everything else, and Gage had told him that the rash only lasted four or five days. Gage hadn't bothered to disabuse him of the notion, there was no point in telling him he'd be sick longer than that. Now Gage could kick himself for not making Denny ride on into town as soon as he had seen that he had a disease. Gage felt he should have known that Denny was weak from being shot, and any illness, no matter how mild, might cause complications.

Denny coughed again, his eyes tightly shut, clutching his side. Gage laid his hand on Denny's forehead and knew he still had fever. Denny seemed not to notice.

Gage picked up both of their canteens, hating to leave Denny without water in case he should want some. But both of them were almost empty anyway. Leading Cayenne, he walked straight east to the spring, the only fresh water source he knew of north of New Orleans. It was an underground spring, bubbling up merrily in a grove of tupelo trees. It must have been from a deeply buried water vein, because the water was barely cool even at the source. The other freshwater springs Gage had known had always been icy. It amused him as he observed that of course in southern Louisiana the underground springs probably ran warm.

He had visited the spring three times in the last two days, because he had no water containers other than his and Denny's canteens. It was the first time he'd seen the spring since the summer before the war had broken out, and he had forgotten how beautiful it was. The source of the spring bubbled up merrily from a small hillock, and just beneath was a waterfall of about a foot, sprinkling and splashing over the tupelo tree roots. The stream running from the spring had cut a wide and deep V-shaped course for about half a mile before it ran down into the lowland swamp. All along it were the graceful tupelo trees, their shallow, thick roots tangled and writhing, but their torturous growth was softened by deep green moss growing on them. Several kinds of ferns, all with lacy delicate fronds, covered the steep banks of the stream. The spring was a shadowed, quiet, cool place, and Gage wished again that they could camp there. But the trees were too thick and so many of the roots were above ground, it would be impossible to find a comfortable place for Denny to lie down.

As they neared it, Gage said to Cayenne, "Better get you a nice, long drink of water, boy. We've got a hot fast ride ahead of us." Gage went ahead slightly to the right, because he liked to fill the canteens from the spring itself, rather than downstream, though the water ran clear and clean all the way to the swamp.

He stepped out of the woods that grew right up to the head of the spring. Instantly he froze and, with a sharpshooter's alertness and precision, took in the scene before him.

About six feet in front of him a young woman was standing in the middle of the spring, bent over another woman who was lying in the small pool that formed at the fountainhead before it gurgled down the waterfall. The waterfall was pink with blood.

The young woman looked up, and her face grew fierce, her eyes narrowed, glittering. In her hand was a knife, she seemed to be trying to do something in the water with it, but when she saw Gage she lifted it to her waist and pointed it at him. Her mouth drew back slightly in a feral grimace.

Gage dropped the canteens and Cayenne's reins and held up his hands. "I'm not going to hurt you, ma'am," he said quietly. The woman didn't move; her savage expression didn't change. Gage went on, "I'll help you, if you need help."

The woman lying in the water sat up, her face a mask of pain, and she half-turned to look at Gage. She said something in a foreign language to the girl. Slowly the girl dropped the knife to her side and said to Gage in a low voice. "Her leg is caught in a trap, and I can't get it off."

Gage waded to them, his boots slipping on the mossy roots. The woman was wearing a long, gray skirt that floated lightly around her. A rusty, saw-toothed trap was closed on her right leg, just above her ankle. Apparently the girl had been trying to force it open with the knife, but either the knife wasn't strong enough, or she wasn't. Gage squatted down and took both sides of the trap in his fingers. Straining, grunting, he pulled with all the strength he could muster. Slowly, so slowly, the gap between the teeth grew apart; an inch, another inch, more and more, and the girl quickly pulled the old woman's leg up out of the trap. Gage let it snap shut again, then picked it up and threw it far out into the forest.

The old woman lay there in the scant foot of water, panting short, quick animal grunts, her mouth a bloodless thin line. Gage, still squatting by her, looked up at the girl. "You have a camp near here?"

"Yes, just back there," she waved to the west. She still stared at Gage suspiciously, though he noted now that she had put the knife back in a sheath on her belt.

"I can carry her," he offered, "or if you don't want me to, she can ride my horse. He's very gentle." The old woman was short, but she was thickly made, almost plump, and he knew the girl couldn't possibly carry her, and the woman wouldn't be able to try to limp along with assistance.

The girl looked at the old woman, whose eyes remained tightly shut. She looked down at her leg. The wound was terrible, a deep tearing on both sides of her leg that was bleeding copiously.

Reluctantly the girl said, "All right, but first we have to let the water wash out the wound." Then she said something to the old woman, who opened her pain-dulled eyes to dark slits, then nodded. Looking back up at Gage, the young girl said, "Help me." She slid her arm around the old woman's waist.

Seeing what she wanted to do, Gage knelt behind the woman's head and put his hands under her arms. As gently as he could, he lifted her and pulled her back toward him. The girl wanted to place the old woman's ankle right in the fastest, strongest bubbling up of the stream. As they maneuvered her, the woman let out a closed-mouthed groan, almost a growl. The girl looked anguished. The woman was so tensed up with pain that she felt as if she were made of wood.

Worriedly the girl muttered, "It was rusty, and muddy."

Gage knew she was talking about the trap. "Yes, ma'am," he said regretfully. "Tetanus, that's a terrible thing."

She frowned. "What's tetanus?"

Now Gage regretted mentioning it, but it was too late for that. "It's—have you ever heard of lockjaw?" She shook her head. "It's a disease you can get from wounds from something rusty, or dirty from animal droppings, things like that," Gage said calmly. "But you're right, letting this strong flow of water wash out the wound is the best thing for it." That was true, he knew.

She looked miserably worried. "How long do you think we should do this? She's bleeding so much."

"Just give it another minute or two," Gage answered.

As they sat there he studied the young woman covertly. She had a sort of beauty he had never seen before, exotic and strange to his eyes, with glowing skin colored like a fawn. Now that he was so close to her he could see that her eyes were unusual, a translucent brown-green hazel. Even in the deep shade her black hair gleamed like an onyx jewel. She was wearing a shapeless blouse that was so loose one side was falling down her shoulder, and a gray skirt that was tattered at the hem. The belt she wore was wide, and of gleaming black leather with an ornate silver buckle. Her movements were smooth and quick and feline. Gage thought that it had been as if he had blundered into a snarling tigress in the woods.

The old woman whispered, "Nadyha, it's enough. Let the *gajo* take me home."

Nadyha's lips tightened but she looked at Gage and nodded. Smoothly he moved to the woman's side and lifted her in his arms. "Follow me," Nadyha said. "What about your horse?"

Gage gave a short, sharp whistle and said, "C'mon, boy." Cayenne started wading across the stream, obediently following.

Nadyha turned and hurried off into the deep woods in the opposite direction from Gage's camp. He carried the woman, who was still stiffened with pain. Her hands gripped around Gage's neck like a vise. Her skirt dripped soddenly along the path, and blood ran steadily from her leg. Every few minutes a low whimper escaped her. Gage thought he could see her growing paler by the minute.

"I'm so sorry this happened to you, ma'am," he said softly. "I really think I can help you, though. I'm sure going to try."

Her dark pain-clouded eyes searched his face, as if she was trying to see inside his mind. Then she said with difficulty, "Pleasant words are as an honeycomb, sweet to the soul, and health to the bones." Gage was amazed to hear her quote Proverbs; with the girl's wild beauty and the old woman's foreign features, he had somehow assumed they were some sort of heathen immigrants.

Nadyha walked quickly, tossing anxious glances over her shoulder, but Gage had no trouble keeping up. Though the woman was heavy, he felt as energetic and strong as when he had carried wounded men away from a battlefield. God gave a man superhuman strength when it was needed, he thought.

They walked about a half a mile, Gage guessed, and suddenly came out of the woods into a clearing. As always, his eyes took in the entire scene in mere moments, and he felt a sort of shock, not of pain but of bewilderment. It was like a bower, or a grotto. Woods and flowering bushes formed two sides of the enclosure, while a low-growing, gnarled weeping willow tree formed a seemingly solid curtain of green on the third side. Beneath his feet was solid, thick, ankle-deep green, and the stringent perfume of mint came strong to his nostrils. Standing end-to-end in a semicircle were three large, ornately decorated, brightly painted wagons. In the front and center of the wagons was a circle, cleared of the mint carpet, with a big fire crackling. Three pots were suspended over it on an iron framework. All this Gage took in and in a flash thought: Gypsies. But that wasn't what amazed him.

On one side was a sort of hoop on a stick, only it was made of thick, twisted vines, and a hawk perched upon it, his predatory lidless gaze fixed on Gage. By the hawk's perch sat a plump black bear, eating an apple, holding it with both paws. By the furthest wagon to his left was a mountain lion, lying Sphinx-like in a ray of sunshine. By the cougar's side sat a black cat, unconcernedly washing its face.

A young woman came running out of the far right wagon, her face twisted with fear. She asked a question in a high, frightened voice, and Nadyha replied shortly in their own language. She motioned Gage to follow her and led him to the middle wagon. There were four steps leading up into the arched doorway. He followed Nadyha in, stooping a little because the roof was exactly six feet high. His impression was of color, dazzling colors of fabrics and paints everywhere. The young woman following them stopped and stood uncertainly in the doorway, wringing her hands. She was weeping silently.

At the back of the wagon was a bed beneath a long, open window with a windowbox full of a grass with small yellow flowers. Nadyha stripped a bright multicolored coverlet from the bed, then reached down under the bed and came up with a thick roll of white fabric. Measuring out several lengths, she nicked it with her knife, then tore it. Folding it she placed it on the bed, then gestured to Gage. Gage laid the old woman down, careful to lay her bleeding ankle onto the pad Nadyha had made. As the old woman settled into the soft mattress she gave a shuddering sigh of relief.

Swiftly Nadyha knelt by her bed, took one of the woman's hands, and asked a question. The woman grimaced and then answered huskily, "Willow bark tea, maybe. And Nadyha, I thank *miry deary Dovvel* for the *elachi*. Make a poultice." The effort of speaking seemed to heighten her pain, for she gritted her teeth and then shut her eyes tightly closed. Her hands and arms began to shake slightly. Gage had seen wounded men's entire bodies go into palsy tremors from extreme pain.

Nadyha said to the woman standing in the door, "Mirella, go get the willow bark, it's in my wagon in a box, labeled. I put the *elachi* out to dry this morning, it's right by the herb garden." Mirella turned and hurried out of the wagon.

Nadyha rose and bent over the woman's lower leg. She looked up at Gage with both uncertainty and suspicion. He said, "I've seen things like this before, ma'am. Can I help?"

Before Nadyha could ask the old woman or even glance at her, she whispered, "*Hai, gajo*. Please."

Nadyha said something in a tone that clearly was an objection, but the old woman said, "No, Nadyha, it is right." Nadyha looked resigned.

Gage bent over the wound, gently dabbing a pad of the fabric to it to clear up some of the blood. Then, with the lightest touch imaginable, he felt around and above and below the wound. Looking up at Nadyha, he said quietly, "Her leg is broken."

"Which?" she demanded.

Gage knew she didn't mean "which leg", she meant "which bone". "The small one," he answered. "But it's going to have to be set." He looked hesitatingly at the old woman's face. "May I ask her name?" he said to Nadyha.

"I am Simza," the woman answered. "I can hear you. What can you do?"

"Miss Simza, I don't know if you—you people have better medicine," Gage said hesitantly, "but I have the best medicine I know of for pain in my saddlebag. It's a strong, even a dangerous drug. But I think I'm going to need to set your leg, and that's going to be a much worse pain than you're in right now."

"I know," she gasped. "Your medicine, is it laudanum?"

"Yes, ma'am."

"Then give me some."

Gage went outside of the wagon and looked around, but Cayenne was nowhere in sight. Then with a jaundiced eye he looked at the cougar, who looked back at him with cool interest. Gage hoped he was interesting because he was a stranger, not because he looked or smelled like a meal.

Nadyha came out of the wagon and plucked at his sleeve. "I'll go find your horse and bring him here. Where is the medicine?"

"It's in the right-hand saddlebag, a blue bottle," he answered. "Ma'am, I'm not sure my horse—" But she was already gone, running back the way they came as lightly as a doe.

Gage went back in to Simza and gently began sopping the blood away from the wound. He could see it clearly now, each sharp tooth of the trap delineated in her skin on each side of her ankle. Across the front and back were long slices as the teeth had slid across instead of digging in. Gage reflected that it had been a good thing it was a wolf trap. If it had been a bigger bear trap it would have cut her foot off.

He wondered—worried—about the wild girl Nadyha finding Cayenne, and thought that likely the horse hadn't wandered too far. Gage was sure he was just spooked at the assorted wild animals in the camp, and Gage didn't blame him a bit for that. He was a little spooked too. Still, maybe she could find Cayenne and at least get close enough to him to get the laudanum—

She came in the door with the bottle, her eyes glittering, her color high, and demanded, "How much?"

"Has she ever taken it before? Or had morphine, or anything like that?"

"No."

"Does she drink liquor? Brandy or whisky?"

"No, never."

"Then give her a good-sized spoonful, and we'll see," Gage said with more certainty than he felt. Nadyha went to a drawer and came out with a large soup spoon, poured the strong-smelling, thick liquid into it, and gave it to Simza. In a few moments she visibly relaxed, but only a little. "Another, I think," she said in a stronger voice.

Nadyha gave her another spoonful.

They waited, as Simza lay still, her eyes closed. Her breathing grew easier, and her hands stopped shaking. They could see her body relax. She nodded and said quietly, "I'm ready, *gajo*. Do it now, quickly."

Gage moved to the foot of the bed and said to Nadhya, "Hold her leg around her calf. Hold it hard." Nadyha did as he directed.

Gage wrapped his left hand around Simza's foot, his right hand around her ankle, and then gave a mighty jerk. Simza groaned loudly, "Uhhh!" And then it was over. Gage nodded at Nadhya, and saw that she had tears in her eyes. When she saw Gage's sympathetic expression she dashed them away as if she were ashamed.

Simza sighed deeply, then said with weak humor, "Ouch, ouch, ouch. That hurt more than I thought but less than it should. Thank you, *rai*."

Nadyha's lip curled derisively. Gage said, "You're welcome, ma'am." To Nadyha he said, "After you take care of that wound, you're going to need to splint her lower leg. Do you need me to help with a splint?"

"No, my brother Niçu can make that when he comes back. He's out fishing," she said heavily, and Gage knew she meant to communicate to him that there was capable man in the camp. As if *she* needed protection, he thought dryly.

Mirella came in, carrying a small iron pot with a handle. As she entered, the most delightful scent Gage had ever experienced filled his nostrils. It was a heavily sweet fragrance, but it had a subtle spicy, piquant aroma interweaving the sweetness. He had never smelled anything like it, and somehow it made him think of the Far East, of deserts and oases and turbanned men. "What is that?" he half-whispered, inhaling deeply.

Simza's eyes were still closed, but she inhaled and a small smile played around her severe mouth. "Ointment and perfume rejoice the heart," she whispered.

"It's *elachi*, Grains of Paradise," Nadyha told Gage. "It's very rare, and precious. The *gaje* call it cardamom."

"I've never heard of it," Gage murmured, "but I'll never forget it."

He started to turn toward the door but from her bed Simza said, *"Av akai, rai."*

"That means, 'come here,'" Nadhya interpreted, then added with some disdain, "'sir.'"

Gage went to Simza's bedside and she held out both her hands. He took them in his own.

Quietly she said, *"Devlesa avilan."*

Nadyha told him, "This is an old Gypsy greeting. It means, 'It is God who brought you.'"

"How do I answer?" Gage asked.

"The answer is, 'It is with God that I found you.'" Then she slowly said the Romany words.

Gage looked at Simza and smiled. *"Devlesa araklam tume*, Miss Simza. I'll pray that God will bless you, keep you, and heal you, ma'am."

He left the wagon, with Mirella and Nadyha talking rapidly in low tones in Gypsy. Going down the steps, again he eyed the big cat who watched him unblinkingly. Looking around, he stared at the bear, who seemed to have fallen asleep sitting up. The hawk was gone, and so was the black cat. And Cayenne was nowhere to be seen.

Sighing, he started toward the path they'd followed into the camp. He'd almost reached the treeline when he heard Nadyha call out, *"Gajo, av akai!"*

I already speak Gypsy, I know that means "come here, you," Gage reflected wryly, and turned back.

She hurried to stand in front of him, her hands propped on her hips. "Baba Simza says we owe you a debt. What can we do to repay you?" She was defensive and defiant.

Seeing her standing there, slim and tall, the unusual beauty of her face lit by the blazing sun, her head held high and proudly, Gage reflected that she had probably had male attention showered on her for a while now, and from what he'd seen of her he thought that most, if not all of it, had been wholly unwelcome. Carelessly he replied, "Well, you could tell me where my horse is, or if that cougar has eaten him. He looks pretty well-fed."

"He is a she, and her name is Anca," Nadyha said with exasperation, "and as much as I love her, I wouldn't let her eat a horse. He's tied up right over there, behind my brother's wagon, see?" Now Gage saw Cayenne, who was contentedly crunching on some tall yellow things that looked like flat sticks, stuck in a bucket. At his puzzled expression, Nadyha said, "It's pasta. Do you never feed him pasta? Horses love it, and it's good for them. I put a piece of sugarcane in there too, but he's already eaten it, the greedy piglet."

"Thank you, ma'am," Gage said. "I'll be going now."

Now she spoke in a courteous, sincere tone. "Wait, *gajo*. Baba Simza isn't joking, and neither am I. We owe you, and I must know how to repay you."

He answered evenly, "Ma'am, I helped you, I mean Miss Simza, because she needed help and I had it to give. There is no debt, so there is no repayment."

She said flatly, "We have money."

"No, thank you, ma'am," Gage said coldly.

After a slight hesitation, softly she said, "I see. My name is Nadyha. Simza is my grandmother. You should call her Baba Simza, it's a term of respect, but with—with—some affection. She'd like that."

"If we have the pleasure of meeting again, Miss Nadyha, I'll sure call her Baba Simza."

"What's your name?"

"Gage Kennon."

For the first time he saw her smile, a joyous, childlike, spontaneous widening of her generous lips. "Your name is Gage? How do you spell it?"

"Hm? Uh—G-A-G-E. Actually, my name is Gabriel, but when I was just small—"

He stopped talking because now she was laughing, a warm, low-pitched pleasing sound. "Your name is gah-jay. Oh, that's funny. You're the only person that's ever had the guts to actually admit it," she giggled.

"Yeah, I've kinda gathered that *gage* isn't exactly a term of endearment," Gage said dryly.

"No, it's what we call all non-Romany peoples. Mostly we don't like them, that's why we make it sound that way. By the way, the *gaje* call us Gypsies, but that's not what we are, we just let the fools call us that because it shows their ignorance. We are Romany, or Rom. Anyway, I won't call you *gajo* or *gaje*, I'll call you Gage, because you were kind to Baba Simza," she said decidedly. "Tell me, Gage, isn't there some way we can help you? Food, or cloth, or tools, or something for cooking, maybe?"

Gage's eyes lit up. "Well, ma'am, there may be something you can do for me, or for a friend of mine. We're camped about a mile from here, on the other side of the spring. He's real sick. I was on my way to New Orleans to see if I could find an apothecary that might give me some medicine for him. But you seem to know something about medicines and tonics. If you know of something that might help him, he and I both would be grateful to you."

Nadyha considered for a long time, staring at Gage with no trace of self-consciousness. She was weighing him, he thought, and he wondered if he would pass whatever tests were running through her mind.

Finally she said, "Go get your friend, and bring him here. I know medicines, I'm a good *drabengri*."

Gage was amazed at the offer; it was the last thing he had expected from this rather hostile girl. But he said, "I don't know if I should do that, ma'am. My friend has measles, and it's catching. Have you all had measles? All of your people here?"

"There are only four of us here," she said quietly. "And we've all had measles. Bring your friend here, Gage. Baba Simza would want you to."

"And you, Nadyha?" Gage asked quietly.

Her chin came up again, but she answered warmly, "I want you to bring him here, too, Gage. He needs help, and I have it to give."

GAGE PUT DENNY IN the saddle and jumped up to ride behind him. Cayenne would do fine with them riding double for a mile and a half or so. Denny lolled to the side, and Gage put his arm around his waist to hold him, and held the reins in his left hand. He could feel fever-heat radiating off Denny. Just then he coughed so hard he would have fallen off if Gage hadn't been holding him so tightly.

"This is the best camp I've ever seen, Denny," he said comfortingly. "I know you're miserable, but when we get settled there you're going to be so much better."

"You say it's Gypsies?" Denny mumbled. "I thought all they did was tell fortunes, and steal stuff, and then run off to do their scamming on the next bunch of dolts."

"Yeah, I know, but I don't think these are those kind of Gypsies. The old woman, Baba Simza, quoted the Bible to me, so unless I'm real mixed up, or they're real mixed up, I doubt she has much to do with nonsense like fortune-telling. Anyway, this Nadyha, she's some kind of herb woman, I guess you'd call her."

"And you said she's pretty?" Denny said a little more alertly.

"I think I said she's bug-your-eyes-out-beautiful," Gage answered airily. Then he cautioned Denny, "But don't let on you think so. Don't even act like you notice her looks."

"Huh? That doesn't make any sense, women always want you to go on and on about 'em, how pretty they are, how nice their hair looks, how their ears look like perfect shells even if they stick out like an elephant's, how their waist is so small, blah-de-blah-de blah blah blah."

"Not this one, she's kind of a no-nonsense girl. And she carries a knife, a long, sharp one."

"Oh. And you said she has a cougar? You mean, a real one?"

"No, an imaginary one," Gage said smartly. "Yeah, it's a real cougar. And a bear. And a hawk. And a black cat with one ear and one eye."

"You forgot to tell me about the cat before," Denny said blearily. He started coughing again, and it pained Gage to feel him convulsing so hard. His whole body shook with the deep hacking. When the spasms stopped, Denny fell limply back against Gage, in a swoon.

"We'll be there soon, Billy Yank," Gage whispered. "You just hang on. I think Miss Nadyha's going to help you, I really do."

Thinking of her, the words came back to Gage: *Devlesa avilan, It is God who brought you. Devlesa araklam tume, It is with God that I found you.*

CHAPTER FIVE

Gage didn't quite know what to do when he and Denny arrived at the Gypsy camp. He heard low murmurs of voices from Baba Simza's wagon, and he was sure that Nadyha and the other woman were still attending her. Denny's fainting spell had passed, but he was still so weak he was leaning back heavily against Gage. Gage thought that if he dismounted, Denny might just tumble off the horse.

Denny was staring around in amazement and Gage took time now to study the Gypsy camp more closely. On their right, looming behind the bright wagons, the tall woods closed in—oak, cypress, water elm, dogwoods, tupelo. All of the undergrowth, the vines and shrubs and briars and scrub pines had been cleared away. Gage saw three distinct paths leading into the woods behind the wagons.

The hawk was back on his perch, glaring at them. The bear was lying on a fat, brightly colored cushion, snoring slightly. Anca, the cougar, was lying under Nadyha's wagon

75

in a bed of slightly taller and thicker undergrowth than the mint carpet of the campsite. She raised her head to look at them when they arrived, but then yawned dismissively and laid back down. A movement caught Gage's eye, and he saw the black cat on top of the nearest wagon, looking down at them with one baleful yellow eye.

Ahead of them, past the circular clearing with the campfire in the center, was more close forest, but for the first time Gage saw that a sizable lean-to was built slightly back into the woods, made of cypress wood with a tin roof. In the deep shadows inside he saw an armorer's forge and boxes, baskets, stands of reeds, folded-up cane chairs, and built-in shelves filled with jars and tin containers.

On their left was the great willow tree, short, with great spreading branches that almost touched the ground. The "weeping" leaves were so thick that seeing the trunk of it was impossible. Tall oaks soared above it, and Gage thought that here was a good place for him and Denny to situate their blanket rolls. It was in the camp, but a discreet distance away from the wagons (and the animals) and the mint carpet ran right up to the woodline. He made a snicking noise and touched the reins, and Cayenne crossed the camp, his eyes showing white at the nearby cougar, even though she could hardly be seen under the wagon in the thick green growth.

Gage dismounted, and sure enough, Denny leaned precariously over and Gage half-assisted, half-lifted him down from the horse. He started coughing, and Gage sat him down with his back to one of the oaks, then quickly made up a pallet for him with the oilcloth and tent. He was studying how to make him a pillow when Nadyha came out of Baba Simza's wagon and walked over to them. She was dressed in the same plain, shapeless blouse and tattered skirt, with the wide belt and knife at her side. She had pulled her hair back severely and tied it with a green ribbon. She stopped, frowning with ill temper as she stared at Denny.

"He's a Blue Beast?" she demanded of Gage. "You didn't tell me that. Are you?" She looked him up and down accusingly. Gage's uniform shirt with his insignia was made of wool, and he hadn't worn it for weeks. He was wearing a plain white homespun shirt, and his wide-brimmed floppy hat whose only adornment was a black leather band. His breeches were his uniform breeches, gray with the infantry blue stripe down the side, but Gage doubted if Nadyha knew about Confederate gray.

Denny was wearing Gage's red Zouave shirt and pantaloons; Gage hadn't put on his gaiters and brogans for the simple reason that Denny could hardly take two steps, and they had ridden to the camp. But he was wearing his forage cap, Union dark blue with captain's insignia on it. Apparently Nadyha did understand that color.

Denny was trying to rise to his feet and was trying to talk, but he coughed so hard he collapsed back down against the tree, clutching his side.

Gage answered her, "I'm sorry I didn't tell you he was a Union soldier, ma'am, it just didn't occur to me. He's discharged now, anyway. And, no ma'am, I'm—was a Confederate soldier."

She stared at him with her mysterious glass-green gaze. "And you're taking care of him? This—this *gam'i choro*? He's your *jostumal*, your enemy!"

"He was my enemy, in the war. Now he's not. But I understand if you don't want to help him. I'll go ahead and take him into town. I sure didn't mean to offend you, Miss Nadyha."

She looked at Denny, who looked pitiful indeed. His skin was covered with the lurid red spots, he had lost weight and looked thin and haggard. He said in a painfully hoarse whisper, "Sorry, ma'am. We'll go," was all he could manage.

Nadyha seemed to come to a decision. "No. Baba Simza told me to take good care of your friend, Gage. She's wise, and understands and sees things. You stay, *gajo*," she said to Denny.

"Thank you, ma'am," he said tiredly.

Looking at the pallet Gage had prepared, Nadyha prodded it disdainfully with her toe. "It'll do for now, while I see him. Lie down here, *gajo*," she instructed Denny. Gage helped him and said, "I had made a grass pillow for him, but I haven't had time to get one together here yet." Gage laid Denny down flat on his back, whipping off the offending cap.

Nadyha knelt down by him and made a disgusted face. "This *lalo* shirt, take it off, Gage."

Gage reflected that with Nadyha's attitude it might not help Denny very much; he was aware of how peculiarly vulnerable sick people were to the people caring for them. Remembering Simza's proverb about pleasant words giving health were particularly fitting, but he also knew that if he tried to quote such to Nadyha she would very likely claw his eyes out. He got Denny's shirt off, folded it neatly, and set it aside.

"*Lalo*, red, it's *mahrime*, unclean," Nadyha said evenly. She pointed to Denny's bullet wound. "He's been shot?"

"Yes, ma'am, almost two weeks ago now," Gage replied. "The wound was healing cleanly, but then when he got the measles it seemed like it opened up again. That's why I've left the stitches in."

She nodded. Then with surprising tenderness, she said to Denny, "Don't worry, *gajo*. I'm going to see what your sickness is, and then ask Baba Simza how to care for you."

"I have measles," Denny said, puzzled.

Ignoring him she laid both her hands on his chest and watched as it rose and fell; his breathing was very irregular. She felt of both sides of his neck, probing a little, and then lightly pressed two fingers right on his Adam's apple. She seemed pleased when he didn't cough. Then she laid her head down on his chest, her ear pressed down to his right side, and stayed perfectly motionless for a few moments. She ordered Denny, "Cough," and he obliged. Her face grew grave. Startling both Gage and Denny, she moved so that her nose was almost touching Denny's bullet wound, and sniffed, long and hard. "It's not septic," she murmured, then laying her head on the left side of Denny's chest, listened as she had before.

She sat up straight and asked Gage, "Will you help me get him up and see if he can lean over his knees so I can listen to his back?"

It was an odd request to Gage; he had seen doctors listen to a patient's chest, and tap and thump them many times, but he'd never seen one listen to their back. Still, he pulled Denny up, then gently leaned him down, supporting his shoulders. First Nadyha sniffed the exit wound in his back, seemed satisfied, and again listened on both sides. Without a word she rose and went to Baba Simza's wagon. Gage gently laid Denny back down. Denny's swollen brown eyes had a very slight sparkle. "Gosh, she's something."

"Told you," Gage said smugly.

"I get the feeling that if it weren't for Baba Simza she might be trying to figure out how to chop me up into little pieces with that knife of hers, instead of worrying about what's wrong with me." In spite of his light words, he looked worried. "Do you think something else is wrong, besides the measles?"

"I honestly don't know, Denny," Gage said. "But I'll tell you this. I've been praying for you, asking the Lord how I can help you, and I feel like this is His answer."

Denny said with some embarrassment, "You know I'm not real religious, like you are, Gage, so I don't know what to say except 'thank you.'"

"Don't thank me," Gage said, smiling a little. "Thank Him."

Nadyha returned with the other young woman Gage had seen before. "This is Mirella, my *bori*. I forget the English, my brother's wife. Mirella, this is Gage and that's the sick *gajo*," she said, pointing out and to the obvious.

"My name is Dennis Wainwright, Miss Nadyha, Miss Mirella," Denny said with an effort. "It's a very great honor to meet you both."

Mirella smiled at Denny, and Gage was struck by the warmth and good humor he saw in her expression as she said to him, "Thank you for helping Baba Simza, Gage. I'm glad we can repay you by helping your friend. Welcome to our home." She turned and went to the lean-to and started searching the shelves.

Nadyha put her hands on her hips and looked at both Denny and Gage in that same daring, defiant manner she had spoken to Gage before. "I want you *gaje* to understand something right now. I don't touch men. I don't touch *Roma*, and I don't touch *gaje*. Except when I'm the *drabengri*, when I'm trying to heal. Do you understand?"

Both Gage and Denny nodded humbly, and Nadyha seemed satisfied. She knelt by Denny's pallet and looked into his eyes. "*Gajo*, you have the water in the chest. This is never good, but you're not so bad. I asked Baba Simza about how to care for you, and she knows all about this, the water in the chest, the coughing, the measles. You'll be much better in two days and in six or seven days you'll be well enough to eat too much and walk around and ride the horse, unless you're too weak from being sick and then you'll fall off."

Denny managed a faint smile. "Ma'am, if I'm well enough to fall off a horse in a week, then you'll be a miracle worker."

"No, I'm not," she said evenly. Turning to Gage, she said, "For two days he's going to need all-day, all-night care. Will you help?"

"Of course," Gage said positively. "In fact, if you can teach me what to do, ma'am, then I'll take care of him by myself. With you sort of supervising, if you would."

"A *gaje* asking a Gypsy woman to be his *ciocoi*, his overseer? Now there is a miracle," she said sardonically, rising to her feet. "Mirella and I will be back when we've finished your medicines. Lie flat, *gajo*. No pillow for you," she finished severely.

"I'm curious to see what they're going to do to you," Gage gently teased Denny.

"Curious isn't the word I'd use," he replied. "What I'm curious about is if she's right, that I'll feel better in two days. I hate to admit it, but now I feel like a ninety-year-old man just about to kick off. I guess, if she is right, in two days I'll feel like a seventy-year-old man that's got a few years left in him." The effort of saying so much obviously exhausted Denny, and after a fit of coughing, he closed his eyes.

"I think she's right, Denny," Gage said quietly. "I think in a week you'll be well." Silently he added to himself, *And that, Lord, will be the true miracle.*

Mirella had been busy making some concoctions in two of the three pots hanging over the fire. Nadhya went to the lean-to, put on an apron with deep pockets, gathered some supplies, then retrieved the two copper pots from the fire. She and Mirella started across the "yard" to Denny's pallet, and Gage saw with bemusement that the bear, who had been watching Nadyha carefully, lumbered after them. Nadyha turned and fussed at him in Gypsy, and the bear turned and dejectedly walked back to his cushion. He looked so disappointed and hangdog that Gage felt sorry for him.

Nadyha and Mirella spread out a clean canvas cloth by Denny's pallet, placed their supplies on it, and knelt down. Nadyha said to Mirella, "Pour some of the *elachi* tea into this small bowl, and break up bread pieces in it until it's like a kind of gummy pancake. Just a little, though, to make two poultices this size." She laid two doubled squares of muslin down that measured about three inches square.

Denny sniffed, then asked, "What's that smell? It's— it's—" he groped for words, and Gage knew exactly how he felt. As Denny inhaled deeply, it made him cough. He snorted hard, for his nose was still running constantly, and then gulped.

Nadyha said, "That's just what you musn't do, *gajo*. Don't swallow that poison from your chest. You have to blow it out of your nose, and spit it out of your throat, into these cloths." She laid down a small pile of squares of unfinished muslin by his hand. "Don't use the cloths more than once," she warned. "Throw them into this." She held up an obviously old, ragged basket. "You understand, *gajo*?"

"Yes, ma'am," Denny said meekly.

Mirella had finished pulping up pieces of white bread into the *elachi* tea, and had put the gummy substance onto the fabric squares. Nadyha picked one up and told Denny, "This is *elachi*, Grains of Paradise. We just got the plants back from the Blue Beasts, and we don't have much of the seeds, which is what you smell. I didn't want to use them for you but Baba Simza is making me." She placed the poultice over his wound, then lifted him up to slide the other one under him. "I'm not going to put bands around you, because of the measles spots, it'll just make them itch more. Here, here, you've been scratching, you'll make sores, they'll get septic. Don't scratch."

"Yes, ma'am," Denny repeated helplessly.

"Now then," she said in a businesslike tone, "I want you to sit up." Gage made a movement to help Denny but Nadyha smoothly put her arm around his shoulders to support him. Her touch was much gentler than her tone. Mirella took a pint bottle filled with clear, thick liquid out of her pocket, poured it into a large spoon, and Nadyha took it from her. "Here, take this. But don't gulp it, let it roll around in your mouth before you swallow it. It'll make the sores in your mouth feel better, and it'll help your sore throat." Obediently Denny took the spoonful. His eyes opened wider, but with pleasure, not alarm. He swished it around in his mouth for a few moments, then swallowed. "That's delicious," he murmured. "What is it?"

"Anisette," Nadyha answered. "It will help you sleep, but not at first." She watched him expectantly.

After a few moments he started coughing, and Nadyha said with approval, "It helps you cough up the poison. Here." She held one of the fabric squares up to Denny's mouth and he coughed and spit, gagged and coughed and spit. When the spasms relaxed, Nadyha threw the soiled cloth into the basket and said kindly to Denny, "That's very good, *gajo*. Now sleep." Denny sighed deeply, closed his eyes, and seemed to instantly fall into a deep sleep. Almost running, Nadyha went to the pump and washed her hands, then returned to Denny's side.

She pointed to the other copper pot, which had steam rising from it, with a clean herbal scent, and told Gage, "This is to bathe him, tonight, when the fever goes high.

It'll be just lukewarm by then, and the herbs will soothe the itch."

"I can do that," Gage said firmly. "And what about that stuff, you said it was anisette? Is it some sort of laudanum?"

"No, it's made from the anise plant, it has a taste like licorice. But we make it with distilled gin, so it's a spirituous drink. That's what makes him sleep, you see," Nadyha explained. "So for the next day, and the next day, he should have a spoonful every two hours, maybe three hours, depending on how much and when he starts coughing in his sleep."

"You mean I'll need to wake him up?" Gage asked. "Even if he's sleeping soundly?"

"Yes, for tonight and tomorrow, and then we'll see," Nadyha said firmly. "He has to get that poison out of his chest. Don't give him a pillow, if he sits up it'll make it all sink to the bottom of his chest and it'll be harder to get it to come up. You see?"

Gage nodded. "Makes sense, though I've never heard of this treatment for pneumonia. Thank you, Miss Nadyha, I'll take care of him."

Nadyha went on, "I'm going to go over there," and she pointed behind and to the left of their pallets underneath the oaks, "and fix our fire pit. These cloths must be burned," she said with emphasis. "And when you touch them, you must go wash your hands at the pump."

"I will. But, couldn't I go dig the pit? I really would like to do something, ma'am, instead of just sitting here like a stump. And then maybe, if Denny would be okay for a couple of hours, I could go hunting for us. These woods are filled with all kinds of game, and I'm a pretty good hunter."

"It would be good for you to bring us some pigeons, maybe a wild hog," Nadyha agreed. "But soon my brother will bring our supper. Maybe tomorrow you can hunt. And yes, I'll show you the fire pit, it's already built but you'll need to gather some small dry kindling for it. While you're doing that Mirella and I will gather moss and herbs to make the *gajo* a good mattress."

The sun was lowering, slowly disappearing behind the willow tree and its shadowing oak giants. Underneath the trees the temperature dropped quickly, and a quiet, soft breeze carried the strong mint smell over the camp. Gage gathered a good-sized pile of dry sticks and knots of pine around the fire pit. He noted the clear path leading to the pit from the direction of the wagons, and wondered what they burned so often, for the tin-lined fire pit was much used. All trace of grass and weeds had been cleared around it, and a deep layer of fine ash lay at the bottom.

Returning to camp, he unsaddled Cayenne, who had been wandering around just inside the woods, nibbling on the thick grasses that grew even in the deep shade. Gage was looking at the pump, for there was a trough by it, and he wondered if that was the animal's drinking-trough or if the Gypsies used it for something else; a freshwater reservoir, maybe, or for bathing. He had just decided to go find Nadyha or Mirella and ask about watering Cayenne when they both came out of the woods from behind the wagon with, Gage presumed, Nadyha's brother Niçu. He was as tall as she, with long legs, but there the resemblance stopped. His skin was as dark as Simza's, and his features were sharp and severe, his dark eyes glittering. He wore a plain white shirt and black trousers tucked into knee-high boots. Oddly, for the first time, Gage now noticed that both Nadyha and Mirella went barefooted.

Both of the women were talking at the same time, urgently, in Gypsy. Niçu was holding a five-gallon bucket in one hand and a stringer of fish in the other. Now he held up the hand with the heavy stringer in an imperative gesture, commanded, *"Chavaia!"* and both women fell silent. Nadyha took the bucket, while Mirella took the stringer. Niçu gave Denny and Gage a dark stare, then went into Baba Simza's wagon.

Gage watched as the women went to the pump, and Nadyha started pumping fresh water into the bucket, placing a tin mesh over it and letting it overflow. Mirella also held the fish under the streaming water, quickly washing each one. They talked in low voices, glancing at Gage and Denny. The bear came up to them, and Nadyha patted his head and smiled at him.

Mirella came to the lean-to and laid the fish down on a table built onto one side of it. She got a bundle of leaves and some jars of herbs from the shelter, then pulled a fish from the stringer and chopped off its head expertly with a butcher's cleaver. Gage went to her and asked, "Ma'am, can I do that for you? I really want to help."

"Yes, thank you," she said. "If you'll chop the heads and tails, I'll wrap them."

Gage took the mallet, chopped off the fish's tail, and slid it down the table to where Mirella stood. She deftly sprinkled both sides of the fish with some spices, then wrapped it in two leaves, and placed it in a big Dutch oven.

"I love catfish," Gage said, for on the stringer were six big fish. "But we usually fry—"

"Don't call them catfish," Mirella said with alarm. "Especially in front of Baba Simza. You must call them mudfish."

"Okay," said Gage, puzzled. "But may I ask why?"

"Because they can't be cats," Mirella said, plainly unsure of how to explain. "Ask Nadyha, she can tell you better than I can."

Gage had been watching Nadyha—indeed, it was very hard for him not to, he found her not only alluring but fascinating—and she had finished flushing out the bucket. With a long-handled, big spoon she reached into it and brought out a pile of crawfish and then dumped them into a smaller bucket. She was smiling and talking to the bear, who was sitting watching with avid interest. After another big spoonful of them went into the bucket, she picked it up, kissed the bear on the head, and walked to his cushion, talking to him all the time. He followed her, and Gage could have sworn he was smiling. She set the bucket down by his cushion, he plopped down, and with relish dipped into the bucket and started devouring crawfish.

Gage compared the bear and the cougar in his mind; the bear was so tame, his ways and even his expressions so clear that he seemed almost human. On the other hand the cougar Anca seemed primitive, unknowable, as if she might spring on one of them at any time. She got up and walked over to the bear's bucket, sniffed it, and turned disdainfully away. The bear seemed supremely unconcerned. Anca returned to the steps of Nadyha's wagon, sat down, and began washing her face. To Gage her paws seemed enormous, the claws nightmarishly long and sharp.

Nadyha dumped the remaining crawfish and a pile of jacket potatoes into an enormous steaming pot on the fire. Then she sprinkled several powders into the pot, and the old familiar, and to Gage terrific, smell of Creole cooking wafted to him, peppery and spicy.

Nadhya came to the table and grabbed the last fish from the stringer. "This is for Anca, if she wants it," she said. "She hunted two days ago, she may be getting hungry now."

Gage watched curiously as she went to the cougar. Nadyha knelt down so that they were eye-to-eye, and spoke softly to her. Nadyha stroked her head, then touched her nose to Anca's. Holding out the fish, Anca, with great delicacy considering such large teeth, took it from her hand.

Lying down in her Sphinx position she began to eat the fish.

Gage went to the pump, where Nadyha was already washing her hands. "I like your pets," he said. "I've never seen such tame animals, even in the circus. They struck me as being obedient, but not affectionate. Your cougar and your bear are."

"To me," Nadyha said shortly. "Well, Boldo is a big baby, he loves everyone. But Anca cares for no one, especially men. She's not really a pet, either. She only stays here when she wants to, like Rai, my hawk. Anca goes out to hunt, and maybe one day she won't come back." Nadyha shrugged. "That's the way it is with her. Matchko, my cat, is under my feet all the time, he'll never go anywhere he doesn't have to, he's so lazy."

"That reminds me," Gage said, "Mirella told me not to say 'catfish,' to call them mudfish. She said you could explain to me why."

Nadyha looked at him curiously, drying her hands on her apron. "Why do you want to know? Why do you care what we call things?"

"I'm curious, ma'am, but I don't mean in a bad way," Gage said uncertainly. "I've never met anyone like you. Gypsies, I mean. Uh—I know you call yourselves the Romany, and we call you 'Gypsies,' you said. But do you consider 'Gypsy' to be an insult?"

"No, not at all. In fact, there's a story behind 'Gypsy' that we think makes us special," she said with a faraway look in her eyes. "Anyway, we'd rather the *gaje* call us that than know or understand the real Romany."

"Good," Gage said with relief. "Anyway, what I'm trying to say is that I'd really like to learn about you, because I think you're very interesting, and I like learning about new things. I have about a thousand questions to ask you, besides the catfish one. And now the Gypsy one."

"Don't say catfish," Nadyha said with exasperation. "And I don't have time to answer those questions, much less a thousand more. When Niçu finishes talking with Baba Simza, he'll want to talk to you. And now Tinar and Saz are here, and we must take care of them."

She nodded her head behind his back, and he turned to see two horses standing to the left and a little behind the lean-to. Both of them were gorgeous, flashy horses, black and white, with long satiny manes and tails, and feathered hooves. They weren't tall horses, about fourteen hands, but very powerfully built, with broad chests and thick strong legs. He saw with amusement that Matchko, the cat, was lying down on top of one of the horse's withers, his front paws tucked neatly under his chest. "Those are beautiful horses," Gage said admiringly. "I've never seen any quite like them. Are they some sort of European draft horses?"

"That's another story we don't have time for right now," Nadyha said, now obviously baiting him. "Are you going to help me or not?"

"I'd love to. I was just about to ask about my horse, Cayenne. Watering him, and so on."

"Behind the lean-to we have bales of hay stored, and the mangers, and they water at the pump trough. Come with me. And go ahead and bring your horse, he'll like Tinar and Saz."

Gage whistled for Cayenne, and he saw the Gypsy horses prick their ears alertly. "Which is which?" he asked Nadyha.

"Tinar is the one that Matchko is sitting on," Nadyha said with amusement. "Matchko always tries to sit on and ride Saz, and not once has he ever let him, but Matchko keeps trying. Stupid cat," she said affectionately.

Cayenne came plodding up, and the three horses all touched noses warily, and stared at each other for awhile. When Nadyha and Gage brought out the three small mangers, they lined up with a will, expectantly. As they were stocking the mangers with hay, Gage asked, "You don't picket them?"

"No, they always come home in the evening, and stay here at night," Nadyha said. "There's very good grazing all around, especially one field that's full of red clover this year. It's about a mile from here. Do you tie up Cayenne at night?"

"Not usually, but since Anca and Boldo and Rai come and go here, I'm not too sure he'll stick around," Gage answered uncertainly.

"He'll stay with Tinar and Saz," Nadyha said confidently. "Now, we need to go see about Dennis."

Gage noticed that she called him "Dennis," a slight crack in her hostility. Denny was stirring and coughing in his sleep. Nadyha woke him up, gave him another dose of anisette, made him cough and spit, and then let him lie down in peace again. "He'll do well," she said with satisfaction. "You'll see."

Niçu came out of Baba Simza's wagon, and his face was now thoughtful instead of antagonistic. He came to sit cross-legged by Nadyha. She said, "Niçu, this is Gage and this is Dennis. This is my brother Niçu."

Niçu nodded to the two men, though he didn't offer a handshake. "My grandmother has told me about how you helped her, Gage. She says that she knows it's right for you two to be here with us, and for my sister to take care of you, Dennis. Now I'll tell you this. I've only known one *gaje* family that ever treated the Gypsies fairly, that ever gave us a chance. That family is almost gone now, except for a widow and two children. I've never trusted any other *gaje* in my life, and if it were left up to me, I would never let you stay here, in our camp. But Baba Simza is our *chivani*, our head *Phuri Dae*, and I trust her wisdom in all things. So I welcome you, and I and my *familia* will help you."

Both Gage and Denny murmured their thanks. Gage said, "Denny here is very ill, and too weak to help out in any way. But I'm not. I'd appreciate it, Niçu, if you'd let me know how I can be of use here. I can hunt, I can chop wood, I can take care of the horses, I'll do anything I can to help."

Niçu's expression lightened a bit with approval. "You'll find that no matter what you've heard about Gypsies, we all work hard around here, and I agree with you, if a man's a guest he should do his best to help out his hosts. But for now, Nadyha tells me you've said you'll take care of your friend. Just do that, Gage. Baba Simza says it's right."

"Then it must be right," Gage said, his blue eyes sparkling. "Would it be—uh—improper of me to ask to see her? I mean, if she would want me to."

Niçu grinned as he rose, and only then did Gage see a resemblance to Nadyha. While Mirella had a pleasant expression, both Niçu and Nadyha had a habitual stern set to their faces. When they smiled, it was a sea change, the sun suddenly breaking through black clouds. Niçu answered, "Baba Simza has already told me, among about a hundred other things, that she wants to see you and talk to you. But no, *gajo*, you shouldn't go into her wagon. Tomorrow, though, she has told me that I'd better have her a chair made so she can sit outside. She said she's already sick of living in the *vardo*."

Nadyha rolled her eyes but she looked amused. "She's not living in the *vardo*, this just happened this morning. Anyway, we do stay outside all the time, except for sleeping," she explained to Gage and Denny. "I know how she feels. C'mon, Niçu, I'll gather the lanterns and help you with the chair. I'm sure she's told you exactly what she wants and how to build it. Gage, supper will be ready in about an hour, and Mirella's fixing a special broth for Denny and Baba Simza."

"Can I help with the chair?" Gage asked.

Nadyha and Niçu exchanged amused expressions. "He doesn't like sitting still, does he?" Niçu asked.

"I don't know what he likes," Nadyha said with a toss of her head. "But he's just going to follow us around, begging for work, like some *gaje* traveling tinker. We might as well let him help."

"I don't know much about Gypsies," Gage said, feigning offense, "but the *gaje* think it's rude to speak of a person as if he's not standing right there listening."

To his relief, both Nadyha and Niçu laughed.

CHAPTER SIX

The garish Louisiana dawning sun sent horizontal slivers of yellow light through the willow-curtain, and one beam fell on Gage's face. He woke up, instantly alert and feeling rested and refreshed. Sitting up, he looked around to orient himself to this still-strange world. The horses, including Cayenne, had disappeared. The cougar was still asleep under Nadyha's wagon; the bear was on his cushion, still snoring; and the hawk looked headless, as he had tucked his head underneath his wing. Denny slept soundly, and Gage thought that his breathing seemed just a little easier than the day before; and it didn't have so much of that wet, mucky sound. He heard soft voices from Baba Simza's wagon.

Then they started what to him sounded like a chant. He grew wary, for though Gage didn't know much about Gypsies, what he had heard about them was pretty much what Denny had said. He'd heard that the women were fortune-tellers, and cast spells, and had the "evil eye," and that the men were lazy and ignorant and con men and thieves. But what bothered Gage most was the occult leanings. *Vaudou*, an African religion, was practiced widely in New Orleans, headed by a "voodoo queen" named Marie Laveau, and her daughter, creatively named Marie Laveau II. Gage knew nothing about voodoo, and didn't want to know; and likewise, he didn't want his fortune told and didn't want to know about Gypsy superstitions, or whatever supernatural practices they held to.

But as the quiet voices came to his ears, they had a cadence, a rhythm, that seemed very familiar to Gage. It was like hearing a far-off strain of music, and knowing that you knew the song but couldn't name it. He concentrated, and realized that it wasn't just his imagination. This was no strange Gypsy chant, it was something he had heard many times, if he could just put his finger on it.

Amaro Dad,
kai san ande o cheri.
Ke tjiro anav t'avel svintsime;
ke tjiri amperetsia t'avel;
ketu keres sar tu kames pe phuv sar ande o cheri.
De amenge adjes amaro manrro sakone djesesko
Yertisar amenge amare bezexendar,
sar vi ame jertisaras kudalendar kai amisaile amende.
Na zurnav amen,
Numa skipisar amen katar o xitro.
Ke tuke si, ande sa le bersh kai avena,
e amperetsia, e zor thai o vestimos.
Anarania.

The chant ended, and Nadyha, Mirella, and Niçu came out of Baba Simza's wagon, talking quietly. Mirella went to the campfire, which was already blazing high, and the homey smell of baking bread came from a big Dutch oven suspended over it. Niçu gave Gage a casual nod, and went to the lean-to.

Nadyha came to speak to Gage, who was standing and stretching. "How was Dennis in the night?"

"He had a high fever three times, and I bathed him in your tonic there, and it broke pretty quickly. You were right, about every two hours he'd start coughing, so I woke him up, dosed him, and made him cough up as much as he could." Gage glanced down at him. He was stirring slightly, but hadn't yet opened his eyes. "It seems like he's breathing a little easier already."

Nadyha nodded. "Today I'm going to make him blow the whistle. And Baba Simza is going to lay hands on him. He'll get much better."

Hesitantly Gage said, "I heard you all chanting, or something. Is that some kind of Gypsy—uh—charm, or incantation?"

She looked exasperated. "I don't know what an incantation is, but I can guess. No, it's not Gypsy at all, we just say it in Gypsy. It was the Lord's Prayer."

"Of course!" Gage said with revelation. "I knew it! I mean, I knew the rhythm, the beat of it. I just couldn't think of what it was."

"Yes, we actually pray, *gajo*," she said spiritedly. "Not all of us cast spells and the evil eye and tell fortunes."

"Sorry, ma'am," Gage said guiltily. "I was wrong to just assume . . ."

Nadyha shrugged carelessly and changed the subject. "Baba Simza says she's coming outside if she has to crawl. But then she ordered you to carry her, and that made Niçu mad but she doesn't care. Will you?"

"Sure," Gage said. "Whenever she's ready."

Nadyha knelt down by Denny, who was awake and coughing now. Gage went to help Niçu, who was setting up the chair they'd made the night before. Niçu was quite a craftsman, and he had already made half a dozen chairs out of light cypress, the seats and backs of woven cane with patterned holes in them for cooling. The clever thing about them was that they folded up, and so were very easy to store in a corner of the lean-to. The previous night Niçu, with a little assistance from Nadyha and Gage, had made a chair like that, only with an extended piece added to the seat, so that Baba Simza's legs were supported, and it also folded up. Gage had seen chaise lounges before, but he'd never seen any that were so light but steady and sturdy, and yet folded up. They set Baba Simza's chair under the tree closest to the campfire, by Niçu's and Mirella's wagon.

"You're the beast of burden," Niçu said sarcastically. "Go get her. You're probably going to have to carry her around half the morning until we get the chair in the right place."

"Okay," Gage said meekly.

He knocked on Baba Simza's door and she called, "Come in, Gage." He went in the wagon and was astonished to see how well the woman looked. She was sitting upright on her bed, with two fat pillows behind her. Her wrinkled dark cheeks had a good color, her eyes were bright. She was dressed in a full skirt made of rainbow-hued cotton and a dark blue blouse with puffed sleeves and three ribbons— yellow, blue, and green—sewn down the front. On her head was a scarf of bright blue and yellow plaid, tied at the side of her neck, and trimming the scarf were silver coins that lay low on her forehead and down the edges of the tie, making a light tinkling sound when she moved her head. Her hair was loose beneath the scarf, thick black hair with startling white streaks all through it. Two light strips of pine, carefully sanded to a sheen, made her splint, wrapped with white muslin. She held a cup in her hand, and Gage could smell chicory and lemon.

"Good morning, Gage," she said brightly. "So you've come to get me out of my prison?"

"Miss Simza, I can't believe how well you look," Gage said. "Aren't you in pain? You had a bad day yesterday, a bad accident."

"I would like for you to call me Baba Simza, if you want," she said casually. "Pain, yes, maybe. But your *gaje* medicine, it works well. I just have to make sure I don't take so much that it makes me silly and dizzy, like wine bibbers. But just enough, and it makes the pain ho-kay," she said with relish. "And a good report maketh the bones fat. I have had a good report from *miry deary Dovvel*, and so my bones are getting fat instead of broken. Now, take me outside, I'm smothering, I need to see *cam*, the sun."

Gage carried her outside, and indeed she did harangue Niçu for several minutes until he got her chair fixed just right. Gage carried her from here to there to here like a queen in a palanquin, as she pointed and gesticulated and fussed. Finally she settled on a spot underneath the overhanging roof of her wagon, facing right across the campsite. Her bare feet were in the hot sunlight, but she said, "When *cam* gets a little higher, I'll be in the shade."

They had breakfast, which was fresh bread with sweet butter, jacket potatoes, and a starchy-sweet crunchy green shoot that the Gypsies dipped in strawberry preserves. "This is good," Gage said, holding up the celery-like shoot. "What is it?"

"Heart of cattail," Mirella answered. "It's very good in salads, in soups, mixed with vegetables."

"Cattails?" Denny said with amazement. Though he hadn't been able to eat much, he had taken a bite of the mysterious crunchy vegetable. "I didn't know you could eat cattails."

"Neither did I," Gage said with a hint of regret. How many times had his army been starving, and had passed by stands of cattails with never a second look?

When they finished breakfast, Simza told Gage, "Bring the *gajo* to me."

Gage went to Denny's pallet and said, "Baba Simza wants to see you. I think she's going to pray for you. Will you come?"

"Yes, if you'll help me," he said. Gage helped him walk to Simza's chair and sat him down by it. Denny had enough strength to sit there, childlike, looking up at her. "Hello, Dennis. I am Simza, and if you like, you may call me Baba Simza. Nadyha has told me all about you, and your sickness. Are you a Christian, Dennis?"

He looked slightly dazed, and answered, "Not exactly, ma'am. I mean, I believe that there is a God, but I don't know much more about all that."

She nodded with understanding, and placed both her hands on Denny's cheeks. "Then you bow your head, and close your eyes, and you say to God whatever you can think of. Tell Him if you're mad at Him, or that you believe in Him, or that you don't believe in Him, or that you thank Him because He can heal you, and He will."

Obediently Denny bowed his head and closed his eyes. Simza laid her hands on his shoulders and closed her eyes. Her lips moved, though she made no sound. After a few moments she smiled and said, "*Anarania*. Now, Dennis, you can look up again. Go on back and take your medicine and do what Nadyha tells you. The Lord is going to heal you, whether you believe Him or not."

"Thank you, ma—Baba Simza," he said.

Denny went back to his bed, which was now, thanks to Nadyha and Mirella, a dreamily thick mattress of Spanish moss with some sweet-smelling rosemary mixed in it.

Nadyha gave him his dose, made him cough and spit, and then said, "Today you blow on the whistle every time you take the medicine. Here."

She took a small hollow reed out of her pocket with one small notch cut in it. Fitting it to Denny's lips, she ordered, "Blow."

Denny blew, but no note came out of the reed, only a weak hissing sound. "Harder," Nadyha said sternly. He obeyed, and for a second one tiny note, high and weak, sounded, but then he started coughing. "That's good for now," Nadyha said. "All day, try to make the note sound on the whistle." Now exhausted, Denny laid down and went promptly to sleep.

Gage was watching them, puzzled. Nadyha said, "It will make his chest stronger. Don't worry, *gajo*, I'm not playing a Gypsy trick on him."

He started to say, "No, I know you wouldn't do that," but she tossed her head and walked away.

Gage went to sit cross-legged by Baba Simza's chair. She was sewing a white shirt, squinting a little. She greeted him with a smile. "I have something to tell you. You taught me a good lesson yesterday."

"I did?"

"Yes, and it took me all night to think on it." She looked down at him and searched his face with her penetrating dark stare. "Because it was a hard lesson, too, for me. For a Gypsy. Do you know how we came to be called Gypsies?"

"No, ma'am."

"It's said that when the baby Jesus and the Holy Family went into exile in Egypt, we sheltered them. For that we were driven out, exiled forever. The name 'Gypsy' comes from Egyptian, *Egyptienne*, 'gyptian, Gypsy. And so we became a lost people with no homeland, and ever since then we've been wanderers. And we have been despised.

We've been cast out, hunted, tortured, hung, burnt, murdered in cold blood. Here in America it's not so bad. But some of our kin tell of Gypsies accused of stealing. They can be hung and all of their possessions taken and not a word said, nothing done. Everywhere Gypsies go they know that threat hangs over them."

Gage said thoughtfully, "I didn't know any of that. I mean, I've heard of Gypsies, and I've seen them once or twice in New Orleans. People think—they think they're—" He hesitated.

"Oh, yes, the *gaje* think we're all fortune-tellers, sorcerers, soothsayers, cheaters, tricksters," Baba Simza said with a dismissive wave of her sewing needle. "If we don't get caught stealing, it's because we have 'wicked devices' as the Proverbs say." She stabbed the shirt vengefully.

"Yes, ma'am, I'm afraid that's true," Gage said unhappily. "I guess I'm just an ignorant *gaje* myself. When I heard you all praying this morning I thought you were chanting, or something. I have to admit it's been a great surprise to me to find that you're such a good Christian, ma'am."

"Pah, who is a good Christian? Anyway, a lot of those sayings are true. Many of my people are just like that; the women want to be fortunetellers, mystical, wise, able to see the future. *Dukkering*, the *chovihani, miry deary Dovvel* hates it. And to most of the Gypsies, it is all tricking, anyway, they tell the silly *gaje* they must have money, only then can they see their futures, then they tell them a bunch of *shesti*. And there are Romany that are liars and cheats and thieves and adulterers and murderers." She shrugged. "We're just like other peoples. There are good and bad, smart and dumb, foolish and wise, heathen and Christian. It's just that we've gotten so that we hide everything about us from the *gaje*. So they see what they want to see."

"Yes, ma'am, I understand," Gage said thoughtfully.

"Anyway, I want to tell you my truth I learned from you," she continued in a lighter tone. "My favorite Bible book is Proverbs. I understand Proverbs, most of them, anyway. And what I've always taught is that the *gaje*, the ones who mistreat us, who hate us, who think we're dirty and liars and thieves, will pay for their wickedness, *miry deary Dovvel* promises over and over again that He will make them pay."

"That's very true," Gage said, mystified. "I hope I haven't done something wicked that you think I'm getting away with."

She chuckled. "No, no, that's not the lesson." Again she put down her sewing to look directly at him. "Yesterday, I needed help, and it was surprising that a *gaje* would take such care of a Gypsy, and then be so generous as to give me the medicine, without taking money for it when Nadyha offered. But the real lesson came when *you* asked *us* for help. No one has ever asked a Gypsy for help. At least, not that I know of. And that was when I started thinking that Gypsies need to help others too. All my life I've thought that since we were so despised, that the *gaje* should give to us, and they should pay when they treat us badly. The only help Gypsies must give is to our *familia*, our *vitsi*, our *kumpania*. And I remembered Jesus said even the publicans, the trickster *choros* do that. How much more should we give?"

Gage grinned engagingly. "Uh-oh. It's been my experience that once the Lord taught me something like that about myself, it seemed like every time I turned around it was slap-up in my face. I hope you don't get run over by needy *gajes*, Baba Simza."

"It would be good for us, maybe. Especially Nadyha. She learns this hard lesson from you too, Gage. She would never admit it, but I know, I see her thinking about it. She's quick. And I can tell you that this is the only reason she ever would have asked you and Dennis to come here, to stay with us. I think the lesson hits her hard, too," she said with satisfaction.

"Is she a Christian, ma'am? I can't quite make it out, with her."

Simza sighed. "She knows God, she knows Jesus from when she was just young, a *bitti chavi*. But now she's angry, she wonders, she can't think of why things are the way they are, she doesn't like this, she doesn't like that. So she draws away, she makes fun, she has the smart lips. *Hai*. She thinks she forgets God, but He won't forget her."

WHILE HE AND SIMZA were talking, he watched the others as they began their day. As Niçu had said, these people worked. Nadyha, tucking her hair up into a wide-brimmed straw hat, went off into the woods with a small spade, a rake, and some hand tools. Boldo the bear followed her, and then with deadly silent grace Anca padded off down the path behind them. Mirella tended to the fire, making preparations for dinner and supper. Then she began to weave baskets. Niçu got his armorer's forge going and began working with sheets of tin.

Gage decided to go hunting, as Denny seemed to be resting quietly. The pickings were easy in this stretch of thick woods, and just to the east of the ridge was a canebrake that covered several square miles. He went there, and came back in the early afternoon, his gamebag full, and carrying a trussed wild boar slung over his shoulder.

He greeted Baba Simza, who was still sitting in her chaise sewing, and went to the lean-to. Niçu was sharpening a knife, and Gage stopped for a moment to watch in admiration. Niçu had made a sword-like handle for a long tapering whetstone, and he sharpened the butcher knife by clashing them back and forth, as if sword-fighting himself. The butcher knife glinted keenly in the sun.

Gage went to the lean-to worktable, threw the boar down on it with a grunt, and began to unload his game bag. Neatly he started lining up his birds, eight doves and two of the large quails called chukars. Mirella, Niçu, and Nadyha joined him. Slowly Niçu reached out and picked up a bird. It was headless, with a piece of twine tied tightly around its throat.

"So you climbed a tree and strangled these birds?" he rasped.

Gage grinned. "Not hardly. But I tied them up at the neck so they wouldn't uh—lose all the—uh—you, know, in my game bag."

"Blood?" Nadyha suggested. "And you also shot the boar in the eye so you wouldn't have to see all that blood?"

"I just—I forgot to ask, before I went hunting," Gage said with some confusion. "You were so upset about my red shirt, and I remembered that we haven't had any meat to eat, and then I got afraid that maybe the red, because it's the color of blood, you know—"

Mirella, Niçu, and Nadyha exchanged amused glances. "Gypsies eat meat, Gage," Nadyha explained as if to a small child. "Yes, the *lalo* color is unclean to us because of blood, but only *mahrime*, unclean blood, from sickness, wounds, things like that."

"Do you tell me you shot the heads off these birds? Really?" Niçu said in wonder. "And the boar, exactly in the eye! You must be a really good shot."

"Yeah, I always have been," Gage said casually. "It just comes naturally to me somehow. So, if you'll show me where I can dress out this boar—maybe somewhere outside the camp?"

Niçu said, "Behind the lean-to, there's a low-hanging branch, we can hang it up. It'll be easier. C'mon, I'll help you, Gage."

"Okay. Ladies, I'll be glad to clean those birds, too. I've gotten really good at it."

Mirella said, "No, Nadyha and I will do it." Her eyes sparkled as she looked at the boar, then at Niçu. "Guess for supper tonight?"

With relish Niçu rubbed his hands together and said, "*Gója!*"

Retrieving a stout rope from the lean-to, he and Gage went to the back and strung up the boar. Gage heard slow heavy breathing behind him and turned to see Anca sitting there watching them. Her deep golden gaze was one of intense interest. Her tongue came out and licked her three-inch, razor-sharp fangs. Her head almost reached Gage's waist. "Uh—hello there," he said weakly, stopping his dressing.

Niçu turned, saw the cougar, and shrugged. "She loves boar, it's just about all she hunts."

"Is that right. Think she wants this one? 'Cause for my part she can have it if she wants it."

"Yes, she's definitely expecting a nice haunch when we get through." Then Niçu went on quietly, "You know, the reason we don't have much meat is because I don't know how to shoot. The Perradoses, they never let us have guns."

"I haven't heard about the Perradoses yet," Gage said. "But if you want to learn how to shoot, I'll teach you."

"You will?" Niçu said excitedly. "So I can shoot like you?"

He was, after all, only about twenty or twenty-one, Gage had guessed. With a pang he realized that, at twenty-five years old, he felt immeasurably older than Niçu. "Maybe," Gage said cautiously. "But I'd want to teach you on my Mississippi rifle. This rifle, my Whitworth"—it was still slung over his shoulder and he pulled it to cradle it in his arms—"is a sharpshooter's weapon, it's so accurate—"

Niçu interrupted him, "What's a sharpshooter?"

"Some of us were very good with a rifle, so we were chosen to go in close to the enemy, find a good 'hide,' and shoot them one at a time. Because most of the time you can't get closer than a half-mile or so, we had these special rifles."

Slowly Niçu said, "You shot them one at a time . . . from a half-mile away?"

"Or maybe a little more." Gage was clearly uncomfortable with the conversation, so he went on in a lighter tone, "So this is a special rifle, and it takes special ammunition, and I don't have a whole lot left. I have a couple of boxes of cartridges for the Mississippi, though. But I do like to use my Whitworth for hunting. It messes up small game too much unless it's a head shot."

"And the boar?" Niçu asked, his depthless eyes glinting.

"Aw, that was just for fun."

They finished dressing out the boar, and Anca took her quarter haunch from Gage's hand as delicately as a lady picking up a *petits four*. Dragging it, she walked out into the woods.

Gage and Niçu went to wash up at the pump, and Gage saw Boldo, whose fat torso was completely wrapped up in honeysuckle vines. The bear was happily pulling pieces of the vines off and stuffing them into his mouth. One long vine was twisted around his head like a garland. Gage laughed. "Seeing that one, it's hard to believe that bears can be so vicious."

Niçu said evenly, "You've seen bears that are vicious, have you?"

"No, I've just heard the stories."

"They aren't, you know, unless you threaten them, or unless you blunder up on a mother with cubs. Their favorite foods are vines and berries and roots and especially honey. Not people."

"And crawfish," Gage added. "He loved them."

"Yes, they do love fish. And occasionally they might grab a rabbit or a squirrel, if they're really hungry. But Nadyha never lets Boldo have any meat. She doesn't want him to get a taste for it."

"Smart," Gage murmured. Boldo was small even for a black bear, which was of the smallest species. He was per-haps five feet tall when reared up, about three feet on all fours. Of course, he had the huge paws and deadly claws, but on Boldo they were just kind of funny, as he tried to handle things like crawfish and honeysuckle flowers.

That night Gage found out what *gója* was, and he thor-oughly approved, and decided that he wasn't, after all, sick of onions. Mirella had stuffed the boar, not with cornbread or white bread, but with grated potatoes, diced onions, tiny pieces of boiled quail, and rice, seasoned it with an assort-ment of herbs, and then had baked it all afternoon long. It was mouthwatering. For Denny and Baba Simza, who were still on rather restricted diets, she had boiled a squab, picked out the tenderest darkest meat, and had made a rich brown broth. They were gathered by Baba Simza's chair in the fall of the evening, drinking the strong black coffee that the Gypsies loved, and talking. Denny sat in one of the cane chairs next to her, while Gage, Niçu, and Mirella sat cross-legged by them in the cool deep mint.

"I want to tell you a *lil*," Baba Simza said. Niçu, Mirella, and Nadyha set down their tin coffee cups and came to attention.

"Long ago was a Big Man *gajo*, a powerful and cruel man with much land, much treasure, and many slaves. He found the Romany camping in one of his pastures, by a stream, and he hated them. He said if they didn't leave by the day after, he would have all of the men hung and he would enslave all of the women and children.

"That night the Romany gathered up their camp and left at dawn. As they were on the road, they saw this Big Man, this cruel *gajo*, on the side of the road. He had been robbed, and stripped, and beaten so bad he might be dying."

Gage noticed that Niçu, Mirella, and Nadyha exchanged rather confused glances. A trace of a smile played on Baba Simza's leathery lips.

"All of the Romany were happy to see the Big Man there, and hoped he would die. They said he should pay for his sins, for he was hated not just by them but by the slaves and freedmen and all the peoples around him. And so they went on, *vardo* and *vardo* and *vardo*, and all of them looked down on him lying there bleeding, and said to themselves that so it should be.

"Now there was one young *romoro*, who did well because he was a goldsmith, and he was to be married soon. As he drove by in his *vardo*, he looked down at the Big Man and felt pity and sorrow in his heart. He stopped, and then the *vitsi* stopped. 'I must help the Big Man,' the *romoro* said.

"And his *vitsi* all called him a *dilo*, and said he was stupid because once the man was found, it might even be said that the Gypsies had done this to him, and he would probably be hung if he tried to help the Big Man. And his young *chavi* pleaded with him, and the *Rom Baro* and the *Phuri Dae* forbid him, but it did no good. And so the *vitsi* left the *romoro* and the Big Man.

"The *romoro* picked up the Big Man and laid him on his bed in his *vardo*, and then went to the next village, to the *gaje* doctor, and said, 'Here are clothes for him, and fine boots, and here is money. Will you take care of him?' And the doctor said he would, because it was a good sum of gold coins."

She sat back and studied her grandchildren, then said with emphasis, *"Amaro deary Dovvel* blessed that *romoro* for his mercy. He married and had many children, and when he died he sat at the Lord's Wedding Feast in a place of honor. *Hai,* Lord Jesus, may it be so for me and mine."

DENNY HAD A QUIET night, with no fever and only three coughing spells. Though he could give himself his medicine now, Gage still woke up and gave it to him, then sat with him until the coughing spells passed, and took the rags to the fire pit. Still, it was more sleep than either Denny or Gage had had for many days.

Niçu wanted Gage to give him a little target practice before they went hunting. Niçu said, "Let me show you something." He went into the lean-to and led Gage around to the back, where the horses' bales of hay were stacked. Niçu tucked the top of a canvas square just above his head between two bales of hay and unfolded it; it was a target, a series of black circles from large to the small center. It already had many holes it it, Gage noticed. Seeing his curious look, Niçu said, "I'll show you." From the lean-to he brought out an upright block with eight knives stuck hilt-up in it. "Hold this," Niçu commanded Gage.

Then, casually but swiftly, *swit-thoomp, swit-thoomp* seven times, and seven of the knives stuck out of the target in a precise small circle around the bullseye. With a flourish Niçu picked up the last knife, threw it, and it landed exactly in the center of the circle.

Gage's blue eyes were alight. "I've never seen anything like that before! That's really something, Niçu. With your eye, I don't think you're going to have any trouble learning to shoot."

"So can we use the target?" Niçu asked eagerly.

Gage shook his head. "Sorry. Rifle bullets travel a long, long way. I'm afraid we'd do some damage in the lean-to, and we might shoot Baba Simza or, heaven forbid, one of Nadyha's pets. No, I'll tell you what we can do. I'll take you out to the canebrake, where I was hunting yesterday. All those tall stalks of cane, it's easy to pick out a target, near or far. And I'll bet you'll bag something today, too, Niçu. Seems like you're a good man with a weapon."

Niçu splintered lots of tall reeds, shot several cattails in the head, and brought down a wild turkey. He lamented that it wasn't a head shot, but Gage said, "It was a clean high chest shot, front-on, Niçu. A good shot, especially for your very first time with a rifle in your hands."

Niçu swelled with pride and, when they got back to camp, told Mirella in excited Gypsy, with much gesticulation, about every single reed, cattail, and the wiles of the turkey.

Gage found Denny now sitting up, his back against a very thick pillow propped up against a tree. To Gage's amusement, Matchko the cat was sitting on Denny's lap, his one eye half-closed, his paws tucked primly under his chest. Denny was stroking his head. "Nadyha said I could," he said defensively.

"What? Sit up, or pet the cat?" Gage said as he sat down beside Denny's pallet.

"Both. But it seems like this dumb cat decided that I must be here for the sole reason of petting him," Denny said with mock disgust. "I'm the only one around here that's not working."

"Yeah, and measles and pneumonia's no excuse for it, either. You should be ashamed of yourself."

"Oh, I am," Denny said unconvincingly. "How'd Niçu do? He looks and sounds pretty excited. Bet he didn't shoot it in the eye like you do."

"He did real good for his first time. And you gotta see him throw knives, I've never seen anything like it."

Denny looked at him curiously. "Hey, Gage? Can you shoot as well with handguns as with a rifle?"

Gage smiled a little. "I had a captain that loved to have competition between us sharpshooters. We were all pretty good, you know, so it kinda got to where one was about as accurate as the other. My captain got bored with the Whitworths, so we started having handgun competitions with the officers' Army Colts. That was fun, I wish I could afford a pistol. Anyway, yeah, like I've told you before, it just kinda comes natural to me. I usually won. Why?"

"Oh, just curious," Denny said casually. He turned to watch the Gypsies.

Gage followed his gaze. Mirella and Nadyha were working at the campfire, Nadyha making coffee and Mirella brewing tea. It was odd, Gage thought, he never really noticed what Nadyha and Mirella wore, because it was so plain, just a faded gray or blue skirt; plain blouse with short, puffed sleeves and high, rounded necklines. They tied their hair up with bright ribbons, the only color on them. Baba Simza had worn the headscarf called the *diklo*, and patterned skirts and colored blouses. Gage suspected she only did it because she wasn't up working. The women, Gage had observed, always went barefoot while Niçu wore boots. Nice boots, of good leather, with one-inch heels, taller than average.

"Nadyha's fixing you some kind of tea, but she's fixing me some coffee. You can't have any," Gage teased Denny. Then his eyes narrowed; close by them, the ground-sweeping willow leaves were stirring a bit. There was no breeze on the stifling afternoon air. Gage caught a single brief glimpse, he thought, of tawny gold behind the leaves.

"I don't want any coffee anyway," Denny sniffed. "This taste in my mouth, yech. Nadyha and Mirella have been making me chicory tea with honey. It's good. And I'm kinda glad not to be drinking anisette all day long, too. It puts me to sleep, even if I just woke up."

"It's good for you, Billy Yank," Gage said firmly. "Sleep's the best thing—"

Anca poked her head through the willow leaves. Staring at Gage with her gleaming yellow unblinking eyes, for a moment she looked disembodied, as if her head was mounted on a green wall. Slowly she came through the willow-curtain and walked toward Denny and Gage, eyeing Gage all the time.

Gage scrambled to his feet and Denny muttered nervously, "What are you doing!"

"I'm thinking about running so maybe she'll eat you first," Gage retorted. He gave Nadyha a pleading look as she stood across the site at the campfire, but she merely crossed her arms and watched with amusement.

Anca padded up to Gage and stared up at his face, directly into his eyes, which made the hairs on Gage's arms rise up in goosebumps. He stared back at her, his eyes wide and a dark royal blue.

Casually the cougar dropped her head and rubbed it on Gage's leg. Then she took a step, rubbing against him as she passed, turned, and rubbed up against him again. She was just like a giant kitty-cat, one who arches its back and threads in between your legs. Gage stood stiff and stock-still, as if his entire body had suddenly frozen.

Nadyha's expression changed to one of disbelief and she stamped over to them. "Anca! You *lubni*, you tromple! What are you doing?"

Anca ignored her and continued her walking caress of Gage's leg. "What do I do?" he asked Nadyha helplessly.

"Pet her, *dinili*," she said acidly. "Seems like it's what she wants." She sat down cross-legged on the ground, watching her cougar with disdain.

Gage reached down and tentatively stroked her massive head. She stopped and butted his hand with her head. He kept stroking her, then rubbed her ears. Just like a pleased kitten, she pushed her head against his hand. Slowly, and with relief, Gage sat down. Anca plopped down just beside him and gave Nadyha a stare that seemed to say, "So? You were saying?"

Nadyha muttered, "She doesn't like anyone, especially men."

"What's a tromple?" Denny said blankly.

"It's a—you know, the bad woman, the *lubni*, the loose woman," Nadyha answered with an impatient wave of her hand.

Aside, Gage told Denny, "Maybe it's like Gypsy for a trollop and a tramp."

"Oh, yeah," Denny said uncertainly. Then he asked Nadyha, "Ma'am, I gotta ask you, isn't that cougar danger-ous? You just said she doesn't like people. Does that mean when she has a bad day she might decide to eat one of us?"

Nadyha visibly softened. "No, no, she would never, never do that. She's not tame, like Boldo, but she wouldn't attack anyone."

"But why not?" Denny persisted. Gage was still stroking the cougar's head and shoulders, marveling at the smooth muscles rippling under his hand.

"It's hard to explain to a *gaje*," Nadyha said. "It's like Gypsies and horses, with Anca and me. Gypsies believe that horses are their brothers. Anca is my *she'enedra*, my sister of the heart. She—I found her, shot. She was about to give birth. She had two kits, one girl and one boy. The little girl one died, but the boy one lived. I helped Anca and the little boy cub, I stayed with her for three days and nights. Then she got better, and she was able to get up and move around. She followed me back here, but she didn't stay, she came and went with the little boy one. Finally he left, and Anca came here to live. Not because I made her do it. Because she wants to. That's why she wouldn't attack anyone. She's chosen to live with people." Nadyha gave Anca another glance, her mouth twisted. "She tolerates Niçu, because he helped me with her at first. But I've never seen her get so *dilo* over anyone else."

"Maybe it's because of the boar," Gage said, now smiling down at the cougar.

"Maybe," Nadyha agreed reluctantly.

Feeling that she was in a talkative mood, Gage said, "So Baba Simza explained to me about Gypsies, where the word comes from, and why you don't consider it an insult. But I'm still dying to know about the catfish."

Now she smiled, and to Gage it seemed that her eyes changed from a smoky brownish-green to a deep emerald color. "Ah, yes, the cat, the dog, and the catfish! You probably won't understand, *gajo*, but I'll try to tell you. Gypsies believe that the world must be balanced, that people and things and animals must be in a—in tune, like music, yes? Certain animals are considered *wuzho*, pure, clean in the spirit. Horses are *wuzho*, vultures are *wuzho*."

"Vultures?" Denny repeated in disbelief. He was petting Matchko in much the same way Gage was petting Anca.

"Yes, they keep the balance, because they clear the world of the unclean dead," Nadyha said earnestly. "*Tale*, hawks, are neither *wuzho* nor *mahrime*, but Baba Simza likes Rai because he flies like the buzzard. But lots of animals are considered *mahrime*, unclean. The frog is the worst, because he is born in water and then creeps the earth."

She spoke with such disgust and dread that Gage was reminded of a girl he'd known who literally fainted dead away at the sight of a spider. Of course, he couldn't imagine Nadyha having the vapors over anything, but the look of horror on her face was the same as the girl's had been. "'Frog' is one of our old names for the devil," she continued. "Also *mahrime* are dogs. Foxes are very impure because they are both dog and cat, and neither. And cats are considered *mahrime* because they are supposed to walk the earth, but they still jump and climb and walk the trees. And so you see, Baba Simza would never eat a 'cat-fish.' That would be even worse than foxes," Nadyha said, now her expressive face alight with amusement.

Gage said with surprise, "But she allows Anca and Matchko to live here with you?"

"Mm. Baba Simza isn't as strict, as—um—Pharisee, as many Gypsies are. She doesn't care much for Anca or Matchko, but she doesn't mistreat them either. I think it's been kind of a struggle for her, to put together our ancient beliefs with her Christian beliefs. When Anca first came, Baba Simza was very angry with me. But I reminded her of one of her Proverbs, the one about the lion, and so she says nothing else to me. She wanted to, though, as Anca stayed longer and longer I could tell Baba Simza was trying not to bursten!" she said with a low, throaty chuckle.

"I don't know the thing, the proverb about the lion," Denny said with interest. "What's that all about?"

"I don't know the Proverbs like Baba Simza, but I know this one," Nadyha said mischievously. *"There be three things which go well, yea, four are comely in going: A lion which is strongest among beasts, and turneth not away for any; a greyhound; an he goat also; and a king, against whom there is no rising up."*

"Poor Baba Simza," Gage sighed. "Right there you have a cat *and* a dog."

Nadyha nodded. "I know she's dreading the day when I see some puppies. Anyway, while we're talking about *mahrime* and *wuzho*, I did want to explain to you some things that we all do take seriously. About the washing, the cleaning of oneself and the clothes." She waved at the lean-to, her tanned skin glowing in the dappled sunlight. "Today we wash. I'll show you, there's one pot for—" She stopped, placed her hands palm-upright at her waist, and brought them up to her neck. "For these parts. Another pot for"—she waved vaguely toward her legs—"those parts. Understand?"

"Yes, ma'am," Gage and Denny said solemnly.

"For bathing. Gypsies only bathe in running water," she said sternly. "Usually on one day Baba Simza and I go to the spring, then Mirella and Niçu go the next, and they went this morning. If you want to go, Gage, you can go this afternoon."

"I would like to have a good bath," he said longingly. Then he said, "I'll go through the whole spring, if I have to, to make sure there aren't any more traps."

Nadyha sighed, a deep, mournful sound. "We've been bathing at the spring for many, many years. Never before have we seen a trap anywhere near it. It was so strange, that trap. Baba Simza always wants to wash the—the—upper right in the spring, and then come down to the stream to finish. How many times has she stood right there . . . ?"

"Even though this is high ground, ma'am, it still gets waterlogged," Gage said. "Maybe the rains just finally washed it on down into the pool."

"Maybe," Nadyha said almost dreamily. "Baba Simza said it was *baxt, baksheesh*. I thought she might be stupid from the pain, the shock, for her to say it was meant to be, even that it was a—a—good path laid before her." Her green-glass eyes rested on Gage.

In a low voice, he said, "She's a wise woman, Baba Simza. Maybe she knows something that we don't."

Nadyha, coming out of her reverie, rose and dusted off her skirt. "She knows a lot of things that we don't," she said crisply. "I'm tired of talking now. Go ask Baba Simza all of your questions. Niçu told me that no one has explained to you why we're the Perrados Gypsies. Baba Simza will tell you that *lil*."

Anca got up and followed her. Gage said dryly, "That's exactly what women are always doing to me. They get tired of me and just jump up and walk away."

Denny was in a brown study. "Gage? Explain to me again about the frogs. 'Cause all I could think of, when she was talking, was how good some fried frog legs would be."

"I wouldn't ask for that particular dish if I were you," Gage warned him. "If you do, I bet we'd get kicked out of here real quick. And I wouldn't like that."

"Neither would I," Denny said, lying back sleepily. "It's kind of like being in another world, isn't it? With them, and this place, and the animals, and all. I feel like we're real lucky to be here."

"*Baksheesh*," Gage said half to himself. "A good path laid before you."

CHAPTER SEVEN

Gage and Denny slept, even though the lazy sun climbed up from the east and as always, one playful sunbeam danced right across Gage's face.

Nadyha said, "Wake up, lazy *gajo*! Baba Simza says to tell you, a little sleep, a little slumber, a little folding of the hands to sleep, and you'll be poor and hungry and, I don't know, something about wanteth and travelleth."

Gage and Denny sat up, bleary-eyed, and Denny mumbled, "Huh? Whassat?"

Nadyha turned on her heel and went back to the campfire.

Gage yawned hugely. "It's a Proverb. I'll read it to you later."

They could tell by the delicious aromas of fresh bread and strong coffee that breakfast was almost ready. Denny coughed, but his congestion was already much better. He got his whistle, took a deep breath, and blew as hard as he could. A loud screeching shrill note rent the air. Boldo started and looked scared to death. Rai flew off with an indignant flapping of wings. Anca looked at Denny with such temper that Denny got nervous and forgot to cough.

Nadyha jumped, then yelled, "That's fine, Dennis! Forget about the whistle, ho-kay?"

He was already much better, it was plain. He had no fever and he ate almost as much breakfast as Gage did. They were all sitting cross-legged around the campfire, except for Baba Simza, who sat in her chaise. She looked up at the hot blue sky, and the enormous blinding sun-disk. A few tendrils of clouds floated slowly across it, coming from the south. "*Hai*. It storms this afternoon."

Nadyha said with resignation, "I picked lots of herbs yesterday, my drying racks are full. I'll have to put the covers on them."

"I'll help you, Miss Nadyha," Gage offered. "I'd really like to see your garden."

She stared at him quizzically. "You would? Why?"

"I dunno, I guess I'm just curious, I like to learn new things. I thought it was so interesting, about the Grains of Paradise, and the anisette. Also I'm kinda curious about where my horse is disappearing to all day, running around with Tinar and Saz. Every evening he comes back I'm afraid he's going to be black and white with a long mane and tail and feathered hocks. He already thinks I'm just another dumb *gaje*."

They all laughed. Nadyha said, "Well, he is a very smart horse, I've noticed."

"Thanks a lot," Gage said dryly. "What kind of horses are Tinar and Saz, anyway? I've never seen any quite like them. They're very showy, their conformation is like Thoroughbreds, but they're built so strong, like solid workhorses."

The Gypsies exchanged sly glances. "The *gaje* call them Gypsy cobs," Niçu answered disdainfully. "We've been breeding them for a long, long time. The Perrados, they let us breed our own stock. We were their horsemasters, you see, and they loved the high breeds, the Arabs and Thoroughbreds for saddle horses, and Percherons for draft horses. So we bred all of their horses, and for a hundred years the Perrados had the finest stables of all. He didn't really know about the horses bred for ourselves, and he didn't care. It was a Gypsy secret."

"I haven't heard about the Perrados yet," Gage said. "So you worked for the family?"

"It's a long story," Nadyha said. "But maybe I'll tell it to you when you come to the garden with me." Baba Simza looked pleased, and Nadyha made a small face at her. Gage pretended not to see.

Nadyha was dressed in her usual gray skirt and shapeless blouse, with her knife at her side. She tucked her wealth of hair up into her wide-brimmed straw hat, and then took the path directly behind her wagon. After about a quarter of a mile of thick woods they came to a flat clearing. Gage was surprised at the size of it; he estimated it must be about two hundred feet square. Adding to his surprise, it was completely surrounded by a six-foot-high ornate black wrought-iron fence. Much of the garden was neat squares, with green and flowering shrubs and bushes and plants, but some of the beds were raised, surrounded by cypress stakes and with Spanish moss at the bottom of the bed. On one side were the drying racks, simple waist-high stands with corrugated tin tops, covered by cheesecloth so the drying herbs wouldn't stick to the hot metal. All along the fence grew a breathtaking array of flowering vines: honeysuckle, trumpet vine, morning glory, jasmine, passion flower, and moonflower.

Pushing open the gate, Nadyha said matter-of-factly, "The fence is to keep out the deer and the raccoons. But I grow the vines for them to eat. And for Boldo, of course, silly old bear." He had followed them, and now he nonchalantly took a step toward the open gate, but Nadyha said, "No, no, Boldo, you know you aren't allowed in here. Go on, go get in the shade, I'll bring you some *habben*." Resignedly the bear went to the back of the garden and climbed an old oak tree, sitting on a branch about six feet from the ground overlooking the garden. His bear-face was filled with longing.

Nadyha, taking Gage at his word, started walking up and down the rows, naming the herbs growing. Standing by a thick rosemary bush, she said, "Pah! I weed all times, and here they are, the dandelions, this nutgrass, the thistle." Falling to her knees, she started rooting in the dirt. Gage walked to the next plant, and they ended up crawling up and down the rows, finding devilish little weed sprouts everywhere. Down on his hands and knees, with his face close to the herbs, Gage was enchanted by the delicate, sweet, savory, spicy aromas.

The covers for the drying racks were stored underneath them, simple squares of two-by-fours with tin tops that set on top of the racks. When they finished they were hot and thirsty, for the sun still blazed in the sky, and the clouds were still weak little wisps. Nadyha said, "I'll get Boldo's treat, then we'll sit in the shade of the trees." With her knife she went to a large bush and cut several stems with big pinkish-white blooms. "Mallow," she told Gage. "It's all edible: blooms, seed pods, leaves, stems, roots. The flowers have a sweet taste that Boldo loves." Then she cut several long vines filled with honeysuckle flowers.

She led him around to the back of the fenced garden, and again Gage was surprised to see a stone bench, delicately carved, underneath the oak tree where Boldo was perched. He took his seat at one end and thirstily drank from his canteen. Nadyha handed the big bunch of flowers and some of the vines to Boldo, and happily he began munching. With a sidelong look at Gage, Nadyha pulled her skirt tightly around her and sat at the very end, on the very edge, of the bench. At his rueful look she said, "In the old days, if a woman's skirt so much as brushed up against a man, the skirt was considered unclean."

"In the old days," Gage gravely repeated. "Do you believe that now?"

"No, of course not," she said hastily, then settled back more comfortably on the bench. Taking her hat off, she shook her head so her hair fell in an ebony flow all around her shoulders. Then she began winding some of the honeysuckle vines around the crown of her hat.

"I wonder so much about you and your people," Gage said. "Won't you tell me about the Perrados? And about your *vitsi*?"

Nadyha told him the history of the Gypsies with the Perrados family, how they had been brought to New Orleans as slaves, but then Xavier Perrados freed them after her great-great-grandfather's heroic saving of the horses. "After that we became part of the Perrados plantation, we had our own little settlement, our own houses and barn and stables. I suppose it's the Gypsy blood," she said with a small secret smile, "because over time some of the Romany left, some stayed to be Perrados Gypsies. By the time the Great War came, there were forty-two of us, and there were twenty-one Gypsy homes in our corner of the plantation."

"But surely you don't mean that you four are all that's left."

"No," she said quietly. "The rest of our *vitsi*, they had to leave." She hesitated, looking out through the deep, quiet woods surrounding them. Gage waited patiently; he sensed she would tell him when she found the words.

Finally she said, "The Blue Beasts came. First they told *Kako* Perrados that his taxes would be $3,000, and he had that much money. Then they came back and said, 'No, it's $5,000,' and he said he could get that much together. And the third time they came back they said, 'No, we made a mistake before, your taxes are $8,000, and you must pay it now, or we'll take the plantation.' *Kako* Perrados didn't have $8,000. His wife had died ten years ago, with the yellow fever, and he missed her. Both of his sons had gone away to the Great War. In a week, his heart, it broke and he died."

"I'm so sorry," Gage said sadly. "It sounds like he wasn't just a *gaje*, that he was different. For you, for the Gypsies, I mean."

She nodded. "*Kako*, that means uncle, but it's really a term of respect and affection, and we called his wife *Kaki* Perrados. For so many years we had been Perrados Gypsies . . . but that was all gone, all over.

"When the Blue Beasts found out we were free, not slaves, they told us we must pay the taxes too. All of us had to pay $500 for our houses." Her mouth twisted grimly. "It could have been $5,000, or $50,000. They knew that, of course."

"What did you do?"

She lifted her chin in that proud gesture that Gage was coming to know, and her eyes sparked defiantly. "We took our houses and made our *vardos*. We had sixteen horses that the Blue Beasts didn't know about. We came here, built our *vardos*, and then it was time for us to leave. But Baba Simza said that she knew, *Dovvel* had showed her, that she must stay, that Mirella and Niçu must stay, and that I must stay." She sounded regretful, and a little sad.

"That must have been hard for you," he said. "Did you have other family?"

"Oh, yes. My father was—is—the *Rom Baro*, the Big Man, of our *vitsi*. My mother is only forty years old, and I have three younger sisters and two younger brothers. It was hard, it is hard. I miss them, I miss all of them."

"I'm kind of surprised you stayed," Gage said slowly. "You seem to have your own mind, your own way, Nadyha."

Dryly she said, "Oh, you've noticed?" Then she shrugged. "My brother Niçu and I, we've always been very close. There's a five-year difference between us and my next sister. And both of us, I guess, are Baba Simza's favorites, though she'd never admit it. And Mirella, poor Mirella. She was expecting a child when the *vitsi* left, and we all thought it might be better if she wasn't on the road, traveling. We're not used to that life, you see, as other Gypsies are. But she lost the baby anyway. And then she lost another baby, just last year."

"That must be really, really hard," Gage said in a distant voice. He couldn't help but think of his own mother and father, and how they had just given him away, had deserted him. Brushing these futile thoughts aside, as he had done thousands of times during his life, he asked Nadyha, "And so now do you believe that Baba Simza made a mistake? That you should have gone with the *vitsi*?"

"No." Again she stared blankly out into the distance.

"What do you believe, Nadyha?" Gage asked softly.

He watched as the color in her cheeks heightened to deep coral, and when she turned to him her green-brown eyes were flashing. "I believe that Baba Simza and our fathers and mothers are right about one thing. This world, it's not in balance. It's not fair, it's a cruel world, with hateful people, and very bad things happen to good people, and those wrongs are never righted, and they're never avenged.

And I don't think God even cares about people like the Gypsies and Mirella and those two poor babies. Even the animals are cruel, even my Anca, when she first came to us she brought her kill into camp—" Her voice broke and she bowed her head, the black fall of her hair hiding her face. "It was a—a—doe, and she—she wasn't dead—" A small choking sound escaped from her.

Gage knew she was weeping, and he wanted, so badly, to put his arm around her and comfort her, as one would a child grieving over a dead puppy. But he knew Nadyha would be horrified if he touched her, so he said in a kind, low, reassuring voice, "I can see how you think God doesn't care, Nadyha, because you are right about this world. It's cruel and unjust, with wicked people that prosper, and good people that suffer.

"But that wasn't God's doing, you know. When He made the world, it was in perfect balance, and it was full of His love. When Adam and Eve fell, not only did all people fall into sin, but the whole earth fell into sin, and it became the hard, brutal place that you and I know now. Even Anca, she isn't wicked, she's just the way she is because of human sin. God didn't make her the way she is now, to be a killer. He made her a wondrous, gorgeous animal, and He gave her herbs and grasses to eat. But once the world fell into sin, it started working by the Devil's rules—predators and prey. Animals *and* humans."

As he had spoken, she had first furtively wiped her face with a corner of her apron, and then, when he started to talk about Anca, she straightened her bowed shoulders and turned to look at him with both wonder and disbelief on her ever-changing features. She said, "Is that true? What you said, you thought of it? And you tell me now, because I don't believe that *Dovvel* cares?"

"It's in the Bible," Gage answered patiently. "I just said it differently, that's all. But it's all true. Just like the only way that God could give us a chance to escape from the devil, and our own sin, was to send His Son, Jesus, to us, to take our place, to take our sin, and to die for it instead of us."

"But the part about the animals," she said insistently. "Is that true?"

"It is all true. You know the story of Adam and Eve, right?"

"Oh, yes, the serpent, and the fruit, and God made them animal skins to wear."

"Yes, I think that must have been from the first pred-ator's kill," Gage sighed. "Because until Adam and Eve sinned, the animals were meant to eat herbs and grass and, I can't remember the exact verse, but I can show it to you."

"I want to see. I want to read it myself."

"I'll show it to you." He smiled at her tentatively. She had lost that dreadfully sad look, and now seemed lively and curious. He went on lightly, "They could talk then, too, the animals. Before the fall."

"The Bible doesn't say that!"

"Maybe not. But it's always kind of struck me that God and Adam kind of interviewed all of the animals to find a suitable mate for Adam. None of them would do, of course, but I can't imagine that they would have wasted their time 'interviewing' the same mute animals that we know. And too, Eve wasn't a bit surprised when that snake started talking to her. It seems like if animals didn't talk, she might have turned and hightailed it away from that tree first thing when that old Devil said, 'Hi, there.'"

Nadyha laughed, the deep bubbling up of delight, as if from her innermost being. "You make me laugh, *gajo*. I never thought—anyway, I don't really know the Bible verses, because most of what I've learned about the Bible is from our teacher and Baba Simza telling us the *lils*."

"Bible stories, yes. It's kind of amazing how many people know the stories but they really don't know the verses. So you had a teacher? You went to school?"

"Oh, yes, the Perrados have been teaching Gypsy children to read and write for a long time."

"I noticed that you all are very well-spoken," Gage said thoughtfully. "Do you go to church? I mean, did you, before you had to leave?"

Nadyha answered evenly, "Always the Gypsies have been forced to take on the religion of their masters. But we've never been allowed to go to their churches." Her eyes narrowed as she went on, "There is a Gypsy *lil*, that I wouldn't know was true except *Kako* Perrados said all of his fathers kept writings about their family and their slaves. Once, *gajo*, our word for God was *Devvell*"—she pronounced it "deh-VEL"—"and one of *Kako* Perrados's fathers, many many years ago, heard the Gypsies in their camp praying to *amaro deary Devvell*. He thought we were praying to the devil, your devil, that we call *beng*." Her jaw hardened. "There were terrible men in the church back then. Perrados told the priests, and four Gypsies were burned."

"And so you had to change it to 'doh-VEL.' But Nadyha, you're smart, you've been educated, you know, that those kinds of things have happened to many, many peoples down through the ages, not just the Gypsies. Surely you understand that that's exactly why Jesus had to come down here, to be a human man, and to die for our sins. He died even for those men that burned your fathers, and He died for me, and for you. You understand about that, don't you?" he said earnestly.

"I know it in my head," she said, laying her hand against her forehead, "but it doesn't help here." She laid her hand on her heart. Then she rose and said, "Baba Simza was right; it's going to rain soon. Come with me, I'll show you where our horses are, and how we hid them, even from *Kako Perrados*," she said gleefully. "And from the Blue Beasts."

Following her, Gage said, "You know, I have to ask—did you say you took your houses to build your *vardos*? You mean, you stole your houses?"

Nadyha tossed her head. "Just like a *gaje*, Gypsies steal all the time. We took them, yes, but we didn't steal them. How can you steal from yourself? They were our houses."

Gage grinned. "Don't get your feathers all ruffled. I just think it's funny, and it's great. No one but the Gypsies would have thought of that."

She looked pleased. Heading due west, they soon came to another big clearing, and it was filled with so much red clover that it looked like a red carpet. Tinar, Saz, and Cayenne were grazing away happily. They raised their heads as Gage and Nadyha approached, and Tinar gave a whinny of recognition. To Gage's amusement, Matchko was lying on Tinar's back, sprawled sideways, his legs hanging limply down on each side. They went to pet the horses, and Matchko took offense, because he jumped down and stalked back off in the direction of the camp, his tail waving high and indignantly. Gage and Nadyha laughed, and Gage said, "I've got to tell you, you have the most interesting pets I've ever seen. They all have the most definite personalities, much more so than some people."

"They do, even Rai. He doesn't stay at the camp much, it seems as if he just gets lonely sometimes and visits." She waved to her left. "Over there is another pasture, and we planted it with *dûrvâ* grass. And then, past that, is Anca's killing ground," she said in a low voice, stepping closer to Saz and stroking his nose gently. "That—that time, Niçu took the doe from her and dragged it out to a clearing.

Since that time she takes her kills there. After she hunts, we see the vultures." She pointed to the sky and made a circular motion.

"I see," Gage said quietly. He stepped close to her, stroking Saz's neck, but not touching Nadyha in any way. "Anca's very smart, then. If she does that, she must sense that that's what you want."

Nadyha nodded. "Yes, I know. I feel more for Anca than I do for most people. Baba Simza says that's wrong, and maybe it is. But I can't help it."

"No," Gage agreed softly, "sometimes you can't help who you love."

IN THE NEXT TWO weeks, as Gage observed the Gypsies, he realized how true Baba Simza's words were. They had a secret life that he suspected very few *gaje* had ever seen. They were different from him, from Denny, from the culture he lived in. They spoke Gypsy some of the time, English some of the time, and a mixture of both some of the time. Gage had trouble comprehending why they went back and forth, and he asked Baba Simza about it.

"Romany, we have the words for—" With both of her hands she touched her mouth, nose, eyes, ears, and then rubbed her thumbs against her fingertips.

"Physical things," Gage said.

"*Hai*. But we have no words for longing, sorrow, heart, soul, spirit, joy. Even our word for love, *camova*, is about the physical. So we use Gypsy for everyday things, for simple things, but we use English for the other things, the ideas."

Gage then asked Nadyha to write down some Gypsy words since he would like to learn some of them. She laughed and said, "Romany, it's not a written language, only spoken, passed down from father to son and mother to daughter since oldest times. And even if it were, I wouldn't write it down for a *gaje*." But she had still been smiling.

That was another thing; they laughed and smiled much more than Gage thought they would. He had the impression from what he'd heard that they were a melancholy, stern people. Indeed, Niçu and Mirella and Baba Simza, with their earthy skin color and dark eyes and jutting cheekbones looked severe when their faces were at rest. Though Nadyha was colored so differently from them, she too had a smooth, expressionless face that gave nothing away when she was concentrating on something. But all four of them seemed to be in a good humor every day, laughing at Boldo's antics, or at each other. Niçu, Nadyha, and Simza had the same type of cutting humor, while Mirella's sensibilities were much more gentle. Sometimes, in fact, Gage caught a look of distant sadness or regret in her face as she worked. Knowing about her two lost babies, he thought he understood.

The other thing that struck him was how industrious they were. All four of them worked from dawn to dusk; he found out that they took their goods to the French Market in New Orleans, usually one weekend a month, to sell. The women sewed, and they had two table-looms and they wove colorful madras scarves and shawls. All of them made baskets; Gage went with Nadyha once to the canebrake, and helped her gather the reeds. Niçu made tinware, some useful, some decorative. He was fascinated with Gage's mucket, for he'd never seen one, and he immediately made a dozen of them, all intricately etched. No two of his plates, cups, buckets, even the tin covers he made for the jars of some of the herbs, were alike. In addition, he made wooden goods, useful boxes with handles, all gaily painted like their *vardos*, and decorative wooden fencing that could be bought in five-foot lengths, with spindles and curlicues and etched designs.

As Baba Simza had said, and Nadyha had told them, Denny was fully recovered within a week. He was feeble, to be sure, but with a will he pitched in to work, helping Niçu handle his tin sheets, working the bellows for the forge, helping Nadyha and Mirella stretch and dry the reeds for the baskets, even helping Mirella cook, for he bragged that he was an excellent chef.

One day Nadyha brought what looked like a pile of black and white fabrics to Gage's and Denny's "camp" by the willow tree. With mock disdain she said, "Baba Simza says, 'Withholdeth notteth goodeth from them to whometh it is due, wheneth it is in the powereth of thine hand to do it.' I didn't check that Proverb, but I'll bet she got it backwards, just like she did the *lil* of the Good Samaritan."

It was two plain white shirts, and two pair of black trousers, just as Niçu always wore. The only thing different about the Gypsy shirts was that they were tightly gathered around the yoke, and had fuller sleeves. Denny was about the same size as Niçu, and so his clothing fit very well. Gage's shirts were just a bit tight across the shoulders, though not so much that they were uncomfortable. His trousers, too, were a little short, but it didn't matter because he always tucked his breeches into his knee-high boots anyway. Gage reflected that Baba Simza was a good Christian, indeed, because she seemed to have learned what must have been a hard lesson for her about charity. It didn't occur to him that she had learned it from his example.

In spite of his growing insights into the Gypsies, Gage was convinced that the only reason he came to know and understand them as well as he did was when, after he and Denny had been with them for five days, the Gypsies began to dance and sing at night. Niçu had told Gage that they did almost every night, but because Denny had been so ill—and, too, because Baba Simza was injured and retired very early in the days after she'd got caught in the trap—they hadn't thought that dancing and singing were fitting.

On that night Baba Simza announced after supper that on this evening they would dance and sing. Nadyha and Mirella clapped their hands, and the three grandchildren rushed into the *vardos* to get their instruments.

Gage and Denny were open-mouthed when Mirella and Nadyha came out of the wagons.

Mirella was wearing a full, green skirt the color of summer grass, with a bright pink scarf wrapped around her waist. Her blouse was in their usual style, gathered at the neck, with short puffed sleeves; this one's neckline was cut a little wider than her workaday clothes and showed more shoulder but not more cleavage. It was sunny yellow with tiny pink flowers. Her *diklo*, or head scarf, was of woven madras in all the rainbow of colors—except for red, Gage noted. It had the coins suspended as a fringe all around it. Gage knew now that they weren't really coins; they were clever little tin ornaments that Niçu made, and stamped with figureheads to look like coins. Mirella was wearing a necklace of these tokens that were so highly polished they gleamed silver in the firelight.

Nadyha was wearing a rainbow-colored skirt and a white peasant blouse. But over it she wore a tight-fitting, low-cut tan leather vest that laced up the front, and she wore her knife, her *churo*, at her waist. Her *diklo* was brown and black and a dark burnt-orange color, with gold threads shot through it and Niçu's coins, covered with gold leaf, fringing it. Around her waist were two scarves, one purple and one striped green and blue, and both scarves had the tin coins fringing it so she made a small clinking metallic sound every time she moved. She was wearing heavy gold hoop earrings and also a gold necklace much like Mirella's, only the coins were smaller and there were fewer of them.

"Gosh! You two ladies look just beautiful!" Denny gaped.

Niçu rolled his eyes and muttered, "*dilo gaje.*" But he, too, had put on some accessories for the occasion. He wore a bright blue sash tied at his side, with a knife stuck in it. His black boots looked new, with a diamond design worked into the uppers with brown leather.

Baba Simza and Nadyha played guitar. Mirella played either guitar or recorder. Niçu played violin. He played first, a solo, and the strains of the song, in a minor key, were so haunting and elusive that Gage felt he was almost spellbound. Every note resounded in him; it made him think of poignant, bittersweet but not depressing memories, such as saying good-bye to Ebenezer Jones, and when his favorite teacher had died, happily going home to Jesus after a long illness. This music made him long for a home that he had never had.

And so it was when Nadyha sang. It was a song in Gypsy, with a simple theme, also in a minor key. She and Simza played guitar, Mirella played the recorder, and Niçu accompanied them in a quiet, tuneful background. Though Gage couldn't understand the words, he knew the song expressed longing and a lost love, though he didn't know what kind of love. Nadyha had a lovely voice, a low throaty contralto. Mirella joined her in the last verse in a soft soprano.

When the last notes died out, Gage wanted to say something, but he was so overcome by the beauty of the music that he couldn't think of anything at all. But the Gypsies paid no attention to him and Denny. They exchanged glances, and began to smile, and Nadyha said, "Ha Ne Ne Ne!"

She handed her guitar to Mirella, jumped in front of the campfire, put one foot forward, and held her arms over her head. They started playing, a jaunty, happy, fast-moving song whose main words were obviously "ha ne ne ne." And Nadyha danced.

Gage was fascinated, and not just because it was Nadyha. He was amazed at the dance. It was wild and exotic, but not at all suggestive or vulgar. Most of it was very clever fast footwork, with acrobatic turns and graceful gestures with her arms held over her head. When she whirled, Gage saw no flash of ankles; instead, she untied the scarves at her waist and used them to create exciting movement all around her. She smiled the entire time, her eyes bright. Unlike the songs, the dance had no motif of longing and desire; it was an expression of happiness and gladness, in the moment and unfettered.

The dance finished, and Nadyha wasn't even out of breath, though the color in her cheeks was high and her eyes flashed brilliantly. "Two guitars!" she said, and held her hand out to Mirella. Now Niçu took the guitar and he and Simza started playing, with Niçu performing some very complicated plucking while Baba Simza played a slow rhythm. It started out slowly, and Mirella and Nadyha danced exactly the same movements. Gradually the tempo increased, and faster and faster they danced, keeping exact time with their footwork and clapping their hands together in unison. Gage and Denny started clapping—Gage watched Baba Simza carefully for approval—and she nodded and yelled, "*Hai!*" After that, on the strong beats, they all at one time or another would shout, *Hai!* The dance went faster and faster—Mirella's and Nadyha's scarves were big whirls of color—and then Nadyha called out, "Boldo! Come dance with us!"

The bear, as if he'd been waiting for the invitation, came to his feet, not all-fours but standing upright, and went to stand by Nadyha. He beat his paws together and put one bear-paw in front of the other in a slow shuffle. He snuffled loudly and looked as if he were having fun. Nadyha laughed, and Gage and Denny found they couldn't help but laugh, too. Boldo seemed pleased, and tried a whirl that made him fall to all four paws, but he heaved himself up again and kept his bear dance going until the dance ended.

When they finished Nadyha led him back to his cushion, gave him a small basket of muscadines, and came to throw herself down by Gage and Denny. "That was *pias, baro pias!*" she exclaimed.

Gage knew that was "big fun," and he said, "For us, too. You're all so talented, so gifted! I can't sing a note, and I've never tried dancing but I think I'd probably be a lot like Boldo."

"I think Boldo dances very well," Nadyha teased.

"I sure didn't mean to offend Boldo. I guarantee you I couldn't dance nearly as well as he does."

"He always makes lots of pennies when he dances at French Market," Nadyha said. "Sometimes more than the rest of us do."

With sudden interest Denny said, "Do all of you dance at Market? Dance, and sing, like tonight?"

"Of course. The *gaje* love it. And we're proud of it, it's how we tell our sorrows, our hopes, our longings, in our songs. *Romoro* dance too, it's different from women's dance. You should see Niçu, he's very good, but he always plays violin or guitar with just the four of us. In our dance we tell our happiness, our joy, our gladness at the Gypsy life. And the *gaje* never even know it, or understand it. They think we're just performing tricks, like Boldo," she finished with disgust.

"That's not true of all *gaje*," Gage said in a fervent, low tone. Nadyha turned to him to search his face, and seemed about to ask him something, but Denny interrupted.

"Nadyha, does Anca go to Market, too?"

"If she wants to. Usually she does."

"Does she do tricks, too, like Boldo? I mean, can you make her, like jump through hoops, or things like that?" he demanded with an urgency neither Gage nor Nadyha understood.

But, being in a good mood from the dancing and singing, Nadyha humored him. "Of course not. I wouldn't embarrass her by making her do silly things, she's not like Boldo. He loves the attention, I think if he could he'd laugh at his own silly self. But . . ." she slid Denny a sly look. "There is one thing that Anca and I do. If she will, I'll show you."

She got to her feet and went to the cougar, who had watched all the goings-on with cool interest. Nadyha put her hand under her chin, and Anca rose to her feet. Then, with Nadyha's hand on her head, they walked together to the campfire and began to circle it. In a low, intense voice Nadyha said, "The wicked man says, 'There is a lion in the way!'" She turned to walk in front of Anca, who paced silently behind her. Looking over her shoulder as if with fear, Nadyha cried, "A lion is in the streets!" Then she turned around and walked backward in front of Anca, bending over to look her in the eyes as they paced. "Yes, the wicked run when no man pursues them—but the righteous are as bold as the lion." Now they slowed, and with a small flick of Nadyha's hand Anca sat down. Nadyha went to her knees in front of her. In a soft, low voice now, she said, "Oh, lion, you are comely in going. The lion is strongest among beasts . . ." Now Nadya raised her head and called out loudly, ". . . and turns not away for any!"

Anca's right paw came up with blinding quickness, cruel claws unsheathed, and she opened her mouth and growled savagely, a loud snarl that seemed to rent the night.

It startled—if not frightened—Gage and Denny, and they both jumped. Gage started to scramble to his feet, but then they saw that Baba Simza and Mirella and Niçu were all smiling. The moment, and Anca's wildness, only lasted maybe three seconds. Nadyha took a piece of meat out of her pocket and gave it to Anca, and then they touched noses.

Denny looked at Gage, his brown eyes wide and gleaming. "I've got such a whale of an idea, Gage, you're not going to believe it. If only . . . if only . . ."

"What?" Gage demanded.

"You're sure, you can shoot a handgun as well as you do a rifle?" Denny blurted out.

"Huh? Uh—yeah, I can. Why?"

But Denny merely shook his head. "I'll let you know. For now, just do this for me: practice up on your sharpshooting, and have Niçu practice up on his knife-throwing. And leave the rest to me."

"Ho-kay," Gage said. Both he and Denny had picked up the Gypsies' whimsical way of saying it.

"But Gage?"

"Yeah?"

"Don't shoot any deer."

ON THE NEXT THURSDAY afternoon, Mirella and Nadyha and Niçu and Baba Simza were wearing all of their finest clothes as the two *vardos* pulled out of camp. Tinar and Saz had harnesses of the finest leather and silver, with head-pieces only, no bits in their mouths. Gage rode Cayenne.

Nadyha and Denny sat together in her *vardo*, Mirella and Niçu drove theirs, while Baba Simza rode in their wagon. Anca, Boldo, and Matchko rode in Nadyha's wagon. Boldo stuck his head out of the side window and occasionally waved at nothing.

All that day they had loaded up the wagons with all the goods that the Gypsies were taking to the French Market to sell: shawls, woven scarves, the *tignons* that the *gens de couleur libres*—the free women of color—wore; dozens of baskets; decorated palmetto fans; all kinds of tinware that Niçu had made; thirty jars of honey that Nadyha—with Boldo's eager help—had collected from the tupelo trees; and jars and tins and bottles of herbs and spices and herbal remedies that Baba Simza and Nadyha specialized in.

Riding beside Nadyha's wagon, Gage asked, "Why are we going to town so late?"

"We want to get there on Thursday night and get our place, so we'll be ready in the morning. Friday is the day that the Blue Beasts get paid," she said, her mobile lips curling in disdain. "Saturday and Sunday are big market days for the *criollos*." The Creoles—the word actually simply meant "native," but in New Orleans it had come to mean those French-Spanish descendants who had been born here, yet retained their own unique culture. Then she smiled brilliantly; she had been happy and excited all day, and she and Mirella and Baba Simza were all wearing their fine "dancing" clothes. "But this time, maybe we get to stay until Wednesday, because it's the big *gaje* party, for the freedom. Or something like that."

"Oh, yes, I'd forgotten, it's the Fourth of July," Gage said. "I'd lost track of time."

Beside her, Denny watched Nadyha curiously. "You really are looking forward to this, aren't you, Miss Nadyha? You like going to town?"

"Oh, yes! I love the town, all of the many kinds of people, the Market, but most of all I love the river and the steamboats."

"Oh, really!" Denny said with a big grin. "You like to watch them? The boats?"

"I *love* to watch them! I look at them, and I think, and I wonder, where do they go? What wonderful sights and places do they see? What's the big river like, away from New Orleans? What kinds of people are so lucky they travel up and down the river in these boats, some of them that look like mansions?" she said eagerly. It was a very long, and unguarded, speech for Nadyha.

Gage was surprised, but then he thought he shouldn't be. Nadyha was daring, and she was adventurous, all the things that he wasn't. But then again, it seemed her dreams were very much like his own. *The Big River, wandering up and down it, seeing all those places and people . . . she sounds just like me!*

He looked at Denny to see if he had noticed that Nadyha had said, almost word for word, the things that he'd told Denny about himself.

But Denny wasn't looking at him; he was looking at Nadyha with a big, wide grin on his face, and then he began to laugh.

Nadyha frowned and said, "*Gajo*, what's the matter with you? I didn't think I was so funny!"

"No, no, it's not that," he said hastily. "I just want to say, Miss Nadyha, maybe you'll find out that sometimes dreams can come true."

Looking with longing, already deep and unwavering, at the Gypsy girl Nadyha, Gage secretly said to himself: *How I hope they do!*

CHAPTER EIGHT

Cara Cogbill walked down the same dusty road that she had traveled every Friday afternoon for the last seven years. On either side were endless sugarcane fields, an untidy jungle pressing close on either side of the dirt track, the tall green stalks looming far over her head. She was slight, only 5'4", and delicately built, with tiny hands and feet and waist. To her bemusement, she had developed an hourglass figure at the late age of seventeen; until then she had been as skinny and straight as a short fence pole. Cara couldn't really be considered beautiful, because she didn't have that sort of exotic look that the word implied. She was kittenish, with a tiny heart-shaped face, and she had inherited her mother's unusual coloring, a wealth of fine strawberry-blonde hair, but instead of china-blue eyes, she had wide, dark, big brown eyes and thick, dark lashes.

But right now Cara was much more concerned about her complexion than her shape or her hair. Her skin was very fair, and tended to freckle with even the least bit of direct sun. On this summer afternoon, she was dressed horribly for the heat and humidity. She wore a big bonnet with a wide brim to shadow her face, a muslin fichu tied tightly around her neck to shield it, a long-sleeved home-spun blouse, and a pair of rough leather work gloves that were two sizes too big for her. Not one inch of skin was exposed, and she kept her head down, staring at the road, so that the high noon sun wouldn't graze her face.

She wasn't surprised to hear a buggy coming up the road in front of her, because this was a well-traveled road, leading to about a dozen farms just east of town. It came close, and she glanced up to greet the buggy, for she would surely have met whoever it was many times before. But to her surprise it was Harrison Stokes. His family owned sug-arcane and cotton fields out this way, but their house was a smallish mansion, in the popular Greek Revival style, in the town of Donaldsonville, Louisiana. Sometimes she had met Reverend Stokes coming out to check on the fields, but she'd never seen his son Harry out this way. He stopped the buggy in front of her, blocking the road, and said, "Hi, Cara. You look awfully hot and miserable. How about a ride?"

"Hello, Mr. Stokes. That's nice of you, but you are going the opposite way," she said pointedly.

"Call me Harry. I'm turning around. I was coming to see you anyway." He hopped down and took the horse's har-ness to lead him in a circle. The road was narrow, and he was no hand at backing a buggy.

Cara sighed. She'd known Harry Stokes for quite awhile, for Cara's family attended his father's church, St. Luke's Methodist Church, and Reverend Stokes had been the pastor for ten years. However, though Cara "knew" Harry, he had never paid her the slightest bit of attention, for her family were poor hardscrabble farmers and Reverend Stokes was a successful planter of high standing in the town. Until Harry had returned a month ago from the war, she didn't think he even knew her name. In that month, however, he had been paying marked attention to her at church. They'd had one "dinner on the ground" two Sundays ago, and he had stuck to her like a burr. She didn't exactly dislike Harry—she really didn't know him at all—but she had always thought that he was a snob, like his three sisters, who openly snubbed Cara. And Harry had the kind of looks that appealed to some women, but Cara secretly had labeled him a "pudding-face." His mouth was too short and pouty, his cheeks too full and rosy, his brown eyes too round and big.

Now Cara was in a quandary. At seventeen, when men had first started paying attention to her, she had been confused and even a little frightened. But by now, at twenty, she knew all about it all too well. She knew what Harry was after, and it wasn't to go to her ramshackle farmhouse and meet her mother and father and nine brothers and sisters and court her. She didn't want to ride with him. But how could she say no? It would be silly for her to keep walking and for Harry, as she knew he would, to keep driving the buggy right alongside of her, hounding her. Resignedly she waited until he got turned around, and then climbed up into the buggy. It was typical of Harry—or at least, of the way he treated girls like her—that he didn't assist her.

He barely snapped the reins so the horse started up the slowest trot imaginable. "I just had to talk to you alone, Cara. I can't believe it, you've changed so much since I left." Harry had formed a company of twenty men from Donaldsonville, and by all accounts had accredited himself well in the Confederate Army.

"Yes, so I've been told, sir," Cara said formally.

"You hardly look like the same girl. You've turned into a really beautiful woman. And now, I understand that you're not Mrs. Tabb's servant any more, you're her 'companion.'" He laughed. "I figure that must have happened about the same time Widow Hacker's niece arrived from Philadelphia to be her 'companion.' Hoity-toity, am I right?"

P. M. Tabb and his wife, Octavia, had hired Cara when she had been thirteen to come and work for them on weekends. Mr. Tabb, though very prosperous, was notoriously tight-fisted, and it had frustrated Octavia to no end that he flatly refused to buy any slaves. They cost too much, he said. Why should he pay $500 for a healthy young slave woman when he could pay pennies to one of the poor farm girls to come clean on weekends? Octavia had told him—rightly— that running a household was a full-time, all-day, everyday job, but he had remained adamant. Octavia had hired Cara to come on Friday afternoons and stay Friday and Saturday night. She then went to church with the Tabbs, worked Sunday afternoons, and went home on Sunday evenings. For this she was paid a dollar a weekend. And she earned every penny of it, too. She didn't just clean, she did laundry and cooking, too. In fact, she worked almost as hard at the Tabb's house as she did on the farm.

But Cara really hadn't minded, because Octavia Tabb, who was determined to be the most sophisticated, elegant woman in town, had decided that if she couldn't have six slaves in her household she would have a maid that was comparable to any snooty French lady's maid that any highborn Creole had in New Orleans. She gave Cara uniforms, dark blue blouses and skirts with ruffled white aprons and a frilly cap. She taught her how to speak, how to walk, how to serve with quiet grace, even how a lady sits, with her back not touching the chair, and how to use a fan gracefully. On Saturday evenings Mrs. Tabb had conducted her musical *salon*, with all of the important people in town in attendance, and they were served by a dignified, unobtrusive white maid that could have come from any elegant drawing room in London. For all of her hard work, and in spite of Octavia Tabb's fatuousness, Cara knew that she had received an invaluable education on how to be a proper lady. She was grateful to Mrs. Tabb.

Now she answered Harry a little defensively, "It wasn't just that, you know. Mrs. Tabb came to see that I had a little musical talent, and she has very generously helped me develop it. In the last two years she's been kind enough to teach me to play the piano and the guitar, and helped me with voice lessons, and has taught me to read music. And your mother has been kind, too, Mr. Stokes. She's taught me to play the organ. Anyway, as time has gone by, Mrs. Tabb allowed me to join her Saturday night salon. But I still work for her, you know, it's not really like I'm a 'lady's companion.'"

Harry grinned, stretching his thick, wet lips wide. "Cara, she did that old cat the Widow Hacker in the eye, and I say good for Mrs. Tabb and good for you. I know you're talented, you play wonderfully and sing like an angel in church, and the Widow Hacker's niece Constance looks as if she'd faint if she had to open her pruney little mouth open wide enough to sing. And I hear you're the shining star of the Independence Day Concert."

"I'm not the star," Cara protested, but her eyes sparkled with pleasure. "I'm just lucky Captain Nettles has given me a solo, there are several really good performers in the Donaldsonvile Players."

"Yeah, Captain Nettles, that slick bluebelly, he is lucky to have you," Harry said. Pulling the horse to a stop, he reached behind the seat and brought out a small bucket. It was filled with melting ice, and held a bottle of lemonade.

"Here, I brought us a cool drink." He popped open the bottle, took a long swig, then held it out to Cara. Sliding his arm along the back of the seat, he pulled her so close to him she was crushed against his side. "'Fraid you'll have to share with me, Cara," he said, and leaned his head down. Before Cara could move, his wet lips brushed hers.

With all her might Cara pushed him, jamming the bottle hard against his ribs, and it tipped and ran down in his lap. He jerked, and she jumped out of the buggy. "I'm not sharing anything with you, Harry Stokes! I knew it, I knew I never should have gotten in that buggy!" She hurried up the road, taking hard angry steps, swinging her arms, all genteel lady's mincing walk forgotten.

"Wha—! Cara! Come back here!" Harry bellowed.

Cara didn't bother to answer. When she came to a side road about an eighth of a mile from where she assumed Harry still sat dabbing his lap, she veered off the road, cutting through the corner of a sugarcane field, and came to a small pasture with one old horse placidly grazing. It was a shortcut to town that she'd known since she was a child, though she normally didn't take it now because cutting through sugarcane is no easy thing to do in a long skirt and petticoat. But she didn't want to hear any further nonsense from the likes of Harry Stokes when he caught up to her on the road. She reflected with satisfaction that his ride back into town was going to be wet, sticky, and uncomfortable. Served him right.

OCTAVIA TABB PUT HER hands on Cara's cheeks and lifted her face. Her small birdlike eyes flew open in alarm. "Cara Cogbill, you're as flushed as a tomato! Don't tell me you've been letting the sun hit you in the face, child, no, no! How many times have I told you that ladies must never be freckled!"

"Many times, ma'am," Cara answered submissively. "But no, Mrs. Tabb, I'm afraid I hurried a little to get here, and it's so hot today."

"Yes, yes, well, put up your things and hurry to help me with Mr. Tabb's supper. You know we must have Mr. Tabb's supper all ready for him so that we can get to rehearsal tonight on time. Captain Nettles is so very strict on punctuality, and I don't blame him, because what about those silly Bastien sisters, always lollygagging around . . ." Her voice faded out as she bustled out the back door to the detached kitchen behind the house. She was a short, rather rotund woman, but was quick and sharp in her walk and movements and speech when she was attending her household duties.

Over the years, Cara, who had a certain insight into people, had come to know and understand Octavia Tabb very well. She was a snobbish, stubborn, and sometimes spiteful woman, but on the other hand, she had shown herself to be kind, patient, and even generous to Cara. It had puzzled her at first, because even at thirteen years of age, when Cara had first come to work for the Tabbs, she understood that she and her family were Poor White Trash, while the Tabbs and the Stokes and the Hackers and the Bastiens were Upperclass Society, and with Mrs. Tabb's pretentiousness it would seem that she would never have thought of Cara as anything but a lowly servant. Cara had seen her and Mr. Tabb together, and their quiet, unassuming enjoyment of each other's company, and she knew that the couple had never had children. Cara thought that Mrs. Tabb would have been much more the nice lady she could be, instead of the fatuous social climber that she was, if she'd had children. Cara didn't fool herself that she was like a daughter to Mrs. Tabb, but she thought that she had brought out some deeply buried maternal instinct in her.

Cara hurried to her stifling box of a room, one that had originally been a pantry but now had a narrow bed and chest. She took off her bonnet, fichu, and gloves and threw them on the bed to almost run out to the kitchen. When Mrs. Tabb said to hurry, she meant it.

It was Friday night, and it was a mutton night. Mr. Tabb had regimented menus, and on Fridays he either had mutton or pork chops. Cara hated mutton night; she didn't like the smell or the taste of the meat. But at least it was easy to cook. Mrs. Tabb was already talking, and zipping around putting pots of water on the stove and getting out the turnips and corn on the cob. ". . . sauce for the mutton, you know Mr. Tabb always says that you make it better than I do. And I got some beautiful sweet potatoes so we can make a sweet potato pie, Mr. Tabb does love them. Hurry, girl, it won't be a minute or two before this water boils."

She stopped for a breath, and Cara murmured, "Yes, ma'am," as she started cutting the hock off the leg of mutton.

Mrs. Tabb was a talker, except, of course, when she was in Polite Society; then she was elegant, cool, and dignified. With Cara she kept up a continual running commentary. "I'm worried we won't have Mr. Tabb's supper ready by six thirty, so do hurry, Cara. It is so exciting to have our very first dress rehearsal tonight, I simply must have you touch up my costume with the iron before we leave, it seems to me that the hem flounce isn't quite as crisp as I'd like, and you can iron so much better and more efficiently than I, and I want to check your dress too, because I won't have it said that your costume isn't quite as good as that Constance Hacker's, though hers is very boring, if you ask me, just a starred blouse and a striped skirt, in fact if Captain Nettles hadn't recommended it himself I'd think it was a little bit vulgar . . ."

The Donaldsonville Players, as Captain Joseph Nettles had named them, were putting on a grand Independence Day Concert for the Fourth of July. Captain Nettles had been assigned to Fort Butler in Donaldsonville since the building of the fort in 1862, and his posting had been a bigger blow to him than if he had been grievously wounded in battle. He wanted to be in New Orleans, for he was from New York, and fancied himself an artistic, sophisticated gentleman who needed genteel occupations such as the theater and the opera, and Donaldsonville offered nothing like that. In spite of vigorous political wranglings, he couldn't escape prosaic Donaldsonville, and so he had proceeded to create his own sophistications, and had formed the Donaldsonville Players, a sort of disingenuous name since they hadn't yet actually put on any plays. They did concerts, with singing and poetry recitals and dramatic readings and historical tableaux.

At first the Players had been Captain Nettles and his wife, Eliza, and five other officers and three other wives. But by 1863, when the Union had gained control of the Mississippi River and had effectively split the Confederacy in half, and the war was so far to the east and west of southern Louisiana, the townspeople of Donaldsonville had slowly become interested in the Players. Captain Nettles was elegant, charming, and courtly, and he had managed to flatter and cajole many town ladies into joining the troupe. That meant, of course, that the audiences grew exponentially, for they were mostly the soldiers stationed at the fort, and they'd go anywhere to see pretty girls.

Mrs. Tabb was still rattling on as Cara was beginning to make the sweet potato pie. By now Mrs. Tabb was sitting at the worktable with a glass of sweet iced tea, fanning herself vigorously. This happened quite often when Mrs. Tabb said that "we need to cook this" or "we need to take care of cleaning those curtains today" or "we should pay special attention to the urns and vases in the drawing room." Most of the time Cara ended up doing all of the work while Mrs. Tabb talked. Cara didn't mind, for she knew that Octavia Tabb was a very lonely woman.

". . . and it's so obvious that Captain Nettles realizes that your musical gifts are far above any of the other young ladies', though of course you couldn't possibly be expected to exceed the talents of the more experienced ladies, such as Mrs. Nettles, and you know that I've been playing an instrument and singing since I was a very young girl, younger even than you," she said placidly. "Still, you outshine the Bastien sisters by a country mile, and no wonder, for Carolyn Bastien is a woeful singer and plays the piano even worse, and her daughters take after her. Naturally, Captain Nettles, being a man of such discriminating tastes, has shown a marked preference for you," she said with satisfaction. In her mind, she was responsible for Cara's talent, and any recognition given to it was in reality a compliment to her genius.

Cara frowned slightly. "I didn't think that Captain Nettles had shown me any special attention."

"Certainly he has! After all, your solo tonight is going to be the grand finale," she said smugly. "Mrs. Hacker badgered poor Captain Nettles unmercifully for Constance's dismal piano solo to be the grand finale, but he stood firm. I think he sees much potential in you, Cara, as I always have, and I believe that he's going to make sure that you are featured in all of the productions of the Players. You know, he said to me once, in strict confidence, that there was a new play he's giving serious consideration, and he said that there's a

part in it that I would be absolutely stunning in performing
. . ."

Cara's thoughts wandered. She thought that Mrs. Tabb
was exaggerating Captain Nettles's estimation of her talents. Captain Nettles was in all ways an average-looking
man in his thirties, average size, brown hair, brown eyes,
with even features. One would scarcely notice him passing in the street. But he was undoubtedly charming, with a
ready smile and he showed great courtliness to ladies.

But Cara, with her heightened sensitivity, was wary of all
men, including Captain Nettles. One hard lesson that she
had learned was that, even with all of her acquired graces,
and though she was very careful to conduct herself with
the utmost decorum and modesty, never flirting or coy
or bringing any attention to herself whatsoever, men still
treated her differently than they did girls of the upperclass
families. At least, the Union soldiers did, and even some of
the older men of town who hadn't gone to war and who,
Cara thought indignantly, should have known better, being
brought up as Southern gentlemen. They called her by her
first name without asking her permission, monopolized her
conversation even when she politely tried to extract herself
from them, and some of them even had the nerve to touch
her, to put their arms around her shoulders or her waist.
They never treated the Bastien sisters or Constance Hacker
that way.

But Captain Nettles had never shown the least unwelcome familiarity to Cara. Once or twice she noticed a
certain intensity in his mild brown eyes as he watched
her sing, but she was shrewd enough to know that that
happened to her a lot with men now; she supposed they
couldn't help it. She had noticed that Eliza Nettles, who
would be an attractive brunette if her face weren't quite so
hard, watched her husband like a she-wolf. Cara had seen

this as simply a woman's blind jealousy, because as far as she could tell Captain Nettles behaved himself with all the girls. And, she thought with a grim inward smile, he'd better. If he didn't, Cara suspected that Eliza Nettles would make him pay.

AT SEVEN O'CLOCK, ALL of the Donaldsonville Players were sitting in the front rows of the Opera House, the third floor of a large brick building that housed Tabb's Apothecary on the first floor and Edwards & Diggs Shipping offices on the second, for the building was close to the river. The third floor had been empty, and with Mrs. Tabb's urging, Mr. Tabb, who owned the building, had cleaned it up and had a stage built and had even furnished benches for a hundred people for the theater.

Captain Nettles took the stage and clapped his hands for attention. The twitterings of the sixteen ladies, and the bass murmurs of the five men, died down. "I'm sorry to say that Mrs. Nettles won't be here tonight, although I don't think she's sorry, herself." He smiled engagingly. "She received an invitation from Mrs. Lavinia Heth, Colonel Rufus B. Heth's wife, to come to New Orleans and attend a performance of *Don Giovanni* at the French Opera House. Colonel Heth, as you may know, is General Nathaniel Banks's adjutant and is the Military Police Commander of New Orleans. My Eliza is a distant cousin of Mrs. Heth's, and was so delighted to receive the invitation, not to mention to see *Don Giovanni*. However, she will be back on Monday. Of course she wouldn't miss our Independence Day Concert." Eliza Nettles was always a star performer in their productions, though she was a rather indifferent soprano.

The rehearsal began, and it was rather confused, as they had never done a costume rehearsal before. The men all wore their military uniforms, but several of the ladies had full dress changes. A small dressing room hardly could accommodate eight women in full hoop skirts, changing clothes, and the atmosphere became very tense, as it was also suffocatingly hot in the tiny windowless room. But Captain Nettles managed to soothe them all, flattering them, praising them, and soon they were all relatively happy and preening. Cara noticed that he was in particularly high spirits tonight, his voice louder than usual, and she thought she smelled liquor on his breath when he was close to her.

Cara's costume change didn't come until the second-to-last song of the concert, so all she had to do until then was to put on her sash, a shoulder-to-waist satin length of red, with blue stars outlined in white, which all of the ladies wore in differing red-white-blue combinations. She was wearing a hand-me-down dress that Octavia Tabb had given her, a simple icy blue with a bit of white lace on her collar and sleeves. Cara didn't have a hoop skirt, so she only wore her petticoat.

They went through their repertoire, the patriotic songs, the heartfelt reading of "O Captain, My Captain" by Captain Nettles, and Constance Hacker's solemn and stately piano solo, Pachelbel's Canon. Then, with some flurry and confusion because Eliza Nettles was absent, came the next-to-last song of the evening, "My Country 'Tis of Thee." Octavia Tabb in her solid crimson red dress with sash, representing Freedom, and Mary Louisa Stokes in her dark blue, representing Independence, were both ready with their flags to sing and march their choreographed steps, but they were sadly disconcerted by the missing Union, Eliza Nettles in solid white. Finally Captain

Nettles got Cara to fill in, and they went through the song and the steps—which Cara had unconsciously picked up—three times, at Mrs. Tabb's insistence.

Then it was time for the grand finale, and Cara hurried to don her costume. She was the Statue of Liberty, with a fine, long, heavy piece of silvery-gray satin to serve as her toga, over her dress, of course. She had a torch made of wood and painted with silver gilt, with stubby candles in it that gave a very convincing flame. Her crown was pasteboard, also painted with silver gilt, but outlined with real silver thread. Finally she got her toga wrapped and draped properly, and Captain Nettles obligingly lit her candles. In great state she slowly walked back and forth across the stage, holding her torch high, singing "The Battle Hymn of the Republic" in her strong, true soprano. It rang throughout the big, empty room. At the final *Glory, Glory Hallelujah!* all of the players joined her in a rousing finish. After a long, stirring *His truth is marching on!* they gave themselves a round of applause, except for Cara, who was still holding her burning torch.

It took about an hour for the company to change back into their regular clothing, carefully pack away their sashes and costumes, and finish visiting with each other and, of course, the endless entreaties of Captain Nettles for this, that, and the other. When almost all had left, he came to Cara and said, "Cara, I really think that we need to go over your solo again. Not that there was anything wrong, oh, no, my dear, you were flawless! But we need to make certain that your costume change goes smoothly, and especially we need to see about this torch thing. Certainly you can't come out on stage and get me to light it as we're all finishing 'My Country 'Tis of Thee.'"

"All right," Cara said uncertainly. "I'll let Mrs. Tabb know. Or perhaps she might wait for me."

"No, no, I've already explained to Octavia, I'll take care to see you back to the Tabbs' house. We shouldn't be more than another half-hour or so," he said smoothly.

There were still four or five ladies about, clamoring to talk to him, so Cara went on back to the dressing room to unpack her toga and unwrap her crown from its protective tissue. She had just gotten her toga unwrapped when Captain Nettles came into the dressing room. Suddenly Cara was wary; this was unseemly, even though she wasn't actually changing clothes. She froze, holding the long heavy length of satin in her hand, and stared at him.

Casually he walked over to her and caressed the satin she was holding. "This is such a lovely, sensuous fabric. It suits you, Cara. You should always wear silk and satin." He put his arms around her and pulled her to him. Cara was so shocked that she was numb, and she looked up at him, and saw that his mild countenance had changed. His eyes were dark, his pupils contracted, and his jaw tensed. Before she could react he bent and planted his mouth on hers, kissing her with a roughness that frightened Cara half to death. With all her might, she pushed his chest, but he was strong and he only pulled her so much closer that she could hardly breathe.

She did the only thing she could think of: she bit his mouth savagely. He yanked his head up and slapped one hand to his mouth, which was bleeding. "You stupid little minx! What have you done!"

Trying desperately to writhe away from him she shouted, "What have *I* done? You pig, when I tell Mrs. Nettles, I hope—"

"No! You filthy little—" One hand kept a grip on Cara's arm, but now she yanked it away from him, pushed past him, and ran out onto the stage. He followed her, and grabbed her again. Cara turned on him and landed a hard stinging slap on his face. They grappled, and wrestled, and Cara fought like a cornered vixen. And then—as suddenly as if they'd been struck by lightning—Nettles fell off the stage. He made a sickening, crashing, crunching sound when he landed face-down. Cara stared down at him in shock. One arm was all awry, obviously broken. A trickle of blood came from his nose.

"I've killed him. Oh Lord Jesus, I've killed him," she whispered. She didn't know how long she stood there, whispering broken prayers and entreaties, hoping he'd open his eyes and get up. But he didn't. She started shaking as if she were palsied.

And then the enormity of it hit her. He was a Union officer, and they were under martial law. She'd be tried, and convicted, and even though she was a woman, she would surely be hanged for murder. Panic set in for a moment, but then as clearly as if Someone had spoken audibly to her, she knew what she had to do.

Run.

IT WAS ALMOST TEN o'clock when she reached her home, and climbed in her brother Wesley's open window. He was asleep, of course, and had been since sunset, for at the Cogbill house they rose at four o'clock and went to bed at dark. He awoke as soon as she touched the windowsill and shot up in bed, his eyes wide. He had only been home a couple of months, and sometimes at night he dreamed he was still lying in some field somewhere, waiting for dawn and the shooting to begin again. "Huh! Oh, Cara—what—"

"Shh," she said quietly. "I need your help." Quickly she explained to her brother, the only one in her large family that she was really close to. "I've got to leave, Wes. I've already got it all planned out, I believe—I think—maybe the Lord has helped me see what to do." For the first time that night, and for that matter in a long, long time, tears stung her eyes.

"Oh, Cara, poor little sis," he said helplessly. "What can I do?"

Cara told him, and he went to fetch some things for her. If someone saw Wes wandering around the house, it wouldn't make any difference, but Cara didn't want any of her family to see her, or know she'd been there.

She looked around the room for Wesley's Bible, knowing that he kept some paper in it. She had intended to write a note to her parents, but then she realized that it might get them into trouble. So she knelt by Wes's bed and prayed. By the time he returned she felt strong and determined, sure in her course.

"I hate this," he said vehemently. "I should help you, protect you. This is wrong, all wrong."

"You can't protect me, or help me, Wes, you know that. No one can now, except the Lord, and He will. Please don't tell Mama and Papa what I've done, it'll only make it hard on them when the provost marshals come. And they will, Wes. People knew I stayed behind with that awful man, alone, like a stupid fool. When they do, lie. Don't tell them you've seen me. I know that seems very wrong, but somehow, now as I was praying, I felt that the Lord was sort of going to excuse you, or something."

"Don't worry, little sis. I won't tell them filthy bluebellies one thing," he said fiercely. He hugged her hard, then pushed a coin into her hand. "Here, Mr. Wetherington gimme a dollar for mendin' his fences last Satiddy. You take it, girl, you'll need it."

Cara shook her head. "No, Wes, really, I've got fourteen whole dollars saved up from my wages from the Tabbs, in a little wallet in my Bible that you brought me. That's more than enough. You keep that dollar in your pocket, and when you think of it, you think of me, and then you pray for me. That way we'll both be rich."

AT DAWN A DIRTY, slight young boy bought a deck passage ticket on the cheap steamboat packet the *Luther Yates*. Luther Yates himself was the owner, the captain, the pilot, the purser, and the ticketmaster of the boat. He didn't give the grubby boy a second look; he'd seen hundreds of ragged little boys, and even some girls, going to New Orleans to try to find work. The boy was short and slight, with a worn floppy hat that seemed two sizes too big for him, half-hiding his face. Only a delicate pointed and very dirty chin showed from underneath it. He wore a ragged, much-patched sack coat over a threadbare homespun shirt, and gray trousers that were too long for him, rolled up at the hem, showing worn brogans that were once tan but were now the color of Louisiana mud. Over his shoulder was slung a canvas bag that seemed large for the boy—Luther Yates was sure he didn't have that many changes of wardrobe—but instead of wondering about it he grew irritated with the boy, because he was fumbling around in an inside jacket pocket for the fare.

"Boy, if you'd take them stupid gloves off—what are they, yore daddy's?—and gimme my eighty cent, mebbe we'd git this boat on the river sometimes today," he growled.

"Sorry, sir," the boy mumbled in a deep, hoarse voice that sounded very odd, if Luther Yates had really been listening.

A woman behind the boy shoved his shoulder and said in a whiny voice, "Hurry up, it's boilin' out here awready, stupid boy!" The boy glanced behind his shoulder to see a crude-looking woman with a greasy tangle of henna-red hair and a grimy red, scandalously low-cut blouse.

The boy struggled and finally managed to pull out a much-wrinkled dollar bill and handed it to him. Yates grabbed it and the boy asked, "My change, sir?"

"Change? Change? Do I look like the Bank of Luther Yates to you, boy? If you got eighty cent, I'll take 'er. If'n all you got is this here dollar, either you take her and git off my gangplank or I'll take 'er and you kin git on my boat."

The boy walked on board.

Deck passage on a steamer simply meant that you reserved enough square footage for your body on the main deck. There were no beds, no chairs, not even assigned spaces for passengers on this, the cargo deck. There was the cargo, which on this trip of the *Luther Yates* was hundreds of fifty-pound sacks of coal, and the deck passengers found a hole or cranny anywhere they could. Cara reflected grimly that she shouldn't have taken so much trouble to dirty herself up in her little brother Hiram's clothing, for the air was filled with choking black dust. She thought that by the time they reached New Orleans, probably all of the passengers were going to be very dirty indeed.

She got up as close as she could to the bow, because at the back of the deck was the boiler room, and such was the heat coming from the room that heat-shimmers showed in front of the doors in the coal-shadowed air. Up at the front was only a little better, except that everyone else had the same idea as Cara, and they all crowded up there, some of them climbing up to spread a pallet on top of the coal sacks. Cara found a small hole she could squeeze into, so she could actually curl up on the deck. But to her dismay, two soldiers heaved some sacks around, widened the narrow space, and sat down right next to her. One of them, sitting so close he was almost brushing against her, turned and said grimly, "Lemme tell you something right now, boy. Don't you be lighting no pipe up in here. This coal dust, it'll explode just as good as gunpowder. Me and my buddies are gonna be the 'Baccy Police on this trip. You can chaw all you want. But don't spit over in my direction, I might take offense."

"Yes, sir," Cara muttered. She punched her big bag and then laid down on it, in a fetal position because of the tight space, her back turned to the soldiers.

"Little tyke's sleepy," the soldier guffawed to his fellows. "I don't think that little feller's going to be lighting up no pipe."

It was seventy-nine river miles from Donaldsonville to New Orleans, and that meant that the trip was going to be about eight hours long. After about an hour, Cara was stiff and felt like she was smothering in the heat and thick dust-clogged air. The soldiers had gone out to the narrow little outside deck on the bow, so she finally dared to move. With every bone and joint feeling as if they'd been hammered, she sat up. Cautiously looking around, she saw that there were other people still very close to her. The woman who had shoved her on the gangplank was sprawled just above Cara, on top of three sacks of coal. She was sitting up, her back propped against another sack, her legs sprawled out in a crude ungainly manner, and seemed to be asleep. There were more soldiers around, some young tough-looking men, and one young hungry-looking woman with a little girl that cried incessantly and an infant that alternately slept and cried.

Cara was exhausted, and so hungry she felt faint, for she hadn't eaten any of the Tabb's mutton supper the previous night. *Was it only just last night?* Cara felt as if she had killed Captain Joseph Nettles a long time ago, and had been running forever.

Digging in her sack, she brought out the little packet that Wes had fixed her, a loaf of bread and a wedge of cheese and an apple. Hungrily she broke off some bread and cheese and started eating. Within a moment, however, she was aware of eyes on her, and glanced over to see the young mother staring at her with longing. When Cara glanced at her, she quickly dropped her eyes. Cara broke off about half of the loaf of bread, most of the cheese, then stood up and took the one step across to her. "Here you are, ma'am," she said in her best imitation boy voice. "The little girl looks hungry."

"Thank you so much," the woman said barely audibly, her head bowed.

When Cara turned back around she saw that the woman perched up above her like a moth-eaten buzzard had grabbed the rest of the bread, the cheese, and the apple. Her hard, dark eyes met Cara's defiantly as she took a huge bite of the apple with her yellowed teeth. With juice running down her chin she said, "I'm a hungry little girl, too. Seein' as how you're such a young gent an' all I figgered you wouldn't mind."

Cara started to answer her, and caught herself with horror, realizing that she'd almost blurted out something in her normal voice. And she was staring straight up at the woman; Cara knew very well that if someone fairly shrewd studied her face they were bound to see she was a girl. So she merely shrugged and sat back down.

The rest of the journey was so hot and uncomfortable and nerve-wracking to Cara that she felt she was in a nightmare. The coal dust made her cough, a dry rack that hurt her chest. To make it worse, she was horribly thirsty, but the only provision for water for the deck passengers was a scuttlebutt, a half-barrel of water with one dipper. After watching all the men, most of them chewing tobacco and spitting into the spittoon just by the scuttlebutt, and then taking drinks from the dipper, Cara simply couldn't face drinking from it. The soldiers came and went, and the awful woman made them lewd offers in such a loud, coarse, and unashamed voice that Cara blushed like fire and wished she were a thousand miles away. The mousy woman across from her looked away and clutched her children closer to her.

Finally, after what seemed an eternity to Cara, she felt the engines slowing, heard the steam powering down, and then three sharp blasts of the steam whistle, like hoarse screams, sounded. They had reached New Orleans.

"Keep your seat, boy," the soldier said. "It'll be awhile before we get situated in this port, there's likely a dozen or so boats lining up to off-load. We ain't goin' nowheres 'til we come to a full stop."

But finally they did come to a full stop, and they heard yelling and calls and the creaks as the landing stages were winched down. A deckhand came in to yell out, "New Orleans! All you folks git up and git goin' so's we kin unload!"

People stood up, muttering and gathering up their scant belongings. They gathered in a big knot, with some pushing and shoving, at the bow, at the door to the landing stage. Cara was right in the middle of the crowd, shorter than everyone, and she clutched her bag tightly to her. Just as she reached the door, the redheaded woman brushed up against her so hard that Cara staggered and almost fell. "Sorry, lovey," the woman leered. "Such a crush, ya see." Then she disappeared into the crowd.

Cara finally got down the gangplank, still mingled in the crowd, who sort of herded her onto shore and through a wide entrance cut out of the six-foot earth levees. Then, like dropped marbles, the crowd streamed off into a hundred different directions. Cara stopped in her tracks, trying to make some sense of everything around her. Her senses were so assaulted that she could hardly breathe. The noise was terrific, from the roustabouts on the docks behind her to the hundreds of people in front of her, shouting, calling, cursing. She smelled the fetid odor of the river, the stench of unwashed sweaty people, the heavy aroma of *café noir*, meat roasting, garlic, spices, and horse droppings.

Finally managing to put some order to her confusion, she realized that just in front of her, across an ancient Spanish cobblestone street, was the French Market. The Tabbs had never been to New Orleans, which was a source of constant irritation to Mrs. Tabb, but the Widow Hacker had visited the sprawling city several times when her husband, the longtime mayor of Donaldsonville, had been alive. Mrs. Tabb had allowed Mrs. Hacker to talk about New Orleans in her Saturday night salon, and so Cara had heard quite a bit about the city.

Swaying a little as she stood there, a little forlorn filthy figure, Cara realized that she was weak from hunger and the overwhelming heat. She swallowed hard, her throat raw from thirst and coal dust. All she could think about was her thirst. How could she just simply get a good drink of water? She was sure there must be public pumps, but she thought of the filthy, stinking river behind her and was repulsed even more than she had been by the scuttlebutt. The French Market? She doubted that they sold water, but maybe juices, or even ices? If she hadn't been so parched, her mouth would have watered.

No one was giving her a second look, so cautiously she reached into her inside jacket pocket for her wallet, so she could go ahead and draw out a single dollar to hold, instead of fumbling openly with her full wallet.

She couldn't feel her wallet.

Surely it was her bulky gloves. Cara had had no choice about wearing them; no amount of dirt would have made her hands look like a boy's hands. Stealthily she stuck her right hand under her left arm, quickly drew her hand free from the glove, and reached into her jacket pocket.

The wallet was gone. In front of Cara's eyes rose the vulgar redheaded woman's leering face as she had shoved Cara.

Panic, so sudden and dreadful that it almost choked her, made her overheated body go cold. Her head began to pound, and for a few moments the raucous noise sounded near, then far, then near, in an odd *RAWR-rawr RAWR-rawr* echo. Black spots danced in front of her eyes.

And then, she heard the Voice in her head again. Before, He had only said *Run*. Now He said, *I am the bread of life: he that cometh to me shall never hunger, and he that believeth on me shall never thirst.*

Cara dropped her head and big, hot tears filled her eyes and dripped down onto the hot cobblestones at her feet. "Thank You, Lord," she whispered.

After awhile, she was calm, and felt a little odd, in a sort of dreamy way. She scrubbed the traces of tears from her face and looked around, now with searching eyes. And just to her left were the most outrageous sights that Cara had ever seen in her life, and for a moment she wondered if she really was dreaming. Slowly she walked over to the spectacle.

A great crowd of people surrounded it, and Cara thought maybe that's why she hadn't noticed the sort of combination caravan-pavilion before. But on Cara's side, the crowd had thinned, and she walked up to a four-foot-high brazier that held a pile of unlit wood, a sort of barrier that kept the crowd from pressing in among the people—and the animals.

Two big wagons, curlicued and gingerbreaded and painted in kaleidoscopic colors, stood side by side up against the levee. On each side of them and in front of them big canvas cloths, also brightly painted, had been erected, held up by slender iron poles with large circular bases. In front of the wagons were spread a dazzling array of goods—woven baskets, some painted with designs; piles of scarves and shawls; jars of honey glowing golden; bottles of olive oil with herbs; jars of herbs and liquids of different colors; tinware twinkling like silver in the white-hot sun, baskets with dried herbs piled in them; and tinware vases filled with flowers of all different shape and hue.

But it had been the women that had astounded Cara. Two beautiful, foreign-looking dark women, dressed in short-sleeved blouses and rainbow-colored skirts, were attending the goods. They were barefoot, and wore their black hair down, with colored scarves hemmed with coins. She saw a young man, handsome and slightly dangerous-looking in his exotic way, sharpening an enormous butcher knife against a whetstone that itself looked like a dagger. An old woman, dressed like the young women, sat just by Cara, with a loom in front of her, weaving a scarf of yellow, green, blue, and orange threads.

Cara's mind was sluggish, and it seemed that she took long moments to comprehend each staggering sight in the scene. Owlishly she looked away from the old woman, across to the other side of their "pavilion," and saw the mountain lion. She was sitting upright, washing her paw and then her face, just as any household cat would do. With fascination Cara watched her lick her paw, cruel long claws fully extended, then rub her paw over her eye and ear and top of her head, over and over again. Cara began swaying a little again, and roused herself.

One of the women, the most striking one, Cara thought, laughed at someone standing just outside their pavilion, nodded, and reached out her hand. A pretty girl of about ten took her hand and the woman and girl walked over toward Cara. *Oh, yes, a bear. How did I miss the bear?*

Sitting behind the old woman on a big fat cushion was a black bear. He was wearing a funny green straw hat, with holes cut for his little round ears to stick up through. In front of him was a neatly lettered sign: *Feed the bear for a penny.* In front of him was a basket filled with muscadines.

Cara was riveted at the sight of the muscadines. They were great globules, looking as if they were going to burst out of their skins, purple, black, and green enormous grapes. The woman and the girl came to the basket, and the little girl picked up one of the purple grapes. Gingerly the girl held out her hand to the bear, who then stuck out his enormous paw, black palm upright. The girl dropped the muscadine in his paw, and the bear gave a polite bobbing little bow, then popped the grape in his mouth.

Cara watched with such longing as she'd never felt in her life; she thought that she could gobble up every single one of those muscadines in two mouthfuls. She licked her parched lips. *Feed . . . the boy for a penny?* she thought dazedly.

Then, to her surprise, she found herself seeing, instead of the bright colors before her, an expanse of hot blue sky. Unaccountably the sky was darkening—why was that? And Cara Cogbill fell down in a dead faint.

CHAPTER NINE

Gage Kennon came home on June 29, 1865, after four long, hard years. He was utterly shocked when the Gypsy Caravan, as he had privately dubbed it, drove onto Esplanade Avenue at the outskirts of New Orleans.

First it was because of the smell. Gage hadn't been in any large city during the war. He must have been accustomed to it when he lived here, because now he recoiled from the stench of 175,000 people all smushed together in hot, wet swampy lowlands right on the banks of Ol' Muddy. And too, he realized that he'd been living in what could only be called a scented bower for the past couple of weeks. Nadyha had explained to him that the mint she'd planted on the campsite grounds kept away all kinds of bugs, and even—most important to Baba Simza—the dreaded frog. Several kinds of plants that repelled insects were planted behind the wagons and around the edge of the camp, and the *vardos'* windows all had boxes with aromatic herbs and plants for that reason too. Until now Gage hadn't realized how accustomed he'd grown to the scent of mint with faint airs of rue and lemongrass and marigolds. Riding beside Nadyha's wagon, she watched him with amusement. He must be making a face, and somehow, feeling disloyal, he arranged his features to look impassive.

The other thing that bothered him were all of the Union soldiers. He'd known they were here, of course, because New Orleans had been occupied since May of 1862. New Orleans was the center of the Federal martial area defined as the Department of the Gulf, and at any one time there were between twelve thousand and fifteen thousand Union soldiers in the city. Still, it brought up some of the old anger in Gage to see bluebellies all over the place, just walking or riding around, talking, laughing, shopping, going into saloons, just living there. They didn't belong there, they never had. To Gage that had been the whole point of the war.

As they paraded down Esplanade the Gypsy Caravan drew an immense amount of attention, even in this thoroughly cosmopolitan town. Passersby, on foot and in carriages and on horseback, stopped to stare. Gage noted that most all of the well-dressed women glared, while the not-so-well dressed (literally) ladies of the streets waved and grinned. The men, except for those accompanying the scowling ladies, grinned and whistled and catcalled and waved. Three Union soldiers ran right in front of Nadyha's *vardo* and then came to lope along beside her, for they were moving very slowly.

"Nadyha, Nadyha!" one of them called, grinning like an imbecile up at her. "I've missed you, my Gypsy queen!" He looked about twenty years old, with a shock of curling brown hair under his kepi and a very thin, pitiful mustache.

Enraged, Gage started to pull Cayenne up to intercept them, but Nadyha turned to him and shook her head. She smiled down at them coolly and said, *"Dinili gaje,* Gypsies don't have queens." Making a snicking noise with her mouth, she flicked the reins and Tinar walked a bit faster.

"I'll see you tonight, Nadyha," the boy soldier called. "Wouldn't miss the Gypsies for nothin'!" Slowing, he elbowed one of his companions in the side and said, "Tonight we make market, boys." It was the peculiar New Orleans manner of saying "we're going grocery shopping."

Gage rode past them, so close that Cayenne almost brushed against the boy. What was Nadyha thinking, flirting with the riffraff? He thought he would have to caution Nadyha about things like that.

But he cheered up as they passed through uptown and then into the French Quarter, seeing that the proud old city was fully intact. Gage was sick of seeing towns and small cities and countryside ravaged by war, pretty little towns like Fredericksburg looted and burned, Petersburg turned into one big slum by a year of siege, Richmond shelled to a haggard ruin. No battles had been fought here, for Admiral David Farragut had overrun two forts downstream, sailed into New Orleans with his battleships, and demanded the city's surrender. There was some resistance, but not much. With typical Gallic practicality, the citizens of New Orleans had accepted the inevitable. Gage was fiercely glad. With piercing poignancy he looked down Dauphine Street, toward his old home, and wondered who lived there now. Probably Union soldiers.

When they reached the French Market, right by the levees of the Mississippi River, Gage finally remembered what it was like to really belong to a city. His own flat with the little courtyard, the Market, and the docks were Gage's favorite places, and he knew he'd never find anything quite like them anywhere else. He couldn't help but smile as they drove around one end of the old open-air arcade. It looked exactly the same, except for the men in blue uniforms, but even they faded into obscurity in the kaleidoscopic panorama of New Orleans' French Market.

It was about six o'clock, and in the west the setting sun sent slanted crimson sunlight-bolts throughout the scene. From the river came the huffing of the 'scape pipes of the riverboats still fired up; Gage always thought the sound was exactly like a gigantic animal breathing. But above it all rose the din from the Market. French butchers from the *Halles des Boucheries* called out their wares; from the fruit vendors came loud, indignant Italian and Spanish exclamations as they haggled; German vegetable vendors shouted with Teutonic energy; here and there one could see Chinese, Hindu, and Moors hurrying by with carts piled high with goods. Everywhere was the babble of French, Creole patois, half-French and half-English, translations of French into English with a French accent, and Spanish with all of the same variations. Upperclass white people dressed in their finery, ill-dressed and loud laughing prostitutes, haughty Creoles, blacks in every shade from African black to octoroon gold, the *gens de couleur libres* ladies with their colorful *tignons* all mingled together without apparent constraint or ill-feeling. With a start, Gage realized now that all of the blacks were free people of color; the age-old New Orleans term was redundant now.

Nadyha guided the *vardo* in a circle along the old Spanish cobblestone street that ran just by the Market, and Niçu followed her. Gage dismounted and hurried to help Nadyha down. She just gave him a disgusted glance and climbed down herself. Already some people were coming to stand around the wagons, staring at the Gypsies.

Niçu, Mirella, Nadyha, Gage, and Denny met in a loose circle to organize. Niçu said, "The first thing we have to do is get Baba Simza out of that wagon, or you'll be able to hear her hollering over in Algiers. Gage?"

"Yeah, I got it," Gage said with amusement. Niçu had made Baba Simza a walking cane of the lovely blond tupelo wood, and he had carved the handle in the shape of a bear's head. Apparently since Nadyha had talked with Gage about the status of animals before the fall and had discussed it with her grandmother, Simza had realized that bears, since they were basically vegetarians, were "in balance." She'd been paying much more attention to Boldo since then, talking to him, singing to him, petting him (though she flatly refused to kiss him as Nadyha did), bossing him, scolding him. As for the cane, Baba Simza liked it and was very spry with it, but many times she demanded that Gage carry her. It seemed to tickle the vinegary old lady, particularly as it obviously irritated Nadyha so much.

So Gage brought out Baba Simza's chair, and then Baba Simza herself, and got her settled, with a cup of lukewarm chicory tea. Denny came up to him and said, "Hey, Gage, I gotta go. I'm pretty sure my Uncle Zeke's here. Do you care if I take Cayenne?"

"No, go ahead," Gage said easily. "See you later." Denny hopped up on the horse and took off at a spirited trot.

Now Gage, Nadyha, Niçu, and Mirella set up what Gage called the Gypsy Pavilion. They unhitched Saz from the rear wagon and dismantled the harness tongue. Then, because the *vardos* were so well-made and delicately sprung, the four of them were able to push it up close to the back of Nadyha's *vardo* and lower the front steps, which were curved, painted sky-blue, and had delicate hand-carved detailing on the sides.

Briefly Niçu explained to Gage how they set up their site. Eight-foot-high iron rods were unloaded from the top of Niçu's wagon and screwed into big, heavy, circular bases. Big bolts of canvas, brightly painted in rainbow stripes and then varnished to make them waterproof, were attached to the top of the pole with grommets, and then they raised the poles, making a canvas roof on each side of the wagons and in the front. Gage and Niçu unloaded twelve braziers, wrought-iron stands with a wrought-iron bowl atop, and lined them up on the cobblestones along the big square defined by the canvas tent-tops. Nadyha and Mirella started unloading the cut-to-size small logs that fit into the braziers and loading them up.

By now a sizable group of watchers had gathered. They had crowded around them at first, until Gage and Niçu got the braziers set up. Then they respectfully stepped back behind them. Gage reflected it was an odd mind-set of humans that they instinctively respected boundaries, no matter how loosely defined. Even the ragged children of all ages that impudently darted around every street in the city, most of them looking for or making trouble, stayed back.

"Now what?" Gage asked Niçu.

Niçu nodded toward the crowd, grinning. "What do you think?"

Gage looked over the people. They were excited. They'd been shouting to the Gypsies the whole time, such things as, "Will you tell my fortune, Old Mother? Nadyha, Nadyha, where's your mountain lion? And the bear, we want to see the bear!" Gage now saw the three soldiers they'd seen on Esplanade, and the one who'd impudently spoken to Nadyha stood so close to the brazier that he was touching it. "Nadyha, you're going to sing and dance tonight, aren't you? C'mon, you're the Queen of the Gypsies, you've got to dance for us!"

Gage sighed. "Guess Anca, Boldo, and singing and dancing are the plan."

"Right," Niçu said. "We don't set out our goods until in the morning. Tonight we'll just give them a little taste, so they'll come back tomorrow."

Nadyha and Mirella started the fire in all of the braziers, for it was now full dark. Gage was astounded to see that they talked to the people, responding good-naturedly to their calls and entreaties, smiling, laughing. "You—it doesn't bother you that Mirella acts like that?" Gage asked Niçu as they brushed and curried Tinar and Saz.

"Like what?" he said evenly.

"I don't know, like talking to people she doesn't know, laughing and stuff," Gage said lamely.

"Mirella doesn't act like a *gaje* because she's not. She's Romany, and she's my wife, and I'm proud of her. Personally, I think that *gaje* women act like stupid little mice, with their heads bowed and looking up at you from under their eyelashes or peeping from behind their fans, or acting like you're invisible because you haven't been *properly introduced*. Of course, it's no wonder they don't have energy enough to move or talk, the way they dress, with about three hundred pounds of clothes on."

"Uh—yeah, I see what you mean. Guess I never thought of it like that."

Now they set up another brazier in the center of the pavilion. It was a big round iron bowl, flat-bottomed, with thick two-inch-high legs. When a fire had been built in it, it made a good likeness to a campfire. As ordered, Gage moved Baba Simza and her chair closer to it.

Nadyha began to bring out the animals. When she opened her *vardo* door, Matchko shot out like a black artillery shell and immediately ran to Tinar. Springing lightly, he jumped all fourteen hands to Tinar's back, sat down, wrapped his tail around his front paws, and stared at the crowd beyond the brazier light. Many laughed, some called "Kitty, kitty," and Matchko, with his one yellow eye and one missing ear, gave them a gargoyle's malevolent glare.

Boldo's black head stuck out the door, then he shambled out on his hind legs. Nadyha held his paw as if he were an oversized child as they walked down the steps. Gage thought that that was quite a trick for the bear, and the crowd seemed to agree, for they oohhed and aaahhed. Nadyha led him to the braziers and said, "This is Boldo, the great ferocious black bear!" Some flinched a little, but then Boldo placed one arm across his chubby middle and gave a clumsy bow. Seeming to love the ensuing laughter, he bowed all around, then lumbered over to Baba Simza. Niçu had already put out his cushion next to her chair.

Next Nadyha came out of the wagon with Anca, and Gage was surprised to see that she had on a collar with a length of chain. The collar was of deep brown leather, and it had dozens of Niçu's coins hanging from it, but these coins were big and heavy and made a solemn, deep, clanking sound when she moved. The chain was slender, with light links, with the coins suspended from every other link. The crowd grew quiet as Nadhya took Anca to the far corner of the pavilion and very slowly walked her along the line of people. "This is Anca," Nadyha told them, "and she is the real queen." Anca, as if she were conscious of the fearful admiration directed at her, held her head high and kept looking at the people with her great glowing golden eyes, pacing majestically. Nadyha walked her back and forth a couple of times. Finally someone called, "Nadyha, can we pet her?"

Nadyha's chin came up. "Tomorrow you can," she answered in a ringing voice, "if you pay. And if you dare."

Applause greeted this sally.

When Nadyha finished displaying Anca, she brought her over to her wagon. Anca, too, had a cushion for coming to town, only it was so enormous it was the size of a full bed, and so thick it looked like it was overstuffed with down. But it wasn't. With amusement Nadyha had told Gage that the herb growing under her wagon was catmint, and that it had a calming, sedative effect on some cats, including Anca. Her cushion was stuffed full of it. Gage took Anca's chain from Nadyha and asked, "Do you keep her chained up? I mean, this pretty little necklace wouldn't stop her for a second if she decided to take off."

"She won't," Nadyha said carelessly. "It's just for looks, so the *gaje* won't be scared. Just let it trail, it's all right, she'll probably just crawl right onto her cushion and go to sleep." She went inside her wagon and Gage sat down cross-legged by Anca's mattress. Anca did lie down but laid her head on Gage's lap, as she often did now. He started stroking her head, and again was amazed that the big cat actually purred like a housecat. Except it sounded like a muted roar.

Niçu played a violin solo, and then Nadyha and Baba Simza played guitar and Mirella played the recorder for one song that Nadyha sang. Mirella and Nadyha only danced one time. The crowd began to beg them for more, but Nadyha made an imperious wave to quiet them and said loudly, "Tomorrow! Come buy our goods, if you spend enough money, we'll sing and dance all night!" With loud grumbles the crowd began to disperse.

Now Mirella laid a big iron grillwork across the campfire brazier and placed a big pot of stew on it. Gage had hunted for several days before they'd left camp, bringing in lots of rabbit, birds, turkeys, and two boars. Niçu had built a smokehouse, and they had smoked most of the meat to preserve it for their five-day stay in New Orleans. Some of it they simply salted, for Anca. On the previous day Gage had shot a boar and then brought Anca to it, out to her feeding ground. She had taken pieces, like tidbits, from him before, but he was unsure if she would accept the boar. She was a hunter and he thought she might be disdainful of a fresh kill from a human. But she accepted it with a will, and he'd left her to it. Since she had eaten the day before they left, she wouldn't need to eat large amounts for several days. When Nadyha had found out what Gage had done, she'd said with great sincerity, "Thank you for feeding Anca, Gage."

"You're very welcome," he responded, pleased.

After they ate, Gage asked Nadyha, "I'm so glad to be here, I've just gotta take a look around. I want to go get a *café au lait* at one of the coffee stands in the Market, and then I'm going to take a walk along the docks. Would you do me the honor of accompanying me, Nadyha?"

She considered, then nodded. "I was going to walk the docks myself. But I guess you can come along."

"Gosh, thanks," Gage said dryly.

She did consent to let Gage buy her a *café noir*. Along with his *café au lait* it cost him forty cents, which now meant that Gage had exactly forty-three cents left to his name. But things like that didn't really bother him. Somehow he had a feeling that the Lord had something in store for him, and he knew that that feeling, though it was vague, was strictly scriptural. *A man's heart deviseth his way, but the Lord directeth his steps,* he thought as he carelessly gave the coffee vendor, a beautiful young mulatto woman, four ten-cent pieces. With a half smile he thought, *I wonder if I'm ever going to get my head out of Proverbs as long as I'm around Baba Simza?*

He watched Nadyha. She had on an orange, yellow, and green striped *diklo* with the coins dangling low on her forehead. Her green-tan eyes were bright, her face lit up and glowing, as she hungrily watched all the comings and goings in the French Market. People stared at her, certainly; but she seemed not to care, or even to really notice. Gage had the most curious reactions to her being so oblivious to the intense raking stares. He thought it was extraordinary, he thought she should pay more attention, he thought she was either blind or amazingly naïve though he knew she was neither, he resented it and he completely understood why everyone did it. He stared at Nadyha a lot himself.

When they finished their coffees they went out and slowly started walking down the century-old, famous New Orleans docks. Every kind of watercraft imaginable was there, from crude flatboats to Indian canoes to pirogues to little fishing boats with sails, and, of course, the river-boats. Cheap little packets, tidy little cargo-haulers, mid-sized steamers that hauled both cargo and passengers, and the big ones, the luxurious mostly passenger steamships. As in the Market, all kinds of people crowded the wharves: roustabouts, crews, passengers, couriers, tradesmen, wood-men, pickpockets, thieves, drunks, whores. Horses, carts, drays, wagons, carriages, buggies, and hacks rumbled up and down. It was impossible to keep a distance from Nadyha as they walked side by side, and Gage tried very hard not to brush up against her, as he knew how much she disliked invasions of her space. Now, however, she seemed not to notice. It was a good thing, too, because in the rush and rumble people and sometimes horses ran against you or even into you, if you weren't careful.

But Nadyha wasn't paying attention to the traffic. Her gaze stayed riveted on the line of riverboats. They came to one enormous four-decker that loomed grandly over all. In gold that glinted dimly from the steamer's deck lanterns they read: *Queen of Bohemia*. She had four decks, all of them lit with hundreds and hundreds of lanterns, even though no passengers were on the promenades around the decks. She was painted white with red and gold trim on the gingerbread tops of the deck railings. The pilothouse, a large glassed square right atop, was also heavily trimmed and topped by an octagonal cupola. The tall smokestacks were topped by golden crowns. Between them was suspended a chain and in the middle hung a shield with a medieval-looking lion, rampant, white on a red background, with a golden crown, a golden tongue, and huge golden claws. The *Queen of Bohemia* did look exactly like the large, luxurious steamboats had been nicknamed: floating palace.

"I've never seen one this huge before," Nadyha said in a voice so low that Gage had to bend a little to catch it.

"I saw her a couple of times before the war," Gage said. "I'm not sure, I'm no riverman, but I think she's the biggest on the Mississippi. At least, she's the biggest I've ever seen here."

"I wonder, I wonder," Nadyha said, "where she's been, the things she's seen, the places. I wonder what it's like up there." She pointed to the top deck, where the staterooms must have been large, indeed, for there were double French doors, instead of windows, lining the deck.

"I would imagine those would be some of the grandest, most luxurious rooms I've never seen," Gage said.

They stared for awhile, then Nadyha resumed her walk, and as she had said, she allowed Gage to tag along. Gage asked, "Nadyha, there are a couple of things I'd like to ask you about. Would you allow me?"

To his surprise, she grinned up at him. "*Gaje*, they're so prissy with 'will you give me permission to say this,' 'will you allow me to say that.' Romany men just say what they mean."

"Okay, I can do that. Uh—er—I, uh—"

She chuckled, that low pleasing sound. Gage blurted out, "Would you mind if I stayed with y'all for a while?"

Now she looked nonplussed. "You mean, with us at the Market?"

"Yes."

"But I thought this was your home. I thought—don't you have any place to go?"

"Sure I do," Gage answered, thinking that he could stay in a cheap flea-bitten flophouse for one night at least, with the money he had left. Or he could go back north of town and camp out again. He would never poor-mouth to anyone, however, so he went on, "I just want to stay with you, all of you I mean, at your camp. If you don't mind, and if the others don't."

"Baba Simza probably wouldn't let you leave anyway," Nadyha said lightly. "And whatever Baba Simza says is what better happen."

"You're right about that. Okay, good. Now you're not going to like the second thing I'm just going to come right out and say like a *Rom Baro*." He turned to look in her face and said somberly, "Nadyha, you and Mirella are very beautiful women. And you are exotic, and even though I know that you aren't trying to be—uh—attractive to men, you definitely are, and not all of those men have honorable intentions. You've just *got* to be more careful." As he spoke, he saw with dread that Nadyha's face grew darker and darker.

"Be more careful," she repeated, biting off the words. "You mean, cover myself from head to toe with layers and layers of stupid, uncomfortable, smothering clothes; cover my arms; wear horrible uncomfortable shoes; never look up and around; never speak because I'm not acquainted with the good people of New Orleans; never sing; never dance. That's what you mean."

Unfortunately Gage thought that somehow that was what he'd been thinking of, though not in such stark terms. After all, that's how respectable women behaved and how they dressed. With confusion he thought, *But that's not what makes them respectable. Properly dressed, perfectly mannered women can be just as wicked as any prostitute roaming the streets. It's just that Gypsy women are so unorthodox, and such enticing-looking women. Even though I know very well that Mirella and Nadyha are virtuous and respectable, they don't look like it or act like it, or at least, what we gajes think a virtuous woman should act like. It's just begging, begging for trouble . . .*

With difficulty Gage said, "It's hard for you to understand, I know, Nadyha. But I swear, the only reason I'm saying this is because I'm worried about you. And Mirella, of course. These men," he made a vague wave all around, "you don't know how they think. You have no idea at all."

"Oh, so you're just trying to protect me," she said gravely. "You don't actually disapprove of me."

"Of course not!"

"All right then. Please explain exactly what you want me to wear, what you want me to say, how often I may smile, show me how to dance, teach me how to sing."

"Very funny."

"Then what do you suggest I do?"

After a moment he made a wry face at her. "Don't change a thing about yourself, Nadyha. It was just another dumb *gaje* going on and on about Gypsy stuff he doesn't understand. The only thing I'll ask is this: Please, please don't go around town by yourself. Please allow me to—I mean, I really think I should be with you when you go out, like now, walking around the docks."

She looked rebellious. "What about if Mirella and I want to go somewhere and we don't want you?"

"Does Niçu allow Mirella to wander around without him?"

"*Allow* her? I'd like to see him try to tell her she's not *allowed* to do something. But no, when Mirella wants to go somewhere Niçu usually goes with her. So, if I wander with Mirella, that means I'll be wandering with Niçu. Will you *allow* me to do that?"

"Of course," he said seriously, ignoring her sarcasm. "All I'm saying is that you ladies shouldn't be out in this town without an escort."

"I see women all the time without a man escorting them."

"I know. But you're different, Nadyha. Men look at Gypsy women differently. Do you understand what I'm trying to tell you?"

"Yes, I understand, *dinili gaje*," she said. "I won't go wandering around alone."

"Good. Now I want to ask you one more thing. You promised when we first met that you wouldn't call me a *gaje* any more. How about that? Maybe I can at least score one thing here."

"Score one thing? That's funny. But you're right, I had forgotten. No more calling you a dumb *gaje*."

"Thanks."

"You're welcome, Gage Kennon."

NADYHA WOKE UP AT about three o'clock in the morning for the simple reason that it was when the vendors in the French Market started opening up their stalls. There was just as much racket now as there would be at one o'clock in the afternoon.

As she dressed she wondered how Gage Kennon had slept. He had put his blanket roll behind the wagons, at the base of the levee on dirt instead of the cobblestones. Then she wondered why she was wondering about it. What did she care how he'd slept?

She put on a skirt striped in blue, pink, green, and orange, with no petticoat. Romany women didn't like full skirts, because they brushed up against men. Her mouth twisted with disdain, she thought of the *gaje* women with their ridiculous hoop skirts. What in the world was the purpose of those things? They looked so silly, with little women's waist, shoulders and head, like a stump set on a huge bell. As for modesty, Romany women made their skirts out of fabric thick enough that one couldn't see through them even in the brightest sunlight.

Her blouse, she decided, would be the peach-colored one trimmed with green ribbon, and she'd wear her green, blue, and yellow plaid *diklo* with the golden coins; her gold coin necklace; and thick, gold hoop earrings. Nadyha, Mirella, and Baba Simza never wore their *diklos* and jewelry in camp, except for sometimes when they felt like dressing up for dancing. But one must give the *gaje* what they want to see, she thought acidly.

Everyone else was already up and about. The campfire was going, Mirella was just setting coffee on the grill next to breakfast stew, Gage and Niçu were waiting by Baba Simza's chair. With resignation Nadyha joined them. All of her life they had begun the day by joining hands and saying the Lord's Prayer, but in the last couple of years she had come to find it a tiresome, meaningless ritual. Buried very deep down in her heart, Nadyha knew that it wasn't true, the fault lay with her, not the tradition. But she had become very successful in smothering these feelings, and so she did now.

It was very odd about Gage Kennon, she reflected. Soon after he'd come to their camp Baba Simza had invited him to join in their morning prayer, and he had obviously been pleased. But he intuitively understood that he couldn't join their circle, for that would mean that he would have to hold one of the women's hands. The first time he'd joined them, he'd stood behind Baba Simza's chair, effectively isolating himself, took off his hat and held it in both hands, and bowed his head. So he did now. Nadyha furtively opened her eyes to look at him as they recited the prayer. His lips were moving, and she thought she could see that he was trying to form the Romany words. He really was an unusual man for a *gajo*.

The thought flustered her so she quickly went to attend to Anca and Boldo without saying anything to anyone. None of them spoke very much as they set up their goods for sale. They had folding tables to unload and position. And Baba Simza was extremely picky about how and where the wares were displayed. Nadyha, Niçu, and Mirella had no complaints about her endless directions to placement, from the largest baskets down to the smallest jar of herbs. She had a proven understanding of what would draw the *gajes'* attention and how to sell the goods, for rarely did they return to camp with anything left in their inventory. It took them a couple of hours to set up and already people were starting to gather at the Gypsy Pavilion.

Nadyha forgot about Gage Kennon, forgot about the restlessness that was her constant companion these days, along with her resentment for the isolated and stultifying life she had led since they'd fled Perrados Plantation to hide in their camp three years ago. She was having fun. Going to the French Market and being in New Orleans was the most exciting thing in the world to her.

"Oh, yes, *madame*, that shawl looks very beautiful on you," she said to a plain, dumpy, well-dressed woman. "And it is one-of-a-kind, everything we make is different from the other, so you won't see this shawl on another woman when you promenade in the park, mm? And only three dollars. Yes, yes, I know, but look at the blue, how it matches your eyes! It's truly exactly the same color, everyone must see your pretty blue eyes!" The woman's husband grumpily handed Nadyha three silver dollars.

And so the day went. She realized that she had gotten very hungry, but she decided that they were simply too busy, business was much too brisk, the people were so eager to buy—and to talk to the Gypsies—that she wouldn't stop to eat. Boldo earned many pennies for performing the miracle of eating muscadines. When the basket by him was empty, still with many people milling around, Nadyha said loudly, "Oh, poor Boldo! No more muscadines! Are you still hungry, little bear?"

He solemnly nodded his great bear head.

"All right then. You may eat your hat." Boldo snatched off his hat and took a big bite of it, and the crowd laughed and laughed and some even gave extra pennies. Nadyha made his hats from sugarcane reeds. As soon as the crowd was renewed, she replaced the basket full of muscadines and set a new hat on his head. Soon the pennies started coming in again.

Any time Nadyha observed people getting too crowded on the side of the pavilion where Anca lay on her cushion, she got a little nervous. She wasn't afraid that Anca would attack anyone; she felt as if she knew the cougar as well as she knew Mirella. But once a filthy, loud little boy had thrown a bottle at Anca, which hit her square on the head. Her eyes suddenly flaming, Anca had turned her head and growled at the boy. He had taken off at a dead run, and people had gotten scared and hurried away. Nadyha hadn't cared so much about that, people always loved the Gypsy Pavilion. They would come back. But she did mind that Anca had been subjected to such treatment, and she would mind very much if they all got into some sort of trouble because of Anca.

Now, seeing a tight bunch of people around the brazier by Anca, talking loudly and starting to call out if they could pet her, Nadyha went to kneel by the mountain lion. "I'll ask if she'll let you pet her," she told the crowd. Anca sat up alertly, looking directly into Nadyha's eyes. "Anca, my queen, are you receiving vistors today?" she asked in a low hypnotic voice, then reached into the pocket of her skirt. If a cougar can look slightly amused, Anca did, and obligingly opened her mouth wide, fangs bared, and roared. The crowd flinched and some started backing up. After slipping the treat to Anca, Nadyha called to them, "She is receiving, and she says you may stroke her head once for ten dollars." At that they relaxed and started laughing. Nadyha halfway wished someone rich would take her up on it. Anca would allow it, she was sure, but she wasn't about to let any spoiled children with a penny come pawing on Anca. Boldo was different.

Once during the hustle and bustle, she saw Dennis Wainwright climbing out of a fine carriage that had pulled up, and Cayenne was hitched up behind the carriage. She had forgotten about Denny, and now she thought dryly that Gage must be a generous friend since Denny had stolen his horse and disappeared, and Gage hadn't even commented on it. Denny came into the pavilion, first going to pay his respects to Baba Simza, then speaking to Mirella and Niçu. Hurrying to Nadyha, he bowed and said, "Miss Nadyha, I see you're in the middle of a selling boom, but I just wanted to pay my respects and tell you hello."

She looked him up and down. He was wearing a cream-colored morning suit with a tight-fitting waistcoat and a pocketwatch with a glittering gold chain. The clothes were finely tailored, obviously expensive. "Hello, Dennis. You look well. Not like a horse thief at all."

He waved one hand dismissively, and she saw he now had on a gold pinky ring with a small square glittering diamond. "Aw, ol' Gage told me I could take Cayenne to go see my Uncle Zeke. Besides, I am returning the horse, so I guess that'd make me a pretty sorry horse thief."

"True. I wouldn't consider trying it for a living, Dennis," Nadyha said. Seeing a lady starting to pick up bottles and tins of herbs and setting them back down any which way, she said hurriedly, "Excuse me," and went to the table.

Behind her Denny said, "But—but ma'am—"

Nadyha looked back and said, "Sorry. Business first." Denny went to sit with Gage on the steps of Nadyha's wagon. Matchko, spotting Denny sitting down, crawled up in his lap and started rubbing his gnarled head against his chest, leaving black fur all over his creamy suit.

Some time later Nadyha became aware that Gage was standing sort of beside and behind her, waiting. Nadyha finished with the sale and turned to him. He was grinning like a little boy. "It's time to take a break. You've been working for hours. C'mon, come sit down for a few minutes—and wait 'til you taste this." He was holding a glass full of pale orange ice shavings, and a fresh slice of peach was perched on top. "Peach ice. Manna from heaven."

Nadyha licked her lips and looked around. Baba Simza, Mirella, and Niçu all had peach ices. Baba Simza waved at her imperiously and said in Romany, "Go sit, rest. I'll sell."

Nadyha gratefully took a seat on her wagon steps, and Gage sat down below her. She took a big spoonful of the ice, closed her eyes, and let it melt in her mouth. It was absolutely delicious. "Mm, did you buy these, Gage?"

"Sure did. Do you like it?"

"No, I absolutely love it. Thank you so much."

"Uh—don't thank me yet. 'Cause it's not exactly a gift, it's kinda like a—a bribe."

"What's a bribe?"

"That's where I pay you to do something that you don't want to do. Or maybe you will want to do it, in which case it would be a gift, not a bribe," he said brightly.

"Talk sense, not like a *dilio*—I mean, talk sense, Gage."

"Ho-kay. Y'all are going to dance and sing tonight, right?"

"Ye-es," Nadyha said warily.

Gage took a piece of paper out of his shirt pocket and unfolded it slowly. "Would you consider sort of adding to your—your show? Aw, forget this! Denny asked me to try to talk you into memorizing this and saying it while you do the thing, you know the deal, with Anca, circling the campfire and making her growl and stuff. I told Denny that I couldn't talk you into breathing if you didn't want to, and if you do want to do something I couldn't talk you out of it for love or money. But he says that it's really important, if you'd do this at about nine o'clock tonight."

Nadyha took the paper, glanced at it, and stared at Gage. "Why?"

"Don't have any idea."

She looked down again at the paper, reading it slowly. A small smile turned up the corner of her mouth. "Ho-kay."

"What?"

"Anca and I will do this," she said, popping another mouthful of peach ice into her mouth.

"Oh. Yeah, that's—that's good." Gage stood up. "Just sit for awhile, Nadyha, and finish your ice. I see those kids over there are gonna bust unless they feed Boldo some grapes. I'll take care of it."

Though it rarely came all the way to the forefront of Nadyha's mind while she was selling, she was always aware of the sounds of the steamboats behind her. She loved the blaring of the steam whistles as the boats came in, and the sonorous gongs of the big bells. Late that afternoon she heard a small steamer's whistle right at the levee entrance by their pavilion. Nadyha knew very well the difference between the small and mid-sized steamers and the big ones. The smaller ones' whistles were shrill, in a high-pitched range, and the huge floating palaces were deep and hoarse. She never paid attention to passengers disembarking from the ships, however, because most of them were hurrying home from their travels, not stopping to shop. The passengers started coming through the levee entrance, and Nadyha barely glanced at them.

But a few moments later she saw that one ragged, skinny little boy, hauling a patched canvas bag that seemed much too big and heavy for him, had come over to stare at Boldo. This boy was particularly noticeable because he was so still. The young beggar boys Nadyha had observed that hung around were rowdy, loud, and always scampering around, probably trying to pick pockets. This boy just stood there, his face completely hidden by his big wide-brimmed floppy hat, motionless.

Nadyha kept curiously glancing at him as she told one woman about the benefits of fennel. "It makes a delicious licorice-flavored tea, and is especially good for ladies, *madame, comprendez-vous*? It's also is good for the aching joints, the back strain—"

The boy had crumpled to the ground. It was like watching a vase thrown out of a second-story window, just down and *bang*, all a heap. In a second Gage was kneeling beside him. He bent—jerked—closer, leaning over the boy. Then he gathered him up in his arms as if he were weightless and went to bend over and whisper in Baba Simza's ear. Simza looked startled, then said something to Gage. Without hesitation Gage went to Mirella's and Niçu's wagon, mounted the steps, ducked under the door, and disappeared inside the wagon with the boy in his arms.

Nadyha's eyes opened wide with outrage and she planted her fists on her hips. Leaving the woman standing there she marched over to Simza and demanded in Romany, "What is all this?"

"I'll explain later. It's nothing you have to worry about," Simza answered placidly, continuing to weave on her table loom.

"What? A *gaje* is taking a dirty little *gaje* boy into one of our *vardos*, and I don't have anything to worry about?"

"Not exactly," Baba Simza said with some amusement. "Get back to work, Nadyha, people are trying to give us money and I want you to take it."

Nadyha stalked over to Niçu and Mirella, who were both talking to customers, but she interrupted. "Did you see that? Did you see Gage taking that dirty little boy into your *vardo*?"

"Yes, yes, Nadyha," Niçu said with a touch of impatience. "And I also saw Baba Simza telling Gage to do it." Mirella just shrugged and they both turned back to their customers.

With exasperation Nadyha returned to her Creole lady, who was now staring at her with impatience. But she had waited, Nadyha noted. As she began explaining about fennel again, in the back of her mind she was thinking, *Stupid* gaje! *What does he think he's going to do, save the world?*

And somewhere from the back of her mind came a small, tiny voice, *Maybe not the world . . . maybe he saves just one person at a time . . .*

Circling the campfire with Anca, Nadyha quoted in her throaty voice:

> *Tyger! Tyger! burning bright*
> *In the forests of the night,*
> *What immortal hand or eye*
> *Could frame thy fearful symmetry?*
>
> *In what distant deeps or skies*
> *Burnt the fire of thine eyes?*
> *On what wings dare he aspire?*
> *What the hand dare seize the fire?*
>
> *And what shoulder, & what art,*
> *Could twist the sinews of they heart?*
> *And when thy heart began to beat,*
> *What dread hand? & what dread feet?*
>
> *What the hammer? what the chain?*
> *In what furnace was thy brain?*
> *What the anvil? what dread grasp*
> *Dare its deadly terrors clasp?*
>
> *When the stars threw down their spears,*
> *And water'd heaven with their tears,*
> *Did he smile his work to see?*
> *Did he who made the Lamb make thee?*
>
> *Tyger! Tyger! burning bright*
> *In the forests of the night,*
> *What immortal hand or eye*
> *Dare frame thy fearful symmetry?*

Anca swung her paw, missing Nadyha's face by a mere inch, and roared, a deafening, savage, fearful sound.

It was long seconds before the utter silence of the crowd surrounding the Gypsy Pavilion was broken. Then they started cheering, whistling, applauding, and shouting, "Bravo, bravo Nadyha, Anca!" Nadyha smiled and nodded, then knelt to throw her arms around Anca, who simply watched them with her mysterious Tyger gaze.

DENNY ELBOWED UNCLE ZEKE in the rounded paunch so hard it almost knocked the breath out of him. "See! See! Didn't I tell you! What did I tell you!"

Zedekiah Wainwright stuck a fat cigar in his mouth and joined in applauding, grinning widely. "Yeah, you told me, and I didn't believe it, but now I do. But you really think you can tame that Gypsy woman? After all, she's not like the performing bear."

Denny shook his head. "No one's ever going to tame Nadyha. But I'll bet you she'll do it. Didn't you see her, didn't you hear her? She's a natural, and she loves it. Oh, yeah, we'll get her all right. 'Cause she's like Anca. No one, and no amount of money, could *make* her do it. She'll do it because she wants to. You'll see."

Chapter Ten

When Denny had hopped on Cayenne and took off, he went straight to the St. Louis Hotel. Before the war, the luxurious hotel had been the centerpiece of Creole High Society, with its lavish banquets and balls, and the best Mardi Gras balls were always given at the St. Louis. During the war it had been transformed into a hospital, and Denny knew that it was still occupied by some wounded who hadn't yet returned home, and that some soldiers were still quartered there. However, he also knew Uncle Zeke, and he knew that he had made friends with Nathaniel Banks, the Military Governor, and had wrangled a suite at the hotel when he was in town.

He threw Cayenne's reins to a red-jacketed stableman and went into the entrance hall, an enormous rotunda with a vaulted ceiling, and up the elaborate flying staircase. Milling all around were Union soldiers and mostly black hall porters. Wryly he thought that before the Great

War, he would have been swarmed by the concierge, *maitre des hotels,* and porters, trying to enter the luxurious hotel dressed the way he was, in plain black trousers, white shirt with no waistcoat, and cheap brogans. Now no one gave him a second look.

He went up to the second floor and down an endless corridor that led to two huge double doors; it had been named the Duc d'Orleans Suite, for that august personage had stayed there in the 1840s. Banging on the door, he called out, "Uncle Zeke! You in there? Let me in, it's Denny!"

The double doors were yanked open wide, and his uncle nearly smothered him with a bear hug. "Denny, we've been worried to death! Where the devil have you been? I thought we were supposed to pick you up in Natchez a month ago!"

Zedekiah Wainwright held Denny at arm's length and looked him up and down. He was a robust, burly man with a big chest and paunch; thick, curly brown hair shot through with silver; long, thick sideburns that were all the current rage; pleasant features that could turn hawkish in a moment; sharp brown eyes; and a rumbling boom of a voice. His clothing was somewhat a contrast to his workmen's build and bluff manner, for he dressed expensively and finely. His suit was of tan broadcloth, perfectly tailored to fit him, and he had a thick, gold watch chain suspended from his vest. Sticking a much-chewed cigar in his mouth he said, "What happened to you? You look like a street beggar!"

"Long story," Denny said. "Can I come in, even dressed like this?"

"Of course, boy, come on in. You look like you could use a brandy. And a tailor. Here's Denny, Hervey. Bring us a couple of brandies."

The sitting room of the suite was as elegant as a drawing room in a great house, with velvet-cushioned furniture and draperies and furniture of walnut and cherry. Denny collapsed onto an uncomfortable Louis XVI sofa and accepted the crystal snifter from the servant gratefully. "Thanks, Hervey. You're looking well. Uncle Zeke hasn't completely driven you lunatic yet, I guess."

"No, sir. We're glad to see you, sir," Hervey said. He was a black man of average size and frame, the only things noticeable about him were his large, intelligent eyes and utterly expressionless poker face.

"So, what happened?" Wainwright insisted. "Where have you been?"

"First things first," Denny said firmly. "How's our lady?"

Wainwright sat back and puffed on his cigar until the end glowed like an inferno. "The *Queen of Bohemia* is now the finest steamer on the Mississippi River, Denny. She's already been making us a boatload of money, and it's only going to get better now that this war nonsense is over."

Denny took a sip of the smooth old brandy. "That's good news. Er—to put it mildly, I'm a little short right now. I saw her, she looks great. And Uncle Zeke, when I tell you the plans I've got for her, you're going to make even more money, and then you can increase my allowance," he said brightly.

"Is that right?" Wainwright said, his eyes glinting. "Since when do you know the first thing about the business end of a riverboat?"

"Since I met the Gypsies," Denny replied with a grin.

DENNY HAD SHOWN UP at the Gypsy Pavilion the next day, all clean and polished and wearing a suit that would have cost Gage a month's wages before the war. Gage had been astounded to find out that Captain Dennis Wainwright, the bluebelly beggar he'd picked up outside of Natchez, was in fact a rich man. Reflecting on it, Gage thought maybe he shouldn't have been so surprised; Denny had that certain air of self-sufficiency and confidence that wealthy people usually had. The thing that had thrown Gage was that Denny had suffered the hardships of the last several weeks without complaint. Gage knew that Denny's experience as a captain in the Union Army had never included a field command, in fact he'd only been in close proximity to one battle, at First Bull Run, so he knew nothing about the difficulties of living a soldier's life. Denny's behavior, both to Gage and the Gypsies, had never shown the least hint of snobbery or irritation at his lot. Gage's respect for Denny had gone up a couple of notches.

"I owe you, Gage," Denny had said, taking a twenty-dollar bill out of his pocket. "Please accept this as a token of my gratitude."

Gage had frowned. "I didn't help you for money. I didn't even do it for your gratitude, Billy Yank."

"I know. But I also know that you don't have any money, and that a lot of what little you had you spent on me. Take it, Gage. If you don't, you'll commit the sin of pride, and I'll tell Baba Simza."

Gage took it.

Aside from wondering about his friend's apparent wealthy status, Gage couldn't stop wondering about Denny's insistence on giving Nadyha the poem by William Blake and getting her to recite it that night. What in the world was that all about? Denny had been very mysterious about the whole thing. Gage watched Nadyha as she almost danced around, selling her wares and talking eagerly to customers. That was all show for the *gajes*, he knew. But their song and dance and even Nadyha's interactions with Anca, was Gypsy, for themselves. He couldn't believe she had consented to perform as Denny asked.

Sitting unobtrusively on the steps of Nadyha's wagon, he saw the thin, dirty boy and noticed, as Nadyha did, that he was behaving oddly for a street beggar. The boy's face was half-hidden by his floppy hat so Gage couldn't see his face. He wished he could; there was something oddly compelling about the small forlorn figure, and Gage would have liked to have observed him closer. That was when he crumpled to the ground in a dead faint.

In seconds Gage was kneeling at his side. Bending over him, he finally saw the face, and stiffened with shock. Quickly he scooped Cara Cogbill up in his arms and went to whisper in Baba Simza's ear, "This is a lady, Baba Simza. Can I take her into one of the wagons?"

Simza's eyebrows shot up, but she recovered quickly. "Not Nadyha's, she'd be angry. Take her into Niçu's *vardo*."

"Thank you, ma'am," Gage said.

Niçu's and Mirella's wagon was much like Baba Simza's, only the bed was bigger. Sighing, Gage thought that this girl was going to get their coverlet dirty, for not only was her face and clothing stained with honest dirt, she was literally covered in coal dust. But it couldn't be helped, and Gage thought privately that Nadyha was probably going to pitch an even bigger fit when she saw the coverlet, even though it wasn't hers. Gently Gage laid the girl down on the bed and took off her hat. A glorious tumble of blonde hair—clean hair, Gage noted—spread out on the pillow.

He studied her face. She was very pretty, with delicate china doll features that wouldn't have fooled anyone into thinking she was a boy, once they saw her full on, regardless of dirt and coal dust. Gage poured some water into a wash-basin and began to sponge her face. Underneath the grime she was paper-white, and her lips had no color. He kept sponging her face, her neck, and he took off the bizarre gloves and bathed her little-girl hands. In spite of the heat of the day, her skin felt cool and clammy. She didn't stir, her eyelids didn't flutter, and no color returned to her face or mouth. Gage got anxious, and wondered about a thing he'd heard of called smelling salts. Would that be the thing to do? Did the Gypsies have such a thing? He didn't know, so he went back outside.

Going to Baba Simza, he told her, "She looks about half-dead to me. I don't know what to do. Will you help me, ma'am?"

She cracked a leathery smile up at him. "Help *you*? That's an interesting choice of words, but I'm not really surprised. Here, carry me in there."

Gage carried her into the *vardo* and sat her on a chair right by the bed. Simza said, "What a pretty child." She bent over her, placing her hand on Cara's chest and bending over her with her cheek close to Cara's nose to gauge her breathing. It was quick and shallow. "I'm going to need some things. Get Nadyha."

"Uh—not Mirella?" Gage asked, half-pleading.

"No, Nadyha and I are the *drabengri*. It'll be good for her." Slyly she looked up at Gage. "You're good for her."

"Huh? But—oh, never mind, I'll go ask her and hope she doesn't set Anca on me."

He went outside and waited until Nadyha had sold half a dozen palmetto fans to a lady. Then quietly he said, "Nadyha, that boy that fainted isn't a boy. She's a lady, and it seems like she's really ill. Baba Simza asked if you would come help."

Her face darkened. "We're busy here, Gage. How are we supposed to sell all of our goods if we're all tending to one of your *gaje* strays?"

"Uh—I'll sell. I'll try, anyway."

Nadyha rolled her eyes. "You don't know a *gaje* shawl from a Gypsy *diklo*. Try not to give away stuff with that tender little heart of yours." She stalked into Niçu's *vardo*.

A finely-dressed lady that looked like a mostly Spanish Creole was fingering a bright shawl contemplatively. Gage sidled up to stand in front of the table. "Hello, ma'am," he said.

The woman looked up and her eyes narrowed. "And who are you, sir?" she asked frigidly.

Gage sighed. "I'm just a dumb *gaje*, ma'am. But that shawl sure would look pretty on you. And it's only three dollars."

BABA SIMZA AND NADYHA did in fact have *sal volatile*, and when they waved it under Cara's nose she stirred, then woke up with a start. Her blue eyes widened with consternation as she looked around the *vardo*, then at Baba Simza sitting by her and Nadyha standing by the bed staring down at her with her lips curled. "Wh—where am I? What happened?" Cara asked weakly, then coughed.

Simza lifted her head and gave her a drink of cool water. "Shh, shh, be still, *bitti gaje*. We are Gypsies, and you're in one of our *vardos*, our living wagons," Baba Simza said soothingly. "You fainted, *whish*, gone. It's the heat, and I think you haven't eaten in a while, *hai*?"

Cara looked confused. "I—I don't remember." She put one white hand up to rub her forehead, then said, startled, "Oh, no. You—you know I'm a girl."

"Yes, we noticed that," Nadyha said dryly. "Don't worry about it just now. Drink small sips of the water. I'm going to fix you a good tea and some broth. I think you'll be fine after you get cool and eat something."

Nadyha left and Cara looked at Baba Simza with trepidation. "What—what are you going to do?"

"Do? Do you mean, am I going to do something to you, or with you, that you don't like? No. Don't be afraid, you're safe here. I'm a *drabengri*, a Gypsy medicine woman, and I know all about what's wrong with you. You feel the stomach roll, the head is pounding, you feel hot on the inside and prickly on the outside. You need to drink water, the tea, the broth, then eat. But for now just rest."

Cara relaxed a little, though her eyes were still darting around, trying to take everything in. When Nadyha returned with green China tea and offered it to her, she shrank a little. The young woman didn't seem to be nearly as sympathetic as the older woman. But now Nadyha spoke politely, though with distinct coolness. "Here, I'll hold your head, I know you're very weak. But it'll pass quickly."

Simza and Nadyha removed Cara's heavy jacket and shoes. Cara was so weak she couldn't even sit up for them to take off her coat. Nadyha asked, "Have you been ill? Is there anything wrong with you?"

"No, I'm usually very strong, and I haven't been ill in—in—a long time. Until today, I mean."

"Then you should be just fine in about an hour," Nadyha said briskly.

She rose and in Romany said, "An hour, that's all, Baba Simza. Then she goes."

"We shall see," Simza said calmly. "Now, go get Gage and tell him to come get me. I need to get back out and sell, and so do you, Nadyha. Just about everyone that comes here wants to see you and Anca and Boldo. Gage can sit with her."

Rebelliously Nadyha said, "Gage? That's stupid! Why should he take care of this puny *gaji*?"

"Why do you care?" Simza shot back.

A swift look of unpleasant surprise came over Nadyha's face, then quickly disappeared. "I don't care," she said in English, glancing at Cara. "I'll go get him."

To deepen her disgust, Nadyha saw that two prostitutes were flirting with Gage. They were both young, but in the unforgiving light of day they looked old and haggard. One had untidy mousy brown hair, one had untidy dark brown hair, and both of them wore cheap, flimsy, revealing clothes. As she neared them she heard the one with dark hair say, "Oh, but you know, sir, we don't have the money to buy that shawl. You're a big, strong, handsome man, and we could show you a real good time, and I think then you might *give* us the shawl. Maybe even two shawls." She gave him her best seductive look.

"Sorry, ladies, they aren't my shawls to—oh, hello, Nadyha. These ladies are interested in buying a shawl," he said hastily.

"That's not what I heard," Nadyha said, glaring at the two women. "If you're buying, then I'll be glad to help you. But if you're selling, go sell somewhere else."

"La-di-da," Brown Hair said mockingly. "Insults from a Gypsy? Get over yourself, lovey. C'mon, Jenny, we can come back and visit with Gage later." She linked arms with the other girl and they sashayed off, looking back over their shoulders at Nadyha and making faces.

Nadyha stared up at Gage accusingly.

"I was just trying to sell them a shawl! But I'm not too good at selling ladies' shawls, there was a lady—I mean, a real lady—awhile ago, but she got offended when I spoke to her and went off in a huff. I'm lucky she didn't slap my face for my impudence."

"You're lucky I don't slap your face," Nadyha retorted, rather unreasonably, Gage thought. "Baba Simza says for you to go bring her back out, and then you sit with the *gaji*."

"Huh? Me? Why can't she take care of her?"

Nadyha stuck her clenched fists on her hips, a warning sign that Gage was beginning to know all too well. "If you pick up a stray dog in the street," she said with ominous slowness, "and take him home, then you're responsible for him. Her, in this case. The only thing I wish is that next time you take the stray to your home instead of mine." She turned her back on him and went to a lady beginning to show interest in the herbal remedies.

"Ouch," Gage mumbled as he went into the *vardo*. The girl looked at him with huge alarmed eyes, periwinkle-blue, he now saw. Quickly he snatched off his hat. "Ma'am," he said. "I hope you're feeling better."

"Yes—yes, thank you," she said, but it was in a low, shaky whisper.

Baba Simza held up her arms for him to pick her up, and as they were leaving the wagon she said in a low voice, "Now you listen to me, Gage. That girl is really in a bad way. Don't you pay one bit of attention to what Nadyha tells you to do about her. You sit with her, you fan her, you keep a cool cloth on her forehead, get her to take some tea and broth and then later we'll fix her some solid food. Let her rest."

Gage set her down in her chair. "Yes, ma'am."

"And she can stay. As long as she wants, if she wants," Baba Simza said firmly.

"She can? But—I wasn't thinking—I didn't expect—"

"I know. You just mind me, *gajo*. And I'll mind that one," she said, jutting her chin at Nadyha's back, which still looked stiff with resentment.

"I got the easy job," Gage murmured. "All right, but if she even starts to look funny I'm coming back out here to get you."

He went back to Cara and sat by her bed. "I know this is awkward, ma'am. But see, I—uh—I have to do what Baba Simza says. That's the old lady, the Gypsy lady. I'll be quiet, and respect your—you. But someone does need to sit with you for awhile, and it looks like it's going to have to be me."

"No—but sir, I—that's not really necessary, I'm feeling better already—" She struggled to get up, and Gage just sat and watched her. Cara collapsed back on the bed. "Maybe—maybe in a few minutes," she murmured.

Gage held her head as she finished the tea, then drank some weak broth. The effort seemed to exhaust her and her eyelids fluttered, then closed. Gage kept dipping the cloth on her forehead in cool water, and fanning her with one of the Gypsies' palmetto fans. It seemed she dozed for awhile, and then she woke up again, startled.

"It's all right, ma'am, you just go right ahead and sleep if you can," Gage said kindly.

She regarded him, now much more alert and aware. "Aren't you going to ask me any questions?"

"Not until you're feeling better."

"I'm feeling better. Go—go ahead," she said faintly.

Thoughtfully Gage said, "Really, I just kinda wish you'd just talk to me, instead of me interrogating you. You know, no one here wishes you any harm. We just want to help you, that's all."

"Not everyone," Cara said, looking down and picking at her threadbare shirt.

"Aw, you mean Nadyha. Don't pay any attention to her, she doesn't like anyone. I've been hanging around with these Gypsies for awhile now, and she hasn't been able to run me off yet. Baba Simza won't let her."

"Baba Simza, that's the old lady. She's nice." Cara grew quiet, then sighed deeply. "I guess I owe you an explanation." She went on to tell Gage all about everything that had happened to her, including the theft of her wallet. "So when I got here, I was just looking around, really trying to find a drink of water. And I saw the Gypsies, and the bear, and the grapes . . ." her voice faltered and then trailed off into silence.

Gage was silent for a long time. This girl was in a heap of trouble, no doubt about it; no wonder she dressed up like a boy and fled to a big anonymous city. After the war, it had seemed that the Union was going to be fairly lenient on both the Southern combatants and noncombatants—until President Lincoln had been assassinated. That had changed the victors' tone and attitude. If the Union captain was dead, then they might very well hang even a young innocent girl. A thought occurred to him, and he asked Cara, "You said this captain is at Fort Butler in Donaldsonville?"

"Yes, that's where I'm from."

"You know his name?"

"Captain Joseph Nettles."

Gage nodded. "I have a friend who might be able to look into this, see if Nettles really is dead, and what they're thinking about it. I mean, maybe they think he just fell. It happens."

"Maybe," Cara said, unconvinced.

Gage said, "There is one thing I would like to ask you, ma'am."

"Of course."

"What's your name?"

She smiled a little. "I didn't tell you my name. How odd. It's Cara Cogbill."

Gage took her limp hand and bent over it. "My name is Gage Kennon, Miss Cogbill, and it's a very great pleasure to meet you." He rose and said, "I think you can sleep some more now. I'll be sitting out on the steps there, so if you need anything just call. In awhile we'll bring you something to eat. And don't worry, Miss Cogbill, for now just forget everything and rest."

THAT NIGHT AFTER NADYHA and Anca had performed, Denny told Uncle Zeke, "I'm going to talk to them right now. If I try to talk to them in the morning Nadyha will be really mad at me for interrupting their sales."

"Take them on the *Queen*," Wainwright urged. "Show it off to them. Talk about a good sale! I'm going back to the hotel. But you'll come back and tell me how it goes, won't you, Denny?"

"You bet. I've got no desire to camp out any more," Denny replied. "Go ahead and take the carriage, if I have to I'll borrow Cayenne again."

Wainwright left, and Denny stood at the edge of the crowd for awhile, for they were still clapping and urging more dancing, more singing, more Anca and Boldo, more Nadyha. Good-naturedly Nadyha waved them away, calling, "It's time for our supper. Anca is hungry. I don't think you want to be too close when Anca is hungry!"

Laughing and grumbling, the crowd dispersed slowly. Two wide, shallow baskets were sitting by the two front braziers, and people tossed coins and even some bills in them. Unobtrusively Denny went forward, half-hidden behind a large chubby man, and tossed two ten-dollar bills in a basket. Then he melted back to wait until everyone left.

Finally he stood alone, watching Gage and the Gypsies. Niçu and Gage started setting out chairs, Mirella was preparing bowls of stew and plates with bread and butter and cheese. Nadyha sat next to Baba Simza, talking urgently in her ear. Denny came into the camp and everyone greeted him. "Will you eat with us, Dennis?" Mirella asked. "Please, we have plenty."

"Thank you, ma'am, but I've already had supper. But I'd like to talk to you while you're eating, if you'll pardon me being so rude." He sat down, they were now all seated in a loose semicircle around the campfire brazier.

"I liked your poem," Nadyha said.

"So did the crowd," Denny said. "Thank you so much, Nadyha, for using it in your performance tonight. And that's exactly what I want to talk to you about—the great shows that you all put on every night. I'd like to offer you all a job. And I mean you too, Gage."

The Gypsies exchanged puzzled glances. Denny went on, "First I gotta explain—uh—about me, and my uncle and father and our business. My family's business is called Wainwright Investments, Limited. It's a partnership that owns some businesses outright, and invests in others to share in the profits. Mostly we own textile mills, and we invest in cotton and machinery and iron and—uh—some other things I can't remember right now. Anyway, one growing concern that we do own outright is a steamboat. My family's company owns the *Queen of Bohemia.*"

"You're joshin'," Gage blurted out.

Nadyha's eyes glinted in the firelight. "You own that riverboat? That great, huge, grand riverboat?"

"Aw, I own a little piece of it," Denny said dismissively. "My father owns forty-eight percent of the company, my uncle owns forty-eight percent of the company, and I own four percent. So I guess you could say I own maybe one stateroom. See, my father and my uncle are about as much alike as Boldo and Anca. They're both good businessmen, but they have very different ideas about things, and all of their lives they've fought over business decisions. Now, my grandfather was one hundred percent owner of the business—he's the one that made it grow from owning one textile mill to a profitable national company. And my uncle and my father used to drive him crazy, arguing about stuff." Denny grinned his boyish smile. "My grandfather liked me a lot, but I was only sixteen when he died, he wasn't about to give me a big chunk of the business, and I don't blame him a bit. But he did make sure that I got a big enough piece to have yea or nay say over decisions. And I'm really glad that he did, because never on this earth would my father have bought a riverboat if Uncle Zeke and I hadn't had fifty-two percent of the company," he said vehemently. "Anyway, so here we are, with the *Queen of Bohemia*. I've tried and tried to figure out how to explain to you all—but I'd really rather show you. Would you please come with me and I'll give you a tour? Then you'll see exactly what I'm offering."

Nadyha jumped up. "A tour? We can go see the big boat?"

"Yes, ma'am," Denny answered. "All of you, because as I've said, what I've got in mind is a job, and I mean a pretty good-paying job, on the *Queen of Bohemia*."

Chapter Eleven

Without any discussion whatsoever, the Gypsies jumped up and started packing away their goods and tables. Denny went to talk to Gage, who was helping Niçu store his tinware into crates. But as Denny neared Niçu's and Mirella's *vardo* he saw a shadowy figure sitting on the steps; the light from the nearest brazier barely made the figure discernible. Curiously, Denny went nearer to the wagon, then stopped abruptly, his face a picture of astonishment. Gage hurried to him and said, "Uh, yeah, Denny, there's something I need to talk to you about. That is, I need to ask you—"

Denny demanded, "Who's that girl? And why's she dressed like that?"

"Yeah, that's—she—it's kind of a long story," Gage said. "I'll explain, but I did want to ask you a favor. Is there any way you could find out the status of a bluebelly captain at Fort Butler in Donaldsonville?"

"Yeah. But who's that girl? And why is she dressed like a dirty little boy?"

Despairingly Gage said, "I'll introduce you, Denny, but try not to stare like that, you look like a goggling goldfish. And don't say anything about her clothes. And don't ask her a bunch of fool questions."

"But—"

Gage took his arm and hauled him to stand in front of Cara. "Miss Cara Cogbill, I have the pleasure of introducing you to my friend, Captain Dennis Wainwright. Captain Wainwright, it's my honor to make known to you Miss Cara Cogbill," Gage said formally.

Denny snatched off his top hat and bowed. "Miss Cogbill, it's a great honor to make your acquaintance. Er—uh—"

Cara finally looked up at him, for she had still been hiding beneath her hat. "Captain Wainwright, it's a pleasure to meet you. May I ask if you are a captain in the—" she swallowed hard—"in the Union Army?"

"Not now," he answered, staring at her, still goggling. "I was mustered out of service about a month ago. Uh—I—that is—uh—"

"Denny, close your mouth," Gage said tightly. "Miss Cogbill, please excuse my friend, he's kinda excitable, if you know what I mean. Anyway, he's invited us to go tour his riverboat, the *Queen of Bohemia*. That's why we're all rushing around stowing stuff."

"Yes, I heard," Cara said lightly. "I'm ashamed to admit I was eagerly eavesdropping. I don't know the *Queen of Bohemia*, Captain Wainwright, but she sounds wonderful."

"But—why—" At this point Gage elbowed Denny sharply in the ribs. Denny mumbled, "Unh—ow. Oh. Um—Miss Cogbill, may I extend the invitation to you? It would be an honor if you would accompany us."

Her eyes widened, and not only did she look very young, but she looked like a very young pretty *girl*. "It would? You—you wouldn't mind? I mean, I—I'm not—you see, my clothes aren't—"

Denny had recovered, and he grinned widely at her. "Miss Cogbill, the captain of the *Queen of Bohemia* is a gentleman, formerly a rear admiral of the Navy, named Edward T. Humphries, and he is just as stuffy as his name sounds. It's going to be so much fun to see his face when I bring Nadyha, Niçu, Mirella, Baba Simza—with Gage carrying her, of course—and you on board. Please, you must allow me this pleasure."

"Far be it from me to deny you," Cara said with a mischievous air that surprised Gage.

"Good! Then it's settled," Denny said happily. "Hmm . . . I wonder . . . can we bring Boldo?"

ALTHOUGH IT WAS AFTER ten o'clock at night, there was the usual hurly-burly on the New Orleans docks. The waterfront of New Orleans was lively pretty much twenty-four hours a day, every day of the year. Denny led them straight to the *Queen of Bohemia*. Stopping at the eight-foot-wide gangplank, he gestured expansively. "The grand entrance is just down there, at the center of the boat. But I want to show you the cargo area and third class first, so we have to board here." He went to the bow, where two great double doors stood open. They all trooped after him: Gage, carrying Baba Simza, Nadyha, Niçu, and Mirella, all talking excitedly, with Cara trailing behind them. Denny had decided that it wouldn't be necessary—this time—to bring Boldo.

They gathered in a big empty space, with a wooden deck and only four windows on each side. At the far end were two more big double doors. "This is the cargo area," Denny told them. "This boat is really a passenger steamer, but it does carry cargo sometimes and there's a particular reason, which I'll explain later, that I wanted you to see it," he said, glancing at Nadyha. "Down there are the crew quarters, then the boiler room and engine room. Now, let's go on up to the Promenade Deck, which is actually for third-class passengers."

"Can't we see the boiler room and engine room?" Gage asked with interest.

"No!" Denny, Simza, and Nadyha all said in unison. Denny said, "It's dirty in there, and besides, right now there's no engineers or firemen on board to explain all that stuff to you. You can prowl around in there all you want later, Gage. So let's go on back outside to the stairs."

Two staircases, at the bow and the stern, led up to the second deck. They went up the bow stairs. A wide balcony had two entrance doors into the staterooms. Denny went into a wide, very long hallway lined with doors on both sides. "Now see, on this deck and in second class there are interior staterooms, that means that they don't have windows out onto the promenade. They're cheaper, of course, but we've furnished them just as nicely as the exterior rooms." Going to the first door on his left, he opened the door and Gage was surprised to see that it slid sideways into the wall. Denny went on, "All of the doors slide. It makes for much more room in the staterooms, see? And of course you can still lock them."

"Put me down," Baba Simza said. Obediently Gage set her on her feet. Niçu was carrying her cane, and she could get around very well with it, though she was slow.

They all trooped into the room and looked around. Gage asked, "You said this is *third* class?"

"Yeah. Third class *interior*," Denny said, his eyes sparkling. "These are the crummiest rooms the *Queen of Bohemia* offers."

The room was fully as large as a middle-class family's parlor. The walls were painted a pleasing soft cream color, the floors of highly polished red oak. On each wall was a gas lamp with brass fittings. Two wrought-iron beds painted white with brass accents were against one wall, with a small chest between them that held a cut glass water carafe and two glasses. In one corner was a round table with two chairs, and in the other corner was a washstand with a mirror mounted on it and a porcelain pitcher and washbowl. All of the furniture was made of cherry. The mattresses and pillows were thick, and the coverlets were red-and-gold striped damask. Above the beds were two oil paintings, Mississippi River scenes. "All of the beds on the *Queen of Bohemia* were ordered from France, and all of the furniture on the boat was special-ordered from Jarrod Brothers in Boston," Denny told them. "Of course, all of the draperies and upholstery and linens came from Wainwright Dry Goods, Limited."

All of the Gypsies were looking around, their eyes wide. Baba Simza went to run her hand down the coverlet on one of the beds. Gage was a little surprised, because it was red. But it wasn't a bright crimson, it was a dark brick red, and he had noticed that it was only the true blood-red that seemed to offend them.

Nadyha went to pick up the pitcher and stared closely at it. "Is this porcelain?"

"Yes, ma'am, it sure is," Denny answered.

She looked puzzled. "So what is 'crummiest'? What does that mean?"

"Not this," Cara said softly, running her hands over the silky cherrywood top of the table. Everyone else was surprised; they had forgotten about her.

Denny said, "Yeah, I was just making a joke. 'Crummy' means—uh—not good, not fine, Nadyha. Nothing about the *Queen of Bohemia* is really crummy. So let's just pop across the hall and I'll show you an exterior room." The room was basically the same, except it had a six-by-six window with damask drapes that matched the bed coverlets. "Just to show you that there's a small difference in price in the exterior and interior staterooms because of the window," Denny explained, closing the door. Waving at the far end of the hallway, he went on, "Down there is the Sumavã Mountains Restaurant, which is the third-class dining room. It also has a small secluded dining room, nicely appointed, for ladies who don't want to eat in a public room, and the Elbe River Saloon for gentlemen. You can see all that later, if you want. Right now I want to take you back out to the grand entrance, which leads up to the Salon Deck."

They went back outside and walked around the promenade to a wide rosewood staircase, fronted by two tall pillars that were topped with the same device, the lion rampant, that was on the shield hanging between the two smokestacks. "Is that design something your company came up with?" Gage asked as he again picked up Baba Simza to mount the staircase.

"It's actually the coat of arms of the country of Bohemia," Denny replied. "My uncle has what you might call a deep interest in Bohemia, and it's really such a coincidence—but I'll tell you about it later. Now, this staircase leads up to the Salon Deck, where the second-class staterooms are, and inside is another staircase that leads up to the Texas Deck. No third-class passengers are allowed on this staircase, which is why they have their own outside entrances. The staircase comes into the Moravian Room, a salon for second- and first-class passengers."

The salon ran the entire width of the boat. In the exact center, as one topped the grand staircase, was an enormous six-tiered granite fountain. The top of the fountain was a beautiful woman in simple robes with a golden crown on her head. Even now, though the boat seemed to be deserted, the fountain was running. Clear rippling waterfalls fell from the lady's feet and down into each successively wider bowl. "She's the *Queen of Bohemia*, of course," Denny said, looking up at the figure six feet above their heads, "or I guess you'd say she represents the *Queen of Bohemia*. They've never actually had a queen, only kings, but a small detail like that doesn't bother my uncle."

The room was filled with sofas, settees, armchairs, side chairs, and tea tables, all made of expensive black walnut. The front and back walls were lined with sideboards that held great samovars for coffee and tea, and crystal glasses and bowls for punch, and silver tubs for ice. On one side of the room, with side chairs set in neat rows by it, was a grand concert piano. On the other side were glass-fronted bookcases, with many books, and also busts and decorative urns and carvings and statuettes.

Denny pointed to two doors on the left, plain wooden sliding doors. "Those doors lead to the second-class staterooms." He walked to the other end. Centered amidships was a pair of real doors, ten feet high, painted white with gold trim and ornately carved golden doorknobs. They all followed him into a wide hallway, plushly carpeted, with many small gold gas lamps with alabaster shades hung over oil paintings. Denny pointed out, "That's the *Queen*, you can see . . . all of these are paintings of our ports of call . . . and that's my Uncle Zeke, and this one is of Captain

Humphries." They gathered around the portraits. Gage studied the one with the brass plate that said: "Zedekiah Wainwright, Owner of the *Queen of Bohemia.*" He saw a man with bluff, heavy features, sharp-eyed. He didn't look much like Denny, Gage thought, except for the thick curly brown hair, although Denny didn't have any gray, and he didn't sport the fluffy sideburns.

They heard a low giggle and again were startled to notice Cara. She was staring up at the portrait of "Edward T. Humphries, Captain of the *Queen of Bohemia.*" He was a man with coal-black hair and bushy black eyebrows over stern brown-black eyes. His face was square, his jawline hard and pronounced. He had a perfectly groomed black mustache. "Oh, dear, he does look forbidding," Cara said. Glancing slyly up at Denny she teased, "Are you certain you want to face him down with this entourage, Captain Wainwright?"

"Aw, I'm not scared of him," Denny replied, then anxiously added, "But don't call me 'captain,' please, Miss Cogbill. He's the only captain on this tub. Not that I care, of course." The others exchanged amused glances.

Denny opened another white-and-gilt door on his left. "This is the Lady of Silesia Salon, for ladies, of course. No, no, let's don't go in there right now, I'm getting anxious to get to the Bohemian Dining Room. On the other side, that's the door to the Lusatia Cardroom, which is just another hoity-toity Bohemian name for a saloon. C'mon, everyone, let's go into the dining room, straight through."

Denny threw open the double doors. It was an enormous room, with tables, each seating four persons, filling it. All of the tables were made of rosewood with intricate satinwood inlay, and the rosewood chairs were ornately carved, with gold or red velvet seats. The floor was of blonde satinwood, so highly polished it gleamed like satin. The walls were wainscoted with black walnut, with red-and-gold striped wallpaper above. Two huge chandeliers of silver and crystal hung from the carved plaster ceiling.

But what everyone particularly noticed, when they had finished gawking, was that at one end was a stage, a big stage, with red velvet curtains pulled to the side. "You put on performances of some kind here?" Gage asked. "That's not just for an orchestra, it's too big."

"Sometimes it is just for the orchestra," Denny answered. "Because we have grand balls in here. We also have had solo artists; Adelina Patti was one of our first performers. We also have operas. And we have theatrical productions."

"Is that right," Gage said dryly, glancing around at the Gypsies. They were still looking around at the lush appointments, and seemed not to have been paying much attention to Gage and Denny. But Cara had a knowing, slightly amused, but very intent look on her face.

"This is all yours," Nadyha said in a hushed voice. "Poor Dennis, all over spots, in a dirty *mokadi lalo* shirt and bloomers. No! Dennis *baro gaje, dhon dhon bestipen!* Dennis *bujo* even Gypsies!" Simza, Niçu, and Mirella all burst out laughing.

Denny looked at Gage anxiously. "What'd she say? Was that good or bad?"

"How should I know?" Gage said, blue eyes alight. "All I know in Gypsy is the Lord's Prayer. That wasn't it."

Denny grumbled a little while the fun, in Romany of course, continued. Finally he said, "All right, I'm glad to be so entertaining to you ladies and gentlemen, but how about we go on up to my uncle's stateroom? We'll have refreshments, and we can talk."

"But we didn't get to see the second-class staterooms," Cara objected.

"They're the same size as the third-class," Denny said, "but the furnishings are better. I will show you a first-class cabin, though, because my uncle's stateroom isn't—er—typical. There's a staircase up to the Texas Deck in the Moravian Room, but let's just go back through the galley and take the servants' stairs." He led them back behind through a big, spotless kitchen.

"Why do you call it the Texas Deck?" Nadyha asked curiously. "Texas is a state in America, isn't it?"

"I know this one," Gage said, with Baba Simza in his arms as they went up the narrow back staircase. "The first passenger steamboats named their passenger rooms after the states, that's why they're called 'staterooms.' Texas was the biggest state, so the biggest and best rooms were named after it, and then the passenger stateroom deck got nick-named the Texas Deck."

"I told you, my uncle has a great love of Bohemia," Denny said. "He's named all 174 staterooms on the *Queen* after towns and cities in that country. No one's ever heard of them and no one can pronounce them, but luckily the rooms are numbered, too."

There were no interior staterooms on the Texas Deck. Denny opened the first room they came to, which had a brass plate on the door: *Lebnitz pokoj* ☛ *315.*

It was fifteen feet wide and twenty feet long, bigger than many cottages. The beds were Louis XV, of ornately carved black walnut. The table, chest, and a sideboard were all of rosewood with marble tops. Instead of a hardwood floor, it had a thick, luxuriant Turkish carpet. The bedcovers were of heavy red velvet, the draperies of gold velvet with red satin tasseled tiebacks. Double glassed French doors faced the promenade, and when they were fully opened they in effect formed a private balcony.

"The promenade on this deck isn't public," Denny told them. "The public promenade is the one down on the Salon Deck. Here, I gotta show you this. All of the first- and second-class staterooms have a private bath, but the first-class bath—well, you'll see." It was a roomy bath, with a large copper marble-lined bathtub and marble sink, and the fittings were of silver. The mirror mounted over the sink was framed in rosewood with silver inlay.

Baba Simza frowned at the bath. "Pah, sitting in *mokadi* water, so like a *gaje*."

"Oh, I hadn't thought about that," Denny murmured, then brightened. "Never mind, Baba Simza, I'll think of something . . . anyway, let's go on to my uncle's stateroom, it's at the end of the hall."

When they came out of the room, they met the august personage of Captain Edward T. Humphries himself. He was dressed in evening clothes, white tie and a tailed coat. His visage was dark indeed. "Mr. Wainwright, what's the meaning of this? Does your uncle know that you've brought these people on board the *Queen*?"

Denny did enjoy the staid captain's outrage, but his delight was slightly lessened by the fact that Gage wasn't actually carrying Baba Simza at the time. "Yes, sir, he certainly does," Denny answered confidently. "In fact, he told me to bring them on a tour of the boat."

Humphries looked at the Gypsies long and hard, particularly noting that Mirella, Simza, and Nadyha were barefoot, and the motley crew was accompanied by a dirty beggar boy. His eyes narrowed. "Your uncle told you to bring a pack of Gypsies on the boat. It's that obsession he has with Bohemia, right? Well, try not to mess anything up, Mr. Wainwright. We're all set for the next boarding." He turned on his heel and went down the hall toward the bow, where he had a private cabin.

"Hey, that wasn't nearly as bad as I thought it would be," Denny said with disappointment.

"What does he think we're going to mess up?" Gage muttered. "Sleep in all 174 beds—no that's 358 beds—, drink out of all the glasses, sit on all the chairs?"

"He didn't call you a pack of Gypsies," Nadyha said, fuming.

"We've been called worse," Simza reminded her.

"I am sorry about that," Denny said. "If it makes you feel any better he calls me a worthless idle lazy ne'er-do-well. Here's my uncle's stateroom, all of you please come in and sit down." It was an enormous room, all red and gold and gilded. An iron stove framed in marble made to look like a fireplace was on the back wall, which was the stern of the boat. Two Louis XV sofas were placed along the side, with Louis XV armchairs all around, and convenient walnut side tables. The Gypsy ladies sat on a gold velvet sofa, while Niçu and Gage took the armchairs. Cara perched on the very edge of a fat, tufted slipper chair, and her ladylike position—back not touching, hands folded demurely in her lap, legs to the side and neatly crossed at the ankles—made a ludicrous contrast to her clothing. Denny smiled at the sight, then sat in a chair by her.

At the other end of the room was a dining table and sideboard, and Hervey stood by. The sideboard held several crystal decanters, bottles of wine, crystal glasses, a silver tea service, and a gold coffee service. Lounging in his chair, Denny said, "Over there is Hervey, my uncle's man. He's so quiet and unobtrusive he's almost invisible, but I spot him whenever I want a drink. What will you all have?"

Hervey came and bowed in their direction. Everyone gave him their orders, and immediately Denny started talking. "As I've explained to you, the *Queen of Bohemia* is so named because my Uncle Zeke has such an avid interest in

Bohemia. But what I haven't told you is why he does. It's all because of an opera called *The Bohemian Girl*. He loves that opera, he goes all over, to see it wherever it's being performed. And his favorite thing about the opera is that it's about Gypsies."

Nadyha and Mirella exchanged knowing glances. Nadyha said, "We've heard something of this. Mrs. Perrados, the wife of the eldest son, Jerome Perrados, used to bring people to our cottages. We built them like we build our *vardos*, and then we are Gypsies, our dress is—well, you know. These people, they walk around, they watch us like when people watch Boldo. They were always saying things like, 'Oh, they really are *so* Bohemian, so exotic, so wild,'" Nadyha mocked in a high persnickety voice. "But I don't know this opera."

"It's about a Polish count named Thaddeus, and he is in exile because he was a Catholic and the Hapsburg Empire—oh, never mind about the politics," Denny said with exasperation. "Anyway, the Polish count is in exile in Austria, and he joins up with the Gypsies. And there's a Count Arnheim who has a child, a daughter named Arline. Arline is attacked by a deer—"

"What!" Nadyha exclaimed. "Attacked by a *deer*! What did he do, try to nibble her to death?"

"Okay, forget about the deer. Sometimes operas have what you might call kind of fanciful plots. Anyway, the leader of the Gypsies, Devilshoof, kidnaps the Countess Arline—"

"All the time the *gaje* talk about us kidnapping their children," Nadyha grumbled. "Why should we want their stupid *gaje* children? We have perfectly good Romany children of our own."

"Uh—actually, that rumor might have kinda gotten started because of this opera," Denny said apologetically. "Sorry. Anyway, so Devilshoof kidnaps Arline—"

"No *romoro* would ever be named Devilshoof!" Nadyha snapped.

"Nadyha, if you don't let him tell this story we're never going to find out what he's been hinting at all night," Baba Simza said impatiently. "Go on, Dennis."

With despair Denny talked very fast, "Thaddeus falls in love with Arline, who doesn't remember she's an Austrian countess, and thinks she's a Bohemian girl, like the Gypsies, and the Queen of the Gypsies falls in love with Thaddeus, Arline gets returned to her father, Thaddeus decides to chance going to her even though he's a wanted rebel, the Queen of the Gypsies tries to kill Arline, Devils—I mean, the leader of the Gypsies stops her and she's accidentally killed, Thaddeus and Arline get married and live happily ever after."

Niçu said slowly, "So now we know that your uncle is taken with Bohemia and Gypsies, we know all about the plot of this opera *The Bohemian Girl*, and we know that whoever wrote it knows nothing about the Romany. What's it got to do with us?"

Denny got excited, jumped out of his chair, and started pacing. He almost bowled Hervey over, who was bent over, handing Simza a cup of tea. "See, this opera started what you might call a 'Gypsy craze' in the big cities—London, Paris, Vienna, Hamburg, of course Prague, New York, Boston—and probably here too, Nadyha, which is why Mrs. Perrados was showing off her real Gypsies to her friends, if you'll pardon me for being so impudent. And actually the music is much simpler and more understandable than most operas; one aria in particular has been performed in drawing rooms all over the world countless times, errand boys whistle 'The Gypsy Life,' clerks hum snatches of the songs, men sing them in saloons. So some of the songs could be performed by even the most amateur singers.

"But the music of the Gypsies, it's nothing like the music I've heard you all perform, it's just pretty standard opera. And your lives, your dress, your—your"—he waved one arm wildly—"your performances, the real Gypsy music and dance and ways, are a thousand times better than the opera. So. How would you all like to star in a production that would be very similar to *The Bohemian Girl*, only it would be really authentic Romany?"

A long, stunned silence greeted this. The Gypsies all looked at each other and at Denny, astounded. Gage didn't look surprised, and he noticed that Cara didn't, either. She was smiling a little, a private expression, and her eyes were focused in the distance, intense and thoughtful.

Niçu asked, "Are you talking about us being in a play, or something, here, on the *Queen of Bohemia*?"

"Exactly," Denny said with satisfaction. "Naturally, you'd live here, in the staterooms, not the crew quarters. And you would be paid."

Frowning, Nadyha said, "But what kind of performance are you talking about? We can't sing an opera. We sing and dance because we love to, but we're not actors."

"You can act," Denny shot back. "That's why I wanted you to recite 'Tyger, Tyger' with Anca. I knew you could act anyway, Nadyha, because of the way you performed that night, with the Proverbs, the religious stuff you said. But I wanted to prove it to my uncle, and to me William Blake could have written the poem for Anca, and I needed something from the arts to show that you really can act. It went so well that I've already decided to use that same exact poem in your opening scene with Anca."

"What?" Nadyha said in bewilderment.

"That's right. And you still don't get what I'm thinking, in fact, the kind of production I've already gotten
about half-written," Denny went on excitedly. "As I said,
it's loosely based on *The Bohemian Girl*, it'll use some of
the songs, but mostly I want the real Gypsy music and it
must have the dancing. And Anca, and Boldo, and I think
we should have your marvelous, showy Tinar and Saz, too!
That's why I wanted you to see the cargo hold, Nadyha, we
could have great stables for them, in fact we've transported
horses and carriages before. This production is going to be
sensational! So, there's a part for each one of you, and you
too, Gage." He grinned like a mischievous boy and went on,
"I've even thought of a part for me, and I insisted my uncle
play the part of Count Arnheim. That could be one reason
he's so enthusiastic. The only thing I don't know about is
the Countess Arline . . . we may have to steal a lady from
one of the opera troupes here . . ."

Cara said something in a voice so low no one could quite
hear her.

Denny stopped striding around and waving his arms. "I
beg your pardon, Miss Cogbill? I couldn't quite catch what
you were saying."

She cleared her throat and looked up at him with starry
blue eyes. "'I Dreamt I Dwelt in Marble Halls.' The most
famous aria from *The Bohemian Girl*. I can sing it."

Chapter Twelve

Denny returned with them to the Gypsy Pavilion. Niçu, Mirella, Nadyha, and Simza gathered their chairs on one side of the camp-fire brazier, talking excitedly in Romany. Cara hurried into the *vardo*, where her bag was stored.

Gage set out three chairs on the other side of the fire. He and Denny sat down to wait for Cara; Gage knew she was packing up her things and was going to try to leave. He was going to try to stop her.

Denny demanded, "Gage, you have got to tell me about that girl! Who is she? Why's she wearing those clothes?"

"You've already asked me that about a hundred times," Gage answered. "And I'm not going to tell you, I'll let her tell you if she wants to. But listen, Denny, before she comes back out, I have to ask you—again, because when I asked you before all you could say was 'Who is that? Why's she wearing those clothes?' So let's don't go through all that again. What I need you to do, if you can, is find out about a captain stationed at Fort Butler in Donaldsonville. His name is Joseph Nettles."

"Joseph Nettles," Denny repeated thoughtfully. "I haven't heard of him. So you mean, find out what about him? His height, his childhood, his favorite color?"

"Find out if he's dead," Gage said shortly.

"Huh?"

Cara came out of the wagon, lugging her canvas sack. Gage hurried to her. "Miss Cogbill, would you please join me and Mr. Wainwright? He would like to speak with you, you know, about the—uh—marble halls thing."

"Yes, he's very excited about his theatrical production, isn't he?" Cara said, glancing at Denny. He was watching her. "But as you know, Mr. Kennon, I'm in such a—a—predicament right now that I don't—that is, I'm not sure. Honestly, I think I'd better be going on now."

"Yeah, that's something that *I* wanted to talk to you about," Gage said gently. "Anyway, what can it hurt? Denny's a friend. I would like to be your friend. So, why don't all of us friends sit down and have a friendly chat?"

"I suppose it couldn't hurt . . ." she said reluctantly.

She and Gage went to the chairs Gage had set out. Denny hopped up to hold the chair when she sat down, his eyes twinkling again with amusement at her elegant drawing-room posture and grace in her tattered boys' clothing. "Miss Cogbill, I realize that our acquaintance has been very short, and maybe a little unorthodox, but I'm going to be presumptuous anyway and ask you a bunch of impertinent questions."

"What a surprise," Cara said evenly.

"No, no, ma'am," Denny said hastily. "Not about your—uh—clothing. What I want to know about is that you said you can sing. Can you sing really well? And have you ever considered being in a theatrical production? Do you think you could perform on the stage?"

Now she smiled. "I see you did mean a bunch of questions." Taking a deep breath, she replied, "I'm told I sing very well, yes. And I suppose it would be a sort of false humility to say that I don't. I believe the Lord has given me a gift for singing, and I also play the piano and the guitar. I have been in—on the stage. In a very small way, of course."

Denny sat up straight. "You have? So you already have theatrical experience? Oh, this is too great! Will you sing something for me now? Please?"

She thought for a moment. "Yes."

Gage stood up, grinning. "I'll go get Baba Simza's guitar."

Denny and Cara stared at each other. Denny looked intrigued and mystified; Cara looked tranquil and secretly amused.

Gage returned with the guitar, and Cara took it, strummed it, and expertly tuned two strings. Without any preamble she started plucking the strings, and a lovely haunting music filled the air.

Are you going to Scarborough Fair?
Parsley, sage, rosemary and thyme . . .
Remember me to the one who lives there.
He once was a true love of mine.

She sang the song through, and Gage noticed that the Gypsies had stopped talking and were watching Cara and listening. Nadyha's eyes shone; it was the kind of song that she loved most.

When the last soft guitar notes faded out Denny breathed, "Exquisite."

"Thank you, sir," she said simply.

"Will you please be my Countess?" he blurted out.

"I beg your pardon?" Cara said blankly.

"I mean—uh—that's the name of my play, only now since I've heard you we can call it an operetta!" Denny said excitedly. "*The Countess and the Gypsy Queen*'. So, will you be Countess—Countess—Cara Czerny of Bohemia?"

Baffled, Cara looked down at herself, her dirty boy's shirt, her frayed trousers, her men's brogans. "Countess?" she repeated. "Look at me!"

The humor of the picture hit her then, and she started giggling, and then of course Denny started laughing. Even Gage grinned.

Cara sobered and said, "Mr. Wainwright, I appreciate your offer, I really do. But at this time I'm afraid I can't—it wouldn't be—it's not possible for me to accept it."

"At this time," Denny repeated sharply. "So how about in the morning?"

Nadyha came over to them then and said to Cara, "That was a good song. We all liked it very much. You sing beautifully, Miss Cogbill."

"Thank you, and please call me Cara. I'll be glad to teach you the song, Nadyha. Mr. Kennon told me that you are an accomplished singer yourself."

"Mm," Nadyha said neutrally, barely glancing at Gage. Then, placing her fists on her hips she turned to Denny. In spite of the pugnacious stance, her eyes were alight, her face glowed. "Dennis, we all want to be in your play, and live on the *Queen of Bohemia*."

Denny got so excited he jumped out of his chair. "Yes, yes, yes! I knew it, I knew it!"

"Oh, you did not, *dilo gajo*," Nadyha said, but with a hint of affection. "So, we're tired, it's almost midnight, and we have to get up in a few hours. We're all going to bed. Miss—I mean, Cara, my *puridaia*—Baba Simza—would like to speak to you."

She turned on her heel and left, leaving Denny standing there dumbly muttering, "But—uh—I wanted to—er—"

Cara got up and walked over to Baba Simza's chair. Denny stammered, "But—Miss Cogbill—"

"It's happened to me a lot, but I gotta say I've never seen so many women walk away from a fellow in such a short period of time," Gage remarked. "You're goggling again, Denny. Sit down, you've heard their decision, that's all you'll get from them tonight. These people just make up their minds and then go to work, haven't you noticed?"

"But I want to talk about it!" Denny complained, sitting down again.

"I'll talk about it. I'll tell you right now that I'm not going to be in any play, or any operetta either," Gage said firmly. "So whatever idea you had for me bumbling around on a stage, you can just forget it."

"Yeah, I kind of figured that," Denny said. "But I owe you, Gage, and I do want to hereby officially offer you the part of Count Somebody from Poland in 'The Countess and the Gypsy Queen.'"

"No thanks."

"Good. No, what I mean is, I pretty much already knew you wouldn't do it, so I kinda wrote the part with someone else in mind."

"Uh-huh. And this Count, this would be the Countess Cara Czerny of Bohemia's love interest?"

"He would be."

Gage leaned back in his chair, stretched his long legs out, and laced his hands across his stomach. "Seems to me like you'd make a good Count Somebody from Poland. You can even sing okay, I know from all those times you warbled 'When Johnny Comes Marching Home' while we were on the road."

"You really think so?" Denny said, genuinely pleased. Then he shrugged. "It's not going to make any difference anyway, we could line up a clothesline full of crows on stage and no one would notice, not when Nadyha's performing. And maybe now . . . Miss Cogbill . . ." He ruminated for awhile, then brightened up again. "Anyway, Gage, I had something else in mind for you. Actually, for you and Niçu, and there he goes, I can't even talk about it to him until tomorrow." Niçu and Mirella were just then going into their *vardo*.

"You can't talk about it to me either," Gage grumbled. "I've never met a man so chock-full of fool ideas."

Denny asked with a sly air, "Oh, no? What if I told you this idea is about you shooting a lot, with guns?"

Gage whipped his head around to look at Denny. "Yeah? Good guns, plenty of ammunition?"

"You betcha, Johnny Reb."

"All right then, Billy Yank," Gage said expansively, "let's talk."

CARA WENT TO BABA Simza's chair and asked quietly, "Ma'am? You wanted to speak to me?"

"*Hai*, sit down, Cara," she said, waving. Cara sat crosslegged down by her chair. "You were thinking of leaving tonight?"

"Well, of course, ma'am. I feel much better, you see, I'm not having the vapors or anything," Cara said with an attempt at lightness. "You've all been very kind, and I'm so grateful. But it's time I went about my own business."

"Is it?" Baba Simza asked. In the dying campfire her dark eyes glittered. "You prayed, today, in the *vardo* when you were so sick. You're a Christian?"

"Yes, ma'am, I am. And so I know that the Lord is—He—" Cara swallowed hard. "No matter what happens, I know that He'll take care of me."

"And don't you think that He already has?" Baba Simza demanded. "You're here. It just happened that you fell down, *boosh*, right in front of Gage Kennon? No, no, *bitti gaji*. *Miry deary Dovvel* made sure you didn't fall down over there, over there, over there." She stabbed the air with a gnarled forefinger in three directions. "You fell down here. I think it's funny that people keep falling down in front of Gage Kennon, and he thinks it's funny that I keep having poor hurt *gajes* show up in my camp. And you are hurt, aren't you, Cara?"

Cara tried to answer, but suddenly her eyes filled with tears, and she choked back sobs. Simza laid her hand on the girl's shoulder. "It's not always bad to weep, you know. But don't weep from fear. *Miry deary Dovvel* has told me, *Be not afraid of sudden fear, neither of the desolation of the wicked, when it cometh. For the Lord shall be thy confidence, and shall keep thy foot from being taken.*"

Cara was startled, and Simza went on, "No, Gage has told me nothing of you, nothing at all. This is just the Proverb I thought of while we were talking. *Hai.* Tonight you sleep in Nadyha's *vardo*, I sleep in Niçu's."

Startled, Cara said, "But—Nadyha—?"

Simza shrugged. "She said this, not me. And that, too, is something that one day you'll have to thank Gage Kennon for."

THE NEXT TWELVE DAYS were the crazy-busiest, but also the most fun Gage Kennon had ever had.

The Gypsies flatly refused to leave the French Market, because they had many goods left to sell. Also, they worked, selling those goods, all day; and because Market started so early, they went to bed early. It drove Denny lunatic that they wouldn't start rehearsals on the *Queen of Bohemia*.

"We're steaming out on the twelfth," Denny pleaded with Baba Simza. "Today is the second. As we discussed, Baba Simza, you're all going to be making pretty good money. Can't you just store this stuff you have left and go ahead and move onto the *Queen* and start rehearsals? Please?"

"Seest thou a man diligent in his business? He shall stand before kings; he shall not stand before mean men," Baba Simza quoted placidly as she wove a *tignon*. "We sell our goods, then we return to camp to attend to getting everything stored."

"Yes, ma'am," Denny said, defeated.

After Simza's talk with Cara, she just seemed to become a part of their motley camp, much as Gage and Denny had. She still wore her boy's clothes and hat, and stayed in the background all day. That afternoon Denny received word about his inquiries about Captain Joseph Nettles at Fort Butler. Gravely he went to talk to Gage, who was sharpening Niçu's throwing knives. "I found out about that captain you asked me about," he said, glancing at Cara, who sat on the *vardo* steps. "The news isn't very good. And now I finally know why she's dressed like that."

Slowly Gage put down the whetstone and knife. "I guess both of us had better go talk to her. No sense in pretending that you don't know any more."

They went to sit by her and her face filled with dread as she saw their expressions.

Calmly Gage said, "Miss Cogbill, I had to ask Denny to make inquiries, and he's had some news. But before we talk about that, I just want to say that I know you're a good Christian lady, and I believe that the Lord has set you in this place, at this time, for a reason. So I'll let Denny talk to you about that."

"Captain Nettles is dead," Denny said soberly. "He fell off the stage and broke his neck. It has become known that he was drinking quite a bit that night, and that's believed to be the cause of his accident.

"The problem, Miss Cogbill, is that there are questions about that night. It became known that you were the last person to see him alive. The provost marshals have said they'd like to question you."

"Is—is there a warrant out for my arrest?" Cara said fearfully.

"No, it hasn't really gotten that far," Denny answered reluctantly. "But right now they are looking for you. Apparently, there is some rumor that you've—you've become some sort of—disreputable—person, unladylike, I mean, and some ladies have apparently gotten Mrs. Nettles to think that—well, not that you actually intended to kill him, but that you—um—"

"Got him drunk, tried to seduce him, and then he fell and I ran," Cara said quietly. "I can see that Mrs. Nettles would want to think that." Then she looked up at Denny, her eyes round with alarm. "That's not what happened!"

Denny grinned; he couldn't help it, really. It was his natural expression, and she was so innocent, so kitten-ish. "I know that, Miss Cogbill. After all, if I thought you were a disreputable person, would I have asked you to be Countess Cara Czerny? Certainly not. And I think that's exactly what you should do for now. It's eleven days until we leave, and then we'll be steaming the Mississippi River for two weeks. From what my contact at Fort Butler said, I think there's a very good chance the whole scandal will be forgotten by then."

Cara glanced at Gage, and he nodded encouragingly to her. She took a deep breath, then said, "Mr. Wainwright, I thank you very much for your generous offer of employment, and I accept gladly."

"Great! Let's all go get fitted for costumes!" Denny said, bounding up.

And so they did; at least, Denny, Gage, and Cara did. Gage had consented to be the Captain of the Guard because he only had two lines. The Gypsies said they'd wear their own clothes, which was secretly what Denny hoped for anyway. He did, however, get a pile of gold coins and a heavy gold chain for Niçu to make Nadyha a *galbé*, the traditional necklace worn by Gypsy women. And he bought thick skeins of real gold thread for her to make a *diklo*.

As it turned out, the Gypsies did sell just about everything the next Sunday morning, Market's busiest day, and decided to return to camp that night, and Denny went with them.

For the next four days they rehearsed *The Countess and the Gypsy Queen*; Niçu, Mirella, and Gage practiced their show; and they all worked. Niçu made dozens of tin plates, some dinner-size, some saucers, and plenty of the small tin coins. Mirella and Simza made *diklos* and *kishtis*, the sashes that Gypsy men wore, for Denny had happily told them that they'd have Gypsy extras, and Wainwright Investments, Limited, would pay them for the costuming.

Niçu taught Denny to dance, and Nadyha taught Cara to dance. Nadyha had slowly and tenuously made friends with Cara. Their relationship improved quite a bit because of the animals. In the play Cara had some interaction with them, and though she was a little frightened of Anca, she soon got over it. Anca tolerated Cara, as seemed to be her attitude toward everyone except Nadyha and Gage. Also, it was necessary to teach Anca, Boldo, and Tinar and Saz some new tricks, and though it was mostly Nadyha, Cara found that she could also help with training them.

Five days before the *Queen of Bohemia* was scheduled to leave, the Gypsies, Cara, Gage, and Denny moved onto the boat. Anca, Boldo, Tinar, Saz, and even Matchko the cat moved onto the *Queen* with them. They rehearsed from early dawn until late at night, and when the twelfth came they were all ready.

Nadyha stood on her private balcony, for Denny had given her his first-class stateroom since she had Anca and Boldo with her. She watched and listened hungrily as the great steamer fired up and began to breathe, its low huffing roar from the 'scape pipes. Hundreds of people lined the docks, watching the *Queen of Bohemia* as she slowly backed out, waving and calling out. Her smokestacks belched black smoke, the gold and red trim glittered in the early morning sun, and then her great whistles sounded, a deep commanding baritone.

"I can't believe it," she said softly to Anca, who stood by her side. "It's like a dream, the best dream . . ."

And it's all because of Gage Kennon.

CHAPTER THIRTEEN

Dozens of passengers crowded around the easel set up by the grand concert piano in the Moravian Room. On the easel was a large playbill advertising the operetta to be performed on the *Queen of Bohemia* on two nights during their voyage to St. Louis. The playbill was expertly done. In large script letters across the top was *The Countess and the Gypsy Queen.* Denny had had a woodcut made of Nadyha and Anca, and they brooded in the left corner. Underneath their picture it read: *Nadyha, Queen of the Gypsies, and Anca, her Fierce Mountain Lion.*

In smaller script it read:

Featuring:

Baba Simza, the Phuri Dae

Mirella, the Gypsy who loves Bulibasha

Niçu as Bulibasha, Leader of the Gypsies & members of the Gypsy vitsi

In the lower right hand corner was a delicate woodcut of Cara, looking dreamily off toward some mountains. Her caption read simply: *The Mysterious Countess Cara Czerny.*

Underneath in smaller block letters the playbill read: "The Illustrious Owner of the Queen of Bohemia, Zedekiah Wainwright, has graciously consented to play Count Czerny of Bohemia."

"Captain Dennis Wainwright, Ret., is also featured as Count Tomasz Adamczyk of Poland."

In red block script was the mild warning: "Wild animals will be featured in the production. They are not dangerous, but any ladies who may be distressed are cautioned." This, of course, guaranteed that every lady on the boat would, if necessary, claw her way in to see the operetta.

At the bottom was a removable board for posting performance times for first-, second-, and third-class passengers. It read: *Performance 9:00 p.m. on Thursday night in The Bohemian Room, Texas Deck Passengers.*

Mrs. Euprosine Dobard sniffed and said loudly, "I think the entire thing is scandalous! Did you know that those Gypsy women go barefoot, and their arms are always uncovered! And those terrible beasts! I have told Mr. Dobard that perhaps we ought to disembark in Baton Rouge and take another boat!" She was a short, plump olive-skinned woman dressed in a traveling ensemble that cost as much as her stateroom. Her husband, Theodule Dobard, was also short and rotund. He looked like a beefy squire, with fat, fluffy sideburns and round, red cheeks.

"Aw, Euprosine, the *Queen of Bohemia* is the best steamer on the Mississippi!" he said jovially, a startling contrast to his wife's priggish sniffs and supercilious expression. "And look, if the animals bother you, you don't have to attend, see?"

The crowd around them, some of them second-class passengers, pressed in to listen closely. "There's really a mountain lion?" one young girl asked shyly.

"There is, and a dirty bear, and a wild tomcat that belongs to *them* that scampers up and down the halls willy-nilly!" Mrs. Dobard fumed. "They're in *first class*! It's abominable!"

Mr. Dobard sighed deeply; it was indeed beginning to sound like they may be disembarking in Baton Rouge. But then his daughter, Monique, came to thread her arm through her mother's and said, "Oh, *Maman*, you are making entirely too much of it. It's exciting! I, for one, wish the performance was tonight instead of tomorrow night, I'm so looking forward to it."

Mrs. Dobard looked up at her daughter, for she was a full four inches shorter than Monique. In fact, Monique could have been a foundling, for she was nothing like either of her parents. She was slender and tall, and had exquisite grace and a hypnotic, musical voice. Her face wasn't beautiful, but it was strong, with a long, straight, patrician nose and firm chin and well-shaped lips. Her eyes and hair were dark brown. It was her voice, and her charm, that made her such a comely woman.

"You are?" Mrs. Dobard said. "But, Monique, just think of my nerves! Thieving dirty Gypsies and wild animals! I thought that you might stay with me tomorrow night during this—this—spectacle."

"No, ma'am," Monique said coolly. "I wouldn't miss it for the world."

ANTICIPATION WAS HIGH IN the Bohemian Room. The first-class passengers had finished their dinners, and lots of interesting noises—including a horse's high battle cry, and the growl of a cougar—had been heard behind the red velvet curtains hiding the stage. Now, as the waiters removed the last white tablecloth, to the passengers' wonder they set small vases of flowers on the tables beside the candle lanterns. The gaslights along the walls dimmed down, the gas chandeliers were darkened while the limelights lining the stage were turned up. Captain Edward T. Humphries, resplendent in a white uniform with gold braid, came to stand in the center of the stage. Some murmurs of conversation broke out.

"Ladies and gentlemen," he said in his commanding voice, "if I may have your attention please. *The Countess and the Gypsy Queen* will commence in a few moments. As I'm sure you've already heard, there will be wild animals included in the operetta. I assure you that no person on board my ship is in any kind of danger, so do not be concerned about that. I would, however, request that you remain silent when the animals are performing; please do not applaud or shout during those times. And I must insist that you keep your seats during the performance. Some parts of the production, you will see, are a bit unorthodox, but it is imperative that you all remain still and quiet. Thank you."

The play that Denny had written was basically the same plot as *The Bohemian Girl*, without some of the complicated subplots.

In Act I, Count Czerny of Austria (played enthusiastically by Denny's Uncle Zeke) tells his Captain of the Guard (played rather woodenly by Gage) that he's had word that a Polish rebel is hiding somewhere in his fiefdom, and charges him to find the rebel and put him under arrest. That rebel, Captain Tomasz Adamcyzk, on the run for his life, meets Bulibasha, the leader of the Gypsies. Bulibasha feels empathy for his plight, and says that Tomasz must join his band. They hear horses coming and Bulibasha tells Tomasz to hide.

Then the Captain of the Guard came on stage. A magnificent chestnut horse took exactly two high, proud steps and then reared and neighed angrily at the sight of the Gypsy. Nadyha had taught Cayenne to do this, and he made the very portrait of a proud war horse. The captain asks Bulibasha if he's seen any strangers, and Bulibasha answers that he had seen a Polish soldier, and points the captain in the opposite direction from the Gypsy camp.

A week later, the Captain of the Guard reports to Count Czerny that no sign of the Polish rebel soldier had been found, and that he must have fled the fiefdom. Count Czerny calls off the hunt. The count asks his servant where his daughter, the Countess Cara is, and the servant replies that she has gone to the meadows to pick flowers. Count Czerny remarks that he worries about her, she often wanders far from the castle, but she has done so by herself since she was a small child. The curtains close.

Then, in the Bohemian Theater, servants standing by the gas lamps along the wall turned them up to make the room well-lit again. As if from far away, soft strains from two guitars are heard. Very slowly the music grows louder, and then Countess Cara Czerny enters from the back of the room. She's carrying a flower basket. Her dress is of sky-blue satin that shimmered richly in the light. It's simply made, with tight sleeves and a tight bodice, a skirt slightly gathered at the waist, and a long train. Her hair is unbound, a cloud of honey-gold around her shoulders, falling to her waist. Around her neck she wears a gold medallion on a long chain. She starts weaving among the tables, picking a flower here and there from the vases, and singing, *Are you going to Scarborough Fair?*

A surprised hum sounded from the audience, and shuffling sounds were heard as they turned in the seats to face the rear of the room. Then a profound silence fell. All that was heard was the distant guitar music, and Cara's sweet voice, singing low, as if to herself.

As she neared the stage the curtains silently opened, and Tinar and Saz walked onstage. Saz, in particular, was a sensational-looking horse. His mane was pure white except for one broad streak of black. The night before, Gage and Nadyha had braided the horses' manes and tails, fastening gold and silver threads in them. Now they were loose, full, and wavy, and the threads glittered in the limelight; Gage had even dusted their hocks with powdered fool's gold, so every time they moved their hooves a tiny shower of gold fell from them. They began grazing on a blaze of red clover at their feet.

Cara stops and looks in wonder, then says, "Have I wandered into a beautiful dream? What are you, such wondrous steeds? Where do you come from, and where do you go?" Very slowly she climbs the stage and nears them. "Is this an enchantment? No, no, I'm not enchanted, but I have fallen under a spell, of amazement of such fantastical beasts. Dare I go near them?"

At this point, as Nadyha and Cara had taught him, Saz looked up straight at Cara, nodded his head up and down as if saying, "Yes," then pawed the ground with his forefoot. Amazed, Cara drops her flower basket and goes to him to pet him (also secretly giving him a lump of sugar). She murmurs endearments, pets both horses, and continues to wonder aloud about them.

And then she's attacked by a ferocious bear. He lumbers onto the stage from behind the horses. Immediately Cara, frightened, starts backing up. The bear stands upright, raises his forepaws, and starts toward her. As he nears her Cara faints, falling and striking her head against a rock. The "ferocious bear" then nonchalantly climbs up the stand of rocks, to where a honeycomb has been hidden. He sits down and begins to eat unconcernedly. Even Nadyha hadn't been able to make him get up and go away after he gets his treat, but it didn't seem to matter to the audience. They looked awed, astounded, and some of the ladies looked extremely frightened. But they didn't leave.

Tomasz, who is looking for the horses and Boldo, finds the unconscious countess. When she fell, the chain around her neck broke, and he picks it up and recognizes the coat of arms of the House of Czerny. Pocketing the necklace, he rouses the girl and finds that she has amnesia; she doesn't even remember her name. Because she is so weak, Tomasz picks her up and carries her in his arms to the Gypsy camp.

The next scene was Nadyha and Anca, alone on stage except for a campfire and trees and shrubs in the background. Nadyha recited "Tyger, Tyger", Anca swatted viciously at her and roared deafeningly. The entire room was silent; no one moved. And then, in spite of Captain Humphries's instructions, applause and cries and halloos and whistles broke out. Many men stood, shouting, "Bravo, Nadyha! Bravo, Anca!" The wives yanked on their coattails to make them sit back down.

The Gypsies were on their way to Prague, where a National Fair was to be held. Although Tomasz knew who Cara was, he kept it to himself, because he had fallen in love with her and knew that if he returned her to her father, he would lose her. Because she has lost all of her memory, he gives her the name "Camova", which in Romany means "love". During their travels Camova, in essence, becomes a Gypsy. Nadyha, who is in love with Tomasz, is jealous of her. Bulibasha also falls in love with Camova.

One scene was particularly poignant. Nadyha and Niçu were on the stage, but at opposite ends, in front of their *vardos*, which were particularly cleverly downsized mock-ups. They are unaware of each other, but they sing a duet, each in turn, each mourning their hopeless loves. It was a lovely, heartfelt song, and complicated, and Nadyha had written it. She had finally found the words to her music.

As always, the scene of the Gypsies singing and playing their instruments and dancing were a big hit. Niçu and Denny danced Gypsy-style, which was a lot of foot-stomping and leaping, and at the end they both jumped over the campfire. During the scene Matchko strolled onstage and nonchalantly leapt onto Tinar's back, which made the audience laugh. The extra Gypsies sitting around were members of the orchestra, for only the Gypsies played instruments in the scene, and some chambermaids who were having the time of their lives. When Baba Simza and Niçu played "Ha Ne Ne Ne" and Nadyha, Mirella, and Cara danced, the audience, again ignoring Captain Humphries's warning to stay silent, began shouting "*Hai!*" along with the extras. Boldo got to dance, too, much to the audience's delight.

But the most moving scene of the play featured Cara and Niçu. Although he couldn't read music, he had learned to play the most famous aria from *The Bohemian Girl* on the violin. With the lights low, he comes to sit outside Camova's *vardo*, in the deep shadows beneath the back window, and begins to play the simple but haunting melody. After playing two verses, Cara, in a flowing white dress, comes out of the wagon and, not seeing Niçu, begins to sing into the night:

> *I dreamt I dwelt in marble halls*
> *With vassals and serfs at my side,*
> *And of all who assembled within those walls*

That I was the hope and pride.
I had riches all too great to count
And a high ancestral name . . .

The song had four verses, ending sadly with "But I also dreamt which charmed me most, that you loved me still the same . . ." As she finishes she goes back into her *vardo*. The last soft strains of Niçu's violin die out, and, crushed because he knows that Camova loves Tomasz, he drops his violin and bows his head. Niçu was actually an excellent actor.

Count Czerny, Cara's father, also attends the fair in Prague, and there sees his daughter. As soon as Cara sees her father, her memory floods back, and they return to their castle. Tomasz lets her go, because he feels guilty for never telling her who she was, nor even who he really is. Here Denny got to sing "Then You'll Remember Me," with the full orchestra, and he sang very well.

In the end, Tomasz decides he must go to Count Czerny, confess who he is, and declare his love for Cara. Nadyha, maddened by jealousy, follows him to the castle and tries to stab Cara. But Bulibasha, though he is forbidden by his Queen to follow her, does so, and wrestles with Nadyha as she flies at Cara, knife held high. In the struggle, Nadyha gets stabbed in the heart and dies. The Gypsies leave Bohemia in sorrow, Count Czerny forgives Tomasz (particularly when he finds out he's really a count), and Cara and Tomasz live happily ever after.

The general consensus, shared by even Euprosine Dobard, was that the play was a spectacular success.

NADYHA WAS AMAZED AT the enthusiasm for every scene of the play, and she was thoroughly chagrined when she found out that it was customary for the actors in productions to meet and mingle with the audience. Denny had brought several people backstage after the play was over, and he had started introducing them to Cara, Simza, Niçu, and Mirella. Nadyha had grabbed Anca and Boldo and fled. After she put them in her room she ran up to the Hurricane Deck.

The top deck of the *Queen of Bohemia* was fully accessible to passengers, but because the salons were so luxurious, and the promenade so inviting with its full complement of deck chairs, there was rarely anyone up there, except for the pilot in the pilothouse, of course. Nadyha loved staying up on the Hurricane Deck, not only for the solitude, but also because it gave such a sweeping view of the river. She was fascinated by every scene, every landmark, every settlement, every stretch of silent forest, and by the river itself. It was ever-changing.

She heard footsteps on the stairs, and turned to see Gage come on deck. "Oh, hello, Nadyha," he said. "Congratulations! You were outstanding." He came to stand by her at the railing at the stern. Below them the great paddlewheel churned, but the *Queen* was so big and heavy that she glided majestically.

"How did you know I was here?" Nadyha demanded.

"I didn't. I just kinda wanted to get some fresh air, and avoid the crush. It's not as if there were hordes of people wanting to meet the Captain of the Guard, anyway." Glancing at her, he studied her profile. She was lovely, and mysterious, and enticing. Her expression was unreadable as she stared out over the river. He continued, "I think just about all of them want to meet Nadyha, Queen of the Gypsies."

"Gypsies don't have queens," she said automatically.

"I know that, but your fans don't." When she didn't respond he asked, "Nadyha, is this thing going to make you unhappy? Because if it is, you don't have to do it. I'll talk to Denny, and I'll pick us all up and move us back to your camp in a hot minute if that's what you want."

She turned to him then and smiled a little. "No, no, not at all. I love being here, on this wonderful boat. I love"—she waved, encompassing the moonlit scene before them—"seeing all this. And I like the play, and performing. It's just that I wasn't quite ready for all the attention."

"It seems to me like you get a lot of attention in New Orleans, and you handle that very well." Gage moved a little closer to her, though as always he was careful not to even brush up against her.

"Yes, but that was different. Here, we're supposed to be introduced to the *gajes*, and talk to them," she said disdainfully. "What am I supposed to talk to them about? I have nothing to say to *gajes*, they don't know or care anything about me. They just want to talk to the Queen of the Gypsies."

"Yeah, that's true. But so what? At the French Market they wanted to talk to you because you had things to sell that they wanted to buy, they wanted to see you with Boldo and Anca, they wanted to hear you sing and see you dance, they wanted to see you because you're an interesting Gypsy woman. You're doing the very same thing now, only you're selling the Queen of the Gypsies instead of shawls and herbs."

Slowly she said, "I hadn't thought about it that way."

"I think if you'll just relax and give it a chance you'll find it's just as easy as talking to customers at Market. And you're great at that. Just like you're great at everything you do."

"That's silly," she scoffed. "No one is great at everything they do."

"Ho-kay. At least you didn't call me a *dinili gajo*. I'm making progress," Gage joked.

Sharply she asked, "Making progress at what?"

"Uh—it's just a figure of speech."

They both turned to watch the scene, and it was a comfortable silence. The moon was a lopsided three-quarter, and the sky was so clear it seemed the points of the stars could be seen. They were traveling a straight stretch of the river, heavily forested on both sides. Although the Mississippi River was known as the Big Muddy, at night it glimmered cleanly from the ship's thousand lanterns.

"It's so different," Nadyha said softly. "Ever since we got past Baton Rouge the land looks so strange to me. Even the sky looks different, the sun and the moon and the stars."

"I have a theory about that," Gage said dreamily. "It may be nonsense, but I believe it's true. I used to look up at the stars and the moon from battlefields in Virginia, and I thought they looked harder and colder and farther away. I believe that because the air in southern Louisiana is so humid, so filled with tiny water droplets all the time, that it magnifies the sky. It softens the moon, makes it look bigger, gives it a luminous halo. And the stars look like diamonds shimmering underwater."

She looked at him curiously. "I think that is a beautiful thought. I believe it too."

"Good. Then if the two of us agree, maybe it is true. Uh, since we're getting along so well, there is something I'd like to ask you, Nadyha. It's a really big favor, but I've found out it never hurts to ask."

She looked amused. "No, I promise I won't hurt you just for asking. Asking what?"

Gage hesitated, then said, "Would you help me with my show? Mirella's helping Niçu, you know, and I could use an assistant. It's a big thing, I know, because you're such a huge star and all, and I'm just plain ol' Gage Kennon the Dead-Eye Sharpshooter, but it wouldn't be much for you to do, just sort of help me with—uh—I thought of a couple of things—but you probably—"

"I heard you tell Denny once that he was blathering on and on," Nadyha said, deadpan. "You're blathering on and on, Gage. Yes. I'll be glad to be your assistant."

"Huh?"

Carefully enunciating, she said, "Yes. I will be glad to be your assistant."

"You will?" he said, astounded.

"For the third time, yes."

"Oh. Oh! Great, that's fantastic! Thanks, Nadyha, I really appreciate it. Can we—can I show you what I want you to do? Now, I mean?"

"If we can do it up here," Nadyha said. "I don't want to be shut up in even my palace of a stateroom for any longer than I have to."

"Sure we can! I'll go get my stuff, and some lanterns, and everything we need. Say, why don't we bring Anca and Boldo up here? They probably would like to get out of the palace for awhile too."

Nadyha laughed, that delightful genuine sound that Gage had come to love. "I think you love them almost as much as I do, Gage Kennon. Yes, I'd love to have Anca and Boldo up here with us. Thank you."

He dashed toward the stairs but then turned and said softly, "You know, Nadyha, you're dead wrong about one thing. I know you, the real Nadyha. And I'm a *gaje* and I care about you."

Before she could respond he had turned and hurried away.

CHAPTER FOURTEEN

It was a bright, sparkling morning when the *Queen of Bohemia* docked at Natchez, Mississippi. As always in a river town, the wharves were teeming. The *Queen* herself was like a stirred-up beehive, too, with some passengers disembarking, some coming on board, and all the while roustabouts trying to load up tons of wood for her ravenous boilers.

Above it all, on the Hurricane Deck, Nadyha watched all the activity far below her. Soon after they came to a full stop she was joined by Stephen Carruthers, the first pilot of the *Queen*. Denny had introduced them to the pilots and the engineers, and Carruthers had been very attentive to Nadyha—when he could find her. He was young to be the first pilot of a steamboat such as the *Queen of Bohemia*, only twenty-five years old. Tall, with far-seeing blue eyes and dark hair, he was a handsome man, and was accustomed to receiving lots of female attention. It fascinated

245

him, and frustrated him, that Nadyha treated him with the same cool courtesy she treated everyone she met.

He joined her at the side rail and noted that she immediately sidestepped a few inches away from him. He had seen that she always did this whenever anyone, male or female, stood too close to her. "Good morning, Miss Nadyha. So what do you think of Natchez?"

"Good morning, Mr. Carruthers. I think this is a very strange city." She pointed first to the docks and the shantytown behind them. "It looks like all of the poor people live there, and the rich people live up there." She pointed to the city proper, up on the bluffs behind.

"You're right about that. Down here, it's called Natchez-Under-the-Hill. It's got a wicked reputation, too, even for a river port," he told her. "But the town, up there, is really beautiful. And it's very well policed, so it's safe, not like Under the Hill."

"Is it?" she said with interest. "What about over there? What is that pretty little wood up there?"

"That's the City Cemetery. I've been there, it's like a lovely, peaceful park. It's old, too, some of the graves are from the 1700s."

"Graves? So they're buried in the ground?"

He smiled at her, flashing deep dimples and straight, even white teeth. "I forgot, you're from New Orleans. Yes, up here you can bury people in the ground and they won't float back up to haunt you. Would you like to see the city, and the cemetery? We're going to be here for about four or five hours, getting our wood loaded. I'd consider it an honor if you'd allow me to escort you on a tour, Nadyha."

"Thank you, but no," she said frostily, noting he had inched closer to her and had dropped the "Miss." "I'm going down to my stateroom now. Good-bye."

As usual, she made her whirling exit, leaving the man standing there with his mouth open.

Anca was sitting out on their balcony, watching the goings-on with interest. Boldo, who had taken over the second bed in the stateroom, was sound asleep. Nadyha stamped out onto the balcony and said to Anca, "What is it about *gajes* that they think they need to babysit you all the time? It's ridiculous! I'm a grown woman, and besides that I have a knife and I know how to use it." Anca's look seemed to be one of agreement. Nadyha went on in a half-whisper, "And I have a cougar, too . . . Anca, how would you like to go for a walk?"

Anca had done very well on board the ship as Nadyha walked her on the Promenade Deck. The passengers greeted them with familiarity, but gave them a wide berth, which suited Nadyha just fine. Now Anca did very well in the slum streets of Natchez-Under-the-Hill, padding along beside Nadyha, who held her useless golden leash close. But the people of Natchez-Under-the-Hill didn't do as well as the passengers on the *Queen of Bohemia*.

Men yelped and backed up; the numerous prostitutes screamed and cursed Nadyha; horses shied and panicked. The commotion was loud and spread up and down Silver Street, the main street by the docks that led up to the city of Natchez on the eastern side. Ignoring the hubbub, Nadyha and Anca walked sedately to the west side of Under the Hill, for Nadyha had seen that Silver Street looped around behind and led straight to the City Cemetery.

Finally they were at the end of the shanties, shacks, brothels, and warehouses that huddled close to the Natchez docks. Climbing the hill, Nadyha breathed deep, for the air was cleaner and much sweeter-smelling than the fug on the docks. On each side of the muddy cart track were open fields, filled with black-eyed Susans and colorful lantana bushes and purple coneflowers.

The cemetery was quiet and deserted. Nadyha and Anca wandered among the graves. Many of the headstones were beautifully carved and had poignant scriptures or sayings on them. Marble benches were placed around. As it was growing warm, Nadyha led Anca to a bench underneath a live oak tree so old that many of the branches nearly touched the ground.

For awhile Nadyha thought about death. But she was so young, and had such a full and rich life, that she had trouble imagining her own death. She thought, *Baba Simza says that young people always think they're going to live forever. But it's hard not to think that, when it seems that your whole life, for years and years and years, lies before you . . .*

Then she thought of Gage Kennon. He was on her mind a lot these days. At times it infuriated her that he filled her thoughts so much; at other times she had a somewhat careless attitude about it. After all, he had been such a big part of all of their lives—Baba Simza's, Niçu's, and Mirella's, not just her own—for awhile now. She smiled when she remembered the first time she had seen him. She must have looked as wild and feral as Anca, glaring at him over Baba Simza's prone body and brandishing her knife. She remembered what he had said: *I can help you.* It seemed that Gage Kennon said that a lot, to many people. Why was that? Was it because he was a Christian? Nadyha didn't understand that "giving" part of Gage. Did he just plaster it on when he saw someone in need? Or did it come naturally to him?

Suddenly she grew exasperated that she'd been sitting there for so long, brooding about Gage Kennon. She hopped up and started wandering among the graves again. Anca walked with her, trailing her leash. Nadyha read a few of them and then abruptly stopped before one sizable white marble headstone. It read simply:

LOUISE

The Unfortunate

Nadyha stared at the simple inscription for a long time. Then, to her consternation, tears filled her eyes.

"Hey, you! You, girl! Whatcha think you're doin'?" a loud crude but distant voice yelled.

Dashing away her tears, Nadyha whirled. Two men were walking along the side of the cemetery grounds, leading their horses. They had on gunbelts with pistols and silver stars pinned on their long frock coats. Nadyha refused to shout back an answer to them like some brawling fishwife, so she picked up Anca's chain and they walked back to the seat underneath the oak tree to wait for the deputies. Nadyha sat down, and to her everlasting gratification, Anca decided at this time to sharpen her claws on the oak tree. The scratches were about three inches deep, over a foot long, and about six feet from the ground. The two deputies stopped in their tracks about twenty feet from the tree.

"What do you think I'm doing?" she answered them in a normal voice. "I'm just looking around, enjoying the peace and quiet. At least, I was."

One of the deputies, a red-faced man with a big beer belly overhanging his gun belt, stepped just a bit closer. "You cain't be here with that wild beast, you crazy Gypsy girl! The City of Natchez ain't no circus, and we don't want none here neither!"

"That's odd, I thought I was in the City Cemetery, not the City of Natchez," Nadyha said with spirit. "And I'm not with a circus, and neither is my cougar."

"Yeah, yeah," Red Face Deputy said. "What you are is disturbin' the peace, and I've of a mind to put you under arrest!"

"Oh, really? And are you going to put Anca here under arrest too? Go ahead."

The two men looked uncertainly at each other.

The first deputy's face flushed so dark it was purplish-red now. "Looky here, you smart-mouthed Gypsy tart!" he snarled. "You jist bring that there lion and come along with us. And if he even looks at one of us funny, then I guess we'll be havin' to put him down!"

Nadyha jumped up and crouched directly in front of Anca, drew her knife, and said with gritted teeth, "If you so much as touch your gunbelt, this knife will end up right in one of your hearts! Then Anca will kill the other one! And that's how this story will end!"

Now the other deputy, a younger man, slender and with a homely, honest face, stepped forward with his hands raised up in surrender. "Whoa, whoa, there, ma'am. Let's all just calm down here. Roy, what's the matter with you? Ain't gonna be no killing of nobody or nothing here. Please, ma'am, just sit back down and put away your knife and we'll talk about this all quiet and nice-like. Please?"

Nadyha kept her flinty gaze trained on "Roy." He grimaced, gave the younger deputy a dirty look, then made a small waving gesture. "Ain't nobody gonna hurt your cougar if he don't hurt nobody first," he grumbled. "But you don't need to be a-wavin' a knife around at dooly appointed deputy sheriffs, neither."

Slowly Nadyha sheathed her knife. With her arm around Anca's neck she knelt beside her. The younger deputy said, "That's much better, thank you, ma'am. I'm Deputy Bart Ingram, and this here's Deputy Roy Maltby. Ma'am, just exactly what are you doing running around here with a mountain lion? I know there ain't no Gypsies buried here. Where are your people?"

"My people are on the *Queen of Bohemia*," Nadyha said, tossing her head.

The two deputies looked at each other and Maltby burst out into guffaws. "Yeah, and my people live in a pink castle and ride unicorns!" he brayed. Then sobering, he said to Ingram, "What a bunch of hooey! A pack of Gypsies on the *Queen of Bohemia*! I say we arrest her right now, see what her story is after spending the night with the lady jailbirds from Under the Hill!"

"Okay," Ingram said, shrugging. "I'll arrest the girl and you arrest the cougar."

The two deputies stared at each other with uncertainty again.

DEPUTY ROY MALTBY DID not have an easy time of it when he visited the *Queen of Bohemia*.

First he was stopped on the grand staircase by the Chief Steward, who informed him that third-class passengers were directed to use the outside entrances. Deputy Maltby informed the Chief Steward that if he didn't get to talk to someone in charge of this here boat in one minnit or less'n he'd arrest 'em all.

The Chief Steward hurried to fetch Captain Humphries, who huffily escorted Deputy Maltby to Zedekiah Wainwright's stateroom. Denny was visiting his uncle, and when they heard about the problem, they both laughed uproariously, which didn't put Deputy Maltby in any better mood.

"Are you people tellin' me that that Gypsy wench was tellin' the truth?" he demanded. "You let dirty Gypsies on this here fine boat?"

"They're cleaner than you are," Denny retorted, eyeing the deputy's dirty fingernails. "And we're privileged to have them, they're performing in an operetta on board."

Maltby stared at Denny and his uncle, bug-eyed. "Well that girl cain't be a-sashayin' through town all by herself with that lion. It ain't safe."

"We'll take care of her, don't worry, I'll protect you, Deputy Maltby," Denny said with exasperation. To his uncle he said, "I'll go get Gage. Don't worry, we'll take care of it."

"Deputy, I'd appreciate it if you'd take special care of Nadyha, she's the star of my show," Wainwright said proudly, jamming his ever-present cigar into his mouth.

"Take keer of her!" Maltby grunted. "If it wasn't for my buddy Bart I woulda had her in my jail by now. Paradin' around with a lion in Natchez. And pointin' a knife at dooly appointed deputies. And disturbin' the peace."

"How can you disturb the peace of a cemetery?" Denny asked. "Never mind, I guess Nadyha can figure out a way. So, Deputy, are you going to accompany me and Mr. Kennon back to rescue you and the other deputy from this dangerous girl?"

"I'll 'company you, all right. But if it wasn't for my buddy Bart—"

"I know, I know," Denny said. "We'd all be in your jail by now. We'll be back soon, Uncle Zeke. And I assume we'll all be in one piece . . . if Deputy Maltby doesn't upset Anca too much."

Denny found Gage, who was down in the cargo hold keeping Tinar, Saz, and Cayenne company. Like Denny and his uncle, he laughed when he heard the story and saw the sanguine-faced, grumpy deputy. "I've got a great idea," he told Denny. "Let's go get Niçu. Natchez is going to have a parade like they've never seen before!"

It was quite a procession that wound its way through Natchez-Under-the-Hill and up Silver Street to the City Cemetery. Nadyha was sitting on her marble bench, with Anca lying at her feet in her Sphinx position, facing Deputy Ingram, who still kept a discreet distance. She watched with wry amusement as they neared her.

First came Niçu, leading Saz, and behind him was Denny, leading Tinar. Then Gage led Cayenne, with Cara riding. Casually Gage came and sat beside Nadyha. "I heard you're under arrest," he said, grinning.

"No, I'm not," she replied, her eyes dancing. "But Anca is. They just can't figure out how to take her into custody, *dinili shanglo*. What are all of you doing here?"

"We're taking you back to the *Queen of Bohemia* in style, Your Majesty. Right down the Main Street of Natchez, Mississippi. Your queenly steed awaits."

Doubtfully Nadyha glanced at Deputy Maltby, who was growling in Deputy Ingram's ear. "But that *shanglo*, the dirty *lalo*-faced one, he doesn't like me and Anca."

"He needs to learn to respect his betters," Gage said, suddenly sharp. "As it happens, Uncle Zeke is friends with the mayor of Natchez, and in fact, the mayor and his family are right now bustling around packing for a free first-class trip to St. Louis. And we're all invited to parade in Natchez, to advertise the sensational new operetta *The Countess and the Gypsy Queen* that's currently being performed on the *Queen of Bohemia*."

IT WAS IMPROMPTU, SO no one really knew who these outrageous people were, but the citizens of Natchez were delighted nonetheless.

Nadyha was wearing a purple skirt with coins sewn around the hem, a new innovation that she had thought up for the play. Around her small waist was tied a green scarf, and she wore a black puffed-sleeve blouse with a tight-fitting leather vest. Her *diklo* was multicolored, and was trimmed with real gold coins. She sat sidesaddle on Saz, though that was perhaps a misnomer because she rode bareback. Sitting tall and erect, her slim back ruler-straight, Saz wore neither bridle nor halter; Nadyha merely guided him with one hand lightly grasping his gold-speckled mane. Beside her rode Niçu on Tinar, his dark features seemingly fierce and alien, the razor-sharp *churo* glittering in the black sash at his waist. Between them Anca marched majestically, her head held high, looking neither to the right or the left.

In complete contrast to the Gypsies, Cara rode behind them, slim and fair, wearing her icy blue satin costume dress with the long train. Her hair was unbound and made a glowing halo around her. Denny was leading Cayenne, and he could hardly keep from glancing behind just to look at her. Whenever he did she smiled shyly at him.

Behind her the two deputies rode side-by-side. Deputy Maltby had begrudgingly gotten in a better mood, while Deputy Ingram was positively enjoying himself. Neither the Gypsies nor Cara spoke to all of the people who stopped to watch them, though they looked around and nodded acknowledgments to the crowd. At first people were silent with amazement as they came out of the stores and offices on Main Street to crowd the boardwalks and see the spectacle. Then they began buzzing, "Who are they? Look at that beautiful young lady! She's not a Gypsy, they're Gypsies, aren't they? Where did they get those horses! And look, look it's a *mountain lion!*"

Deputy Ingram lifted his hat to some ladies and called out, "These are some of the actors in *The Countess and the Gypsy Queen*, ladies. They're performing on the steamer the *Queen of Bohemia*. They've decided to bring out their animals to get some fresh air, and to see our lovely city."

One fresh-faced young buck called out, "Can the Countess and the Queen please stay for awhile?" Laughter greeted this sally—at least, from some of the men.

Walking unobtrusively along the boardwalk, keeping up with the "parade," Gage enjoyed seeing people's reaction; he even chuckled at the young man who watched Nadyha and Cara so longingly.

Every once in a while, Nadyha looked directly at him. She didn't smile, but Gage could have sworn he heard her voice in his head.

Thank you, Gage Kennon.

CHARITY SUFFERETH LONG, AND *is kind; charity envieth not; charity vaunteth not itself, is not puffed up, doth not behave itself unseemly, seeketh not her own, is not easily provoked, thinketh no evil; rejoiceth not in iniquity, but rejoiceth in the truth; beareth all things, believeth all things, hopeth all things, endureth all things. Charity never faileth . . .*

Gage read the words over and over again, and tried to figure out if he was really in love with Nadyha.

I do suffer long, he thought with arid amusement. *And I think I'm a kind man, at least I try to be. But envy . . . jealousy . . .* Gage was jealous of Nadyha, he admitted to himself. He had seen the marked attention that the pilot Stephen Carruthers paid her, and there were some young men, passengers in second class, that hounded her every step when she left her stateroom. Although Nadyha kept them all at her customary arm's-length, Gage couldn't help it, he wanted her all to himself, and he wanted other men to stay away from her.

So here I am, behaving unseemly, seeking my own, easily provoked. Is this love? Or is it just desire, just a physical hunger? Gage struggled with himself, trying to answer this exceedingly important question.

She is such an enticing, alluring woman, what man wouldn't desire her? But really, it's so much more than that . . . just thinking of spending my life with her, with waking up to her every morning, each day would be sweet-spicy, just like elachi, *Grains of Paradise . . .*

After awhile, he made himself stop trying to analyze his own heart. *What difference does it make anyway? Nadyha isn't attracted to me, sometimes I think she really doesn't even like me much. I guess I better just concentrate on "bearing all things". . .*

Denny came in, and looked alarmed at Gage sitting at the table with his Bible open in front of him. "Are you—uh—praying?"

"No, just sulking," Gage answered. "Come on in."

Though Denny and Gage were sharing a second-class stateroom, Denny was hardly ever there. He mostly stayed with his uncle, schmoozing passengers in the Moravian Salon or on the promenade or playing cards in the Count of Lusatia Cardroom. Now he was holding a crystal tumbler with ice and a brown liquid, and he took a deep drink as he sat at the table with Gage.

"Please tell me you're not drinking whiskey before the show," Gage grunted.

"No, it's sweet tea," Denny retorted. "Why, are you nervous?"

"No, I'm not nervous. I just don't want you tossing plates up in the air that sail to Vicksburg or come crashing down on the passengers' heads."

"I'm dead sober, sir, so don't worry about it, I'll toss 'em so good even Boldo could hit them. But what I still can't believe is that you talked Nadyha into being your show assistant. How'd you manage that?"

"I dunno," Gage said dryly. "I just asked her, and she said yes. She had to tell me 'yes' three times before it got into my thick head."

Denny cocked his head and stared at Gage curiously. "You really care about her, don't you, Gage? I mean, you're falling for her, aren't you?"

Gage rose and went to stand in front of the window, watching the shores of the Mississippi River glide past. Quietly he said, "Once Niçu and I were talking about Gypsies' marriages. Did you know that they don't celebrate birthdays, that their wedding is considered the most important event in their lives, and that they celebrate their anniversaries always? And Niçu said that it sometimes happens that a Gypsy man will fall in love with a *gaji*, and if she consents to completely become a Gypsy and live their life, the *vitsi* will accept her, and she becomes one of the husband's family." Brooding, he fell silent.

"What about a Gypsy woman and a *gajo*?" Denny asked quietly.

It was a long time before Gage answered. Finally he said, "Niçu said that if a Romany woman fell in love with a *gaje*, she'd probably be shunned, cast out of the *vitsi*. But he said he'd never heard of that happening. As far as he knew, no Romany woman had ever wanted to marry a *gaje*."

Denny seemed at a loss for words. Finally Gage turned to him and said in a blustery voice, "Well, I ain't nervous but I sure am going to be hot." He went to the hooks lining one wall and put on a black satin vest. Then he buckled on a black leather gunbelt with two Colt .44 pistols in holsters at each side, and pulled on a long, black frock coat. "And I look like an undertaker. Another one of your fine ideas, me dressing up all in black. I look weird, and I'm hot."

"Niçu's dressed all in black and he's not crying like a girl about it."

"He's not wearing a vest and coat. Why do I have to wear the vest and coat?"

Denny explained carefully, "Because you're not a Gypsy. You're Gage Kennon, Dead-Eye Sharpshooter."

Gage rolled his eyes as he put on his black hat. "Sometimes I really wish," he grumbled, "that I was a Gypsy."

THE STEWARDS HAD PUT out sixty deck chairs on the port side of the Hurricane Deck, and they were full, and there were about another fifty people standing. Denny made a mental note to set out a hundred chairs for the next show. He was a little surprised to see so many women; he hadn't really thought that Gage Kennon the Dead-Eye Sharpshooter and Niçu the Knife-Thrower would be such a draw for females.

Bales of hay were stacked up, three deep and six high, at the stern end of the deck, and two tables were on either side of them. Twenty feet in front of the hay were two more tables. Mirella stood by one, dressed in Gypsy finery, her face glowing with excitement. On the table was the butcher block holding Niçu's throwing knives.

Nadyha stood by the other table that held a long wooden case, black velvet-lined, and ammunition. Denny was amused to see that she had dressed in one of her theater costumes, a black *diklo* with silver threads and coins, a black blouse, black leather vest, black skirt, and a serpent-green scarf around her waist. *She and Gage would look like a pair of crows if they weren't such handsome people,* he thought. *It's sad about Gage . . .*

Gage and Niçu came on deck, grinning and waving at the audience, who spontaneously started applauding. Denny stepped in front of the railings that had been set up to keep the people from getting too close to the firing range. "Good afternoon, ladies and gentlemen! Welcome to our show. You're going to see some of the best shooting, and the most miraculous knife-throwing that's ever been performed.

"Everyone please stay behind the railings until the show is over. But"—Denny grinned devilishly—"after the show, Gage and Niçu want to invite you to come over and talk to them, see their weapons, and it's possible that they may even let you show off your marksmanship and knife-throwing skills!"

At this announcement, which Denny had just thought of at that moment, Gage gave him a look that would have melted polar ice. Nadyha laughed.

Before the show began, Nadyha and Mirella allowed the audience to inspect the weapons. Gage put the pistols in the case, and Nadyha walked very slowly down the line of people, holding out the case and saying, "You will see that these are Colt .44 handguns, six-shot revolvers. There is nothing special about them, any one of you can buy this same gun in any armory. You will see that Gage Kennon is a tricky shot, but there are no tricks about the guns!"

Then Mirella brought the butcher block of knives over to display them. She walked up and down the line of people, pulling out a knife every few steps, and holding it high to glitter dangerously in the late afternoon sun. Finally she

259

stopped and said, "I don't suppose any of you would like to offer an article of clothing for a demonstration? No, of course not. Nadyha?"

Nadyha stepped up, threw a madras shawl into the air, and Mirella held out two of the knives straight in front of her. As the heavy shawl fell on the blades, the material cleanly split on the blades. "Oohs" and "aahs" sounded from the audience.

Mirella and Nadyha then set up two targets. The one on the left looked exactly like the six of spades from a pack of cards, and the one on the right looked like the six of clubs. In turn, Gage shot the center of a spade, Niçu landed a knife right in the center of a club, until all of the designs had holes straight through.

Next, Denny threw plates into the air—on the starboard side, of course—and Gage shot them. At the Gypsy camp they had carefully measured out the square footage for Gage's rehearsals, so Denny knew just where to stand and how to throw the plates so that they would fall to the deck instead of overboard. Gage had found that if he shot them in the center, they would fall fairly straight, but if he hit the edge of the plate it ricocheted. Denny had spent a lot of money on ammunition for Gage's practice, but now every single plate had a hole in the exact center. After shooting a dozen plates, Nadyha and Mirella picked them up and held them high so that the clean center holes could be seen.

Niçu did his newest trick, one he had thought up himself. He juggled four knives, impossibly fast, the blades flashing a silver blur. Then, with a flourish, he took one step backwards and the knives all landed, *thwack-thwack-thwack-thwack* in a row on the deck, blades half-buried. That earned him a long, enthusiastic ovation.

Mirella and Nadyha set up new targets with different designs, and Niçu and Gage in turn stood with their backs to the targets, whirled, and landed shots and knives in whatever was the bull's-eye. Gage admitted to himself that in spite of his complaining about his clothes, he had consciously practiced whirling around with a flair, and making showy quick-draws.

To end the show, Gage stood at his table, his stance easy and relaxed, his hands down at his sides just by the deadly looking guns. Nadyha tacked up a target; it was a completely blank sheet of white pasteboard, and it was small, only eight inches by ten inches. The audience was silent, puzzled. Nadyha came to stand by the railing. Gage took a deep breath, then drew both guns and started firing. Twelve shots sounded so close together they were almost like one enormous explosion.

When the smoke from his heated guns cleared, the audience was still staring blankly at the target. It was so far away that they couldn't see what Gage had done. Gracefully Nadyha went to the target, pulled it down, held it high over her head, and walked very slowly down the rows of people.

On the tiny target, outlined in bullet holes, was the head and shoulders of a man. Where his heart would be, there were two holes exactly one-half inch apart.

Even the people seated leaped to their feet for a standing ovation.

Denny walked to the railing, his hands held high. "We hope you enjoyed the show, ladies and gentlemen! Gage and Niçu will be happy to talk with you and answer questions now. Thank you!"

It seemed that every person wanted to talk to them. The second- and third-class passengers had no societal constraints, so they crowded around the tables and introduced themselves and fired questions. But the first-class passengers required introductions, and Denny was very busy making Gage Kennon and Niçu properly known to several ladies and gentlemen.

Theodule Dobard, with his habitual happy expression, came up to Denny with his grim wife and lovely daughter in tow. "We'd all like to meet Mr. Kennon," he told Denny. "Would you be so kind as to introduce us?"

"Of course, sir." Denny led them through a crowd of two couples, four men, and a family of five to get close to Gage. He was standing at the table, his guns laid out and unloaded, gesturing and talking with animation. Denny cleared his throat and Gage turned to him. "Mr. Kennon, I have the honor of making known to you Mr. Theodule Dobard, Mrs. Euprosine Dobard, and Miss Monique Dobard, of New Orleans. Mr. Dobard, Mrs. Dobard, Miss Dobard, it is my pleasure to introduce you to my friend, Mr. Gage Kennon, also of New Orleans."

Theodule Dobard immediately started firing questions at Gage, about the guns, about his skills, about his experience as a sharpshooter. Mrs. Dobard sniffed and looked bored. But Denny noted that Monique Dobard was watching and listening to Gage with a certain feral, hungry look in her dark eyes that Denny recognized very well.

When her father took a breath, Monique stepped forward to stand close to Gage and gaze up at him appealingly. "Mr. Kennon, I've never shot a gun in my life, I've never even held one. Would you be so kind as to do a small demonstration . . . just for me?"

Gage smiled pleasantly, the exact same smile he gave everyone, from the wealthiest first-class gentleman down to the ten-year-old boy in third class. "Certainly, ma'am. I'll show you how to load the gun, but I'm sure you understand that right now, with everyone around, I can't allow it to stay loaded."

"Mm, then I suppose you can show me how to load and how to unload," she said, smiling back at him. "And then, perhaps, you might show me how to hold it, and point it? I'm really very interested, after your magnificent show. I may take up target shooting myself."

"Monique, what are you talking about?" her mother demanded. "Ladies don't go about shooting pistols like some back alley gunslinger!" She gave Gage a very dark look.

Monique, still looking up into Gage's face, said sweetly, "*Maman*, it's really very warm up here, you know you feel faint when you get too warm. *Papa*, perhaps you might want to take *Maman* into the salon and get her an ice or a sherbet."

"All right, but I did want to talk to you some more, Mr. Kennon," Dobard said begrudgingly. "Perhaps we might meet later, sir, in the card room?"

"Perhaps Mr. Kennon will join us at our table for dinner," Monique suggested, giving her mother a warning glance. Euprosine Dobard's mouth shut with an audible click. Monique entwined her arm with Gage's and gave him a melting look from beneath her thick, dark eyelashes. "Would you be so gracious as to dine with us tonight, Mr. Kennon?"

"Thank you, ma'am, I'd be happy to," Gage said, looking slightly bewildered.

Denny kept watching with the utmost enjoyment. It seemed that Gage not only had to show Miss Dobard how to hold a pistol, he was required to stand behind her as she extended her arms, and place his hands over hers to help her point it properly. *Those sultry, sassy Creole women! No wonder I love New Orleans!* Denny reflected.

Then, abruptly, he wondered where Nadyha had gone. Mirella was still with Niçu, but there was no sign of Nadyha

263

in the crowds at either of the tables. He searched around and saw her, standing against the port rail. She stood stiffly, her arms crossed tightly across her chest. She was watching Gage and Monique Dobard, and the expression on her face was of barely concealed fury.

Denny thought, *How about that? Maybe it's not so sad about Gage after all . . .*

CHAPTER FIFTEEN

 "Baba Simza, your lace is so much better than mine," Cara sighed. "I'm afraid when I add my pieces to yours, it's going to look like I found some of it in a secondhand shop's ragbin."

"*Shesti, bitti gajo,*" Simza chided her. "You teach me, mine looks just like yours." Cara had taught Simza and Mirella how to tat lace. The truth was that even though Cara had been tatting lace since she was eight years old, the Gypsies' lace was finer than hers. Nadyha, Mirella, and Simza all loved any kind of needlework. Nadyha had quickly learned tatting, but in the last few days she had been so restless and preoccupied that she hadn't done much sewing or needlework.

In the days on board the *Queen*, they had all fallen into a routine. Nadyha adored her first-class stateroom simply because she had a private "verandah" but she did get lonely and bored. Simza, Cara, and Niçu and Mirella all had second-class staterooms, so Nadyha invited them to come to her stateroom every morning. She had also invited Denny and Gage. Denny declined because he always slept late—the Gypsies still started their day at dawn—but he had obligingly arranged for them to have breakfast brought to Nadyha's room. They stayed there until luncheon (as it was called on the *Queen of Bohemia*), unless the ship made a wood stop, which they did twice a day. Then Nadyha, Niçu, and Mirella always took a walk, usually taking out Tinar and Saz and Cayenne. Nadyha hadn't tried taking Anca for a walk again, but Denny had told her that his uncle was making arrangements for the theater troupe to "tour" at all of their ports of call on the return trip.

"I know Anca needs to get out of her cage," he'd told Nadyha with his mischievous grin. "And we'd hate for her to get arrested again."

They all enjoyed their mornings together, but the women had noticed that for the last four days Nadyha hadn't invited Gage to join them. When she first suggested spending their mornings together in her staterooom, her family and Cara had understood that it was to be an every-morning routine. But Gage, of course, would never presume to go to a lady's stateroom without being invited, and Nadyha knew that. But since the first day of their trip, Nadyha and Gage had met down in the cargo hold at dawn. Nadyha insisted that she alone take care of Tinar and Saz instead of letting crewmen do it, and Gage had done the same. So every morning before breakfast they mucked out the horses' stalls and fed and groomed them. Then Nadyha asked Gage to come to her stateroom for breakfast with everyone.

The last four mornings Nadyha had told Niçu to check on the horses when he woke up, and she would go down after breakfast to do the work. Niçu, who was after all a man's man and not very insightful, hadn't asked any questions, and had merely told Nadyha that he'd muck out and feed the horses, and Nadyha could groom them anytime. Nadyha hadn't said anything else, and she had started going down to do the grooming while everyone else was having luncheon. She knew she wouldn't meet Gage there then.

Cara, Simza, and Mirella were all sitting at the table, tatting lace. Nadyha, Anca, and Boldo were out on the deck. Nadyha stood at the rail, watching the rising sun begin to light up the western shore of the river. As it had been since they had passed Memphis, the land was mostly wide stretches of farm fields with the occasional little river landing for surrounding plantations. Nadyha still loved to watch the scenes as they glided along the great river, even miles of flat farmland. The landscapes were alien to her eyes, and with each moment the quality of light made the river change its persona. Right now, just after dawn, the sun tinted the Big Muddy with gold-tinged rays.

Inside, the three women exchanged meaningful glances at they watched Nadyha standing so still and silent. Baba Simza sighed and shook her head, then continued the conversation. "Cara, you're going to be the—the—what is it they call it? The bellringer of the ball?"

Cara smiled. "It's the 'belle' of the ball, spelled with an 'e.' And I doubt that very seriously. There are so many pretty ladies, so many pretty *rich* ladies with such fine dresses. And I don't even have a hoop skirt." Then, her eyes growing wide, she hastily continued, "Oh, please, please forgive me for complaining! It's so kind of you, Baba Simza, and you, Mirella, to help me with my dress. I would have thought that you would think I was just a foolish, silly *gaji* to want to go to a ball. But now I know one thing, I'll have finer lace than any fashionable woman there."

The *Queen of Bohemia* would reach St. Louis this evening, and the boat overnighted there, its last port of call. Tomorrow night was the Captain's Ball, the grandest entertainment on the *Queen's* two-week round-trip journey. Denny had asked Cara if he could escort her, and she had very politely declined, saying that she would rather stay with the Gypsies, who, of course, wouldn't attend. But Baba Simza had found out that it was because Cara didn't have a ball dress, and she had taken it upon herself to tell Cara that they would fix her old sky-blue muslin and then proceeded to accept Denny's invitation on behalf of Cara.

Simza smiled at her. "Why should we think a dance is foolish? We dance much more than *gajes* do! And I for one will be glad when my ankle is so well, I can dance again!"

Niçu came in, smelling of horses. He sprawled on one of Nadyha's beds, putting his hands behind his head. "They were making bacon for breakfast down in the Sumava. The smell just about starved me to death. You might know they think about ten o'clock's the right time to serve breakfast to first-class people, like my hoity-toity sister."

Nadyha came in to sit cross-legged on the other bed. "You're complaining about getting first-class breakfast served to you in a first-class stateroom. So who's hoity-toity? And get your filthy boots off my bed."

"It's not your bed, it's Boldo's," Niçu said, but he did angle up his legs to take his boots off without rising. "Hey, Nadyha, Gage asked me about you this morning. He said he hasn't talked to you in days, he was just wondering if you were ho-kay."

"I wonder he's had time to worry about me, with that *lubni* and her wretched mother and babbling fool of a father hanging all over him all the time," Nadyha snapped. "What did he say?"

"Huh? I just told you, he said he hasn't talked to you, he asked if you were ho-kay."

"What did you say?"

Niçu looked puzzled. "I said you were ho-kay. What was I supposed to say?"

"Nothing," Nadyha said moodily. "It's stupid anyway, we did the show last night, I saw him then."

"Yeah, but he said you didn't talk to him," Niçu said uncertainly. "Why didn't you talk to him?"

"Because I have nothing to say," she said, flouncing out onto the promenade again.

Thoroughly bewildered now, Niçu asked the women at the table, "What's going on? What'd I do?"

Mirella said soothingly, "It's nothing you did, Niçu. How are Tinar and Saz and Cayenne?"

They talked about the horses, the show, the ship, and the people until breakfast arrived. Niçu had exaggerated, they were served breakfast at about eight o'clock every morning. Nadyha came back in and they all settled down at the table and began pulling the silver covers from the platters of bacon, soft-boiled eggs in eggcups, toast, chops, and hashed potatoes. Niçu said a blessing and they began to eat hungrily. Even 8:00 a.m. was late to them.

Nadyha burnt her finger on a piece of bacon, it was so hot. Then she cracked her egg so hard it shattered, bits of shell and runny egg sliding down the sides of the eggcup onto the marble top of the table. Jumping up, muttering darkly to herself, she went into the bathroom and they heard water running. "I don't think I've ever seen Nadyha in such a *narkri* mood for so long," Niçu complained. "Isn't anyone going to tell me what's the matter with her? I am her brother, after all, I want to take care of her."

Nadyha came back in, holding a steaming-hot rag. Rubbing savagely at the egg-and-shell mess on the table, she said sharply, "There's nothing wrong with me, I am not in a *narkri* mood, and I don't need anyone to take care of me, not even you, *Prala*."

"But *Phei*—" Niçu began but stopped as Simza shook her head at him, a warning. "Sorry, *Phei*," he finished lamely.

Nadyha dropped her head and stopped scrubbing. Then she looked up at her brother and said repentantly, "No, I'm sorry, because I am in a *narkri* mood. I don't know why. I mean, there's no reason why. I mean—oh, forget it! I'll just be better, that's all." She whirled and stalked out of the stateroom.

"Don't try to tell me anything," Niçu said to the women, holding up his hands in a gesture of surrender. "Because now I don't even think I want to know."

THEY DIDN'T SEE NADYHA again until they went to the Sumava Mountains Restaurant, and in this, the restaurant for third-class passengers, it was still called dinner when you ate at noon. Denny had tried and tried to get the Gypsies to eat in the Bohemian Restaurant, which was for first- and second-class passengers, but after two dinners they had avoided it assiduously. The women stared at them and made faces at them, and on both nights one couple, the fabulously wealthy and highborn Creoles, the St. Amants of New Orleans, had swept out of the restaurant and gone to complain to Captain Humphries. Captain Humphries had passed on their complaints to Zedekiah Wainwright, who had talked to Denny about it.

"So the women go barefoot," Denny said carelessly. "That's one of the things that makes them so exotic, Uncle Zeke. And don't you dare tell me about their bare arms, when we have the Captain's Ball I'll bet you'll be able to see Mrs. St. Amant's arms and a lot more besides that, if you know what I mean." The current fashion for ladies' evening dresses was to show lots of bosom.

"But not at dinner," Uncle Zeke said. "And she'll be wearing shoes."

"Then you explain it to Nadyha," Denny retorted. "I'm sure she'll be reasonable about it."

"Er—can't you talk to her?"

"Oh, no, huh-uh. I'm not the one who doesn't want them in the Bohemian. Personally, I think most people are so fascinated by them they don't give a fig if they're barefoot. In fact, I think we ought to let Anca and Boldo eat in first class, too."

And so neither Denny nor his uncle said anything to them, but on their own the Gypsies decided that they preferred the Sumava anyway, and Cara agreed with them. People still stared, and they made themselves free to come to their table to talk to them, but in general they were just curious about them, and often asked them for autographs.

However, as Gage had noted, there were three young toughs that came very close to making nuisances of themselves over Nadyha. Now, as they enjoyed a sumptuous meal (on the *Queen of Bohemia*, even third-class food was always fresh and well-prepared) of tenderloin steak with an assortment of summer vegetables, Frank Yargee, E. B. Aikin, and Leroy Hinkle stopped by their table for a friendly chat. Without an invitation, they drew up three chairs and sat in a semicircle surrounding Nadyha. Frank hitched his chair so close to her that Niçu frowned and said, "Yargee, give my sister some elbow room, she can hardly lift her fork."

"Aw, she don't mind, do you, Yer Highness?" Yargee said.

"Actually, I do, Mr. Yargee," Nadyha said evenly.

He hitched his chair about a half-inch away. "Here you go, wouldn't want you not to be able to git to your grub."

Frank Yargee was squarely built, seemingly as wide as he was tall, just like an ox. His head was square too, with long, tangled, greasy brown hair and small, dark eyes and an iron jaw. He dressed in a manner that, even to the Gypsies, was cheap and flashy. He wore a brown felt bowler hat that he never seemed to remove, even in the dining room, sack coats that were usually in garish checks or plaids, and his favorite waistcoat was a bright crimson satin with yellow lapels and big gold buttons. He also had two gold teeth, his two front uppers, and he thought that they were so dashing they made him simply irresistible to ladies.

His two friends, as often happened with loud overbearing bullies, were mousy and timid. Both of them worked at a barrel-making factory, and because they were both heavy drinkers they had become Yargee's best buddies. E. B. Aikin, whose name was actually Edra Boaz although he never told anyone that, was a short man with long, straight hair that would have been like straw, except that it was such a neutral sandy brown color that it was nondescript. He had rather vacant watery-blue eyes that were usually red-rimmed from drinking. Leroy Hinkle was average-sized, prematurely completely bald on top, but he had let the black fringe that started just above his ears grow down to his shoulders. He, too, wore a dirty bowler hat that he never removed, mimicking his best friend, who he thought was a real tough. Hinkle was a tad smarter than E. B., but his favorite joke in the world was his friend's name. "He be achin'," he'd always say, and laugh like a lunatic howling at the moon. He had been laughing at this joke since they had been friends, for twenty years now.

Yargee leered at Nadyha. "Y'know, Nadyha, I've seen some dancing girls in my time, but I don't think I've niver seen one that can shake it as good as you did last night. When's the next show?"

Niçu slammed down his knife and fork and leaned over the table. "Yargee, you're out of line. Leave my sister alone."

"Oooh, the little Gypsy knife man's gittin' upset, E. B.," Yargee said. "Why don't you tell him what my nickname down on the docks is?"

E. B. Aikin smirked. "It's 'Scargee.' Not, Yargee, yer git it? 'Scargee.'"

Yargee's thin lips curled as he leaned over toward Niçu. "See, my old dad owns a saloon down in N'awlins, name of Yargee's Levee Saloon. And I've allus kept the peace at Yargee's Levee Saloon, which ain't no simple thing with them roustabouts and wharf rats and all that trash. And you know how I done it, ever since I were fourteen year old? I don't fool around with no fist-fightin' nor no clubs nor even no guns. I done it with my knife, my real-true Bowie knife I named Belle. And Belle, she's left some scars on some folks that I done thought got outta line, and I know when folks get outta line, and I'm a-tellin' you, Gypsy, for all your fine toothpick-juggling, I ain't outta line with Nadyha."

Niçu jumped to his feet, his face dark and fierce. "I want you to leave right now, Yargee. And from now on you stay away from my family."

Yargee hopped up too, knocking his heavy black walnut chair backwards into Leroy Hinkle's lap. "And what are you gonna do if I don't, Gypsy?"

Niçu's black eyes glinted. "You want to settle it with knives? I'll be happy to oblige, right now."

Yargee's lip curled. "Yeah, I bet you would. And I'd cut you up, and then me and my buddies would git kicked off the boat. Oh, no, huh-uh. But you ain't gonna tell me where I can sit or walk and who I can talk to, little man. So from now on *you* just better watch *yerself*."

He marched out of the dining room, with his two friends trailing him, glancing back at Niçu with expressions of idiot glee. Niçu sat back down and resumed eating.

Baba Simza shook her head and said with a hint of regret, *"The way of the wicked is as darkness; they know not at what they stumble."* With relish she took a big bite of steak.

Cara glanced around at her in disbelief. The Gypsies all were calmly finishing their dinner. "But aren't any of you—upset? Niçu, that man is like a brick wall, he's twice your size! Mirella, aren't you afraid? And Nadyha, what are you going to do?"

Mirella answered, "No, I'm not at all afraid. It doesn't matter how big a man is, it's how smart he is. Niçu's got more sense—and courage—in his pinky finger than that *didlo gaje* does. Niçu can take care of himself. And he can take care of us."

Cara watched Nadyha as she took a sip of coffee. "But Nadyha, what if that man somehow gets you alone? I honestly think he's dangerous!"

Nadyha shrugged. "You're never alone, if you're not in your stateroom. It won't happen."

But she was wrong.

MIRELLA, SIMZA, AND CARA usually spent the early afternoons after luncheon sitting on the promenade on the Promenade Deck. It was ten feet wide, with a six-foot overhang for a roof, and so it was shady and cool, with the constant breeze as the *Queen of Bohemia* steamed along. Nadyha rarely sat with them; most of the time she enjoyed walking Anca or Boldo around. But on this afternoon she sat with them, tatting in her lap un-tatted, as it were, simply watching the shore. She had taken a chair next to Baba Simza. Her grandmother let her sit in silence for awhile, but finally, in Romany, she asked, "Are you going to tell me what's wrong with you, child?"

Nadyha came out of her dark reverie, looked down, tatted two stitches, then dropped the sewing again to look straight into her grandmother's wise old eyes. "I can't. I can't even think about it, much less talk about it."

"You do think about it, too much. Maybe you should talk to me, maybe not. But I do know you don't pray about it, Nadyha," Simza said gently. "I mean, you don't pray about *him*. And I think that's really what's wrong with you."

Nadyha wasn't at all startled by her grandmother's shrewdness; Baba Simza knew her as well as any human being can know another. But it irritated her, partly because of her much-hated tangle of emotions for Gage Kennon, and also because deep down she knew she was rebelling against God, and she felt guilty. "Grandmother, please. I am a grown woman, and I can work this out myself. I just need—need—some time."

"Away from him? Hmph, that's not going to be so easy," Simza said dryly. "Oh, maybe today, though. It's going to storm, so Gage and Niçu won't have their show this afternoon. So for tonight at least you can run away from him."

Nadyha stared out over the railing. All she could see was a bright sunlight happily lighting up miles of cotton fields, and a strip of periwinkle-blue sky.

But as usual, Baba Simza knew. By three o'clock that afternoon, it was as dark as midnight. The black storm clouds were so low they seemed to hover just above the *Queen of Bohemia*'s smokestacks. The thunder was deafening, and angry bolts of lightning flashed all around them. The warm soupy rain was almost horizontal, and everyone was forced to go inside.

Nadyha retreated to her stateroom, grateful that she didn't have to do Gage's show tonight. It never occurred to her to simply refuse; she had said that she would do it, and she was a woman who kept her word. But she felt vast relief, and she was enjoying the storm. To her it was a kind of dancing-close-to-danger that she loved. She wasn't at all afraid. Throwing open the French doors, she stood on the threshold, getting soaked but reveling in the spectacular storm. It made her forget about Gage Kennon.

After some time she realized that the carpet of her stateroom all around the doors was getting soaked, and with regret she closed them. Anca was in the far corner of the room, watching Nadyha with disdain, while Boldo was crouching down behind the bed, anxiously sucking his paws. "Oh, poor Boldo bear," she said, patting him on the head. "Don't be scared, it's just a silly old thunderstorm. Here, you sit up here on your bed and I'll get you some grapes." She went to the sideboard and unlocked the cabinet below; if she didn't keep it locked, Boldo got into it and ate all of the fruit, bread, and cheese that the *Queen* stocked for all of the first-class passengers.

After Nadyha set a bowl of big purple grapes on the bed, he lumbered up there and started eating, all fears forgotten. Quickly Nadyha changed into dry clothes, one of her old shapeless blouses and a gray skirt with the ragged hem. Taking off her *diklo*, she wrung it out—it was dripping wet—and then hurriedly toweled her hair.

She got a horse's curry brush from her closet and began to brush Boldo. It relaxed him when she groomed him. When the next roar of thunder sounded he didn't even flinch. "Foolish bear, I wish you'd be this good when I give you a bath," she grumbled. "You act like I'm sticking you with Niçu's knives." The thought reminded her of Niçu's and Gage's show, and in the perplexing confusion of her mind she regretted that she wouldn't see Gage that evening.

"Oh! I call you foolish!" she rasped to Boldo. "I'm as stupid as a *gajo*!" She went on talking nonsense to the bear, and he finished his grapes and started nodding. Finally she got him to lie down and go to sleep.

The *Queen of Bohemia* was steaming placidly along; no amount of wind or rain could slow her down. But suddenly the great brass bell sounded half-a-dozen urgent deep gongs, and the steam whistles screamed. The *Queen* immediately started slowing, then with a wrench it slewed sideways. The entire boat gave a mighty jerk and then started shuddering. Nadyha was knocked sideways to the floor. Everything fell off of the sideboard. The French doors, which she hadn't locked, swung open and banged against the walls.

Quickly Nadyha jumped to her feet to close the doors, then anxiously went to hover over Boldo. He had drowsily opened one eye when the crash had happened, and as Nadyha bent over him he merely looked back up at her and his eye slowly closed again. He snored a little. Anca, lying on her cushion by Nadyha's bed, looked annoyed and began cleaning her face.

Nadyha thought, *Tinar and Saz! And Cayenne! What if they fell, or got slammed into the stall? I've got to go see about them . . . especially Cayenne, he's so much more high-strung than Tinar and Saz . . .*

She ran out of her stateroom.

WHAT HAPPENED WAS THIS: Stephen Carruthers was steaming along just past the quaint old town of Ste. Genevieve, along a straight stretch of river that was like a ruler for about twelve miles. He knew every current, every snag, every low bottom, even every tree through here, just as he knew most all of the Mississippi River from New Orleans to St. Louis. That was why, though it was so far in front of him, when lightning struck a blinding flash on the right-hand bank, he figured that it had hit a giant pine tree that he used as a mile marker, for the tree was about eight feet in diameter and soared up fifty feet high. Instantly he stood on the wheel to turn her to port, rang the bell—the "Emergency!" signal when a steamer was underway—and blew the steam whistle. Like the queen she was, the boat answered and yanked hard left. Coming side-on to the teeming storm current, she rocked side-to-side, hard.

Everyone immediately picked themselves up and ran outside, heedless of the pelting rain, to see what had happened. Frank Yargee, E. B. Aikin, and Leroy Hinkle had been in the Elbe River Saloon since they'd left the dining room after their confrontation with Niçu. They had all been drinking straight whiskey steadily, and were all three very drunk. Yargee had been bragging about how he was going to "fix" Niçu, and how he was going to make Nadyha see that he was the man for her, the stuck-up Gypsy wench.

When the ship crashed, all three of them, who were bellied up to the bar, fell down. It would have been comical to watch the three of them stumbling and staggering around, trying to get to their feet, if they hadn't been cursing so foully. Then, like everyone else, they went out onto the promenade to see what had happened.

The saloon was on the starboard side of the boat, so they were dumbfounded to see that they were broadside-on to the raging river, with the Queen's bow just nosed up against the left-hand shore.

And then Frank Yargee saw Nadyha running down the steps. Her blouse was falling off of one shoulder, her hair was unbound and wild, and the sight of her filled him with drunken rage and lust.

"C'mon, boys, I know where she's going," he told his two friends. Shoving, pushing, cursing, they made their way through the crowd to the steps down to the Boiler Deck.

Yargee had been watching Nadyha, and he knew she would be going down to check on her horses. He also knew that with whatever accident had happened, none of the crew would be loitering around in the cargo hold.

The stalls were set up on the starboard side of the hold. They were of a good size, eight feet by ten feet, so the horses had plenty of room to move around. Lined up, first was Cayenne's stall, then Saz's, then Tinar's. Next to his stall was another stall that they had built for Anca, for her feedings. It was smaller, six by eight, and aside from the fresh sweet hay they kept on the floor, Nadyha had made a second cushion, filled with catmint and Spanish moss, for her. After she ate Anca usually took a good wash and then napped for a couple of hours.

Now, as Yargee and his friends came into the hold, they saw Nadyha standing at Cayenne's stall. She stood in front of the door, but hadn't gone in, for the horse was frightened and was shaking his head and trembling, his skin running with shivers, his eyes white. But he was calming down as Nadyha petted his nose and spoke softly to him. The storm was so loud that she couldn't hear the three men. When they came past Anca's stall she saw them out of the corner of her eye. Immediately she flattened herself, back up against Cayenne's door, and her hand went to her waist. But she wasn't wearing her belt, so she didn't have her knife. Her eyes shifted to the right, but Yargee saw it and took two running steps and grabbed her arm. "Oh, no, you don't," he said in her ear. "They're going to be too busy in that there boiler room for you to go running around in there bothering 'em."

Nadyha tried to yank her arm away, but it was as if it was stuck in an iron vise. Yargee yanked her closer and put one arm around her waist. Still muttering into her ear, he said, "Now, me and you are gonna have us a little talk, and we're gonna come to an agreement. And you're not gonna say one word to nobody about our little talk, or our agreement. 'Cause if you do, your old granny just might find herself limpin' even worsen than she does now. You got that, you Gypsy whore?"

Nadyha opened her mouth wide and screamed as loudly as she could. But she might as well have been mute, for all the good it did. The rain was still hard and deafening, and the cargo hold was always noisy from the nearby boiler room and engine room anyway. But her scream did affect the three men. Aikin and Hinkle, who had been smirking at Yargee and Nadyha, suddenly looked uncertainly at each other.

Frank Yargee, in a fast whipping motion, took out his Bowie knife. He held it to Nadyha's cheek, a twelve-inch long glittering blade with serrations lining the curve of the tip. He hissed, "You do that agin, I'm gonna cut your pretty face. Nah, I ain't a-gonna kill you or really even hurt you bad, I ain't that kind of man. But I will mark you up, Nadyha, and that would be a real shame for a fine-looking wench like you."

Nadyha's eyes were huge with horror, and her mouth trembled. But she remained perfectly still. "Thass much better. Now I know you got your pretty little cushion for your tiger down there in that stall. What say we go have us a seat and talk?"

He started walking Nadyha down the stalls. Nadyha's horrified gaze slid to the horses. Tinar and Saz watched them alertly, but they didn't seem to sense her anguish. Wildly Nadyha wondered why; she thought she was as in tune with her horses as she was with Anca. But then she realized that Anca was a predator, and she could sense a prey faraway, and she would know that right now, Nadyha was the prey. But the horses didn't.

The two men half-stumbled along behind Yargee and Nadyha, and Aikin mumbled, "Frank? You sure . . . I mean, people like this girl . . ."

"Shaddup!" he snarled over his shoulder. "Open that stall door. Then close it, and you two idiots just stand there and mind your own business!" Hinkle opened the door and after Yargee and Nadyha went in, he closed it. He and Aikin stood in front of it, shuffling and looking down at their feet and casting alarmed glances all around.

Just for the fun of it, Yargee slammed Nadyha into the far wall and, still holding the knife just a hair away from her cheek, pressed himself against her. "See, I been watching you, Nadyha, and I know you're a girl that likes to have fun. So we're gonna have us some fun, ain't we?"

Yargee had his back to the stall door, so he didn't see Gage come running in. Gage grabbed him by the scruff of the neck and around his waist and, lifting him about six inches into the air, slammed him face-first into the wall. Yargee's nose broke, and the rough wood dug splinters all into his face, and blood began pouring down. But he was a fighter, and he still held the knife. He tried to turn it and backward-stab Gage in the belly.

Gage let him drop to his feet, grabbed his right wrist, and yanked it up hard, back between his shoulder blades. With satisfaction Gage felt his shoulder dislocate, and then, even in the din, heard the crack of Yargee's upper arm break. He let out a screaming yowl that, for a moment, gave both Nadyha and Gage a great deal of pleasure. Gage let go of him and he crumpled facedown to the floor, his left hand scrabbling in the hay, still shrieking from his blood-filled mouth.

Gage looked at Nadyha. She still stood, flattened against the wall, staring down at Yargee with horror-filled eyes. Slowly her gaze rose to Gage, and she began to tremble, her entire body started shaking as if she had suddenly become palsied. Her face was a sickly yellow color, as if she were going to be horribly sick.

Throwing Yargee's knife out of the stall, he went to her and very gently took her in his arms. She buried her face in his shoulder, shaking tremulously. Gage stroked her hair and whispered reassurances to her. They stood that way for a long time, unmindful of Yargee, who was now moaning and sobbing on the floor. Very slowly Nadyha stopped trembling.

Then, with a violence that shocked Gage, Nadyha pushed him away. Her face was now flushed a painful crimson, her eyes blazed. "You—you men! What's the matter with all of you! All you want—all you care about—is to—is to—filthy brutes!" She ran out of the stall and fled to the steps.

Now Gage felt faintly ill himself. He glared down at Yargee, cringing and crying on the floor, and considered breaking his other arm and both of his legs. "Sure would make me feel better," he muttered to himself. "So I guess maybe she was right. I guess that just makes me a filthy brute."

CHAPTER SIXTEEN

Nadyha ran to Baba Simza's stateroom and burst in. Simza was standing at the window, watching the rain and wondering what had happened and why the boat was turned sideways so that she only saw the river flowing fast and brown behind. When she turned and saw her granddaughter, she felt a shock of dread shake her to her very bones.

Nadyha's hair was wild, her face was a pasty yellow hue, her eyes were stretched wide and filled with horror. Her blouse was torn, and there were angry red marks on her lower neck and shoulder. *"Puridaia!"* she cried with an anguished voice that Simza, in her worst nightmares, never thought of hearing from a loved one.

Quickly, ignoring the pain from her still-healing ankle, Simza ran to Nadyha and threw her arms around her, hugging her close. Nadyha began to shake and sob. Gently, murmuring wordless soothing sounds, Simza led her to the bed and they sat together. Nadyha clung to her and, in between sobs, managed to tell her what had happened. She spoke in Romany, and was barely coherent. There is no Romany word for rape; but to Simza she might as well have been screaming it in English over and over again. After a long time, Simza finally got Nadyha to lie down. She curled up in a fetal position, still weeping, but the storm of breathless gasping sobs were subsiding. Simza covered her with a light sheet and whispered, "I'm going to get Niçu and Mirella. Just one moment, *bitti chavi*, I'll be right back." Nadyha nodded tremulously.

Simza hurried next door and banged hard on their stateroom door. "Niçu! *Av akai!*" Immediately Niçu wrenched it open, his expression already alarmed. Mirella hovered behind him.

Briefly Simza told them what had happened. Mirella's eyes filled with tears and Niçu looked deathly angry. Simza said, "You need to go down and talk to Gage, and you men can decide what to do. Mirella and I are going to take Nadyha to her room, she'll never rest without Boldo and that cat." She was, of course, speaking of Anca. "And Niçu, don't let anyone come to Nadyha's stateroom to see about her, not even maids. All she wants right now is us, her *familia*. So when you get the business settled with that *narkri mokadi mahrime gaje*," she spat out, "you come back to see what we're going to need."

NIÇU RAN DOWN TO the Boiler Deck and found Gage, still standing over Frank Yargee, staring at him with narrowed flint-blue eyes. His jaw was tensing over and over again as he clenched his teeth.

Niçu regarded Frank Yargee, and instead of wanting to kill him he just felt a sickening disgust. He was still facedown, wallowing in hay that was smeared with the blood from his face and nose. His right arm was crooked at such an awkward angle that Niçu immediately knew that Gage had broken it. He was making pitiful mewling sounds alternating with bellowing groans.

"What are we going to do?" Niçu asked Gage.

"I dunno. Now I wish I hadn't broken his arm so I could beat him to death in a fair fight," Gage growled. "I was thinking about just leaving him here and nailing the door shut but I hate that he's dirtying up Anca's stall."

"That's the truth, the filthy vermin," Niçu agreed venomously. He had an urge to kick Yargee then; after all, his left side wasn't hurt. But he resisted the impulse and merely said, "I guess I'd better go find Dennis."

"Yeah, he's probably in the Moravian," Gage said, then added dully, "That's where we were when we wrecked, or whatever happened." Gage was filled with bitter regret; he had been in the salon, with Monique Dobard hanging on his arm as usual these days, listening to Cara playing the piano and singing. When the ship had been yanked around, he had taken long moments to see that Miss Dobard and her parents were all right before he had hurried down to check on the horses. And *this* had been happening to Nadyha. Gage really felt murderous then; it was hard for him to restrain himself.

Niçu did find Denny in the Moravian Salon, along with his uncle. They were reassuring the passengers that the obstruction was being cleared, and there was no danger at all, and they would still reach St. Louis that night. Niçu walked up to them as they were standing talking to a group of first-class passengers and rudely interrupted Wainwright as he was speaking. "I need to talk to both of you. Now."

They stepped out into the passage and Niçu told them what had happened. He was surprised as he observed these two hearty, back-slapping *gajes*; Zedekiah Wainwright looked as aghast and horrified as Niçu himself had been, and he reflected, *I never thought a grinning fool like Dennis Wainwright could look so dangerous.*

They all went back down to the cargo deck and, as Niçu had, Wainwright and Denny regarded Frank Yargee with utter disgust. "I wish I could just roll him over the side right now," Zedekiah Wainwright grunted. "But I guess that would hardly do." He sighed deeply. "We have a doctor on board, I'll ask him if he'll see to him. But first I'm going to ask him to attend Nadyha," he told Niçu.

Niçu shook his head. "Baba Simza says she's not hurt, not physically, anyway. And she doesn't want anyone but us right now." They all understood he meant the Gypsies; and it rent at Gage Kennon's heart.

"Those other two imbeciles that run with him were here, standing guard," Gage said coldly. "They ran like scared little mice when I came in, and I'm glad they did. If they would have just walked up to me and started spouting some of their drunk babblings, I might have . . . I might have been . . ." *Too late*, were his unspoken words.

Denny snorted. "Those two weasels? They were probably so scared gutless I'm surprised they had sense enough to run. It's not going to do them any good anyway. We're going to have all three of them arrested in St. Louis for assault, battery, and attempted rape. Until then, they can just rot in their stateroom. I'll post an armed guard at their door."

"That would be me," Gage asserted flatly. "And I really hope they try to escape."

Dr. Hypolite Dauterive was a tall man, with a proud, erect posture and a wealth of salt-and-pepper hair. At his knock at the door, Gage opened it, gave the three men inside a deathly glare, and let the doctor out into the hallway of the third-class passengers' deck.

Dauterive's sharp gaze assessed Gage for a moment, and Gage met his eyes with a hard stare. "You know, Mr. Kennon," Dauterive said evenly, "when Mr. Wainwright asked me to attend that man, he told me that he was going to jail when we reach St. Louis tonight. I insisted upon knowing the particulars because it was unclear to me why Mr. Yargee was going to jail, and not you. Although Mr. Wainwright was very reluctant to explain, he did tell me exactly what happened." Now Dauterive stuck out his maNiçured hand. "May I shake your hand, sir."

They shook hands firmly, and Dauterive continued in a clinical voice, "His shoulder was dislocated, but his arm is so badly broken that I couldn't relocate the shoulder again. I've just splinted and bandaged up his right side. His nose is broken, both of his eyes are going to swell shut, and the worst injury of all is that he sustained a severe skull fracture. Pooling blood is putting pressure on his brain, and if he doesn't have surgery to relieve it soon he may die."

"Surgery," Gage repeated. "I don't guess you can do it?"

"There are no surgical instruments here, and I've never done that sort of surgery in my life. I wouldn't attempt it even if we had the best operating theater on board. At any rate, Captain Humphries has said that we'll likely reach St. Louis before midnight. That will be plenty of time for him to have surgery at St. Louis Charity Hospital," he said with relish. "They let the students do surgery there."

"Will he die before then?" Gage asked coolly.

"Unfortunately not," Dauterive replied, "and now I'll have to go to confession for saying that, and thinking it, and feeling it. Is there anything I can do for you, Mr. Kennon? Anything you need?"

"No, thank you, sir." They shook hands again and Dauterive left.

Gage resumed his pacing. A chair had been set out in the hallway by Yargee's stateroom door, but Gage couldn't keep still. Passengers came and went, and he had met most of them and knew them by name, but he didn't speak to anyone. Sometimes they came toward him with a smile, but the smiles faded when they saw his grim face. He was dressed in black trousers and a plain white shirt, but he was wearing his gunbelt with both Colts at his sides. Passersby gave him a wide berth as he paced up and down.

I should have asked Niçu to come at least let me know how she's doing, he fretted. *Niçu has no idea how I feel about her, how this whole thing is like a waking nightmare to me . . . we're all friends, of course, but Niçu doesn't know how much I love her . . .*

The thought brought him to an abrupt standstill in his pacing. *I do love Nadyha. All those other things, all that jealousy and desire and passion I've felt, they're nothing to me now. All I want is for her to be well, to be happy, to be free from fear . . . even if it's without me.*

He started pacing again, more slowly.

Vaguely he became aware of the boat moving again, and he heard three triumphant short blasts on the steam whistle. About half an hour later Denny came down. Without preamble he said, "It seems like, from what I'm getting that Baba Simza told Niçu, that she's kinda in shock. They tried giving her some brandy, but just as they lifted the glass to her face she got really sick. She said it smelled like *him*," Denny said with his fine lips curling. "So I got some laudanum and sent it up, and Niçu said she's gone to sleep."

"I guess that's the best thing right now," Gage said. "Nadyha"—he swallowed hard before he was able to continue—"Nadyha's strong, but this would make any woman suffer terribly."

"I know," Denny said helplessly. "Uncle Zeke and I have told them that we'll send them right back to New Orleans by train if they want, or we'll put them up in the St. Louis Royal Hotel, or we'll do anything, anything . . ."

"Are they going to leave?" Gage asked sharply.

Denny shook his head. "Baba Simza says not, she thinks it would be better for them to stay on board the *Queen*, instead of racketing around on a train for three days or staying in some stupid *gaje* hotel that might not have running water. But she did say she's going to ask Nadyha what she wants to do, in the morning."

Gage was vastly relieved; he knew that Nadyha would trust her grandmother's choices. "They'll stay, thank the Lord. We can—they're safer here."

"Uncle Zeke is in the most tearing rage I've ever seen," Denny said with heat. "And for that matter, so am I. This should never, *never* have happened on board this boat. We've worked hard to make it safe and secure for our passengers, and for our ladies, yes, even the third-class ladies that manage to make enough in some fancy New Orleans brothel to take a trip on the *Queen of Bohemia*, like those two silly girls Susanna Melton and Fanny Griffiths." Denny knew almost every passenger, even those in third class, by name.

He continued, "Even people who look down on Gypsies would be outraged. But listen, Gage, my uncle and I and Captain Humphries have decided not to tell anyone what's happened. Not because we're worried about the boat's reputation! But because we just don't want Nadyha to be bothered. Even Captain Humphries agrees with that. The old buzzard's kinda gotten to admire her."

"Who doesn't?" Gage said, his spirits lifting a little. "I agree, too, I'd hate to think of all the gossip about her. The only thing is, I wish Niçu would understand that I need to know about her, how she's doing, if she needs anything, and so on."

Denny's brown eyes glinted. "Yeah, Niçu's kinda blank on you and Nadyha. Oh, don't look so outraged, we both know exactly what I'm talking about. And I've got some pretty good news for you, buddy. The Guidrys are disembarking at St. Louis."

"Who are the Guidrys, and why should I care?"

"The Guidrys," Denny said with relish, "occupy the stateroom right next to Nadyha's. And it's not booked on the return trip."

Gage managed a small lopsided smile. "Oh, yeah? Well, now it is."

THE *Queen of Bohemia* steamed into St. Louis, majestically as always, half an hour past midnight. For the rest of the night and the next day, Gage and Denny were very busy.

They and Captain Humphries and Zedekiah Wainwright went to the harbormaster and explained that they had three criminals on board the ship that they wished to be arrested and taken to the St. Louis jail. Unfortunately, one of those prisoners would need an ambulance to take him first to Charity Hospital for emergency surgery, and if he lived, then he would certainly be sent to jail. The harbormaster promptly sent two stout men of the harbor watch back with them, and assured them that he'd send deputies and arrange for an ambulance.

After conferring, Captain Humphries, Gage, and Denny and his uncle had decided not to have Yargee charged with attempted rape, because in that case Nadyha would have to go to the sheriff's office to make a statement. They decided that it would be best if she could be completely left out of it. And so Gage Kennon made a complaint against Frank Yargee for deadly assault. "He tried to stab me, and I was unarmed," Gage explained to a curious deputy sheriff. Gage didn't mention that it was after he'd already broken his nose and fractured his skull. "And E. B. Aikin and Leroy Hinkle were aiding and abetting him in his assault." Which was exactly true.

Getting Yargee, Aikin, and Hinkle into custody took most of the night, and then Gage and Denny moved up to the first-class stateroom next to Nadyha's. Just before dawn Baba Simza met them out in the hallway to give them a report. "She's sleeping much. The laudanum makes her very droozy," she said, and Gage and Denny knew exactly what she meant. "It's best, for now. But I know Nadyha, by tomorrow she'll be tired with the droozy. And *miry deary Dovvel*, He'll take care of her. You pray, Gage, and you too, Dennis, you young heathen."

"I'll leave that to Gage," he said. "But Baba Simza, please, tell me what else we can do. What can we get her? Any medicines, herbs? Her favorite food? What is her favorite food?"

"Crawfish *gombo* and peach anything," Gage said promptly. "But listen, Baba Simza, I have another idea for a gift for her, but I need to talk to you first."

Simza gave an exaggerated sigh. "That means something I'm not going to like. But go on, *gaje*, I'm listening." Gage had a talk with her, and with much grumbling Simza gave him permission to get a special gift for Nadyha.

Gage and Denny had important errands to run, so they immediately returned to the city without bothering to go to bed. Since the *Queen* hadn't sustained any damage from the almost-wreck they'd had, they were going to leave St. Louis at six o'clock that evening. Gage wanted to ride, but Denny said they'd have to take a carriage. "Why do we have to take a carriage?" Gage asked as they walked up the wharves to Main Street. "I'd rather ride."

"No, you wouldn't," Denny said confidently. "Because we have to buy a hoop skirt, and you would look really silly carrying a hoop skirt around on horseback."

"A hoop skirt?" Gage said blankly. "What's that?"

Denny needed to call on his parents, of course, and Gage accompanied him. He found Lucius Wainwright, Denny's father, to be a hatchet-faced martinet who criticized everything about Denny from the moment they walked into the grand mansion. Denny resembled his mother, in that she had the same thick, healthy, bright brown hair and brown eyes, but there the resemblance ended. She had a long-suffering, rather petulant manner, nothing at all like Denny's good nature. The visit left Gage wondering about the nature of bloodlines, and how capricious they were sometimes. Denny was much more like his uncle than he was his father or mother.

And Monique Dobard, he thought as they left Wainwright House in relief, was like neither of her parents. Gage had been flattered, at first, by her obvious partiality; he had never made the acquaintance of an upperclass New Orleans woman, much less have one flirt with him so outrageously. But he felt a slight disdain for her now. He had come to understand that her obsession with him was not because she wanted to get to know him—Gage Kennon. She was flirting with the dangerous Gage the Dead-Eye Sharpshooter. And, he thought with dry amusement, she was driving her mother crazy, which Monique seemed to enjoy.

They managed to complete all their errands, although it took them an unconscionably long time to find crawfish. Finally Gage found a hole-in-the-wall dive down on the docks with five pounds of live crawfish, and when the greasy owner found out how anxious they were to buy, Denny had to pay five dollars for them. "Only about a hundred times what you'd pay in New Orleans," he said happily. "And she's worth it."

They had to drive out of the city to get Gage's gift for Nadyha, and that took another couple of hours. Finally they made all of their purchases, including a hoop skirt, which Gage realized would indeed be awkward to carry on horseback, for it was a flat circle about six feet in diameter with concentric wires. Denny explained to Gage, "Baba Simza told me to buy this for Cara, because she has a nice ball dress but no crinoline, and that's all the current rage, you know. So Baba Simza gives me some money, and I told her that the *Queen* would finance this purchase and consider it part of the Countess's costumes. But Baba Simza got really mad at me—she does that a lot—and she snapped, 'Oh, so you think Cara will accept this gift from you, from a man? What's the matter with you, *dinili gajo?*'

"Yeah, well, she was right," Gage said. "I may not know the difference between a hoop skirt and an anvil, but I know ladies like Cara. It would shame her to accept any gift from a man, especially—uh—delicates."

"Yeah, I realize that now," Denny said thoughtfully. "Cara really is special, she's charming, kind, has lovely manners and graces. And so gifted. You know, whenever she's in the Moravian people always ask her to sing. I was thinking that maybe we should consider a separate show for her, a concert."

"Uh-huh. Good idea," Gage said vaguely. All of his thoughts were intensely focused on Nadyha.

They got back to the *Queen of Bohemia* at six thirty. Captain Humphries grumbled at them making their departure late, but Denny said, "Aw, he's not happy unless he's got something to complain about. I guarantee you, if he had done what we've done—and he would, for Nadyha, I suspect—he couldn't have gotten here on the dot either."

The Captain's Ball had been planned for this night, but because the accident had thrown them off schedule they decided to have it on the next night, Friday. Matter-of-factly, Denny told Gage, "Of course now there'll be no play. So I was wondering, would you and Niçu do your show Saturday?"

"If Niçu wants to," Gage said. "If he doesn't, I'll go up there and show off all by myself."

"You don't show off," Denny said with a hint of envy. "You're just you. I guarantee you, if I could shoot like you I'd be the biggest swaggering fool in history."

"Who says you aren't anyway, Billy Yank?" Gage said.

ALTHOUGH CAPTAIN HUMPHRIES, ZEDEKIAH Wainwright, and Gage and Denny had solemnly decided to keep Frank Yargee's attack on Nadyha a secret, they had forgotten to tell Dr. Hypolite Dauterive. Dr. Dauterive told his wife and a couple of the other men in first class, so the whole truth was known to first class by early Thursday night.

The *Queen of Bohemia* was much like a small town, admittedly a luxurious small town. Porters and stewards and chambermaids and waiters overhear conversations, and the third-class passengers had all noted Gage Kennon's armed guard of Yargee's and his friends' stateroom. Many passengers were still up milling around when the deputies came to arrest them and the ambulance came to pick up

Yargee. By Friday afternoon, when they stopped at Cairo, Illinois, the entire boat knew about the assault, if not the specifics.

The knowledge affected the passengers, and had repercussions, some seen and some unseen. As was inevitable and what Gage and the others dreaded, gossip was rampant about Nadyha. What none of them had realized, however, was how much she was admired and respected, even liked. By the time the Captain's Ball commenced on Friday evening as they left Cairo, Nadyha's stateroom looked like some kind of combination greengrocer, fruiterer, and hothouse.

Captain Humphries had, of course, sent a discreet note of apology, along with a huge bouquet of flowers. This idea had also occurred to many passengers, and Mirella had to start putting flowers out on the promenade. Even the crew chipped in and bought Nadyha a dozen red roses and had Niçu deliver them to her, along with a crudely spelled but endearing note from the Crew Chief. Stephen Carruthers sent her a box of chocolates. The orchestra worked together, and handwrote on fine parchment the music and lyrics to "Scarborough Fair."

Zedekiah Wainwright had practically cleaned out all of the fresh peaches in the city of St. Louis. In fact, he bought so much from two fruitsellers that they were able to close their shops early. He sent all kinds of fresh fruit to Nadyha, which everyone knew Boldo would probably eat.

Denny had bought an enormous basket filled with French-milled scented soaps, talcum powder, perfume, and five different kinds of scented shampoos and rinses for a ladies' hair. "She'll probably dress me down for buying something so personal," he joked to Gage. "But then again, when she sees your gift she'll probably forget all the rest."

NADYHA OPENED THE FRENCH doors to a cool evening that had no moon. Music from the Captain's Ball wafted up to the first-class deck. Nadyha sat down on her cushioned chaise—another gift sent from Zedekiah Wainwright—and Anca sat beside her. Nadyha stroked her head and listened to the music and savored the night. Although the *Queen* was lit with all of her golden lanterns, she didn't light the far shore. All Nadyha saw were the shadows of trees against the sky.

Behind her Simza and Mirella sat at the table, reading the Bible and talking quietly. Their voices were just soft murmurs to Nadyha, but by some chance zephyr she heard her grandmother say, "Pah, wheels within wheels, fiery creatures that fly but don't turn, who can know what it means? But always, in the Bible, *Dovvel* will show you something. Even in this Ezekiel, listen, Mirella. *I will seek that which was lost, and bring again that which was driven away, and will bind up that which was broken, and will strengthen that which was sick . . .* That could be about the Romany, you see?"

Nadyha thought, *That could be about me. I feel lost, and I think I'm broken. Will I ever be whole again? Will I ever be—strong, and happy, and feel good again? I don't know, I can't see it, I'm afraid I really have been broken. Afraid . . . afraid . . .*

Restlessly she went inside and joined the two women at the table. "*Si tut bocklo?*" Mirella asked.

Nadyha started to answer no, but then she said, "Actually, some fruit would be very nice. If Boldo's left me any, that is." Mirella and Simza exchanged quick glances; it was the first time that Nadyha had made an attempt at even a weak joke. Mirella rose and went to the sideboard to prepare a platter of fruit; Wainwright had bought peaches, of course, and plums and bananas and plantains and red, green, and purple grapes, apples, pears, and even some guavas and mangoes, which none of the Gypsies had ever seen. Mirella decided to peel and quarter some of them and see what they were like.

Hearing his name, Boldo lumbered over to Nadyha and with a big breathy bear sigh, sat down beside her. She kissed his head and scratched behind his ears. "He knows something's wrong," she said in a low voice.

"*Hai*," Simza agreed. "Even the *cat* does." Simza always put special emphasis on "cat" when she was talking about Anca, to communicate her disdain for such an animal. In the last two nights, however, since she had been staying in Nadyha's stateroom with her, Nadyha had caught Simza— twice, actually—stroking Anca's head. It was the first time Nadyha had ever seen her grandmother touch the cougar.

Nadyha said hesitantly, "*Puridaia*, I must ask you something, and you must tell me the truth."

"*Hai*, I will do that."

Nadyha frowned and chewed on her lower lip. "Do you—do you think that sometimes Gypsies should try harder to—to—be like the *gajes*? I mean, if we're going to live with them, among them, instead of by ourselves with only our *vitsi*, I was thinking that maybe we should—look more like them, act more—"

Simza put up one hand, an imperious gesture. "*Hush kacker!* I know what you're trying to say, Nadyha, and you're wrong, very wrong. You're thinking that because we dress the way we do, with our bare arms and bare feet and dancing and singing, that that's why that *mokadi jook* attacked you? Because you look like you do, and dress like you do? So, you think that in some way, it's really your own fault?"

Nadyha dropped her eyes and fingered her skirt nervously. "We're so different from the *gajes*, Baba Simza. Men are bound to think—they must see us, and think—"

"'Men think, men see,'" Simza interrupted her. "There is no 'men,' there is only a man, a woman, a person, who makes choices, for good or for evil. That Yargee man chose evil. It wouldn't have mattered if you wore *gaje* mourning clothes and covered yourself from head to foot, Nadyha, he still would have done what he did."

Mirella set a scrumptious-looking tray of fruit, bread, and cheese on the table. "Let me ask you a question, Nadyha. If Yargee had attacked me, do you think that I would have deserved it?"

"What? No!"

"No," Mirella repeated. "But I dress like you, I dance in front of people like you, and no, that could never mean that I got what I deserved if a man raped me. Never. Just like you."

Nadyha looked thoughtful; but she did start to eat. All of them ate in silence for awhile, then she said, "We're supposed to do the show tomorrow night."

"No one expects you to do the show," Simza said calmly. "Mr. Wainwright has told me that we are very welcome to do whatever we'd like, even if it is to stay in our rooms until we reach New Orleans."

Nadyha said quietly, "I might just do that."

Simza frowned and then asked, "Do you remember when that *narkri bitti gajo* hit Anca in the head with that bottle?"

Puzzled, Nadyha answered, "Of course."

"And what did she do?"

"Do? She got angry."

"Yes, she did. You see, she knew it was nothing that she had done to deserve that boy throwing things at her, and she got angry. She got angry, but she didn't lash out at the boy. You're like Anca, Nadyha. You're strong, and you know yourself. You can be angry, but be angry at the sin; and you cannot make the man pay, for that judgment is for *Dovvel* Himself. So be angry, and sin not."

Nadyha thought: *Am I angry? I just feel sickened and weak. And I don't care what Baba Simza says—I don't even care what You say, God! I wish I could make that man pay!*

The more she thought about their conversation, the angrier she grew; but the part about "sin not" escaped from Nadyha's fevered mind.

CHAPTER SEVENTEEN

Niçu and Mirella came to Nadyha's stateroom at dawn, as usual. As they had their morning prayer Simza noted again with regret that Nadyha refused to say the prayer, merely standing with them and holding their hands, her head bowed.

When they finished, Niçu said, "It's feeding day for Anca, Nadyha. I think I'll take Boldo down too, walk him around a little. He likes it so much, everyone wants to feed him."

"How are Tinar and Saz and Cayenne?" Nadyha asked. It was the first time she'd asked about the horses since the attack. "I miss them terribly."

"They're fine, they miss you too, *Phei*," Niçu said affectionately as he herded Anca and Boldo out the door. "But you know that Gage and I take almost as good care of them as you do."

Simza saw the longing in Nadyha's eyes, and how she seemed a little restless this morning, roaming around the room, aimlessly plucking at the flowers and fingering the many notes she'd been sent, but not reading them. Simza followed Niçu out into the hall and said, "Tell Gage it's time."

He grinned at her. "You're sure about this, *Phuri Dae?* I've never heard of a Wise Woman of the Gypsies to permit this kind of *mahrime.*"

"It's not *mahrime*, if it was I wouldn't allow it, and it's in the Bible," Simza retorted. "Now, get along with you. Oh, wonderful, now that the *cat* is leaving here comes the other one."

Matchko strolled in, his tail held high, and started weaving in between Nadyha's legs. "Matchko, you silly cat, where have you been?" she murmured, then picked him up and went to sit on her chaise on the deck. He settled down in her lap, paws tucked neatly beneath his chest, and started purring.

Mirella brought Nadyha a glass of juice and smiled down at the beat-up tomcat. "I think he's had more adventures on the *Queen* than either Anca or Boldo."

Matchko had pretty much made himself the mascot of the boat. He wandered at will, and nothing and no one could dissuade him from strolling nonchalantly into the Moravian Salon or the Bohemian Room. He always took part in the shows, in one scene or another. Most nights he stayed with Denny; when they had first boarded, Matchko had dashed out of Nadyha's stateroom and nosed around until he'd found Denny in second class. He spent a lot of time down in the cargo hold, with Tinar and Saz. Most of the crew had been horrified the first time he came down there. They thought that cats were bad luck, especially black ones. But Matchko had caught two rats down in the hold, and the crew suddenly reversed their opinions, because they had been even more horrified to think that their Queen of the Mississippi River had rats.

"You're getting fat," Nadyha said, pinching Matchko's big belly.

Mirella sat down by her. "Do you know what that *narkri* tomcat has done? He went down to third class and charmed those two *gajis*, you know, the ones that dress that way, that are so flirty? Yes, the *lubni*, I suppose they are, but you have to admit they're more—more—refined than most of the ones we've seen."

With interest Nadyha said, "Yes, I know, Susanna and Fanny. *Gajes* call them 'ladies of the evening.' What about them and Matchko?"

"Dennis told me that Matchko started following them around, and they got silly over him, like he's a baby, or something. Susanna and Fanny have made friends with some of the cooks and the bakers, and they beg for cream for Matchko all the time. That's why he's getting so fat."

"*Dinili* Matchko," Nadyha said affectionately, scratching behind his one ear. Looking up, she watched the shores flying by; they were going downstream now and were traveling much faster. They were passing a particularly lovely forest, with deep secret glades and soaring oaks and elms and pines. "I wonder about women like them, what kind of lives they have? How can they be happy, how can they—do what they do?" Nadyha murmured, and had a small involuntary shudder of revulsion as she remembered so vividly Frank Yargee's rough hands mauling her, his fetid breath and body odor, of the touch of the slimy cold knife steel on her cheek.

"I've wondered, too," Mirella said. "Those two girls are so young, but there's not a shred of innocence about them. It's very sad." She studied Nadyha for long moments, then continued quietly, "I've also thought about them a lot since that *mokadi jook* attacked you, Nadyha. What if he had raped Susanna or Fanny? I really don't think anyone would have been so outraged as they have. Isn't that very odd? We've always thought that *gajes* had nothing but disgust for us Gypsies. But so many of them have been so kind."

Nadyha considered this. It was true, she had almost been dumbfounded by the kind attentions she had received since Yargee had attacked her. Would a *gaje* prostitute have received the same consideration? She didn't really know, she didn't understand *gajes* well enough.

Then a tiny, timid thought came up from her heart into her mind: *Would God have sent Gage to save Susanna or Fanny? Maybe, maybe not . . .* Deep down, Nadyha knew that the Lord had sent Gage down to the cargo hold. But she shied away from thinking about Gage Kennon. As she reflected so often now, she felt as if she were *broken*, bruised, tender, not in body but her mind and in her spirit.

Nadyha knew that Gage and Denny had moved into the stateroom on her left, and her gaze wandered to the open French door. It reached from the stateroom wall to the railing, blocking the view of the promenade next door, but Nadyha knew that Gage and Denny never opened their balcony doors. It was another example of the extremely sensitive respect they were showing for her privacy.

But Nadyha didn't really want to think much about other people and their concerns right now. Her anger, and the slight resentment she'd been subject to for a long time, was turning into bitterness. Truth to tell, she didn't care a bit about anyone but herself, though this particular tiny, timid thought never made it to the forefront of her mind.

In the stateroom Baba Simza had been preparing some fruit to add to their breakfast. A knock came on the door, and she promptly went to answer it, as she always did now. To her shock, Mrs. St. Amant, in all her glory, stood in the hallway. When Simza opened the door, the lady took a step backwards, and made a small, graceful gesture to signal Simza to step outside.

Ynes St. Amant was three-fourths Spanish, one-fourth French, considered an extremely aristocratic Creole mixture. She was a tall woman, five feet ten inches, with a flawless olive complexion and heavy-lidded dark eyes. Her hair was shining ebony black, thick and luxuriant. On this morning she was wearing what was called a "walking dress," or "promenade costume." It was a deep moss green Basque jacket, trimmed with black satin frogs and jet buttons. Expensive Austrian lace peeped out at her collar and cuffs. Her skirt was of yellow, blue, and green plaid taffeta, and the width of the skirt nearly filled the hallway. From a matching moss green satin reticule she took two small white cards and held them out to Simza, who took them slowly. She read, in gold gilt script: *Mrs. Toussaint St. Amant, 12 Dauphine Street.*

Mrs. St. Amant said in her well-bred, slightly French-accented voice, "*Madame*, I must beg your pardon for my presumption, intruding on you in this manner. But I am very anxious to make your acquaintance, and that of your family. I am Mrs. Toussaint St. Amant. Of course, I am aware of your stage names, but I haven't had the privilege of learning your proper names?" she finished delicately.

With growing wonder, and sly amusement, Simza replied, "Gypsies have Christian names, Mrs. St. Amant, but by long tradition we keep them secret from non-Romany people. You may call me Simza."

"Oh, I—I see," she said uncertainly. It took a lot to make Mrs. St. Amant stammer. "Then—then please call me Ynes." She cleared her throat and began again, obviously a prepared speech. "Simza, my husband and I were appalled to hear about the unfortunate incident. I understand that you all are in seclusion, and again I must beg your pardon for intruding, but I knew that I must call on you and let you know personally how very much I regret what's happened."

Simza simply asked, "Why?"

"Because good people should not be silent in the face of evil," she said vehemently, then added in a more hesitant tone, "And because I—I realized that I, personally, should not think myself above this . . . above you, any of you. Will you accept my most heartfelt and sincere apologies, and please communicate to your family my sentiments?" she finished in a rush.

"*Hai*, I will do that," Simza said. After a long moment in which she could see that the woman was still struggling, Simza said softly, "We forgive you."

Ynes St. Amant's eyes filled with tears, and fumbling a little, she took a handkerchief out of her reticule and quickly dabbed them away. "Thank you. Before I release you, Simza, there is one more thing I would like to tell you. My husband and I are *patrones* of the French Opera House. We believe that you all are so gifted, so talented, and such strong performers that you should consider the stage. Please talk to Nadyha and your family about it.

"Also, I would like to extend you all an invitation to call on me, at your earliest convenience. My at-home days are Tuesdays and Thursdays, and I will always be at home for you. Usually Fridays are family days, but if you should call on Friday, I shall be at home then too."

Simza was puzzled; and there was no guile in her. "I don't understand. You don't live at your home every day? You only live there on Tuesdays and Thursdays and sometimes Fridays?"

Mrs. St. Amant looked taken aback, but then she smiled wryly. "No, Simza, that is the conventional way of letting people know when you receive visitors. And I hate to admit it, but sometimes I am 'at home,' but then I tell my butler to tell some people that I am 'not at home'. This is a very common circumstance, but I think I'm seeing that you probably would not excuse me for it. Anyway, all I was trying to say is that whenever you call, I will be so glad to receive you." And then Ynes St. Amant did something she had never done before. She held out both of her hands to Simza.

Simza clasped them warmly. "Thank you for explaining it, Ynes," she said lightly. "It would not have been good for us to call when you were not at-home. *Gaje* things like that, we don't know."

"Maybe not, and that may not be a bad thing at all. I'll take my leave of you now, Simza. Thank you for allowing me to speak with you, and explain to you . . . and apologize to you."

"Go with *miry deary Dovvel*," Simza said, and went back into the stateroom, closing the door behind her, and leaning against it to stare down at the cards she held. Nadyha and Mirella were still sitting out on the deck. Nadyha turned to see her, and called out, "Who was that?"

Shaking her head, Simza joined them and related what had just happened. Even Nadyha laughed when Simza told about her confusion at Ynes's being "at-home." "All my life I've thought *gajes* were crazy," she grumbled. "Then, no! *Miry deary Dovvel* says I mustn't think that. Still, I wonder . . ."

"I can't believe that she apologized," Mirella said thoughtfully. "I thought she was the haughtiest, most arrogant person I had ever seen."

"Maybe she was, and maybe she still will be, who knows?" Simza said. "But you must see, God can take a bad thing, a very bad thing, and turn it to good? I think the only reason this proud *gaji* ever thought twice about her behavior was because of what happened, Nadyha."

"Yes, but the bad thing happened to *me*," she said fiercely. "And no good can ever come of it for *me*."

Simza started to answer, but just then another knock came on the door. Nadyha complained, "I really wish people would leave me alone."

Rising, Simza said, "No, you don't," and went to answer the door. This time it was what she expected. A basket was set on the floor in front of the door, with no sign of anyone in the hallway. Looking down at it, Simza sighed heavily and thought, *If I don't watch out I'm going to turn into a stupid old* gaje *woman!*

This time Nadyha and Mirella had watched her, and now they came to see who was at the door. Nadyha's eyes grew wide, and she cried loudly, "Puppies! Puppies! Oh, oh, aren't they just beautiful, just darling!" Instantly she picked up the basket and set it on her bed. Inside were two chubby round balls of fur. One of them was quite a bit larger than the other, about eight pounds, with black and tan markings. The other smaller one was a lovely golden color with white markings. Both of them had long sharp noses and feather-soft ears that prettily flopped over at the tips. The big one had a yellow satin ribbon around his neck, and the smaller one had a green ribbon, and to it was attached a folded note.

Slowly Nadyha opened it and read: *From an admirer who wishes you the best of all things. I pray you will know God's comfort, His watchcare over you, and above all, His love.*

Tears filled Nadyha's eyes and she bowed her head. In a muffled voice she said, "Baba Simza, please go tell Gage that I said thank you."

Matchko jumped up on the bed to look in the basket. Flattening his one ear, he hissed a little, then jumped off the bed and scampered out the door behind Simza. Nadyha laughed and picked up first one puppy, then the other, to feel of them, to let them lick her face, to smell their warm sweet-puppy scent.

Simza came back in, grumbling. "He says you are welcome, and I say that you should be thanking me. I'm the one who has to now, besides all the other *narkri* beasts around here, put up with two little *jooks*."

"They're not *narkri*. Besides, dogs are in the Bible," Nadyha said, her eyes now sparkling. *"There be three things which go well—"*

"Those things are not greyhounds which are comely in going," Simza retorted. But she was filled with joy to see simple delight shining on Nadyha's face, and reflected that even those two silly dogs were well worth it.

NADYHA WAS SO ENCHANTED with the puppies that she forgot all about the last few dark days. She played and played with them. Niçu brought Boldo back, and the breakfast cart. Nadyha "introduced" Boldo to the puppies, and they immediately seemed to fall in love with him. They climbed all over him, licked his nose, batted at his paws. Nadyha laughed and laughed at their antics, and at Boldo's long-suffering expression.

All morning she had so much fun with the puppies that she hadn't a care in the world. At about lunchtime she suddenly said, "Baba Simza? Would you mind going to see if you can find Gage? Maybe he'd like to have luncheon with us."

"I wouldn't mind a bit, it's about time," she huffed, heading to the door. Nadyha said, "And, too, I'd like it if Cara could come see me, after luncheon. I'm sure you can find a porter to take her a message."

"Yes, Madame Queen of the Gypsies," Simza said sarcastically, while secretly rejoicing.

Gage came into Nadyha's stateroom in about two seconds. He looked relieved, happy, and wary. "Hi. So, do you like my gift?" he asked casually.

"You know I do!" she said. "Come, sit with us, tell me about them." She was sitting cross-legged on the floor, playing with the puppies.

Gage joined her, and the poignance of the two of them, sitting down with some pet between them, swept over him. Watching the playful little dogs, he couldn't help but grin. "These are called rough collies. They're herding dogs, but they also make good house pets.

"When we were on the way to St. Louis," he continued discreetly, "I told Denny that I wanted to get a couple of puppies for you, and I asked him if we might be able to find some, young puppies but already weaned. Of course he and his family know everyone in St. Louis—or maybe Missouri—and he knew Mr. Cyril Hull, of Hull's Dairy, which seems like a big to-do dairy farm and business. For years Mr. Hull has been using rough collies as their farm dogs, because they're such good shepherds and watchdogs, and he breeds them. It just happened that he had an eight-week-old litter, and I got you the biggest one, and the runt."

"Runt? What is runt?" Nadya demanded.

"It means small, stunted. With puppies it just means the smallest of the litter."

"Mm. He is small, isn't he?" Then she laughed, and Gage thought it was the sweetest sound he had ever heard in his life. "Like this other is big! They're both just—just—darlings!" She lifted them both up and kissed them both soundly, right on the mouth.

"Better not let Baba Simza see you do that," Gage sighed. "I got a feeling she might rinse your mouth out with carbolic soap, and she'd probably do mine too, just to make me pay."

Mischievously Nadyha said, "I can't believe you talked her into letting me have dogs. She's always said she draws the last line at dogs in the camp."

"Ah, it's my famous charm, none of the ladies can resist it," Gage joked, and immediately regretted it when he saw a shadow cross Nadyha's face. But then she went on talking about the dogs, and how she was having trouble thinking of names for them.

Gage thought, *It's not her . . . it's not Nadyha. Not the Nadyha I know. This girl is cold, and hard . . . Nadyha was always so warm, glowing, so fiery . . . is all that gone forever? Oh, Lord, I pray not!*

Baba Simza came back in, and behind her came a steward with the luncheon cart. A thin, earnest young man, he seemed to know that he was the only one of the crew that had been allowed in Nadyha's stateroom for the last four days, because he bowed to Nadyha at least half a dozen times as he set the table. Nadyha gave him a polite nod, and Simza was relieved to see that she now accepted a more normal routine as a matter of course.

They had luncheon, although it was hard for Nadyha to sit still, she kept jumping up to look at the puppies, who had played until they had simply fallen over, asleep. "Nadyha, sit at the table, put the basket down by your feet if you can't keep from hopping all over like a rabbit," Simza ordered her. "And no! Don't set the basket *on* the table!"

Niçu told them of Anca's feeding that day. "Mr. Wainwright bought two sides of beef, just for Anca! I told him that if Gage could just get into some little patch of woods somewhere and shoot a couple of hogs she'd like it much better. But I don't think Mr. Wainwright wants any of us to leave the *Queen*, ever. I think he wishes we'd all just move in and live here, like it's all one big *vardo*."

"But we're not going to do that, are we?" Nadyha said sharply. "We're going back to camp when we get to New Orleans, aren't we?"

"Of course, *bitti chavi*," Simza said, reaching over to pat her hand. "If that's what you want, that's what we'll do."

Gage's heart sank.

CARA CAME IN AND went straight to sit on the floor by Nadyha. "I've missed you," she said simply. "I'm so sorry."

Nadyha nodded stiffly. "Thank you. Look! See what Gage bought for me!"

"So I heard," Cara said, picking up a wiggling puppy to hold him close. "We had dogs on the farm, and I always loved them."

They talked about the dogs for awhile, and then Nadyha said, "Tell me about the Captain's Ball. Was it *pias, baro pias*?"

Cara blushed, and her blue eyes shone. "It was. I had—so many nice gentlemen ask me to dance. And Dennis was so kind, he made certain that I was properly introduced to everyone. It's so funny, and silly, so many of them ask me if I'm a real countess! Can you imagine that?"

"Yes, I can. And what do you answer?"

"I say no, of course. But some of them act like I'm really just being mysterious." She smiled then. "Maybe I am, because of what happened—to me, with Captain Nettles, you know. But I'm sure not trying to make anyone think I'm a countess. Anyway, Dennis really made me feel comfortable. He has such a courtly manner, when he's not being a silly show-off little boy. And he made sure that the gentlemen weren't too—too—attentive."

"Annoying, you mean," Nadyha muttered. With an effort she said more lightly, "You call him 'Dennis' now? I'm surprised at you, Cara, such improper familiarity!"

She blushed. "I know, it seems silly to you, but it's an important *gaje* rule, really. Young unmarried ladies don't allow men to call them by their first names, and they don't call young men by their first names. But Dennis said that when I called him 'Mr. Wainwright' he always looked around for his uncle, and it was really such a needless bother, considering. So, yes, I call him 'Dennis' and I gave him permission to call me 'Cara.' At first I said he could call me Countess Cara, but that didn't go over too well with him."

Nadyha smiled a little. "I think Dennis likes you very much, Cara. Maybe more than you realize."

Cara looked down at the puppies and started petting one of them. "No, I realize," she said soberly. "It's just that nothing can come of it. Dennis isn't a Christian man, you see. And besides that—we all know I may be in big trouble in Donaldsonville. Oh, I hope, I pray, that all of that is over when we get back! I miss my family so much. I even miss Mrs. Tabb."

Cara kept talking, and Nadyha was thinking, *Cara, she went through exactly what I went through! Well, maybe that captain that attacked her wasn't as dangerous as Yargee, but she still must have been just as afraid as I was. And no one showed up to rescue her. And then that captain died, and that must have been so horrible anyway, and then she had to run, because she might have gotten into trouble, when she was the victim, she was the prey! She seems so innocent, so delicate— but she's doing so much better than I am. What's wrong with me?*

"... Dennis said that he thinks I should do concerts, here, on the *Queen*," she was saying. "I hadn't really thought of it before, because I've been so happy with the play."

Nadyha said, "Yes, we have been, haven't we? Happy with the play . . . happy here. You know, Cara, I know that I couldn't possibly do the play tonight. But please tell Dennis that we'll be performing on Monday night, the night before we reach New Orleans."

"Really?" Cara said excitedly. "Do you—do you think you'll be all right, Nadyha?"

"I don't know," she said wearily. "But I'm going to try."

ON MONDAY NIGHT, THE play commenced at nine o'clock that evening. Normally, during the *Queen's* round trips, separate performances were given for first class, and then a second night reserved for second and third class. This time, because it was the only performance given on their return voyage, all of the passengers on the *Queen of Bohemia* were invited to attend. It was standing room only. Captain Humphries gave his usual warning for all of the audience to remain seated when the wild animals were on stage, but then the absurdity of it—there were about a hundred people standing up—hit him, and his granite face cracked into a smile. "Just don't run up here and crowd them, people," he finished in a deep grumble.

The audience was very quiet and still. No whispers, no fidgeting or even feet-shuffling from the people standing up were heard from the first moment the curtain rose, with the enraptured silence lasting all through Cara's entrance and song.

And then the curtain opened on Nadyha and Anca. The entire room erupted into a noisy din. The first-class passengers who were seated rose to applaud, even some of the women. Both men and women shouted, "Nadhya! Nadhya! Brava, Nadhya!" Rowdy young men from third class stamped their feet and whistled.

Nadyha stood, slim and tall and dignified, her eyes great dark pools glinting in the dimmed light. Her hand rested on Anca's head, who sat calmly by her, watching, motionless. The applause went on and on. Finally Nadyha crumpled a little, sank to her knees, and threw her arms around Anca's neck. She faced the audience, and they could read her lips as over and over she said: *Thank you.*

AFTER THE SHOW, DENNY and Gage sat down in the empty Bohemian Room to talk to the Gypsies. "I can easily make arrangements for all of you, and all the animals, to get transported back to camp," Denny told them.

Niçu was adamant. "We don't want a bunch of *gajes* to know where we're camped. The property is part of the Perrados plantation, and if that Major Wining finds out we're camped there I'll bet he'd just love to charge us about ten thousand dollars in taxes. Or throw us in jail. No, we've already talked about it, and we've decided that Mirella and I will double on Saz, Nadyha will ride Tinar, and we'll go to camp. Then Mirella and I will bring two *vardos* back to get Baba Simza and the animals."

"You can take Cayenne," Gage said. "I'm going to be staying at the St. Louis for the next week, he'd be a lot better off with you anyway."

Nadyha made it clear that she didn't want a lot of attention as they left the *Queen*. "I just really would prefer to leave quietly, without having to deal with—" She made a vague waving gesture, in a peculiarly awkward manner, for her. She looked drained and utterly exhausted.

Niçu said, "Sure, *Phei*. We'll wait until everyone disembarks, and by then the crew will be so busy they'll probably hardly notice us."

With relief Nadyha said, "Good. So, I'll say good-bye for now, Dennis, Gage. Thank you for everything." Then she got up from the table and left, her head and shoulders bowed.

The *Queen of Bohemia* came into New Orleans on Tuesday morning. It was a brilliant day. Even the Big Muddy glinted gold-splinters in the sun. But Gage felt little cheer. He stood on the Hurricane Deck as they docked. The wharves, as always, were a kaleidoscopic jumble of people, carts, and animals. The French Market was bustling. The usual hurly-burly of crews working to dock and passengers getting ready to disembark went on, down on the decks below him. He felt oddly alone and disjointed, as if he were watching a scene that he had nothing to do with, as if he weren't really there, and didn't belong there.

But this is my home, he thought despairingly. *If I don't belong here, then where do I belong?*

Unbidden, the echoes sounded in his mind: *With Nadyha . . . always and only with Nadyha.*

Chapter Eighteen

Gage looked around his room at the St. Louis Hotel. He found it rather shabby after the second-class stateroom on the *Queen of Bohemia*. The two wrought-iron beds were elegantly made and sturdy. The springs didn't creak, the down mattress was thick, the bedlinens were of fine Egyptian cotton. But they were smaller than the beds on the *Queen*, and Gage's legs were too long for the bed, and he had had a restless night.

A small cherry tea table sat underneath the window, with two armless slipper chairs upholstered in blue satin damask, but one of the chairs had a very noticeable stain on the seat. Since the St. Louis didn't have bathrooms *en suite*, a serviceable marble-topped oak washstand with pitcher and bowl was provided. Gage missed the fine bathroom on the *Queen*.

So now I'm a nimby-pimby gentleman of discriminating tastes, he thought acidly. He set his Bible on the table but found that he couldn't sit still and concentrate. Rising to stare out the window onto St. Louis Street, which was already busy just after dawn, he wondered what in the world he was going to do with himself for the next week. The *Queen of Bohemia* was scheduled to leave next Tuesday, August 1.

So I'm wondering about this week? Lord, what am I going to do for the rest of my life? Go back to being a clerk at Urquard's Sugar Refinery? The idea of spending his life as a clerk was anathema to him. How could he go back to such a dreary life? After the war, after living with Gypsies, after the *Queen of Bohemia* . . . after Nadyha?

Roughly shoving the thoughts of her out of his mind, he tried again to read and pray, but found that he simply couldn't calm down. He was so restless that his body almost felt chafed, a sort of skin-crawling itch such as he got when he drank too much strong coffee. He started pacing, which usually helped him to think, to figure things out.

At first his thoughts were just a jumble tumbling over and over in his head—sugar clerk, Gypsies, sharpshooter, Nadyha singing, the *Queen*, Nadyha and Anca, Nadyha and the puppies, the river, the fog of his future, the weary look on Nadyha's face as she had said her listless good-bye to him.

By nature Gage was a disciplined man, and eventually he was able to wrench his thoughts away from Nadyha. He thought of the *Queen of Bohemia*, how much he had enjoyed the last two weeks, how exciting it had been, how traveling on the river had been just as thrilling as he'd always imagined it would be, on those long-ago days before the war when he spent so much of his leisure time down at the docks. Slowly he realized that, regardless of his previous criticism of the very fine St. Louis Hotel, it really didn't have anything to do with comparing the hotel to the trappings of the *Queen*.

It dawned on him: *I loved being on the river. So now instead of a hoity-toity gentleman I'm a river rat?*

The thought was alien to him. Gage recalled his life before the war, and how he had been such a loner. Even his single courtship of one woman in his life had really been just going through the motions because, he thought, *I have to get married. Everyone gets married.* He realized now that he had never seriously considered it, and obviously she must have known that. No wonder she married someone else as soon as he was gone. It hadn't really bothered him very much.

And what about all of those longings after the surrender, to be alone again, to be solitary again? On the *Queen of Bohemia*, as large and roomy as she was, Gage had been cheek-by-jowl with people all the time. That's how it would be, working and living on a riverboat. Could he truly be seriously considering such a life?

It was true; he was. Gage had gotten to know all about the steamer in their two-week voyage. He had made a nuisance of himself, he suspected, with the Chief Engineer and the Chief Fireman, down in the boiler room and engine room asking hundreds of questions. He had found it fascinating that, once he understood the mechanism, the steam engines that drove a steamboat were actually less complicated than the boilers and engines necessary for refining sugar. He found everything about the boat interesting: how the engines drove the paddlewheel, how the firemen gauged the steam necessary to drive the engines, how the pumps worked for the fountain, how the galleys obtained fresh milk, how big the paddlewheel was, where the cleaning supplies were for the chambermaids.

Could I actually work a riverboat? Is that—possible, feasible, Lord? What would I do? It takes a special kind of training to be a fireman, to really understand the boilers, it seems like that only comes with experience. Engineer, now . . . I could do that, the engines are really pretty simple. But there are a hundred engineers on every dock in every port that have been on the river all of their lives. Could I be content just starting out as a crewman on some little freight crawler?

He didn't know the answer to that question. Already weary at seven o'clock in the morning, he realized the hard truth: any future without Nadyha was bleak and dreary to him.

He sat back down at the table and turned to Psalm 119. With a great mental effort he made himself read. Whenever Gage couldn't concentrate, he knew he could always read Psalms. Soon he was absorbed in this, the longest psalm.

When he finished, he prayed, and it was as if he were some sort of imbecile, sitting there mumbling to himself. But he prayed just the same. Gage had been a Christian since he'd been eight years old. He knew that even if it seemed that God wasn't there, He really was. Gage knew that if he prayed and asked God for answers, he'd get them. They may not be as fast as he preferred, and they may not be the answer he wanted, but He would always answer. By the time he'd finished it was time to meet Denny for breakfast.

Down in the Grand Rotunda, Gage eyed all of the Union soldiers milling around with a jaundiced eye. "This place is crawling with bluebellies," he grumbled.

"Yeah, all of the hotels are," Denny said. "Quit complaining, Johnny Reb, you're lucky I got us a room here. It's only because Uncle Zeke is such good friends with General Banks, you know. Anyway, how about Madame Borski's Russian Tea Room for breakfast?" They went outside and

Denny instructed an attendant to summon them a hackney cab.

"Are you kidding? I'm hungry, really hungry. I don't want watery tea and little poom-poom cakes for breakfast. We're going to Tujague's. They serve a man's meal there."

Tujague's was a small café down in the French Quarter by the docks. They served only breakfast and dinner, mostly to rivermen and French Market vendors. The place was crowded, the atmosphere was steamy, the conversations always at a constant low roar. But the food was outstanding.

"Have Guillaume's Creole Casserole," Gage advised Denny. "It's my favorite." The dish was a rich, hearty egg casserole made with German sausage, bell peppers, onions, garlic, and thickened with clotted cream and cracker crumbs. Tujague's always served fresh-baked French bread and sweet cream butter, and of course, all of the strong black coffee you could drink.

As they were finishing up Gage asked, "So, what do hoity-toity gentlemen of leisure do with themselves all day? I sure don't know."

"My, we are irritable this morning, aren't we?" Denny said. "Oh, we just fritter around. Today we're going to go to Corbette's Hair-Cutting and Shaving Saloon, and then we're going to Bustamente's Turkish Baths. That'll take most of the day. After that we'll just fritter around until we figure out where to have dinner."

"Supper, I still call it," Gage said. "And I want to go to Antoine's. I've never been there."

Denny's eyes brightened. "As it happens, Uncle Zeke—"

"Yeah, yeah. He's Antoine's long-lost cousin, or Antoine owes him ten thousand dollars, or something. Great, as long as you can get us in. So what is a Turkish bath, anyway?"

Gage felt better after he got a haircut and a professional shave. But he enjoyed the Turkish bath more than anything.

He had heard of them, of course; there were at least four Turkish baths that he knew of in New Orleans. But he'd never had the money to indulge before.

First was the "warm room," where the bather sat in a room that had small hot fires in front of the vents, to dry the air, so that the bathers had a purifying sweat. Attendants stood in front of the vents and fanned so as to circulate the air. Next was the "hot room," which had a big coal-fired kiln in the middle that heated up rocks. Attendants poured water on the rocks so that the room was filled with hot steam. Next was a room with several fountains spouting ice-chilled water, and the bathers leisurely splashed themselves all over. Then came the baths, and one could choose between cool, lukewarm, or hot; Gage chose lukewarm. The water was exactly the temperature of his body, so that he felt he was submerged in fine liquid satin. He reveled in it for half an hour. Then he got a massage by a huge black man that was so thorough and soothing that Gage felt every lingering bit of tension in his body just melt away.

Denny, sensing Gage's mood, hadn't tried to talk to him much during the baths. But as they were getting their massages on stands right next to each other, Gage started talking to Denny. "You know, I was thinking this morning, life on the *Queen of Bohemia* is great, but it's not real life. It's just one big party, really."

"Yeah, to the passengers. But to owners, running a riverboat is hard work. And it is a lucrative, legitimate business."

"Maybe. It's just that I feel like some kind of idiot. I feel like I need to get a job. Playing around shooting up the place isn't really a job."

Denny gave him a sharp sidelong glance from his stomach-down position on the marble massage stand. "What are you talking about? Of course it's a job. Hey, you're my friend, Gage, but I'm telling you right now that the *Queen of Bohemia* is no charity concern. Uncle Zeke wouldn't pay you if he didn't think he was getting a return on his investment."

"I just can't see it."

Patiently Denny said, "So, do you think that the Gypsies don't have a real job, that they don't deserve to be paid? Or Cara? No, you don't think that. I know you're like a babe in the woods in a lot of ways, Gage, but what you need to realize is that, just like the Gypsies and Cara, you're what they call a 'draw.' You have a really outstanding, unusual skill, and besides that, people like you, they want to talk to you, they think you're interesting. Even women," he added slyly.

"Yeah, and you know how much stock I put in that," Gage said. "Who knows what's going to strike a woman's fancy in the next minute-and-a-half?"

"I do," Denny said. "I know women. They like you and they instinctively trust you, because it doesn't take very long for even a half-wit to see that you're a good, decent man."

Denny let Gage ruminate on that for awhile, then he continued, "About Cara. Uncle Zeke asked a friend of his, an aide of General Banks's who has some kind of distant connection to that captain that died, to make some really detailed inquiries about that situation in Donaldsonville. I'm hoping by tomorrow we'll hear some good news about it."

Gage realized he hadn't thought about Cara since the last performance on the *Queen* two nights ago. "I forgot to even ask. Where is she? Where did she go?"

"I tried to get her to stay on the *Queen*, because you know that Captain Humphries and the pilots really live on the boat, along with about fifty crew members, so we have one galley and the laundries going all the time. But she wouldn't do it, she said it would be taking charity, and she had made so much money that she could stay at a boardinghouse. A respectable ladies' boardinghouse, of course."

"Of course. Cara is really a courageous, independent-minded young lady."

"That's putting it mildly. She looks like a fluffy little kitten, but she can be as tough as iron." Very casually Denny continued, "I've been thinking a lot about her, and her situation. And Nadyha."

"Nadyha? What do you mean?" Gage asked alertly.

"It's just so odd. Nadyha seems like the daring, flamboyant, world-wise one, and then there's Cara, the innocent little farm girl. But I've realized that Nadyha has really had a much more sheltered life than Cara has. That fierce Gypsy loyalty to *familia* and *vitsi*, and the way they shun *gajes*, really effectively shuts out the real world."

Thoughtfully Gage said, "I never thought of it that way. You're right, Denny. I guess maybe I really am just a dumb *gaje*."

"Nah. You're smart. Especially for a Johnny Reb."

The famous Antoine's fulfilled all of Gage's expectations, with his menu choices of Oysters Meuniere, Pompano *en croute*, and succulent tenderloin *flambé*. Afterwards, Denny was telling the *maitre'd* to summon one of his endless cabs, when Gage finally protested. "Why can't we just walk down to the *Queen*? It's only five blocks. It'll take more energy to hop in and out of the cab than it will to just take a nice after-dinner brisk walk."

"Ha! You called it 'dinner.' And taking cabs is what fritterin' hoity-toity gentlemen like us do. Never mind, I guess I can stagger down to the docks."

As always, the July night in New Orleans was sultry, but it was refreshing after the close atmosphere of Antoine's. The first three blocks of St. Louis heading toward the river was mostly residential, old Spanish colonial homes that reminded Gage of his apartment. As they neared the docks there were more coffeehouses, restaurants, and, of course, saloons and brothels. Gage and Denny were propositioned four times by "ladies of the evening" just crossing Chartres Street alone.

As she always was, the *Queen of Bohemia* was fully lit by her deck lanterns, even though there were only crewmen on board. Gage savored the sight of the grand steamer towering over them. As they boarded and went up the Grand Staircase Denny said, "She is beautiful, isn't she? A real, true queen. But I'm kinda surprised you wanted to come along with me, Gage. I'm afraid you're going to be bored. I'm afraid *I'm* going to be bored."

"Bored? Not me. What else am I going to do with myself? Besides, I'm really interested in everything about the *Queen*, even the business side of it, which I can see you really aren't. So why are you bothering to meet with your uncle anyway?"

"I just decided that if I was going to play at big riverboat owner I might better get some idea of what I was playing at," Denny said cheerfully. "I hate to admit it to anyone, me bein' such a ne'er-do-well idle lazy fritterin' gentleman and all, but after this last trip I have gotten interested in the crass commercial side of the business."

They went up to Zedekiah Wainwright's palatial stateroom, and he greeted them in his usual hearty manner. The ship's purser, A. J. Ruffin, was there for the business meeting. Gage had met him once, and as he shook hands with him, he thought of his earlier reflections about riverboat crews. Ruffin was nothing like a clerk; he was a thickly built man with shaggy black hair and shrewd black eyes and a craggy face. He had probably been on the river since his childhood, and was likely self-taught as far as bookkeeping for a steamer went.

"Let's sit down and have a drink before we get to the heavy lifting," Wainwright said. "Mr. Kennon? I just today took delivery of a case of fine French brandy, how does that sound?"

"No, thanks, just coffee, if Hervey's already got some made," Gage replied.

"He doesn't drink spirituous liquors," Denny said.

"Ever?" Wainwright said in astonishment.

"I tried it once," Gage said. "It doesn't agree with me."

"You and your buddies stole a barrel of cheap beer when you were eleven years old," Denny scoffed. "That's hardly comparable to enjoying a good brandy."

"I was sick for a week, and believe me, even though it's been fifteen years I still haven't forgotten it," Gage said with a wry smile. "Seems like it's just more trouble than it's worth."

"That's my buddy Gage," Denny said in an aside to his uncle.

As the silent Hervey served Gage his coffee and the other men their stronger brews, Denny asked Ruffin, "So, A. J., how'd we do this trip? Seems like we must have done pretty well, the old girl was full to the brim coming and going."

"So she was, but as to how well we did, exactly, is a mystery to me," he answered with a harassed air. "This is the first time since before the war that we were fully booked, and back then we had a very different pricing structure, and all of the costs were a lot lower. It's going to take me and my assistants at least a week before we can nail it all down."

"And we steam in a week, and I'm already seeing problems," Wainwright said, puffing on a newly lit fat cigar. "For one thing, first class out of New Orleans is booked full, round trip, so I couldn't take anyone on in St. Louis, and they're clamoring there, you know. I think we're going to have to figure out a waiting list there and maybe even in Memphis.

"And then, on top of that, I am now officially over-booked one cabin in first class. General Banks finally made his hints strong enough that it got through my thick head I'd better accommodate him and his family or I might be staying at a cheap flophouse on Bourbon Street next time we're in port," he finished irritably.

"You aren't going to kick Nadyha out, are you?" Denny asked in alarm.

"Are you joking? Not hardly! I've got no intention of los-ing her to the French Opera House."

"French Opera House?" Gage repeated in surprise.

Denny said, "Did I forget to tell you? The St. Amants are patrons, and they're interested in a production starring the Gypsies. And Cara, too."

"I can't believe Ynes St. Amant tried to steal my Gypsies and my countess from me," Wainwright growled. Then with a worried air he asked Denny, "You're pretty sure they are coming back, aren't you? I mean, they are Gypsies."

"Nadyha said they're coming back, and so I know they are," Denny replied. "All she would promise is for this next trip, but I think once she gets a little peace and quiet, and then has another successful run like the last one, which I'm sure it will be, she'll want to stay. I really think she, and Niçu and Mirella and Baba Simza too, had the time of their lives. Until that vermin Frank Yargee showed up."

Ruffin suddenly said, "Mr. Wainwright, it slipped my mind until right this minute, I apologize, sir. The sher-iff's office in St. Louis sent us a telegram. The surgery was successful, but Yargee's still in a deep stupor. They don't seem to know if he's going to come out of it or not."

Wainwright shrugged. "Not our problem. Fact is, the longer he's out of commission, the longer it'll be before you have to go deal with a trial in St. Louis, Mr. Kennon."

"Fine with me. It's not something I was looking forward to, anyway."

"And I'd hate to lose Gage Kennon the Dead-Eye Sharpshooter, too," Wainwright said expansively. "You know, it's funny, I knew that would be a hit for the men, but I was amazed at the interest the ladies showed in yours and Niçu's show."

"Told you," Denny said snootily to Gage, then to his uncle he said, "I know you never thought you'd hear these words come out of my feckless mouth, but can we get back to business? What are we going to do about the first class overbooking?"

"I wish I knew. All I can think of is to offer a discount if anyone in first class will take two second-class staterooms instead. Second class is only about two-thirds booked. But I know almost everyone booked in first class, and I can't think of anyone who might settle for second class. Maybe I should talk to the Chalmers, or the Dutreuils. I know them best. I could offer them a discount on a later trip."

"That sounds more likely to happen than talking a first-class into taking second class," Denny said.

Gage said, "I may be sticking my nose into something I don't know anything about, but that would be Denny's fault for inviting me here in the first place. You do understand, don't you, what all this problem with first class really is?"

All three other men looked blank. Gage continued, "You're not charging enough. If you're fully booking round trips out of New Orleans, and you have a waiting list for first class, then that means your demand has outstripped your supply and you can charge more."

"I think that actually made some kinda sense," Denny said slowly.

"Of course it does, I should have seen that, it's basic market economics," Wainwright rasped. "I know that sometimes I just think of the *Queen* as more a personal thing than I do strictly business. Especially since I now have my successful stage career. Don't laugh, Denny, you know you're in the same shape I am, just doing it because we're the owners, so we can, and it's so much fun. Any other observations to make, Mr. Kennon?"

"If you're asking, then I'll just observe that I already thought your second-class fares are a little too high for second-class kinds of people, which are successful tradesmen, owners of retail businesses, owners and higher management of mercantile and manufacturing concerns. Second class is just a little too pricey for some of them, and that's why you might not have it fully booked.

"As far as third class goes, in my opinion the fares look about right. But I think you're spending way too much money on the food in the Sumava. You could serve crawfish stew instead of oysters. You don't have to serve third class the same cut of steaks that you serve in first. You could serve third class red snapper or sheepshead instead of pompano. Little things like that could cut down your costs considerably, and I don't think the third-class passengers would ever perceive a reduction in the overall quality of a voyage on the *Queen*."

Denny stared at Gage. "Is it just me, or does he sound really smart?"

"It's not just you," Wainwright said. "A. J., how about if we go into a little more detail with Mr. Kennon, here, about his suggestions?" Ruffin looked wary, and Wainwright added hastily, "Don't ever worry about your job, A. J., you've been with me since the *Queen* was built and you're a good man. I just think it might help you and me both, and even my lazy worthless nephew, if we get, shall we say, a fresh perspective."

With obvious relief Ruffin said, "Yes, sir, I think you're right."

Denny said, "And besides, A. J., Gage already has a job. It's to shoot up the place."

BY THE TIME THE Gypsies and their animals got settled back into their camp, Nadyha was so exhausted that she felt dull-witted. She could hardly focus long enough to eat their late supper, a delicious beef and vegetable stew sent from the *Queen of Bohemia*. She fell into bed in her *vardo*, feeling a rush of warmth for the security of her home.

After a long dreamless sleep, she was surprised to wake up late. She could tell by the light filtering in through the flower-veiled windows that it must have been about ten o'clock in the morning. The puppies were nestled close to her, and she snuggled with them for awhile, not thinking of anything in particular except how much pleasure the dogs gave her.

When she finally got out of bed Nadyha had the most peculiar feeling. It was as if she had stepped through a doorway. A confusing, noisy, busy, hot, but exciting world was behind her, and as soon as she crossed the threshold she stepped into a completely different, but utterly familiar serene, quiet, certain and sure world. Nadyha had never been a lazy person, but on this day she allowed herself to forget about everything but bathing in the spring, playing with the puppies and Boldo, grooming the horses, and sitting with Baba Simza and Mirella and tatting lace. All of them really enjoyed this new kind of needlework.

The only thing that troubled her, all day long, was that her two imaginary worlds kept colliding, and it was all because of Gage Kennon. He was *gaje*, and he belonged to that other world, the crazy world at the French Market and on the *Queen of Bohemia* that she had so gladly turned her back on. But everything in her own world, the Gypsy camp, reminded her of him. There was Cayenne, placidly "home" again with Tinar and Saz. Over by the old willow tree was where Gage had slept on his old bedroll. As Niçu worked in the lean-to, she remembered Gage helping him with the forge, and trying to learn to make fake Gypsy coins. When Niçu practiced with his knives, she recalled Gage trying to learn to throw knives, which he had been oddly clumsy at, to his irritated surprise and the Gypsies' amusement. Every time she looked at the puppies, she couldn't help but think of him. Even—or perhaps especially—when she bathed at the spring she thought of him. This was where she had first set eyes on him, and her mind overflowed with visions of him and the sound of his voice.

That night, as they sat around the campfire and talked about the *Queen of Bohemia* and their travels, Nadyha finally found a mental solution to her odd disjointed feeling. That world, the troubling, even frightening one that she had fled from, was the *gaje* world. This world, her home, was the Romany world. Gage Kennon was a part of both of them; he had intersected them as surely as if he, too, were walking back and forth between the doorway. But it didn't necessarily follow that it had to be that way forever.

Why not?

Just those two words popping into Nadyha's head shocked her. What was she thinking? Whatever she might do tomorrow or next week or next year, Nadyha belonged in this world. She was Romany. Gage was *gaje*. It was just that simple.

She didn't sleep so well that night.

Nadyha was, indeed, a strong person, and she was young and had a natural wellspring of vitality that she vaguely associated more with inheriting from her grandmother than with her parents. The next day the thought of remaining idle all day, as she had dreamily done the day before, bored her. She tended the garden, and that took almost all day of hard work, for the weeds had grown more than the herbs and flowers. She was gratified to find that her *elachi*, her transplanted Grains of Paradise, were thriving. Although she was unaware of it, little by little she was forgetting the horror of the attack she had suffered, and she was being healed.

One thing she was aware of, however, was that she constantly thought of Gage Kennon. It irritated Nadyha in the extreme, and she struggled to put him out of her mind, with little success. Still, she had a wonderful day, and that night she told the others that she'd like for them to sing after supper. She and Niçu practiced their duet from *The Countess and the Gypsy Queen*. Nadyha and Mirella had found that "Scarborough Fair" was even more beautiful when Mirella accompanied Nadyha's guitar and lyrics on the recorder. They stayed up late, as they had when they were on the *Queen*, and Nadyha was more animated, and laughed more, than she had since the day that Yargee had found her down in the cargo hold.

The next morning after breakfast she announced, "I'm going to the canebrake to cut some reeds. We have almost none left, and who knows? Next month we may need to make baskets to sell at the French Market."

"Do you want me to come with you?" Niçu asked.

"What? Why should you? Of course not," Nadyha said, a little too emphatically.

Her pirogue was just where she had left it, and just as sound as ever. As she maneuvered it out into the shallow water and began to cut cane with her *churo*, she recalled the last time she'd been here. Gage Kennon had been with her. The memories were pleasant, like the marshy smell of the canebrake, the hot sun making a tiny lacework on her face as it streamed through her straw hat, the cry of the loons.

But slowly as Nadyha worked, she became uneasy. The sudden *thrip-thrip-thrip* sound of a startled dove taking flight made her jump. She started looking around nervously, but the canebrake was like a solid wall of reeds encircling her. Nearby she heard a *plop-plop*, which could have been a bird or, more likely, just a despised frog, but Nadyha found herself straining hard to hear more sounds. Her eyes started cutting this way and that way in alarm.

She began to feel slightly panicky, and started rowing her pirogue quickly toward the shore. When she got out of the canebrake and could clearly see the old worn path into the woods, she thought she would feel relieved. She did, after a fashion, but still she urgently felt the need to get back to camp. Gathering her rather scant bundle of reeds, she almost ran up the slight hill into the forest. As she hurried along the familiar path that she had treaded since she had been a small child, she abruptly stopped and threw down the reeds.

"What's wrong with me?" she whispered.

I've never been like this before, I've never been afraid of the canebrake or the forest . . . or of being alone. Is this . . . is this because of him? That Yargee? It is, isn't it! I'm actually frightened, and it's because of what he did to me! How dare he ruin my life like this!

Nadyha suddenly felt herself full of rage. She was angry with Frank Yargee for what he had done. She was angry with God for letting it happen to her. Obscurely, she felt anger against Gage Kennon. Although he could never be compared to a man like Yargee, he had been intruding on her thoughts too much, and somehow she felt that it was his fault, not hers.

Suddenly weary, Nadyha sat down on a fallen pine tree that blocked the path. Dully she thought that she needed to tell Niçu to come cut up the tree and clear the path.

Reluctantly she returned to her previous thoughts. *Dear God, why, why! How could You punish me like this! How could You let that man make me so afraid?*

She listened for an answer. But the heavens might as well have been one of Niçu's sturdy tin pots; smooth, unbreakable, and dead.

Nadyha sat still and silent for a long time, staring out into the deep, quiet woods. Gradually she became aware that she wasn't afraid any more. She realized that she didn't have to be afraid. She could choose to let the fear overwhelm her, as it had done in the canebrake, or she could choose not to give it place, as she had just done, here, in this solitude. She could make a conscious decision that Frank Yargee would not affect her life.

Nadyha realized that God had given her an answer.

THAT NIGHT THEY SANG again after supper, and Nadyha and Boldo danced. The others applauded and laughed long at their antics, for Nadyha was as playful as the bear.

Mirella made chicory tea with lemon and they all settled down companionably by the dying campfire. "Niçu and I have something to tell you," she said to Simza and Nadyha.

Her face was glowing, and her eyes were as starry as the night sky, while Niçu's face was wreathed in a proud smile. "I'm expecting a child."

"*Nais tuke, deary Dovvel*," Baba Simza said with satisfaction. "It's early yet, *hai?*"

"Yes, only six weeks," Mirella answered. "But I'm sure."

"This is wonderful, *te' sorthene*," Nadyha said happily. "I'm so glad for you, *Phral*."

"Me too," he said rather nonsensically.

Nadyha grew sober. "So—this changes things, doesn't it? I mean, are you two still thinking of going back on the *Queen?* Or do you think that maybe we should just stay here?"

Niçu answered, "We've talked about it, of course, but we really feel we need to ask you, Baba Simza. After all, you are our *chivani*, our *Phuri Dae*."

Simza sat for a long time, staring at the dying campfire. Nadyha, Mirella, and Niçu sat crosslegged around her chaise, waiting in silence.

"*A man's heart deviseth his way: but the Lord directeth his steps,*" she said quietly. "You will ask me what that means, and I will tell you a *lil* that *miry deary Dovvel* has taught me today.

"Our lives are like this, the tatting of the lace," she said, holding up the intricate fall of lace she had been working on. "I decide on the thread I use, and I decide what I want the lace to look like, the design. Now, tatting lace is not like sewing, it's really just making the knots, over and over again. And I say that I might decide on the thread, and what I want it to look like when I'm done. But none of that does me any good if the knots aren't tied right."

She gestured around the campfire. "We decided, three years ago, to stay here, in this place, instead of leaving and traveling with our *vitsi*. That was our choice, and I believe it was the right one. It is a good thread, and we make good knots, with our garden and herbs and remedies and baskets and goods at French Market.

"And then, suddenly, like lightning, *boom!* there is a wolf trap, and there is my ankle, and this was surely not my choice. Then there is Gage Kennon and there is Dennis Wainwright, and that was surely not our choice. But they became part of the design, some of the knots that make up the whole.

"And then there is the *Queen of Bohemia*, and I think this was a very good thing. You may say that such was our choice, but I tell you now that we wouldn't have had that choice to make if this *narkri* wolf trap had not gotten my ankle, and if Gage Kennon hadn't met Dennis Wainwright on that dusty road so far away, and if Dennis hadn't had the measles and pneumonia, and if Gage hadn't been at the spring that day. All of those things are steps that the Lord directed. He tied those knots Himself.

"And so you see my *lil?* As before, Niçu, Mirella, I won't tell you what to do; it is for your hearts to devise your way, to choose your design. But I say that I see that *deary Dovvel* has directed our steps, and those steps led us to Gage and Dennis and the great river and the *Queen.*"

MIRELLA AND NIÇU DECIDED to think on Baba Simza's *lil* for awhile, and they went to bed. The dew had long fallen, and Nadyha's skirt was wet, so she pulled up another chair to sit with Simza. "I need to think about your *lil*, too, *Puridaia*," she said. "I never thought of this before."

"Neither have I," she said impishly. "God thinks of this."

"And so you think it was God's will for us to have Gage Kennon in our lives?" Nadyha asked abruptly.

"*Hai*. You don't?"

"I don't know, but I wonder why? Why did all of this happen to us? Just so we can have *baro pias* on the *Queen of Bohemia*, and make money?"

Simza chuckled. "Maybe, maybe not. God said He'll direct our steps, but does He say He'll always tell us why? No, no. I ask Him why the trap closed on my ankle, and for awhile it seems He doesn't answer me. Then finally I know that He does answer me." She gave Nadyha time to absorb this, then said lightly, "I think you wonder about Gage Kennon much more than you say."

"I do," Nadyha said in a low voice. "I wish I didn't. I try very hard not to."

"Why?"

Nadyha stared at her incredulously. "Because he's *gaje*."

"Yes, and five years ago I would have been very angry to think that my *chaveske chikni* was thinking so much about a *gajo*. But today there is a *baro* cat and a *bitti* cat in my camp, and there are two *jooks* in my camp, and today I'm remembering that we found out on the *Queen* that not all *gajes* are wicked and not all of them despise us. Things change, and people change, even hard-hearted people like Mrs. St. Amant—and an old cranky *Phuri Dae* like me."

Nadyha merely stared at her in bewilderment, so Simza went on, "Nadyha, he is a good man. And he's handsome, isn't he? For a *gaje*, I mean. Why shouldn't you think about him?"

"But—I never thought—I didn't think that I would *ever*—he's a *gaje*!"

"You said that already."

Darkly Nadyha said, "It's just not possible. And I'm angry with myself for wasting my time worrying about it. It doesn't matter anyway. Gage is to me just like he is to everyone. He's nice and kind and thoughtful. He doesn't treat me any differently than he does Cara, or Mirella, or you. Why, he was just as nice to that Dobard *dilo gaji* as he is to me!"

And here Baba Simza's wisdom failed her. She knew very little about *gaje* relationships between men and women, and she knew nothing at all about their courtship. Pondering, she reflected that there did seem to be truth in what Nadyha said. Gage was a well-mannered man who treated all women with special courtesy.

But hadn't she seen the warmth, the happiness on Gage Kennon's face when he was with Nadyha? Didn't he seem to esteem her in a way different from the respect, and even affection that he gave to her and Mirella and Cara? As for the Dobard woman, Simza knew a flirt when she saw one, and she knew good manners in a man when he dealt with a flirt. But Nadyha's tone of voice had told her much; she hadn't realized the depth of Nadyha's feelings toward Gage, and now she was very unsure about Gage's feelings toward her granddaughter.

Simza just had a feeling, deep down, that Gage was in love with Nadyha. But she wasn't sure enough of this vague belief to give Nadyha any very strong encouragement. If she was wrong about Gage, and she gave Nadyha a false hope, she now realized it would be very bad for Nadyha.

Nadyha was waiting, with a hint of anxiety, for her to respond. Simza reached over and patted her hand. "*Bitti chavi*, all I will say to you is what I do know. God directs Gage Kennon's steps, and if you will let Him, He will direct yours. And then you'll be happy."

Such comfort really didn't make Nadyha very happy.

CHAPTER NINETEEN

On Friday morning Gage and Denny were just leaving the hotel for breakfast when Niçu came riding up at a reckless gallop on Cayenne. Nimbly hopping off the horse, he came to them, grinning. "You look surprised to see me."

Denny said, "I am! I know you all said you'd come back, but after you melted away on your *vardos* into your mysterious woods, I was beginning to think I had imagined the whole Gypsy thing. What are you doing here?"

Anxiously Gage asked, "There's nothing wrong, is there?"

"Huh? No, nothing's wrong," Niçu said. "Nothing at all. No, Dennis, we're not imaginary Gypsies, we're coming back to the *Queen*. That's why I'm here. This time we need to make some other arrangements for carting the whole Gypsy zoo back and forth."

"Sure, we can do that. We're just going for breakfast at Tujague's, Niçu, won't you join us?" Denny asked.

"I've already had breakfast, but the ride's made me hungry again, so I'll be glad to. Are you on foot?"

"He never goes anywhere on foot," Gage said dryly. "I'm just glad they don't have hacks small enough to fit in the hotel halls."

"Aw, shut your trap," Denny said. "Just 'cause you Johnny Rebs can march a million miles doesn't mean you have to all the time. Here, Niçu, give Cayenne to the attendant and we'll take a cab." They piled into the hackney.

Niçu was curious; it was the first time he'd ever been in a *gaje* carriage. "*Vardos* are much better," he said disdainfully. "This is really rickety and uncomfortable. Anyway, the *vardos* are what I wanted to talk to you about. We've decided that this time, when we get back here, we don't want to have to do that whole thing with us riding out to camp and getting them and then bringing them back to pick up Baba Simza and Anca and Boldo and Baro and Bitti—"

"Who are Baro and Bitti?" Denny asked.

Niçu grinned. Gage noticed that he seemed to be in particularly good spirits this morning. "That's what Nadyha finally decided to name the dogs. She says, I'll name him this, and I'll name him that, but no, that won't do, so this won't do, and on for days. We all were just calling them the *baro* one and the *bitti* one, so she finally gave up and just named them that. She's more *dinili* over those dogs than I've ever seen her, Gage. You did good."

"Thanks. Baro and Bitti, Big and Little. I like those names."

"Anyway, back to carting us all around. We can make it fine into town with the two *vardos*, but this time I don't want to have to take them back to camp and then have all of that back-and-forth when we get home. So, Dennis, do you think we can store them here somewhere?"

"There's only about five hundred warehouses here. When we finish breakfast we can go take a look at a couple of them and see if they would do."

"Good," Niçu said with what seemed to Gage an almost overwhelming relief.

Niçu had gotten angry with Mirella over their ride back from the *Queen* to the camp. At that time she hadn't told him then that she suspected, in fact was very sure, that she was pregnant. Niçu—and Gypsies in general—didn't believe that expectant mothers should be treated as if they were fine delicate pieces of porcelain that might break if they moved around too much. Even though Mirella had lost two children, Niçu never thought that it was because she had lived much as she had always lived, working, sewing, cooking, weaving, even dancing, in the early months. But, sensibly, he did believe that she shouldn't be lifting heavy loads, and she shouldn't be horseback riding.

"How could you do such a foolish thing, Mirella?" he had demanded when it occurred to him about their long horseback ride.

"Because it was the only way that we could help Nadyha," she replied softly. "Don't you see, Niçu? She had to get here, and just with us."

"Yes . . . yes. You're right, I see. But you're not doing it again," he said forcefully. And so he had ridden in this morning.

He had no intention, however, of telling Denny and Gage the real reason for his concerns. Niçu had come to regard them as friends, but they were still *gaje*. The centuries-long habit of keeping all personal things secret from the *gaje* was deeply ingrained in him.

They reached Tujague's, which was packed, as usual. After ordering from a red-cheeked, harried waitress, Gage asked with elaborate casualness, "How is everyone?"

"We're all just fine. It was really great to get back home, but after four days the women are already all looking forward to getting back to the *Queen*."

"Even Nadyha?" Gage asked intently.

"Especially Nadyha. I admit, with what happened, I wondered, too, if she'd really want to come back. And for the first couple of days she was moody and distracted, and I think maybe we're back at camp again," he said philosophically. "But then she got more like the old Nadyha, and I can see she's excited now."

"That's good," Gage breathed. "That's very, very good."

"As a matter of fact, she's the one who says now that we're coming in on Monday afternoon instead of Tuesday morning, like you tried to tell us, Dennis, and Nadyha said no, but now she says yes. She says it'll be much easier to get everyone settled in on the night before we leave."

"I'm really glad about that," Denny said. "And my uncle will be too. We just want you all to have a really good, easy, *baro pias* time of it this trip."

"So, what about that Yargee *mokadi jook*? Is he still in the hospital?"

Denny told him about Yargee's surgery. "He's still unconscious, they can't get him to wake up and they don't know if he ever will. Those other two little worms are still in jail in St. Louis, and if they just kinda get forgotten about, well, that's just too bad."

Darkly Niçu said, "I just don't understand men like that. And to tell the truth, I don't want to understand, I just want to forget it. I sure hope my *phei* can, too." Brightening, he went on, "So, I have a whole list of things the women say I have to ask you, like they aren't going to see for themselves in three days. What about Countess Cara? What's her situation?"

"That whole thing has died down so much that I arranged for Cara to go visit her family," Denny replied. "It sounds like this lady, this Mrs. Tabb that Cara worked for, had a lot to do with it blowing over. Apparently at first Mrs. Tabb was as loud as everyone else in denouncing Cara. Then she must have come to her senses, because suddenly she started saying that Cara wasn't the kind of girl to have a liaison with a married man, and that she—Mrs. Tabb— had particularly noted that this captain had been drinking heavily that night. She told everyone, from the commanding general of Fort Butler down to the streetsweeper, that this captain must have fallen off the stage in a drunken stupor, and Cara must have gotten scared and run."

Niçu nodded thoughtfully. "We know that's not the whole story. But I guess Cara's like my sister. She doesn't want to drag the whole thing out and make a big *lil* out of it. That's kind of a shame, isn't it? I mean, men like them should be publicly exposed, at the least."

"I know, I feel the same way," Gage said. "But I think we ought to let the women decide what's best in their situation. Kinda makes you feel like a big bumbling idiot, trying to help them."

"No. You helped, Gage. You helped both Cara and Nadyha. And for Nadyha's sake I'll always be grateful to you," Niçu said soberly. "Now, how about these warehouses?"

GAGE HAD THOUGHT THAT the week of waiting to see Nadyha again would crawl by painfully slowly. But it really didn't. He stayed very busy, because after the business meeting, both Denny and his uncle started consulting him on all kinds of things about the *Queen*. He and

Denny went to the boat every day. Gage spent long hours with the Chief Purser and his four assistants, combing over their bookkeeping system and making suggestions on how to streamline it, and helping them to get some bottom line figures on the last voyage.

He and Denny also did a complete check of the sets for the play, coming up with new ideas that required some carpentry work, which Gage supervised. Also, because of Gage's natural curiosity, he often went down to the engine room and boiler room to ask more questions of the crew. He got the Chief Engineer to give him a tour of the holy pilothouse, which he had never seen. He really was interested in everything about steamboats.

So Gage was vaguely surprised when he realized that it was already Sunday night, and Nadyha was coming in the next day. He went down to Denny's room and banged on the door. Denny answered wearing a burgundy satin dressing gown, holding one of his uncle's cigars and a crystal tumbler filled with brandy. When Gage saw his finery, he said, "For a working man, you still dress like a posh."

"Is that why you're here? To make fun of my apparel? This, from a fellow who wears all black like an undertaker and a gunbelt with two Colts. What's going on?"

"I was just thinking, wouldn't it be a good idea if we checked out Nadyha's stateroom before she gets here? Maybe have some flowers, and fresh peaches, and stuff? And everyone else's room, too, of course."

"Of course," Denny said ironically. "I'm way ahead of you. It's already done. And that reminds me, I forgot to tell you, if you think we're fussing over her, Uncle Zeke's got us both beat." He sat down and puffed vigorously on his cigar, then started coughing.

"Ever thought about quitting?" Gage asked.

"I just started," Denny said in a strangled voice, "and I enjoy it so much." Finally he cleared his throat, carefully ground out the cigar, and was able to continue. "A. J. had already assigned the staterooms, but Uncle Zeke insisted that Nadyha be in the cabin right next to his. You know, his cabin extends the whole width of the boat, so obviously no cabin is on his left or right. But because of the design of Uncle Zeke's stateroom, the two staterooms directly in front of his are about a foot wider than the other first-class rooms. He said that's why he wanted to put Nadyha in one of them, and shuffle everyone around, which drove A. J. nuts. But I think that Uncle Zeke is really worried about watching over her, you know. I think he feels better with her safely tucked in right by his stateroom. Hervey's always there, and most of the time the pursers or the engineers or the pilots or Captain Humphries are in and out, because he keeps so many of the records there and he meets with them all the time."

"I think that's a real good idea," Gage said deliberately. "Good for Uncle Zeke."

The Gypsy Caravan arrived at the docks at four o'clock the next afternoon, drawing the usual attention from passersby. Gage found that he was so nervous he hardly knew what to do with himself. His strongest impulse was to go grab Nadyha and look her up and down to see if she'd lost weight, if she was still pale, if her eyes still had that dull lost look they'd had when she left, and to fire a dozen questions at her to see what she was thinking. Of course, Gage could never do such a thing to any woman, especially Nadyha, so he tried to make himself calm down and not stare at her too arduously. She pulled the lead *vardo* up at their old Pavilion, the levee entrance by the French Market. Boldo's head was stuck out the window, and he was wearing a sugarcane hat and waving. In spite of his agitation

Gage grinned. "I see nothing much has changed in the last week. Hi, Nadyha."

"Hello, Gage and Dennis," she said, lightly dropping down from the driver's seat. "No, nothing much has changed. Except that now I have two baby *jooks*, and all the time we're afraid Baba Simza is going to have the apoplex."

"Apoplexy," Gage corrected her. She looked good, he thought, much like the old Nadyha. Her brown-green eyes were bright, her complexion was golden again instead of yellow ocher. Her greeting was certainly more lively and welcoming than her good-bye had been. Gage murmured, "You look beautiful, Nadyha. I'm so glad, I—we've really been worried about you."

Lightly she said, "No need. I'm fine, really. So, are you two going to help us get everyone boarded or are you just here for decorative purposes?"

It took a lot of time to get everyone and their musical instruments and the luggage unloaded and then loaded onto the *Queen*. Nadyha said in an aside to Gage, "At least you don't have to carry Baba Simza around this time."

"I wanted to, but she said no," Gage said. "Just like a woman, love 'em and leave 'em." He watched Nadyha carefully to judge her reaction to this. It was the kind of joke he used to make with her that she seemed to enjoy, but after the near-rape she had recoiled with distaste from such things.

To his relief she smiled. Gage noted that it wasn't the same free, easy, sparkling smile she usually had, but the sally amused her just the same. "Oh, well, this time she brought her table loom and two baskets full of yarn. I would guess you'll be lugging all that into and out of the Moravian Salon and the Bohemian Room and my stateroom and the promenade and wherever else it enters her mind to go seven or eight times a day."

After this exchange Gage felt overwhelming relief. He thought, *Ho-kay! Maybe we can get back to where we were before . . .*

Where were we before?

Now Gage grew confused again. His emotions concerning Nadyha had been such a whirlwind, so kaleidoscopic and baffling, that he had trouble now discerning exactly what the "normal" relationship with her had been. *I was attracted to her, and I think she was attracted to me, but then there's the gaje-Romany thing, and did she ever act any differently to me than she did to any of the other men standing around gaping at her? I know it started out differently, because of the bizarre way we met . . . and then I got tangled up with them, because of Denny . . . and then we all got tangled up with the* Queen *. . . but all along, was Nadyha falling in love with me, as I was with her?*

Looking back, Gage honestly couldn't figure it out. He had been so absorbed in his own dilemma that now he thought he had never really had any insight into Nadyha's feelings. Maybe all along she had just been grateful to him, because he'd helped Simza, and Simza had encouraged her and Niçu and Mirella to accept him into their so-exclusive circle.

Gage got tired of this mental overwork, and managed to put it out of his mind as he went to bed. *Two weeks*, he thought. *I have two weeks. By the end of this trip, I'll know.*

GAGE WONDERED IF NADYHA would fall back into their old routine and come down in the mornings to attend to the horses. With great trepidation he went down to the cargo deck at dawn, and found Nadyha already there, mucking out Saz's stall. "Lazy *gaje*," she teased.

"Hm . . . I seem to remember . . . somewhere back there . . . was it you? Yeah, I think you were the Gypsy that promised not to call me a *gaje* anymore," he reminded her as he led Tinar out of his stall and tied him up.

"Oh, yes, I was that Gypsy, wasn't I? Sorry. I forgot."

"I forgive you." Gage heard little whining sounds coming from Anca's empty stall, and looked over the door and grinned. "I see you brought Big and Little."

"Yes, I haul them everywhere," Nadyha said as she vigorously shoveled hay. "And that basket is just so heavy, and awkward to handle. But they're still too little to walk very far. I can't take them out on the promenade, so just to get them out of the stateroom I'm going to bring them down here in the mornings."

It made Gage very happy to hear her say that she'd be coming down every morning. "You know, if you'd like, I think I can fix up a canvas bag for them, with a shoulder strap. I'd make the bottom of it flat and solid, with pasteboard, maybe, so it wouldn't sag."

"Would you? That would be wonderful. Chubby little *jooks*, I won't be able to carry them for long. But maybe by that time they'll be big enough to be able to walk some."

"Yeah, and then I guess it'll be time for the gold leashes. Your pets have better jewelry than most women."

"Hmph. *Gaje* women. All Gypsy women have *galbés*, they're passed down in families from mother to daughter."

"*Galbés*, is that those coin necklaces that you wear? I thought those were just trinkets that Niçu made."

"They are. We hardly ever wear our real *galbés*, just for special things like when we have parties to celebrate the birth of a child."

"And weddings?" Gage said in an offhand manner.

"Yes, weddings too," she murmured. Then, in an artificially bright voice very unlike her own, Nadyha asked, "And so? Do you still want me to help you with yours and Niçu's show tonight? Or did Countess Cara do so well with the last one that I've lost my job?"

"Huh? No! I mean, of course Cara did fine. But I really want you," Gage blurted out.

She looked over the stall wall at him and smiled, her eyes flashing. "Oh? Maybe you'd better come to breakfast with us. We'll see if Cara and I have to fight it out."

It was the last time Nadyha invited him to breakfast. It was the last warm and personal conversation that Gage and Nadyha had the entire trip.

IF GAGE HAD FELT entangled by Monique Dobard on the last trip, on this trip he was positively swarmed by the Chalmers sisters.

Denny called them "The Three Graces" and not because of their grace. Their mother, Grace Steptoe Chalmers (of the Virginia Steptoes, as she told everyone), was a blonde, blue-eyed coquette and her three daughters could have been handmade copies of her. Lavinia was the eldest, nineteen years old, and slightly taller than her mother and sisters, but she had the same exaggerated, prettified manners as her mother and her sisters Josephine and Flora Louise. Josephine was seventeen, but it was Flora Louise, who was only fifteen years old, that made Gage extremely wary. She was spoiled and flirted outrageously with Gage, and her mother and sisters did nothing to curb her behavior. Their father, Boothe Chalmers, was a bluff, black-haired, big man whose family had made a fortune in shipping. He seemed to spend most of his time trying to avoid his all-female family, and so he seemed barely aware of what went on with his wife and daughters.

Again, it all happened after Gage and Niçu's show. Mr. Chalmers had escorted his family to see the show, but immediately afterwards he fled back down to the Lusatia Cardroom, where he spent most of his time. Mrs. Chalmers and her three daughters, however, lingered and button-holed Denny to wrangle introductions to Gage. As soon as they were introduced, Lavinia locked arms with Gage, so tightly that he could barely move. A very small sort of scuffle ensued between Josephine and Flora Louise to try to snatch Gage's other arm, and Flora Louise won. Gage was so entangled and baffled, that, again he didn't see Nadyha slip away. This time she didn't linger by the rail and watch them, she hurried off the Hurricane Deck. He never would have imagined that she was crying.

The inevitable insistence that Gage have dinner with the Chalmers came, and Gage was sadly puzzled as to how to refuse. The invitation was extended to Denny, and the six of them had what to Gage was an interminable torture. The girls, and even their mother, giggled and simpered and gazed coyly up at him from beneath their eyelashes. By the time the dessert course had arrived, it seemed that Josephine had taken a slight bent toward Denny and some of the attention was diverted from Gage, but it wasn't enough. He still felt positively smothered.

As soon as dinner was over, Mr. Chalmers said heartily, "I believe I'll have a brandy and cigar in the Lusatia. Would you two gentlemen care to join me?"

Gage almost knocked his chair over jumping out of it. "I'll join you, sir," he said hastily.

Denny smirked at him as he, too, rose and took his leave of the ladies. Gage never went into the saloons on the *Queen*. As they made their way to the hallway Gage stepped close to Denny and muttered, "Help me. Hide me."

"Sorry, buddy. Like I told you, goes with the territory."

The first performance on this trip of *The Countess and the Gypsy Queen* was scheduled for the next night. After a very quick mineral water and no cigar, Gage excused himself to Mr. Chalmers. "We have to do some special grooming of two of the horses the night before the play," he explained.

Mr. Chalmers said, "Oh? What do you mean?"

"We put a conditioner on their manes and tails and braid them and leave it overnight. It takes a long time, so if you'll pardon me—" Gage's voice faded as he hurried to the door. Again, he had high hopes that Nadyha would come help him, she always had before.

This time his hopes were dashed.

The next morning, Nadyha was again down in the cargo hold before Gage arrived. She had half-finished mucking out Saz's stall, and she seemed to be in a tearing hurry. She hadn't brought Baro and Bitti this time. Gage tried to talk to her, but her responses were short and barely polite, and after awhile they worked in silence. When they finished she said in a distracted manner, "Niçu said he'll come down to help finish Tinar and Saz for the performance. I'll see you tonight."

What have I done? Gage thought. *She's angry, I can tell. What have I done to make her mad at me?* Despairingly Gage realized that he had lost all insight into Nadyha. It seemed as if they had somehow become completely disconnected from one another. He really had no idea any longer what she wanted, what she was thinking, how she felt, even who she was.

The play got the same enthusiastic reception as it always did. The Chalmers ladies were the first people backstage, and they latched onto Gage like leeches. He didn't see Nadyha backstage at all.

This time, because second class wasn't full, Gage and Denny had separate staterooms. But they were next door to each other, and Gage met Denny in the hallway late that night. Following him into his stateroom he said, "Look, I don't think I can eat three meals a day with those Chalmers females," he said with frustration. "I know you want me to be in the Bohemian Room all the time, acting like some big goof, talking up the passengers. But unless the Three Graces give me a little room, that's not going to happen anyway. The only passengers I'll be talking up are Lavinia and Josephine and Flora Louise."

"Probably true," Denny agreed with his habitual grin, which at the moment Gage found truly maddening. "So, you're going to eat down in the Sumava? That's where they all eat, you know."

Gage was downcast. "I didn't think of that. No, guess that won't work."

Curiously Denny asked him, "Gage, what is going on with you and Nadyha? How has she been with you?"

"I don't know. Yesterday morning we seemed to be doing fine, we were laughing and joking like we used to do. But now she seems upset with me, and I don't have any idea what I've done."

Denny hesitated. He had seen Nadyha hurry off the Hurricane Deck after he had introduced the Chalmers to Gage after the show, but he hadn't seen her face and had no idea that she was weeping. He did know that on the last trip Nadyha had seemed very jealous of Monique Dobard, but that had been then and this was another time and another place. Denny knew very well that her jealousy then might have been the result of just a passing infatuation; it happened to everyone, he thought, and for all he knew now Nadyha might not care one whit about Gage Kennon.

Finally he said heartily, "Oh, come on, Gage, who knows with women? She's a hot-tempered girl, but she gets over it fast. You know they'll all be glad to have you eat with them. I've tried to get Cara to start eating in the Bohemian, but she says she's more at home with the Gypsies. And so you will be too."

But Gage just was not the kind of man to intrude where he may not be wanted. *What if she really has no feelings for me, and has come to find my company tiresome? That sure seems like what's happened . . . Oh, Lord, no, please, could she feel about me like I do about those stupid Chalmers girls? No, no, I can't bear that thought . . . I can't just show up at the Sumava, knowing Baba Simza and Niçu and Mirella and Cara would insist that I join them. I would never do that to Nadyha. I'll just have to see . . . if she keeps avoiding me . . .*

And so she did, and so Gage became convinced that he was right. Nadyha cared nothing for him, and she had sensed that he had fallen in love with her, and she found it wearisome. The only times he saw her were in the mornings, and even then she had gotten into the habit of coming down to work on the horses earlier than he, so their time together was shorter. He saw her during the play, and she continued to be his assistant in his show, but they never shared a single private word before or after. He knew that Nadyha and the others stayed out on the Salon Deck promenade a lot, and he began to avoid it, and go down to the rowdy third-class deck promenade. His sole consolation in this was that the Chalmers ladies would never let their satin slippers touch the third-class deck.

As promised, he did get Niçu and a crewman, a former sailor that was clever with sewing canvas, to help him with making a bag for Baro and Bitti. It was long enough for the two dogs, but not so wide that it couldn't be carried on the shoulder comfortably. When it was finished Niçu said,

"Why don't you bring it up to Nadyha's stateroom? We haven't seen you in days!"

"No, you take it to her," Gage said. "Tell her I hope it suits Big and Little."

The days, along with the ports of call, went by. Zedekiah Wainwright had done what Denny suggested, and made arrangements for Nadyha, Niçu, and Cara to "parade" with Anca, Tinar, Saz, and Cayenne in Baton Rouge, Natchez, Vicksburg, Memphis, Cairo, and St. Louis. Word of the *Queen of Bohemia's* colorful entertainers had spread on the river, and also Wainwright had shrewdly posted playbills in every shipping office along with the *Queen's* schedules.

Denny asked Gage to join their parade, but he refused. "You don't need me to go tramping around with you. It works really well to have Nadyha and Niçu leading on Tinar and Saz, with Anca, and then you leading Countess Cara on Cayenne. What would I do? Lumber along behind with funny ol' Boldo the Bear?" He had been so vehement that Denny said nothing more. When they came into port, Gage stood on the Hurricane Deck alone, watching them leaving the *Queen*, usually to much fanfare on the docks. Once, in Memphis, Nadyha had turned and looked up at the Hurricane Deck, and Gage thought she might have been looking for him. But she turned away so quickly that he decided he was mistaken—again.

The last performance of the play was on Sunday, August 13, the night before they would reach their home port of New Orleans. By this time Gage was so disheartened and low that he was barely polite to all of the people from second and third class that came backstage. As usual, Nadyha, along with Boldo and Anca, had disappeared as soon as the performance was over. Overwhelmingly grateful that the first-class people didn't attend the performance—he hoped he had seen the very last of the Chalmers women at dinner that night—he fled up to the Hurricane Deck for some solitude.

Nadyha was there. She stood on the starboard railing, staring out at the bayou country they were passing. There was a perfect half moon, hanging low and glowing orange-yellow in the starry sky. The dim light glinted on the coins on her *diklo* and around her neck, and lit her face with a mysterious glow, and Gage thought he had never seen such a beautiful sight in his life. She turned, startled. "Oh, Gage. I—I didn't know you came up here—after—anyway, if you'll excuse me—"

He quickly walked to her, then stopped, careful to keep his distance. "Wait, please, Nadyha."

"Why?" she asked brusquely.

"I just would like to talk to you. Please."

She stopped, and stood before him, but with her head bowed.

Quietly Gage said, "I just wanted to ask you a question. It's—I don't understand, really. I thought we were getting to be friends. Good friends."

"Yes, I thought—" she murmured, then, with a jerk, stood up straight to stare at him defiantly. "That's not a question."

Helplessly Gage pleaded, "Have I done something to make you angry with me, Nadyha? If I have, please tell me."

Unthinking, he reached out to her, and she recoiled. "Don't," she said coldly. "No, Gage, I'm not angry. Not any more."

She brushed past him and disappeared.

With despair Gage thought, *I know, Lord. I can't always have the answer that I want . . .*

CHAPTER TWENTY

It was almost noon as the *Queen of Bohemia* came into New Orleans. Mid-August, it was a sweltering, glaring day, with wavy heat-shimmers rising from the city. The light hurt Gage's eyes, and he pulled his wide-brimmed hat lower to shadow his face. He had the beginnings of a headache.

He stood in solitude on the Hurricane Deck, far at the stern, on the starboard side of the boat. He was watching their smooth glide through the busy port. They were nearing the *Queen's* permanent slip, at the levee entrance by the French Market. At the Port of New Orleans, the smaller steamers could dock nose-in, but the larger ones were required to always dock starboard, or right-hand side, when facing the front of the boat, alongside the dock. First Pilot Stephen Carruthers always docked the *Queen* in the major ports, and Gage observed, as he had before, that Carruthers was something of a hotshot, seeming always to come in too fast, make the right-hand angled turn rather sharply, and at the very last minute signal "Slow" to the engine room, so that they had to let off almost all of the steam at once, and it screamed sharply and dramatically from the 'scape pipes as they came into their portage.

Below him, on the Salon Deck and the lower third-class Promenade Deck, all of the passengers were gathered. It was customary for the passengers to go out on the decks when they were coming into port, especially when they were coming into home port. Always a crowd gathered when the *Queen of Bohemia* docked, families and friends of passengers, and onlookers who just wanted to watch one of the floating palaces in her stately grace.

Gage watched as they passed the solid line of riverboats docked in New Orleans. He saw the *Sunset West*, a rather small steamer, but with fancy gingerbread work and bright white paint trimmed in blue and yellow. Then came the *Matoaka Maiden*, and Gage studied her, for she was a side-wheeler, and idly he wondered about the difference for passengers from a sternwheeler. Did the two wheels make twice as much noise? Could you hear them throughout the boat? Then he thought that it wouldn't matter on the *Matoaka Maiden*, for she was clearly only a cargo hauler, with no Texas Deck. Right now roustabouts were just finishing up loading her with barrels and crates.

Next was the *Imperious*, a mid-sized passenger steamer, and then the *C. J. Berkeley*, a businesslike, trim cargo vessel. Gage wondered about the *Imperious*. Denny had told him that although she was only about two-thirds the size of the *Queen of Bohemia*, she had fifty-six nicely appointed staterooms and a Grand Salon and Ballroom, and ladies' salons and men's cardrooms and saloons. She did a very brisk business, Denny had said, and his uncle considered her one of the *Queen*'s main competitions for second-class passengers. Gage wondered if she needed a purser. He now knew that he was fully competent to be a chief bookkeeper for a steamer. Although the *Queen*'s purser, A. J. Ruffin, was a riverman, it was rather unusual for a lifelong crewman of a riverboat to become a purser. Gage had learned that most all of the larger passenger boats hired bookkeepers, not rivermen, to manage their finances.

The thoughts depressed him. He didn't want to be on the *Imperious*, or on any other passenger steamer. He wanted to stay on the *Queen of Bohemia*. But it was impossible. He realized that now it was just too painful for him to be here, around Nadyha. Glancing behind him, he looked across the boat, over to the port side, where Nadyha's stateroom was just below. She would be there, he knew, not out in the crowds on deck. Her doors would be open. He wondered what she was doing now. Probably sitting on the deck, watching the eastern bank of the Mississippi River. Dully Gage reflected that now he could see one reason for his beginning headache; low, black threatening thunderclouds were coming in from the southeast. Often Gage had a headache before a big storm; he thought it must have something to do with the air pressure.

The *Queen* was out in the middle of the river. As they passed the *C. J. Berkeley*, Stephen Carruthers made his signature sharp right-hand turn, angling in toward the *Queen of Bohemia*'s berth. Gage admired Carruthers; he may be a showoff, but he knew his piloting. Though the turn was hard and fast, it was exactly timed and coming around left just sharp enough to be flashy but not jarring. Gage watched as they slid gracefully toward the docks, waiting for the scream of the 'scape pipes.

But that wasn't the screams that he heard next.

THE *MATOAKA MAIDEN* WAS owned and piloted by a German man, a stern and businesslike sailor who had been in the German navy. She was strictly a freight hauler, because Captain Arnim Schulteiss would have no nonsense with passengers on his boat. Shrewdly, during the war, he had figured out the most lucrative freight to haul on the Mississippi River: arms and munitions. The New Orleans Armory, taken over by the Union in 1862, supplied arms to every fort along the Mississippi River. Still now, after the peace, the armory was working at full capacity, making more rifles, more artillery shells, more cannon.

And more gunpowder. That was what was in the barrels that Gage saw.

Captain Schulteiss was a careful, methodical man. When the *Matoaka Maiden* had first gotten the contract to haul gunpowder, Shulteiss flatly stipulated that the Federal Army would pay for special racks to hold the barrels, to make them completely secure, instead of just stacking them on the deck. These were simple square wooden racks made of pine, with crosspieces to make a square compartment for each barrel with about two inches of clearance on all sides. The compartments had a thin layer of hay that helped stabilize the barrels. This system had worked marvelously. The *Matoaka Maiden* had never had loose barrels, never had any leaking barrels, and the racks had stayed strong and fast all that time.

But now, after three years, a single screw had worked loose from one of the crosspieces of one of the racks. It thrust out from the wood about a half-inch, and was hidden in the hay. A crewman set the barrel into the compartment, and it seemed to him that the hay was too thick, for the barrel wasn't settling evenly. He pushed. The screw caught one of the metal barrel hoops. It caused a spark.

Of course, these last few seconds of the *Matoaka Maiden* were never known.

MAYBE I SHOULD JUST get a room at some little boardinghouse in the city and look for a job. Stay off the river and away from—

Gage lost his conscious thought, his breath, his hearing, and his connection to the earth. The blast blew him ten feet backwards. He landed with a painful thud on his back and lay there, stunned. He saw an enormous scarlet and black fireball rising above him. Then the fiery debris started raining down.

It took him a few seconds to recover his senses, although to Gage it seemed like a long time, struggling to breathe, staring around with uncomprehending eyes, the only sounds in his head that of stupendous roaring.

His pants leg was on fire. Gage jumped up and smothered it with his hands. Looking around, he saw that there were many big chunks of flaming wood falling on the Hurricane Deck, too many and too fiery for him to pick up and toss overboard. Already the wooden deck had caught fire in several places. He tried to run to the steps leading down to the Texas Deck, dodging the flaming wood shards, but as he neared it he could see that the steps were on fire.

Without breaking stride he made a U-turn and ran to the port side of the boat. He vaulted over the railing, then grabbed two uprights and slid down them. Making a kicking motion with his legs, he swung, then landed. He was on the deck in front of Nadyha's stateroom.

Horror was in his mind, and it only increased when he saw the scene.

Boldo was between the beds, trying to cower down against the wall. The sounds he was making were wrenching; he bawled, a loud moan that sounded like a man wailing: *NNOOOooh, NNNOOOOoooooh, NNOOOoooh!* Baro and Bitti were in their canvas bag on the bed, shivering with fear.

Anca was at the stateroom door, and smoke crept in from underneath it, hellishly wreathing her. She was standing upright, clawing at the door, her ears flattened completely, snarling. Gage saw dozens of long deep splintered scratches in the wood, and blood on the door from her paws. She looked back at Gage, her eyes narrowed to fierce glowing slits. Savagely she roared.

Nadyha was standing a couple of feet behind Anca, holding onto her leash. She sobbed fitfully and kept screaming, "Anca! Anca, no! Anca, please!" and yanking hard on the leash.

Instantly Gage crossed to Nadyha, put his hands on her upper arms, and roughly turned her around to face him. Her terrified stare held only panic. "Nadyha!" he shouted. "Nadya! Listen to me!" She still stared up at him, her eyes stretched impossibly wide, her gaze uncomprehending. Gage shook her, hard.

A slight flicker of anger showed in her eyes, and she kept jerking around to stare at Anca, but she didn't struggle against Gage.

The room was filling with smoke, even though the French doors were standing wide open. Boldo cried; Anca roared. From faraway they could hear screams and hoarse shouts.

In a slightly quieter tone Gage said, "Nadyha, please listen to me. Anca is frightened because you're frightened. If you can calm down, then we can get Anca calmed down."

Nadyha stopped sobbing and yanking uselessly on Anca's leash, but Gage could tell that he still wasn't getting through to her. He put both of his hands on Nadyha's face and gently turned her to face him. "Nadyha, please listen to me. I love you, my darling, I love you more than my own life. If I have to stand here and burn with you, I will. But we don't have to die. I can get us out of this, all of us. But you have to calm down."

"Wh—what?" She kept trying to wrench around to look at Anca. With soft but insistent pressure on her face Gage kept her focused on him. "You need to be calm, and get past the fear. It's time to pray, Nadyha. Just forget everything, close your eyes, and pray."

After long moments, she swallowed hard, then bowed her head and closed her eyes, and Gage dropped his hands from her face. He heard her speak: *"Amaro Dad, kai san ande o cheri, ke tijiro anav t'avel svintsime . . ."* He joined her, saying the Lord's Prayer in Romany. By the time they finished Nadyha was calm, her face composed, and she had stopped crying.

She stepped close to Gage and gave him a fierce, hard hug. "Thank you," she said simply. Then she turned to Anca and very slowly walked to stand by her. The cougar still was snarling and clawing. "Anca," Nadyha said as quietly and calmly as she could. "Anca, *te' sorthene.* Anca, it's all right," she kept saying over and over again. Anca finally dropped down on all fours and looked up at Nadyha. Her ears were still flattened, and her eyes still spit yellow fire, but she stopped growling and snarling. Nadyha stroked her head a few times, still murmuring soothingly. Then she dropped to her knees, and leaned forward, and they touched noses. Anca was calm.

Nadyha walked to Boldo, knelt down, and enveloped him in a hug. "Boldo, silly old bear, it'll be all right, don't cry any more, *dinili* bear . . ." Finally the bear stopped moaning, though to Gage his foolish bear-face still looked as frightened as a child's.

Nadyha came to her feet and asked Gage, "What do we do?"

"We get off this boat," he said. Slinging the puppies' canvas bag over his shoulder, he pointed to the door and said, "We can't go that way, it looks like the hallway's on fire. We'll have to go to the servants' stairs."

"Along the deck?" Nadyha asked.

"Yes, that little door down in about the middle of the boat. Keep hold of Anca's leash. Will Boldo follow?"

She turned to the bear and said in a normal, everyday voice, "Boldo, come on, we're leaving now." The bear obediently got on all fours and followed Nadyha and Anca out onto the deck.

When they got outside, Gage quickly closed the doors and he and Nadyha looked around.

The *Queen* had staggered at the concussion of the blast, and then she had slewed around so that now the port side of the boat was directly facing the east bank. Gage wondered, because he had seen several boats along Algiers Point before, but now no other vessel was in sight. On their left were the windows of Zedekiah Wainwright's stateroom, which were regular windows, not French doors. They were open, and grimly Gage saw smoke billowing out of them. He could see nothing past the stern of the boat because of the thick, dark cindered clouds.

The *Queen* was wallowing, aimlessly floating back away from the docks, toward the middle of the river. The sun was now shrouded with a black pall of smoke. The air was filled with the harsh smell of burning, and was clouded with ash. Even as they hesitated, a chunk of burning overhang from the Hurricane Deck fell down onto the deck, just a few feet from them. "C'mon," Gage said, and grabbed Nadyha's hand. They ran down the deck, and Gage was grateful that the French doors of the first-class staterooms were all shut. It would have been time-consuming to have to ram all of those doors closed to clear the way on deck.

The problem, Gage thought as they fled, was that the only outside steps that ran all the way from the Texas Deck down to the main cargo deck were at the stern on the starboard side. Gage had already seen up on the Hurricane Deck that the stairway was on fire; he was fairly certain that much of the starboard side of the ship was burning. Even if he and Nadyha had been able to go down the first-class hallway to the interior stairs that went down to the Moravian Salon, those stairs were on the starboard side of the ship. Gage said a hurried prayer of thanks that he knew of this tiny servants' stairs, which were on the port side.

Because Gage had been so curious, he knew about the interior servants' stairwell amidships, and he knew that it ran from the first-class deck down to the third-class deck but not all the way down to the main deck. Gage thought fast. When they reached the third-class deck, they could use the port steps at the bow that all third-class passengers used when they boarded, since they weren't allowed on the Grand Entrance staircase that led only up to the Moravian Salon. After boarding, because passengers were strictly forbidden to go down to the main deck, the stairs were barred by an iron gate. Gage told himself that he would take care of that, even if he had to chew it open. He glanced over the side. It was a full thirty-foot drop down to the water from here. Gage knew that he had to get them down to a lower deck.

They reached the narrow door leading into the stairs and Gage wrenched it open. He smelled smoke, but it didn't come roiling out. Holding it open, he motioned Nadyha to go first. She went, with Anca's leash in her hand, but then the leash tightened. Both Anca and Boldo hesitated. Clearly they didn't want to go into the dark, tight, smoky place. "It's ho-kay, Anca," Nadyha said. "Come with me, Boldo." She walked in, and they followed. The stairs were steep and narrow, and almost as tightly wound as a spiral staircase. The stairwell was windowless, and the only lights were one small gas lamp on each landing, but they were out, and they groped along in almost complete darkness. Gage went weak-kneed when he saw the darkened lamps, because it was the first time he'd thought about the gas lines. The crew must have gotten to the mains very quickly to shut them off.

Gage thought now that his hearing was returning. The stairwell was deserted and quiet, although they could still hear the 'scape pipes huffing, and it occurred to Gage that they were still under power.

Nadyha walked in front; behind her, Anca glided down the steps, her haunches lowered. Boldo went down the stairs on all fours with surprising agility. Gage brought up the rear. The puppies were wiggling, and kept trying to climb out of the bag. Gage wished he'd fashioned the bag so that it would close. He kept his left hand on the bag, pinching the middle of it shut so that the puppies could only just stick their heads out.

Nadyha started coughing, but she wasn't choking. The stairwell was filled with smoke, but it wasn't thick and suffocating. Gage asked, "Are you all right?"

"Yes, I'm fine. Gage—where are we going? What are we going to do?"

"When we get down to third class, don't go out into the stateroom passageway, just go out the door onto the deck. Then we'll go up to the bow and use those stairs to get down on the main deck."

They reached the landing on the second-class deck, and now they could hear shouts and screams, a continuous din that was curiously muted because they were at the end of such a small, narrow hallway. As Gage had known she would, Nadyha hesitated. "Gage, what about Baba Simza and Mirella and Niçu? And Cara?" she asked with anguish.

"I've been praying," he said simply. "I have to save you, Nadyha. Niçu will take care of the others. After you're safe, if I can, I'll come back."

She nodded and dashed tears from her eyes, then continued down.

They burst out of the door onto the promenade of the third-class deck. The harsh noise of a panicked crowd assaulted their ears. They looked to their right, toward the bow, blinking in the daylight glare after being in the dark stairwell. A mass of people were on the deck, crowding around the narrow stairway, pushing, shoving, cursing, shouting. Even as they watched, a man shoved a woman and she toppled over the railing to fall screaming to the river below.

Gage turned to Nadyha and said grimly, "We can't go that way."

Her face crumpled. "I thought—I thought we might be able to get down to the cargo hold and—Tinar, and Saz, and Cayenne—they can swim—"

"I know," he said fervently, "they're your brothers. But they're Niçu's brothers, too, and I know that he'll take as good care of them as you or I would. We just can't go and try to fight that crowd at the stairs, and there's no other way down to the main deck from here. We're going to have to jump."

Nadyha looked over the railing. It was about ten feet down to the river, which was filled with debris. She looked back up at Gage, and she looked frightened. Still, her voice was steady as she asked, "You and I can go over the railing, but what about Anca and Boldo?"

"Stand back." Nadyha stepped back against the ship's side. Gage leaned over and hit the railing with a piledriver kick. It loosened it. He kicked it again, grunting with the effort. The top crossbar splintered and with one final kick the railing separated, leaving an opening about two feet wide. As Gage was taking off his boots he asked hesitantly, "I don't even know . . . can cougars swim? Can bears swim?"

"I don't know either," Nadyha answered. "But I'm praying that they can."

"Me, too. Now I don't know how deep the water is here, but I know that we're close enough to the shore that we probably will only have a short swim before it shallows out. When you hit the water, go straight in feet first, then pull your knees up fast. It'll keep you from sinking too deep."

Nadyha nodded, then stepped up to him and caressed the puppies. "Baro, Bitti, don't be scared, Gage will take care of you." Gently she shoved them down into the bag and folded the top. Placing her hand over Gage's, she said, "I thank God for you." Then she dropped to her knees in front of the two animals. "Anca, Boldo, we have to jump. It's all right. I know that *miry deary Dovvel* will take care of us." She stood again, and took a deep shuddering breath. She removed Anca's leash, walked to the edge of the deck, and said, "Come on, with me. It's time." Anca and Boldo both walked and looked over the edge. In an instant, Anca launched herself into the water. Nadyha grabbed Boldo's paw and jumped. It all happened so fast that Gage was stunned for a moment. Then, holding the puppies in the canvas bag far over his head, he jumped.

He did as he'd instructed Nadyha, going into a crouch as soon as he slid into the water. Then he straightened out and gave a hard scissor kick in order to surface. With vast relief he felt his toes barely scrape the bottom. Surfacing, he saw that the puppies' bag hadn't even been dunked. Nadyha was on his right, swimming steadily. With bemusement he saw that Anca was gliding easily through the water far ahead of them, with Boldo not far behind her. He, too, swam with a grace that he never had on land. Gage carefully set the canvas bag down in front of him and saw with relief that because of the pasteboard bottom it would float, for a little while at least. He started kicking, pushing it in front of him.

They had to swim all the way around the bow of the boat, which was about forty feet. Gage now comprehended the debris in the water; some of it was not debris, but bodies. He wondered about the woman who had fallen overboard. Above their heads, on the third-class stairs, the crowd of people had grown but it seemed that the panic had lessened. They were streaming down the stairwell now.

As they rounded the bow Gage saw that the broad platform on the main deck, where the giant capstans stood that winched down the landing stages, was crowded with people. Even with her immense size, the *Queen* still had a shallow draft, so the main deck was only about two feet above the water. Gage thought, *Once Nadyha's safe, it would be easy for me to swim back out and pull myself up onto the deck.*

He rounded the boat and finally could see the docks. The *Queen* was still drifting, but she hadn't drifted far out into the river. The shore was about two hundred feet away. Just ahead of him Nadyha swam; Boldo was still in front of her and Anca was already about halfway to shore. Gage kicked harder and began to move faster, until he was alongside Nadyha. "You're doing great. Just a little farther on, and I think it might shallow out enough for us to be able to wade."

She was breathing hard but not gasping. "I understand."

They swam; they swam. Gage watched Nadyha anxiously but she kept a steady, strong rhythm. Finally he stopped kicking and went vertical. His feet touched the bottom, but it was still neck deep. "Just a little further," he called to her. With determination she did three hard, heavy strokes, then stopped. She stood up, and the water was chest-deep. Now slightly breathless, she said, "Thank You, Lord, thank You." Gage put his arm around her, and they waded. Ahead of them Anca and Boldo reached the shore.

Now Gage was able to look around and assess the situation. The Hurricane Deck of the *Queen* was burning from the stern to amidships; the pilothouse, just a few feet from the bow, was still intact. As Gage had suspected, the Texas Deck was burning on the starboard side. The lower decks, however, seemed to be intact, but then he saw smoke was pouring out of the grand staircase. The Salon Deck must be on fire too. When the explosion had first happened, he had immediately thought of the accident that happened all too often on riverboats: *boilers exploded*. Later he knew that such couldn't have been the case. At least, the *Queen of Bohemia*'s boilers didn't explode, or it would have blown the entire ship to pieces. Now Gage understood that there had been an explosion up the docks, and the *Queen*'s stern and starboard side had been shocked by the concussion, but the worst damage had been done by the lethal rain of debris. That had set the *Queen* on fire.

Past the *Queen*'s berth, the *C. J. Berkeley* was burnt almost down to the waterline. Right in front of her berth, the docks were on fire. Catching glimpses through the roiling smoke, with a shock Gage saw that the *Illustrious* had disappeared. It simply wasn't there.

The scene was of utter chaos on the *Queen*. On the third-class deck a panicked crowd still gathered at the bow, fighting to get on the staircase down. Below, on the platform in front of the cargo hold, so many people had fled there that some of them were getting pushed off into the water.

They reached the shore. Boldo was sitting down, watching them. Anca paced; she was keyed up but no longer panicked. Gage laid the canvas bag at his feet and stared back out at the crippled *Queen*. "I can swim back, and pull myself up onto the main deck at about amidships, where the exterior door to the firebox is."

Nadyha came to stand in front of him, looking up at him with the most tender expression he had ever seen on her face. "Back there, you told me that you loved me."

"I told you that I loved you more than my own life," Gage said hoarsely. "That's the truth."

She put her arms around his neck and pulled his head down. Whispering in his ear, she said, "I love you, Gage Kennon. I love you more than I can ever say."

He kissed her, passionately, and she clung to him.

A deafening growl sounded in the heavens, lightning forked through the smoke, and it began to rain.

NIÇU AND MIRELLA WERE in their stateroom, next to them was Baba Simza, and next to her was Cara. They heard the explosion, and felt the *Queen* stagger. All of them were looking out of their stateroom windows, and they saw the fiery wreckage landing all around them. Niçu was galvanized into action. *"Av akai!"* he commanded, grabbing Mirella's hand. They ran out into the hallway and Niçu started banging on Simza's door, while Mirella went to Cara's. When they were all out in the hallway Niçu said, "Follow me." They were in second class, but instead of going to the Grand Entrance stairs in the Moravian Salon, he turned left and headed toward the bow. They reached

the outside stairs on the starboard side. They knew that
the decks above them were on fire, but for now, at least,
these stairs were clear and they hurried down as fast as
Baba Simza could hobble. Down on the main deck they
went through the double doors into the cargo hold. Tinar
and Saz were relatively calm, but Cayenne was nervous,
rearing to paw at his stall door and giving the high, snorting
whinnies of a frightened horse. Niçu calmed him. Then he
told the others, "Get into Anca's stall and stay there. You'll
be much safer there than with all the *gajes*. I'm going to go
try to find out what happened."

Mirella said with distress, "Niçu, what about Nadyha?"

He answered, "Gage will find her, and he'll take care of
her. I know that, we all know that. I'll be back as soon as I
can."

He went back to the boiler room and was relieved to find
that the doors weren't locked. Inside were only four firemen; usually there were eight. The boilers were still going,
though the ship was idled. "What's happened, Mannie?"
Niçu asked the nearest crewman, a big black man that was
usually jolly but now looked as tightly wound as a watch
spring.

"Seems like one of the boats down the docks exploded,"
he answered. "We thought at first it was the boilers, o'
course. None of us saw the explosion. But now the Chief
thinks there's way too much fire a-rainin' down, so we
don't know."

"What about the *Queen*? Any idea of the damage?"

"Firebox is fine, you can see. Engine room's fine, she's
still purring along. But we got no steering, thinking maybe
Pilot Carruthers got killed. The top decks are on fire, so no
one's been able to get up to the pilothouse."

"What are we doing? What's the plan?"

Mannie shrugged. "Cap'n Humphries ordered us to stand by, keep her runnin', and they're hoping one of the other pilots will get up there before we get into trouble down here. Cap'n says we're close enough that if we could get her piloted we might still have time to pull 'er up to the dock."

Niçu frowned and considered for a minute. At last he asked, "What do you think, Mannie? Do you think we ought to swim for it?"

Without hesitation he replied, "Not just now, I don't. The crew's got a bucket brigade going out there on the stern steps, and I say they'll get a pilot up there before long. This old girl is the soundest, sweetest boat on the river. I say she'll make it."

As a rule, Gypsies didn't shake hands, but now Niçu stuck his hand out and Mannie grasped him with a firm, solid handshake that comforted Niçu even more than his confident words had. "Thanks, Mannie. I have to ask, is there anything I can do?"

"Go take care of your people, Niçu. And pray."

That's exactly what Niçu did. He returned to the cargo hold and went into Anca's stall, where the women were gathered. "I want us to say our prayer, and then, Baba Simza, will you pray?"

"I already am," she said, "and *miry deary Dovvel* has told me that no matter what happens, He is right here with us and will comfort us and give us peace. *Hai*, I will pray so that you can hear me, and then you all will know, too."

They stood in a circle and held hands and said the Lord's Prayer, the Gypsies in Romany and Cara whispering in English. Then Simza prayed a fervent prayer aloud, and she was right. All of them felt comforted and unafraid.

STEPHEN CARRUTHERS NEVER KNEW a thing. The concussion blast blew all the pilothouse windows to bits, and he was killed instantly.

The captain, pilots, and owners had a routine when they were coming into home port. Captain Humphries stood on the main deck at the prow, in solitary splendor. Denny and Zedekiah Wainwright mingled with the passengers on the Salon Deck promenade. The purser, A. J. Ruffin, and the two other pilots went to Wainwright's stateroom, because right after they docked Wainwright had a meeting with the captain, the pilots, and the purser.

In the stateroom, when the explosion happened, the men were situated like this: Hervey stood at his usual post by the sideboard, which was on the starboard side of the boat. A. J. Ruffin was standing at the sideboard, preparing himself a cup of *café au lait*, because he always said that he was the only one who could fix it exactly as he liked. The two pilots were sitting at the opposite end of the room, on the sofas, sipping the coffee that Hervey had just served them.

The second pilot of the *Queen of Bohemia* was a young, rowdy riverman named Joshua Swain, and he had been on the river since he was six years old. The third pilot was an older man named Hiram McCullough, who had owned a small cargo hauler that had blown up in a boiler explosion, and he had never been able to get the finances together to buy another, so he was grateful to accept piloting a fine steamer like the *Queen*.

The *Queen* started her turn, and Joshua Swain said to McCullough, "As usual, Carruthers is racing her in like a Thoroughbred. Did you know—"

BOOM!

The blast blew in the starboard windows. Hervey was smashed against the sideboard, and his neck snapped. Ruffin was blown sideways into the dining table, breaking his left arm and leg and giving him a severe concussion. Because the pilots were seated all the way across the room on cushioned sofas, they were pressured by the blast but uninjured.

In mere seconds blazing chunks of debris smashed in and set the wall and the floor on fire.

When Swain and McCullough recovered, their first instinct was to put out the fire. They used everything on the sideboard, except the flammable liquor, of course, to douse it. When all of those liquids were gone, they grabbed ice buckets and ran back and forth from the bathroom, which was at the bow end of the long room, inside Wainwright's bedroom.

The wool carpet on the floor charred but didn't burn, so the fire didn't spread on the floor. But they soon realized that running back and forth from the bathroom with ice buckets wasn't going to put out the fire traveling fast along the starboard wall. The room was filling up with smoke.

Choking, McCullough gasped, "This isn't going to work. Seems like we're still under power, so you need to get up to the wheelhouse and see what's going on. I'll get A. J. out of here. The blast came from starboard at the stern, so I'm going to try to get him up into one of the bow staterooms."

"Are you sure?" Swain asked. "I'm stronger, I can drag him easier."

"No. You're a better pilot. The stern steps are on fire. You're going to have to do some running around to get up there. Go."

The pilots and the Chief Engineer had interior staterooms on the third-class deck. Enclosed in the middle of these four staterooms was a small stairwell, for private use only by them, that went up all three decks to the pilot-house. The only access to these stairs were from interior doors in the staterooms, for Zedekiah Wainwright wisely knew that if passengers had a stairway to get to the pilot-house, no amount of monitoring would keep them out.

Swain went out into the hallway, and he saw that it was as black as midnight, filled with choking smoke. But he saw no flames—yet—so he went to the servants' stairwell on the bow side and flung himself down it, taking three steps at a time. He continually cursed under his breath, because he was running *down*, when he needed to be running *up*. But he couldn't think of anything else to do.

He came out of the servants' hall into the corridor where the third-class staterooms were. Men and women were running up and down, crazily, in blind panic, screaming and shouting and pushing each other. As soon as Swain stepped into the hall he was knocked down by two young men who bowled right into him, stepped on him when he fell, and kept running. Swain got up and savagely pushed everyone else who got close to him, even women, and finally fought his way to his stateroom door. He went inside, noting in the back of his mind that there was no evidence of any fire down here; the air was clear. Jerking open the small door into the private stairwell, he bounded up them. As he came up onto the level of the Texas Deck, his heart sank. The stairwell was filling with smoke. Fighting his way up, he saw. Up on the Hurricane Deck, at the top right by the pilothouse, the steps were on fire. Joshua Swain went four steps down, then took a running start and launched himself through the flames.

THE RAILING ON BOTH the second-class and third-class promenades was lined with people from bow to stern, watching as the *Queen* steamed majestically into her home port. As they rounded the *C. J. Berkeley* and started their turn, they could plainly see the huge crowd gathered on the docks to meet them. Even though the boat wasn't yet within earshot of the docks, people started cheering. Men waved their hats. Women pointed out the *Queen's* home berth to their children.

Then the world exploded.

The *Queen of Bohemia's* orientation was that she had two boats between her and the *Matoaka Maiden*, and she was making a left-hand turn away from her and was therefore at an angle. The brunt of the explosion hit the starboard stern side of the *Queen*. The *Matoaka Maiden* blew up and out. Because there were two sizable boats between the *Queen* and her, some of the lateral force was blocked, so that the lower decks of the *Queen* didn't sustain much concussion damage. But she was also two decks higher than the surrounding boats, so the starboard side of the second-class deck, the Salon Deck, and the first-class deck, the Texas Deck, toward the stern, sustained the worst damage and was hit by more of the flaming debris.

One hundred twelve people were standing along the Salon Deck railing. Six people were killed by the blast, all of them standing at the stern starboard end of the Salon Deck promenade. Of the approximately fifty people standing close to them, eighteen were critically injured, while everyone was knocked down and many sustained broken bones and severe concussions. Almost everyone had some scrape or wrenched muscles.

On the third-class deck below, fifty-two passengers lined the railing on the promenade. Half of them, closest to the stern, were knocked all the way to the deck, while the rest were staggered by the blast. One passenger, a young man, was killed, when his head hit the wall behind him with such force that it broke his neck.

Denny and Zedekiah Wainwright were standing at the open doors of the Moravian Salon, behind the passengers lining the railing. Both of them were knocked backward about three feet. When they recovered from the shock, passengers were already starting to panic, running around aimlessly. Denny and his uncle, aided by General Banks and his aides, and some other men who kept their heads, started trying to corral them and direct them to go down to the main cargo deck by way of the Grand Entrance stairway. They then discovered that one piece of burning debris had shot into the opening down on the second deck, and the steps were on fire on that level. Denny organized the porters and stewards into a bucket brigade. Wainwright and the other men started assisting the wounded, carrying them into the salon. It wasn't long before Captain Humphries reported on the situation to Wainwright.

"What can we do?" Wainwright asked shortly.

"Just what you are doing. There was no damage to the main deck, so the firebox and engine room are fine. Carruthers isn't answering engine room hails, so I think he must be dead. Swain and McCullough, as you know, were up in your stateroom, and we know the stern's on fire up on the top decks, but we don't know how bad it is up there. I've got the crew working a bucket brigade on the stern steps; I suspect the worst fires are up on the Hurricane Deck, and we need to get to them fast. Right now I'm going to go to the pilot's stairs and see if I can get up to the wheelhouse that way."

"You're a good man, Humphries. God be with you," Wainwright said.

"God be with us all."

SOUTHERN LOUISIANA HAD SPECTACULAR afternoon thunderstorms, and this one was no different. No small spitting of warning drops, no rolling of far-off thunder, just crash, and then the flood.

By the time the stricken *Queen of Bohemia* made it into her portage in New Orleans, the fires on the Hurricane Deck were already out. The starboard side of the Texas Deck still burned in places, but the bucket brigade was quickly dousing them. Precisely because Zedekiah Wainwright had spared no expense in the construction of the *Queen*, the fire damage she sustained was much less than it would have been on any other steamer. The pumps working the water system to the bathrooms kept going, so the crew had access to water on every deck. The fine plush Turkish carpets were of wool, which not only didn't flame on top, but also effectively smothered the fires that caught underneath, from the walls burning into the floorboards. The fires on the Texas Deck moved along the outside walls and along the roof, but not into the staterooms. Only half a dozen staterooms, including Zedekiah Wainwright's, lost part of their roofs.

Gage and Nadyha stood far down the docks from the *Queen* as she came in, because Boldo and Anca and, of course, the puppies, were still with them. At the *Queen's* berth there were fire engines and ambulances crowded around, and they were already having to deal with an unruly crowd of people, mostly the friends and relatives of passengers on the *Queen*.

Though she was injured, the *Queen of Bohemia* was not cowed. Joshua Swain guided her into port as gracefully and strongly as ever. In record time the crew had the landing stages down. People flooded off the boat, first running and shoving, but as the crowd thinned, they grew more orderly.

"They'll be last, you know," Gage said to Nadyha.

"I know," she said, but with anxiety.

When all of the passengers had cleared the landing platform, they came out of the cargo hold and made a procession down the gangplanks. First came Niçu leading Tinar, then Mirella leading Saz, and Cara and Simza with Cayenne. Gage and Nadyha looked at each other, then burst into laughter.

For the first time in his life, Matchko had managed to hitch a ride on Saz.

CHAPTER TWENTY-ONE

 Gage Kennon was a very busy man during the next few months. The very next day after the accident, Zedekiah Wainwright said, "A. J. is going to be out of commission for a long while. Can I interest you in a chief purser's job?"

Gage said, "Acting chief purser I'll accept. Until A. J. comes back."

"Good enough. Maybe by then we can all get back to pursuing our lucrative acting careers," Wainwright said, slapping Gage on the back. "Providing you can talk Nadyha into it, that is."

"I can't talk Nadyha into anything."

"You talked her into an engagement."

"No, I didn't," Gage said with a grin. "She asked *me* to marry *her*. It has to be her idea, you see?"

Denny made inquiries, and found out that the Perrados plantation was for sale. Major Wining had, in fact, been disciplined for his poor stewardship of the estate, and he and his staff were now lodged in a shabby boardinghouse in town.

"I can't possibly buy that forty-thousand-acre estate," Gage moaned. "Even if I wanted to, which I don't."

"As it happens, it's possible that the estate can be broken up into parcels. If, for example, someone wanted to buy that useless strip of woods that joins onto that useless canebrake."

"I'm someone," Gage said eagerly. "And I need some money, and I want you to help me get it."

"Already done, Johnny Reb," Denny said cheerfully. "Wainwright Investments, Limited has interests in four banks. Take your pick."

Baba Simza's and Niçu's and Mirella's cottages, which were at the old campsite, were finished in October. Gage's and Nadyha's cottage, which was a slight distance away, closer to the spring, was finished in November.

Gage and Nadyha stood together, with Gage's arm around her waist, hugging her close. Once he had permission to touch her, he wanted to keep her close all the time. They gazed at their home; the very last touches of bright green paint had been done on the elaborate gingerbread trim just that day. "Never in my life did I imagine I'd live in a house that looks like a circus wagon," he said.

Nadyha gouged him in the ribs with her elbow. "*Dilo gaje*, that does not look like a circus wagon. It's so much better, it looks like a Gypsy *vardo*."

He turned her to face him and encircled her in his arms. "You're right. And believe me, I do love everything about Gypsies."

He kissed her, but lightly, without heat, because Gage had realized that he was going to have to control his passion for her until they were married. If it had been up to him, they would have been married the day after the accident. Nadyha had wanted for them to get engaged, but she insisted that Gage had to wait to set the wedding date until she knew it was time for them to get married.

She returned his kiss, then pushed him away. "Pah, you always want to kiss. Niçu and Mirella don't kiss all the time."

"Bet they do when they're alone," he teased, and drew her back into his arms.

After long moments Gage reluctantly let her go. "You know, you really should go ahead and move in."

"No," she said vehemently. "It's our house, for me and you to live in, together. Why would I want to be there all alone? I'll stay in my *vardo*, with Baba Simza and Niçu and Mirella, until we get married."

"When is that going to be?" Gage demanded. "I'm tired of sleeping under the willow tree."

"Soon," she answered softly. "I promise you, *ves'tacha*. Soon."

Every morning at dawn Gage rode into town to meet with Denny and Zedekiah Wainwright, and though they often pressed him to stay when business lasted until late evenings, he always refused, and returned to the camp. Although now Mirella was obviously expectant, and so didn't dance, Nadyha still did. And Gage wouldn't miss that for the world.

NADYHA'S *VITSI* MADE THEIR way back to New Orleans in December. Nadyha's father, Dimas, was the *Rom Baro* of the *vitsi*, which was an elected position, so he was more like a president than a king. However, he was positively feudal in some of his views, and that included the marriage of his daughter to a *gaje*.

"You've all gone *dinili*," he told his mother, Simza. "You and Niçu and especially Nadyha. What do you think you're going to do? Turn into *gajes* and go your merry way?"

"We'll never be *gajes*," she replied. "Especially Nadyha. Her betrothed is a special man, a good man, and he knows Nadyha will always be *Roma*. I think he even loves her more because she is a Gypsy."

"Well, I'm not paying him a bride price," Dimas growled. "As I see it, *he* should pay *me*."

Although Dimas was so angry about Gage, and looked at him only with disgust, he did decide that the *vitsi* would stay for a couple of months. They were comfortably camped out around the original campsite. As the days wore on, Dimas came to cautiously respect Gage, and eventually he even came to like and trust him. As did the king, so did the people, and by the end of January most of the *vitsi* had come to accept Gage, not as a Gypsy, but as a relatively sane and sensible *gaje*.

The week before Christmas, Gage told Nadyha, "We're fairly sure now. The *Queen* should be fully repaired and restored next month. Mr. Wainwright's set the first sailing for February 5."

"Then I have a question to ask you," Nadyha said, her hazel eyes sparkling green-gold. "Will you meet me on the *Queen of Bohemia* on February 4, and marry me?"

"Huh? You—how did you know that the *Queen* would be ready then?"

"I didn't, until now. But it's what I've been waiting for. Our lives have been all entwined with her, and I believe that our lives will be entwined with her for some time to come. I wanted to get married on the *Queen of Bohemia*, for I think it will be good *baksheesh* for us. And *miry deary Dovvel* has said to me that this is a good thing."

"It's not just a good thing, it's the best thing," Gage said, grabbing her around the waist and lifting her up high in his arms. "Just like you."

A GYPSY WEDDING IS a four-day celebration, with feasting, music, singing, and, of course, much dancing. Zedekiah Wainwright experienced several moments of half-regret that he had invited Gage and Nadyha to wed on the *Queen* when they boarded along with the forty-two other Gypsies from their *vitsi*. However, they were very respectful, did their own cooking and cleaning, didn't drink too much, and were on the whole a very joyous and merry people. By the wedding day Wainwright was already talking to two of Nadyha's brothers and one of her sisters, trying to persuade them to join their theatrical troupe.

The ceremony was attended by Denny and Cara, who were growing closer every day, and Zedekiah Wainwright and, of course, Anca and Boldo and Matchko and Bitti and Baro. Dimas and the *vitsi* had been almost as horrified at Nadyha's dogs as they had been with her choice of husbands, but as they had been with Gage, after a month they philosophically accepted the half-grown puppies.

Nadyha had told Gage that Gypsies didn't have formal wedding ceremonies, and she consented to have a *gaje* ceremony. Gage got his pastor, a humble, sweet-natured old Methodist preacher, to preside. Gage and Nadyha stood in front of him in the Moravian Salon, facing each other, and holding each other's hands as they recited their vows. But of course, there must be some part of Romany's heart in their dedication to each other. After they finished their Christian vows, Nadyha's maid of honor, Mirella, handed Nadyha a piece of bread and a small sewing needle, and

Denny, Gage's best friend, handed him the same. Gage and Nadyha pricked their fingers, and placed a tiny drop of blood on the bread. Then they exchanged the bread and said to each other, "By this bread and this blood, I promise you that my heart, my life, belongs to you forever." Then Nadyha and Gage ate the bread.

It would have been shameful to Gypsies to exchange a public kiss, so Gage turned again and took Nadyha's hands in his.

His voice ringing throughout the room, he said, "*Devlesa avilan*. It is God who brought you."

Nadyha smiled sweetly. "*Devlesa araklam tume*. It is with God that I found you."

Gypsy Glossary

amaro deary Dovvel	our dear God
anarania	amen
av akai	come here
baksheesh	a good path laid before you
baro	big
baxt	meant to be
beng	devil
bitti	small or young
bitti chavi	young Romany girl
bori	brother's wife, sister-in-law
bujo	to swindle, scam
cam	sun
camova	physical love
chavaia!	Stop!
chaveske chikni	granddaughter
chavi	Romany girl
chivani	wise woman
choro	a thief

chovihani	a person of power
churo	knife
ciocoi	overseer
devlesa avilan	It is God who brought you
devlesa araklam tume	It is with God that I found you
Devvell	at one time this was their word for God
dhon dhon bestipen	very much wealth
didlo	crazy
diklo	head scarf
dilo	fool or imbecile
dinili	silly, stupid, foolish
Dovvel	God
drabengri	healer
dukkering	fortune-telling
dûrvâ	marshland grass
elachi	Grains of Paradise—cardamom
familia	family
gaje	non-Gypsy, peasant
gaji	non-Gypsy, peasant (female)
gajo	non-Gypsy, peasant (male)
galbés	coin necklaces
gam'i choro	evil thief
gója	a favorite Gypsy dish of a pork roast stuffed with grated potatoes, rice or corn flour, onions, garlic, and other spices
habben	food
hai	yes
Hush kacker!	Shut up and listen!
kralisi	queen
jook	dog
jostumal	enemy

kaki	aunt, also a respectful form of address for an older woman
kako	uncle; these are also terms of respect
kishtis	sashes that Gypsy men wear
kumpania	a group of Gypsies of several *vitsis*, or clans
lalo	blood red
lil	story
lubni	loose or immoral woman
magerd' o choros	wicked thieves
mahrime	unclean
miry	my
misto kedast tute	you did very well
mokadi	spiritually unclean
mokadi lalo	refers to the particular red color that is considered unclean
nais tuke	thank you
narkri	unpleasant or troublesome
phei	sister
phral	brother
Phuri Dae	wise woman of a clan
pias, baro pias	fun, big fun
prala	brother
puridaia	grandmother
purodod	grandfather
rai	sir
Rom Baro	the Big Man of the *vitsi*; male leader
Roma	as the Gypsies refer to themselves, Roma or Romany
romoro	Gypsy/Romany men
shanglo	police
she'enedra	sister of the heart
shesti	nonsense

si tut bocklo?	Are you hungry?
tale	hawks
te' sorthene	friend bonded by heart, spirit
vardo	living wagon
ves'tacha	beloved
vitsi	Gypsy clan
wuzho	pure, clean in spirit

Also Available in

THE WATER WHEEL SERIES

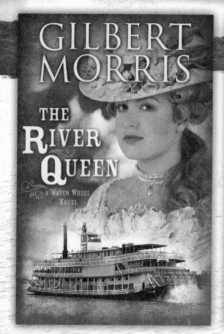

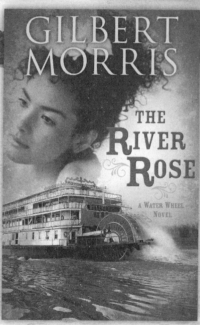

THE RIVER QUEEN

Beloved historical romance novelist Gilbert Morris discovers inspiration aboard an 1850 riverboat where a prideful woman and a drunkard captain seek restoration and find it, by God's grace, in each other.

THE RIVER ROSE

When two very different people jointly inherit the same steamboat in Memphis during the mid-nineteenth century, their shared need for a new livelihood steers them toward falling in love.